FAMILY FEUDS . . .

— DuPont
— Rockefeller
— Gucci
— Johnson & Johnson
— Marshall Field
— Onassis
— Vanderbilt
— Trump . . .

These are just a few of the families chronicled in shocking detail in the pages that follow. Read all about it — the high stakes inheritances, the adulterous scheming, feuding spouses and ex-spouses, vengeful children. The secrets behind America's wealthiest dynasties are all here in

FAMILY MONEY

FAMILY MONEY

—GEORGE MAIR—

PINNACLE BOOKS
WINDSOR PUBLISHING CORP.

PINNACLE BOOKS are published by

Windsor Publishing Corp.
475 Park Avenue South
New York, NY 10016

The P logo Reg U.S. Pat & TM off. Pinnacle is a trademark of Windsor Publishing Corp.

First Printing: May, 1994

Printed in the United States of America

This book is dedicated to my grandchildren
Jordan and Megan
and the other grandchildren yet to come

Thanks to my agent, Jane Dystel, for representing me so ably and to my editor, Beth Lieberman, at Zebra Books, for her patience and guidance.

The Beginning . . .

When Seward Johnson, heir to the great Johnson and Johnson pharmaceutical fortune, was fourteen, his mother turned him over to one of her women friends for ten days as a sex slave.

The woman initiated Seward into every imaginable form of sexual pleasure, technique, and intercourse. Following that, Seward's mother left for England forever to marry a British nobleman leaving her son behind in the care of the servants.

For the rest of his life, Seward had only three enduring interests: sailing, breeding cattle, and seducing every female who came within reach, including his own daughter, Mary Lea.

He started an incestuous affair with Mary Lea when she was eight that continued for eleven years in a bed they often shared with Seward's wife. The affair, in turn, distorted Lea's relationships for the rest of her life during which she became the sex slave to most of the men who wanted her along with being a successful Broadway and movie producer.

But the Johnson story is just one example of what has happened in the lives of the very rich heirs to great fortunes. In *Family Money* we examine the effect of money on bloodlines. The children and heirs of the rich often grow up in luxury, but they also grow up haunted with anxiety about themselves— their own identity and destiny. The effect of having a huge fortune-in-waiting can generate havoc with the lives of the children of the rich.

For example, loving relationships that would be normal between ordinary parents and children or among brothers and sisters are virtually unknown with the very rich. Honest relationships between the heirs and children of the rich and lovers, friends, and colleagues are rare and marbled through with fear and suspicion.

We will see how a huge fortune-in-waiting breeds greed, murder, suicide, incest, forgery, revenge, drugs, sex, insanity, lust, and hatred. How it nurtures the dark side of the human psyche. As Seward Johnson's daughter said during the court battle over the half billion dollar estate, "This isn't about money. This is about revenge." In that instance, it was also about perverse sex, attempted suicide, incest, and greed.

As easy as their life may seem to an outsider, the children of the rich often become alienated from their parents, friends, and the world.

W. Clement Stone, Charles Tex Thornton, and Joseph Hirschhorn were raised like girls by their single parent mothers while Averell Harriman had a bad relationship with his aloof and authoritarian father. William Randolph Hearst and Howard Hughes were alienated from their fathers and Hughes was an orphan when he was 19.

Barbara Hutton hated her father and spent her life trying to marry men who could become second fathers. Peggy Guggenheim, had mismatched parents who ignored her and she was raised and terrorized by governesses and nurses. She fled to self-imposed exile in Venice, Italy.

The whole life of Eleanor Medill (Cissy) Patterson was scarred by her bitterness toward her mother, drunken father, and their disastrous marriage. Mrs. Harold F. McCormick, an unhappily married Rockefeller daughter, saw her children by appointment only.

Generations of Vanderbilts were plagued with miserable childhoods from a long sequence of matrimonial catastrophes and the stunted emotional growth of their elders. Commodore Vanderbilt, like his own father, was distant and brutal toward his own children. "Every Vanderbilt son has fought with his father" said the third-generation Cornelius Vanderbilt II after a long court battle that lost him most of his inheritance.

Alva Vanderbilt wielded absolute power over her children and forced one daughter to marry the Duke of Marlborough at a cost of $12 million. Gloria Vanderbilt was the pawn in a sensational custody fight in the 1930s between her mother and aunt.

John D. Rockefeller, Jr., Barbara Hutton, Howard Hughes, several Vanderbilts and Peggy Guggenheim remembered years of intense loneliness. Rich children can be very lonely.

They can also be severely depressed, which may account for the high rate of suicides among heirs. Jacqueline Thompson in her work, *The Very Rich Book,* claims 80 percent of the acknowledged suicides in the U.S. are among the wealthy. Some notable examples:

Roger Annenberg, 22, son of the very rich publisher who founded *TV GUIDE.* J. Frederick Byers, III, 38, son-in-law of CBS chairman and legend, the late Bill Paley. Harvey S. Firestone, III, 32, grandson of the tire company founder. Clifford S. Heinz, II,

26, heir to the Pittsburgh condiments fortune. Ethel du Pont Warren, 49, heiress to the du Pont fortune and former daughter-in-law of President Franklin D. Roosevelt.

The profile of the one who founds the family fortune has an important effect on his children and heirs. He usually is almost always a "he" and a renegade, religious elitist or rectal obsessive—depending on which theory you believe.

America is a nation of renegades—escapees from the traditions and established order in some other place. In short, if any of our ancestors could have made it in "the old country," they would never have left.

The Guggenheims left the anti-Semitic repression of Switzerland to become street peddlers in Philadelphia. The Reynolds' fled the poor northern counties of Ireland to grow tobacco in rural North Carolina. Sutter fled the police in Europe to build a ranch in California where the Gold Rush began.

The renegades had the initiative and ambition to fight for survival and a better life. This, with a touch of freebooting morality, made the fortunes of the Rockefellers, Astors, Vanderbilts, Hunts, Hughes', Morgans, Harrimans, and the Guggenheims.

Religion played an important part in the fortunes of some families. Among some of the pious, the accumulation of wealth was convenient proof God smiled on them because they were one of the faithful. The religious teachings of John Calvin carried that message and justified money-making because God rewarded hard work with financial success.

In the early 1900s, the Rev. Russell Herman Conwell, a Philadelphia Baptist minister, crisscrossed the country preaching his famous "Acres of Diamonds" sermon to huge crowds. He preached, as does Reverend Ike today, that going after money is an honorable crusade and a test of one's usefulness to God and others.

Dr. James A. Knight, professor of psychiatry at Tulane University of Medicine, says that, "The promise of protection and power is also found in religion: God promises protection, help . . . provided [you] fulfill certain ethical requirements."

Some psychologists relate control of the rectum with the drive to make money through obsessive control over the world. This was a theme of Sigmund Freud's.

Dr. Henry Clay Lindgren, professor of psychology at San Francisco State University, said, "Sigmund Freud . . . maintained that our attitudes and behavior toward money were determined during toilet training, when we established control over the anal sphincter. Habits of thrift, Freud said, were derived from the pleasure of retaining the contents of the large intestine."

According to Freud's theory, such an anal-based character develops three main traits in later life: excessive orderliness, parsimoniousness, and obstinacy.

We will explore the bizarre, tragic, unusual lives of children born into families of great wealth. It is a different life from which most of us have lived.

One

Wrong Heirs Who Got Howard Hughes's Millions

Money is a mystery in our lives.

Experts in human behavior say money often brings pain, happiness, mayhem, and murder, but we're not sure what money is, how it works and why it affects us so much.

The meaning of money is like a Rorschach blot, says Arlene Modica Matthews in her book, *If I Think About Money So Much, Why Can't I Figure It Out?* The meaning of money is in the mind of the beholder. "It intermingles with fantasies, fears, and wishes, blending with a grab bag full of blind spots, embellishments, denials, distortions, and impulses," contends Matthews.

Oddly enough, talking about money is taboo. People will talk about orgasms, fatal diseases, and ax-murdering cousins before they will talk about money.

Money lives in the dark side of our souls for some reason. One of the most astonishing experiences in life is what happens to rational, kind, civilized people when a relative dies. Before the body is cold, the relatives swarm through the dead relative's possessions like giant, carnivorous soldier ants devouring everything in their path.

John Cohen, writing in the March 23, 1990, *Washington City Paper*, said that when an inheritance goes sour, "you truly are better off dead. At least that spares you the sight of people clawing through your material world like it was so much carrion, snapping at one another for silver trays and shares of stock."

Even among the many bizarre cases cited in this book, the fight over the inheritance of the Howard Hughes estate stands out as unusual.

He was so misanthropic and enigmatic that his name has become a common noun phrase meaning a mysterious recluse as in, "He was the Howard Hughes of the Canadian cabinet" or "He was the Howard Hughes of baseball."

The *real* Howard Hughes, one of the most mysterious rich men in America, died April 5, 1976, of kidney failure which his personal doctor said was due to massive doses of aspirin taken over a long period of time.

After his death, there were too many wills that had been talked about, but no valid will could be found. So, Howard Hughes was judged to have died, in effect, without a will and the court had to decide who was heir to his multimillion-dollar estate. Many "heirs" jumped up claiming they should be included.

People claiming shares of his estate included: Melvin Dummar, a Utah garageman named in the "Mormon Will" and movie actress Terry Moore who claimed to have secretly married Hughes on a yacht off the California coast. A court awarded Moore some money but rejected most of the other claims.

Beyond that, Texas, California, and Nevada each claimed Hughes as a resident for tax purposes even though Nevada doesn't have an inheritance tax. It took the courts five years to sort out who was a legitimate heir and who wasn't. It was a monumental search and the outcome was just as weird as the life and death of the man who triggered it.

When Howard "Sonny" Hughes, Jr., became an heir to the $872,000 estate of his father, "Big Howard," in January 1924, he was a eighteen-year-old orphan.

The other heirs were his grandparents, Felix and Jean Hughes; Felix, Jr., Big Howard's older brother; and Howard, Sr.'s sister, Greta.

His uncle Rupert, Big Howard's younger brother, was left out of the will and he wasn't happy about it. Rupert tried to get control of Sonny's part of the estate — ownership of the Hughes Tool Company. The great value of the company came from its revolutionary cone-shaped oil drilling bit, which was acknowledged to be the best in the world.

Rupert's claim was based on his contention that Sonny, being a minor, needed a guardian. Up until then, Sonny had been attending Rice Institute and was only interested in three things: airplanes, Hollywood, and the saxophone. However, that changed when he became an heir. At age 18, he applied to the court and convinced Judge Walter Monteith, a friend of the family, to designate him an adult.

That done, Sonny bought out his grandparents' and uncle Felix's interest in Hughes Tool; married his sweetheart, Ella Rice, and rushed off to Hollywood. Over the next 52 years, Sonny parlayed Big Howard's stake into a billion-dollar empire.

He died like something out of a Stephen King story — he had voluntarily shriveled his 6'2" frame to 92 pounds, his fingernails were several inches long, he had hair over his shoulders with bedsores and needle marks all over his body. He died in the security-tight suite of a Las Vegas hotel he owned and surrounded by a ominous phalanx of Mormon bodyguards. And he died without leaving a valid will.

He had made his first will in 1925 a few days before he married Ella Rice. He also made later wills or discussed them with his secretary, attorney, and close colleagues. His secretary of many years, Nadine Henley, said that Hughes repeatedly postponed decisions and, while she typed a number of wills over the years, he failed to sign them.

In the search for a valid will, some odd things happened. A California Judge, Neil Lake, ordered a search for a Hughes will. However, the man he appointed to make the search was Richard C. Gano, Jr., one of Hughes's first cousins on his mother's side, and someone with a vested interest in finding or not finding a will depending on what it said about bequests to various family members.

Then, came the group of Hughes's close business associates who testified that he intended his estate to go to the Howard Hughes Medical Research Institute. These same associates controlled the Institute.

Of course, there was the famous Morman will that claimed to be Hughes's hand-written testament and mysteriously appeared under the door at Mormon Church headquarters in Salt Lake City. Both Nevada and Texas courts rejected it.

The final arena for determining who were the legal heirs to the Howard Hughes estate became the Texas Probate court of Judge Pat Gregory. The proceeding was divided into three parts. Part I would weigh the claims of anyone alleging to be a direct heir.

If that failed, Part II would be to determine relatives on Hughes's mother's side, and Part III would focus on his father's side. To help, the court enlisted a professional genealogist, Mrs. Mary Smith Fay.

Part I quickly turned into crazies-time in July. Several women claimed to be directly related to Hughes after having met him in unusual circumstances. There was the older, stylish strawberry blonde, Alyce Hovsepian Hughes. She said she met Hughes in a Philadelphia hospital after which he forced her to shoplift some jewelry and, then, they were married. Afterward, he asked her to use the name, "Jean Peters," which she did and they remained married even though they never lived together. This and most other claims were summarily thrown out by Judge Gregory.

The real Jean Peters, a Hollywood actress, had been married to Howard Hughes for a number of years although they did not see each other for the final four years of the marriage. It was a strange marriage for other reasons, as well.

At first Jean had been apprehensive about meeting him because she was an actress and he was the biggest playboy movie producer in Hollywood who went through a steady stream of bosomy starlets.

Attracted to each other, they dated, but he didn't want to get married, so she did—to someone else. Then, he became determined to have her and mounted a campaign of attention and intimidation that so disrupted her marriage that her new husband left her. Reclaiming her for his own, Hughes flew her to remote Tonopah, Nevada, and married her on January 12, 1957, in a small motel.

In spite of her wanting a decent home, he insisted on living in several bungalows at the Beverly Hills Hotel. He rented five or six of these very expensive and exclusive bungalows for a number of years and neither asked for nor was given a long-term discount. He paid regular daily room rates for all the bungalows.

He and Jean lived in one bungalow, he used another as an office, and several others housed his infamous armed Mormon body guards. When a leaky roof caused part of a ceiling to fall in one of the bungalows, he refused to let anyone enter the premises to fix it. It was just left open to the sky.

In addition to the bungalows, Hughes also rented several rooms in the main part of the Beverly Hills Hotel. In one of these he usually kept at least one aspiring starlet whom he could visit for sex when he wanted it.

Hughes loved to talk for hours on the phone late at night and would get so involved that he forgot everything else. Room service at the hotel caught on to this trait quickly. So, when he called room service at 3 A.M. for his usual steak and potatoes dinner, it was cooked and brought over. .

The kitchen waited fifteen minutes and cooked and delivered another steak dinner identical to the first. By the time the second arrived, the first steak dinner was cold and untouched by Hughes who had been on the phone. This process was repeated several times before Hughes stopped telephoning long enough to eat. He was charged for all the steak dinners delivered.

His transportation arrangements were very odd. He feared assassins, kidnappers, or just plain nosy people. So, he never went in or out of the hotel through the lobby. By living in the bungalow area, he could simply walk out to Crescent Street on one side of the property and get into a rented Cadillac that he kept at the curb. He could, but he almost never did. He kept that Cadillac parked at the curb for several years paying several times more in rental fees than the car cost new.

In addition, he kept a car and a beat-up pickup truck in the basement garage of the hotel's main building so he could sneak into the garage from the rear grounds and drive out in either of the vehicles by himself. Or, have one of his Mormon bodyguards do the driving while Hughes hid on the floor.

He once read a recipe for a pineapple upside-down cake that intrigued him. About 1 A.M. one morning, he called the chef in the room-service kitchen to have a cake baked according to the recipe. The chef sent a bellman to an all-night market [a rarity in those days] in downtown Los Angeles for the ingredients and several hours later the cake was delivered to Hughes's room.

Hughes enjoyed the cake, but not the bill afterward. The chef billed him $25 for the cake and he complained to the owner of the hotel, Ben Silverstein, whom Hughes had never met in person. The owner was a crusty old real estate promoter from Detroit years before and he had one simple rule: everybody paid full price or got it free.

When Hughes objected to the $25, the owner said they would take it off his bill and it would be a gift to Hughes from the management. Stubborn, too, Hughes refused. He wanted to pay something, but not $25. Both men dug in their heels and, eventually, Hughes paid the $25 — a pittance compared to his normal daily charges over the years at the hotel.

These were only a few of the oddities of this true American eccentric. Early in the hearings, Judge Gregory decided there were no direct heirs qualified to share in the estate. Next, attention was focused on Hughes's relatives on his mother's side of the family.

This turned out to be fairly simple because of William Rice Lummis who was the oldest son of Frederick and Anent Gano Lummis, Howard Hughes's mother's sister and Hughes's aunt. The 16-year-old Hughes lived with Gano Lummis after his mother died and while he attended Rice University.

William Rice Lummis thus was Howard Hughes's

first cousin on his mother's side. Ironically, Lummis practiced law at Andrews and Kurth in Houston, the firm that did Hughes's legal work, but the two cousins never worked together.

Howard Hughes hadn't been dead but a few days when Lummis swung into action on behalf of the family as if he had planned it all out before. He got a Delaware court to appoint him temporary sole stockholder in the Summa Company, Hughes's main company, and named temporary coadministrator of the Hughes estate in Texas and Nevada.

He took a leave of absence from his law firm, moved to Nevada and took charge of Summa's operations pending a determination about the estate.

Lummis quickly claimed Hughes's body when the Las Vegas authorities released it. He had assumed temporary control of Hughes's business by simply seizing it, but knew there would be many challenges down the road because of the vast amount of money involved.

No matter what happened, Lummis would be a rich man either as the heir of his mother, if she was declared Hughes's sole heir — which was possible under the laws of Nevada and California — or by Lummis being one of Hughes's cousins if she wasn't the sole heir.

Then, Lummis called a meeting of the twelve people on Hughes's mother's side who qualified as first cousins. He convinced them all to join in a 16-page "Settlement Agreement." The 12 cousins agreed on splitting their part of the inheritance privately no matter how it turned out in court.

Of course, this did nothing about the question of heirs on Hughes's father's side of the family, which turned out to be quite controversial.

While the family bloodlines on Hughes's mother's

side of the family—the Gano side—were fairly clear and simple, that wasn't so on his father's side. On the paternal wing, the bloodlines were convoluted. They involved murder, a messy divorce, a drowning, uncertain marriages, an incredible massacre, confused identities, impotence, and family betrayal.

As noted before, Howard, Sr. had two brothers. Felix, Jr., and Rupert, plus one sister, Greta. All three had died before Howard Hughes, Jr. and, therefore, had no claim on his estate.

However, their children would be the next in line and could claim inheritance as first cousins. The court investigators spent five years trying to find out who was really a bloodline cousin and who just seemed to be. The one thing that was definitely established was that Felix had lived as a vocal coach in Los Angeles, was married three times, but had no children by any of these wives. So that took care of one relative.

Greta, likewise, did not appear to have any children, but her life was so marbled with mystery that the investigators checked very carefully for fear that an unknown child existed somewhere. In their digging, they found some strange things. For example, Greta was supposed to have died February 21, 1916, and it was rumored that she had committed suicide.

Investigators found her death certificate stating the date of her death, but the date of the coroner's written signature on the certificate was *five years earlier*—April 23, 1911.

This contradiction made investigators dig deeper into Greta's life and death and that meant digging deeper into Rupert's life since they seemed linked. Rupert, a Hollywood movie producer whom Howard, Jr. hated, supposedly had one daughter, Elspeth Hughes Lapp, but she had also died before Howard, Jr.

So, the bloodline, if intact, would flow from Rupert to Elspeth to her three daughters: Barbara Lapp Cameron, Elspeth Lapp DePould, and Anges Lapp Roberts. These three might be eligible for one-half of the Hughes estate just as the Gano side of the family was eligible for the other half.

It didn't turn out to be that simple, however, because the court investigators and the genealogist, Mary Fay, all believed that there was something definitely wrong with Elspeth's status that clouded the inheritance claims of Elspeth's three daughters. The problem for the court investigators and the genealogist was that a lot of what they uncovered could not be legally introduced as evidence in court.

For one thing, two large groups of relatives on the Hughes side of the family showed up to claim that Rupert Hughes never had a daughter named Elspeth. Each had a different scenario, but both insisted that Elspeth was not Rupert's natural daughter.

If that was true, the inheritance bloodline on Howard, Jr.'s father's side would jump back to Howard, Jr.'s grandparents, Judge Felix Turner Hughes and Jean Summerlin Hughes. The middle name of the judge is important as you will see in a moment.

If the bloodline jumped back a generation to Howard, Jr.'s grandparents, then Barbara Lapp Cameron, Elspeth Lapp DePould, and Anges Lapp Roberts would not be direct bloodline heirs and a whole different set of relatives would inherit in their place.

The first of the two groups of relatives in this controversy were from Midwestern communities centered around Keokuk, Iowa, where Howard, Jr.'s father, uncles, and aunt grew up. We'll call them the "Keokuk Group."

The second group were from a different branch of the Hughes family that settled around Kentucky and Georgia and we'll call them the "Kentucky Group."

The Keokuk group brought forth a series of family witnesses saying that it was "common talk" in the family that Rupert was sterile from having mumps as a boy. Therefore, Elspeth couldn't have been his daughter. She was in fact, they claimed, the illicit daughter from an affair Rupert's wife had with another man.

Family members claimed that Rupert had often told them that he wished he could have had a child. On his visits back to the Keokuk area from Los Angeles and at family reunions, he never mentioned a daughter to any of his friends or relatives. The Keokuk group also produced some documents executed by Rupert during the time that Elspeth was alive in which the line or box that asked about children was left blank by Rupert.

The attorney for Elspeth's daughters, of course, dismissed most of this as gossip, hearsay, and inadmissible in court. While it cast doubt on Elspeth's legitimacy, he said, it failed to prove that she was not Rupert Hughes's daughter.

Then the Kentucky group came forth with their arguments. They agreed with the Keokuk group that Elspeth was not really Rupert Hughes's daughter. However, they had a different explanation that not only didn't require medical proof of Rupert's sterility, but claimed that he did have a daughter by another wife, Agnes.

The Kentucky group claimed that this daughter was named Leila and she drowned in the family swimming pool in California in 1921. Then, the drowned girl was secretly replaced by another girl of her age who was the daughter of Rupert's second wife by another man. If this were true, the end result would be the same, namely, that the three women, Barbara Lapp Cameron, Elspeth Lapp DePould, and Anges Lapp Roberts, were not legitimate heirs of Howard, Jr.'s estate.

But, the Kentucky group gave their claim a bizarre twist. The Kentucky group claimed that Howard, Jr.'s grandfather, Judge Felix Turner Hughes, was a fraud and not a member of the Keokuks' Turner branch of the Hughes family. He was, instead, a renegade from the Kentucky branch of the Hughes whose real middle name was not Turner, but Moner.

Their claim was that Felix was born into the Kentucky branch of the family, but had turned against his family in the Civil War and joined the Northern branch of the family. He was such a despicable renegade that he and some members of his adopted Hughes family ambushed his eight brothers as they were en route to join the Confederate Army and massacred them.

Then, when the rest of the family fled farther south, Felix secretly followed them and stole their life savings of $140,000 at gunpoint.

When Felix moved north to become a member of the other branch of the Hughes family, he changed his middle name from Moner to Turner. Thus, the bloodline, according to the Kentucky group, traced back from Howard, Jr. through his father and to the Kentucky Hughes — not the Keokuk Hughes. That meant still another set of heirs.

For the next five years, court investigators tracked down every bit of information about Rupert Hughes that they could find in court records, interviews, newspaper articles, government forms, statements, and memories of relatives no matter how obscure or distant. This massive effort would produce a result after Howard Hughes's death almost as bizarre as his life before his death.

The investigators followed the claims of the Keokuk and the Kentucky groups in minute detail trying to verify every statement, claim, fact, and nuance.

In the end, the verdict was as odd as one could expect. The conclusion was that there was an enormous amount of material backing up the contention that Elspeth Rapp was not the natural daughter of Rupert Hughes and the investigators personally felt that her three daughters were not, therefore, entitled to be heirs to the Howard Hughes fortune.

However, most of the material the investigators had collected was not admissible in court. It wasn't acceptable by legal standards and, therefore, Judge Pat Gregory felt he had no choice but to accept the claims of Elspeth Rapp's three daughters.

In the end, the Hughes millions was split up among the tax collector, the lawyers, and 21 warring heirs—most of whom Howard Hughes didn't know.

Seventeen years later, writers would still be exploring Howard Hughes's arcane life. For example, in the summer of 1993, Putnam and Sons published *Howard Hughes: The Secret Life* by Charles Higham who had written previous biographies of Errol Flynn claiming the actor was a Nazi spy in World War II and the Duke of Windsor claiming he, too, was an agent of Hitler's.

Higham alleged that Hughes was a major force in the Watergate scandal and had worked closely with the CIA including having owned an island 40 miles north of Cuba that the CIA used as a base of operations against Castro.

The final twist of the Howard Hughes inheritance spins around to its curious end to the career of probate judge Pat Gregory. The judge had been on the Houston bench since 1968 and eventually became supervisory judge over all Texas probate judges. He has been hailed as the father of the Texas probate code.

As such, he has been involved in a number of famous and infamous inheritance cases in Houston to the point of writing a book detailing his experiences. Besides the Howard Hughes case of the 1970s, he was more recently involved in the hottest inheritance case of the 1990s in Houston over the Sakowitz estate. That's treated in a later chapter.

The judge was indicted in January 1993, for money laundering, filing a false income tax return, and misuse of campaign funds. On July 8, 1993, he cut a plea bargain and pled guilty. He faces six months in the slammer and a fine of $250,000. Another curious end to someone connected with the perplexing blood-money war over Howard Hughes.

Two

How Money Destroyed The Dodge Family Heirs

Unlike the Howard Hughes case, there was no question about who the heirs of the Dodge brothers were. The sons and daughters of these two giants of the American automobile industry lived in controlled luxury awaiting the outcome of the dark maneuverings of their parents before coming into their rewards. Then, the children were outraged at the outcome.

The family history of the Dodges has been called a tragedy in which the sons and daughters were the prisoners of money and the family's wealth was the main villain.

John and Horace Dodge had a bicycle shop in Niles, Michigan, and began making parts for car manufacturers such as Ransom E. Olds and Henry Ford. In fact, the first Ford Model-Ts were made by the Dodge brothers with only the tires and wooden buckboard seat being added at the Ford plant.

When Alex Y. Malcolmson and Henry Ford

formed the Henry Motor Company, they got the Dodge brothers to sign up as exclusive suppliers of many parts and gave each of them 5 percent of the new company and made John a director.

By 1913, however, Ford began getting parts from other suppliers, too, and the Dodge brothers were afraid that their only customer, Ford Motors, would cancel its contract with them and leave them high and dry. So, John left the Ford board of directors and the two brothers started the Dodge Corporation using the dividends they were getting from their combined 10 percent share of Ford.

Ford was angry about the Dodge boys going into competition with him and struck back by putting a upper limit on dividends that Ford Motor would pay out in the future. The Dodges immediately sued. The case took three years, but the Dodge brothers won and Ford was forced to pay out $19 million in back dividends.

However, Ford pulled a fast move on his enemies by quitting as president of Ford Motor Company and announcing he was starting a new company in California to build his cars and he and his son would be the only stockholders. So, whether they won or lost the lawsuit, there would be no more dividends coming from the old Ford Motor Company. This made the value of the old Ford company stock plunge and devalued the Dodge brothers holdings along with those of other stockholders. Meanwhile, Ford's agents were secretly buying up Ford stock at 50 cents or less on the dollar and, very soon, Henry was in total control of his old company.

Henry had snookered John and Horace, but they

still ended up with $25 million between them. By the time the Dodge brothers died in 1920—curiously within a few months of each other—they left their heirs a combined fortune of around $200 million. In 1994 dollars, $200 million in 1920 is the equivalent today of $1.5 billion!

John left the most curious of the two wills in which he specifically named a variety of clothing items as part of his bequests to his heirs. These included ten overcoats, a hundred items of underclothing along with 109 shirts. It is best left to a psychologist to explain the reason for this.

One Dodge biographer, Caroline Latham, observed the family was left with a huge fortune that none of them had the slightest idea of how to manage nor did any of them have a clue on running the business that created the fortune. "There was no connection between the money and the source," Latham contended.

The will left Matilda and Anna, the two widows and their children, a major car manufacturing business producing half a million cars a year with some good people to run it. Horace, a few weeks before he died, had personally selected one of these, Frederick J. Haynes, to be president of the Dodge Corporation. It was a wise and happy choice for all the Dodge families because Haynes ran the business well and generated millions of dollars in profits for the heirs of the two former bicycle mechanics.

The down side, of course, is that all that money also created jealousies, envy, anger, and greed among the heirs. Another family feud was about to erupt.

If the Dodge brothers had been successful in creating a big, wealthy corporation, they were equally successful in creating a big, wealthy family. John married three times and Horace married once. The two brothers had sired seven children between them.

So, when they died, they left behind a total of eleven possible heirs — four wives and seven children — in the first generation after themselves.

John married Ivy Hawkins in 1892 and they had three children, John Duval Dodge, Winifred Dodge, and Isabelle Dodge.

Later, he dumped Ivy for Isabelle Smith with whom he had a childless marriage that lasted from 1903 to 1907. He divorced Isabelle and immediately married his secretary and the daughter of a Detroit German saloon keeper, Matilda Rausch, by whom he had two more children, Frances Dodge and Daniel Dodge. So, John left three widows, two sons, and three daughters.

Horace married Christiana Anna Thomson in 1871 by whom he had two children, Horace, Jr. and Delphine.

Each brother set up a trust with all of the income from Horace's trust to be paid to his widow, Anna. When she died, the principal of the trust was to be split between his children, Horace, Jr. and Delphine. So, during Anna's lifetime, Horace and Delphine would be at the mercy of Anna's good will.

The income from the trust set up by John was split six ways with equal shares to his widow, Matilda, the children of his first marriage [Winifred and Isabel] and the children of his last marriage

[France, Daniel, and Anna Margaret]. His son, John Duval Dodge, was cut off without a penny.

So, Horace produced two children while John produced five, but Horace's two made up for their small number by the size of the newspaper headlines they generated in the years after inheriting Horace's fortune.

They did this in a variety of ways including numerous marriages. Delphine married three times and Horace, Jr. five times and each one was instructive. Their goal in life seemed to be to have a good time and see just how much Dodge money they could squander in the shortest period of time.

Delphine first married James H.R. Cromwell, the son of Mrs. Lucretia Stotesbury. Mrs. Stotesbury had been the widow of a well-to-do Philadelphia lawyer who died in 1911 after which she quickly married Edward T. Stotesbury, twenty years her senior, a multimillionaire partner in the Wall Street financial house of J.P. Morgan. She always regarded her marriage to Stotesbury as the "most profitable financial transaction" she had ever made.

In 1926 Delphine and James got entangled in a bad Florida real estate development that went down the porcelain to the tune of $3 million, which Delphine and James's mothers made good, but Anna was not a happy benefactor and wrote to Jim's mother, Eva Stotesbury, just before she helped with the $3 million bailout,

> Once or twice I have settled up Jim's debts to the extent of $100,000 or more. This I will not do again, nor will I participate in helping to settle them. If the children cannot live on

an income of $200,000 a year with gifts from me that I give them from time to time, then it is high time they began to learn to do so.

Unfortunately, the stock market crash of 1929 and her extravagant ways effectively destroyed the $100 million Stotesbury fortune, but Edward probably didn't care because he doted on Lucretia and regarded her beauty and luxury-loving lifestyle as a certification of his own success.

Lucretia's daughter, Louise, would marry three times: a Baltimore man was the first, short and not so sweet marriage; and a not-too-successful movie actor, Lionel Atwill, was the last with an ambitious army officer sandwiched in-between. The army officer was Douglas MacArthur.

Lucretia's oldest son contemplated working, but decided marrying rich women was more fun and there was no heavy lifting.

While not opposed to marrying rich women, Jimmy Cromwell did do his bit to earn his way. He prepared by graduating from the Wharton School of Finance and then married Delphine Dodge. He became involved in the Dodge Corporation and handled the public sale of the company after his father-in-law and uncle-in-law had died.

So it was that in March 1925, Cromwell arranged the biggest cash deal in American history up to then with the investment firm of Dillon Read buying the Dodge Corporation for $146 million. Eight days later, Dillon Read sold its Dodge shares for a $28 million profit.

Unfortunately, Jimmy and Delphine didn't make it. Delphine was, according to Jimmy, emotionally unstable, moody, and likely to do bizarre things. Meanwhile, Jimmy tried his hand at the stock market and then had a string of bad luck losing big money in the Florida real estate crash, writing three modestly successful books, and finally returning to the old tried-and-true device of marrying rich. This time it was one of the poor little rich girls that America had learned to envy, hate, and regard as a national curiosity, Doris Duke of the tobacco fortune.

The Jimmy-Delphine marriage did produce a granddaughter for Anna Dodge, Christine Cromwell, but the divorce between Jimmy and Delphine was so abrasive with a notorious custody fight over Christine, that the court decided it was not in the child's best interest to be in the custody of either her mother or her father. Christine was awarded to grandmother Anna Dodge.

Christine followed the Dodge family pattern of high living, spending, matrimonial musical chairs, and lawsuits. In 1953, she sued the Dodge estate and her grandmother claiming that the trust had not been invested wisely by the trustees and her inheritance had been reduced because of it. It took over a year to have her allegation dismissed by the court, but she did succeed in making her 86-year-old grandmother unhappy.

After Delphine divorced Jimmy, she married Ray Baker, who soon decided to divorce her, but he died in Reno, Nevada, while waiting for the divorce to be final. Then she married Tim Godde, but wanted out of that marriage after two years so she went off to Nevada to wait out the required residence.

The time dragged slowly and Delphine's romance with a boxer, Jack Doyle, helped it to pass more quickly. Unfortunately, Jack's estranged wife was also a fighter and sued for alienation of affections to the tune of $2 million. Mama Anna came to the rescue as usual and paid Mrs. Doyle off, but Mama extracted a price. She insisted that Delphine call off the divorce from Godde.

Delphine's life had been spent in what became an unsuccessful lifelong quest for love involving numerous flirtations, affairs, and three unremarkable and unfulfilling marriages. She ended her days a virtual alcoholic recluse in her Rye, New York, mansion amid costly furniture and art and a wardrobe regularly replenished by a department store in Detroit. They had a mannequin that was the exact duplicate of Delphine's body and regularly sent her new clothes tailored on the mannequin. She died at the age of 43 in 1943.

Immediately following Delphine's death, her widower husband, Tim Godde, married Delphine's maid.

Naturally, there was a lawsuit. Delphine's husband, Timothy, sued Delphine's mother, Anna. Godde claimed that, when Delphine died, her mother promised him $48,000 a year for life if he gave up all claims as an heir to Delphine's estate. This was settled out of court.

Like his sister, Delphine, Horace, Jr. engaged in the same lifelong search for happiness. In the process, he dissipated his father's fortune even though his father tried to keep that from happening. The old man's will left Horace, Jr. only $2,500 a year income, but he harangued his mother until she finally increased that by ten times to $25,000, which still wasn't enough for the boy. So, Horace joined with his sister and got Momma to let them become trustees of the estate that they would eventually inherit anyhow.

Then, armed with money, Horace began his search for happiness and love.

Happiness for Horace, Jr. apparently meant whiskey, fast cars, women, and swaggering around town. Later he would add speedboat racing.

He was regularly arrested for speeding and one time flashed a deputy sheriff's badge at the arresting policeman with the threat of arresting the policeman for meddling in official county business. On that occasion, Horace pulled a gun on the policeman as well, but was disarmed after firing one shot into the ground. Horace, Jr., like his cousin, John Duval Dodge, liked to show off what a spoiled brat he was in the worse tradition of the playboy rich kid.

In the next 17 years, he twice married Detroit society women, Lois Knowlson and Muriel Sisman, and had two children by each. He had been carrying on with Muriel while still married to Lois, but after marrying Muriel, Horace got more and more involved in boat racing and boat building. This lead to frequent separations that became a permanent separation in 1933, but no one filed for divorce.

By this time, Horace was involved with a New York showgirl, Mickey Devine. Muriel reacted by filing several lawsuits against Horace for custody of their kids and a half-million dollars. This was a joke for the money-strapped Horace who was deeply enamored and in debt because of both the divine Mickey and boat racing.

In April of 1937, Horace struck back and filed for divorce on the grounds of mental cruelty because, he said, Muriel was saying terrible things about him in public. That didn't quiet Muriel who responded with more terrible things about Horace including his affairs with "a certain woman." Of course, Muriel meant Mickey and in going public about "the other woman" ignored that she, herself had been "the other woman" in Horace's life some years before.

All this public washing of dirty linen depressed Horace's mother, Anna, who was a quiet woman trying to lead a quiet life. She certainly was one of the happy ones when it ended in 1939 with divorce and Horace married Mickey. Unfortunately, the notoriety of the Dodges didn't end with that. Mickey loved headlines, too, and knew how to get them.

Mickey complained about Horace's drinking and finally made public charges of continual drunken brawling and wife beating that prompted the army to remove Horace—Major Horace Dodge—from active assignment as being unfit for duty.

Four years of this sort of thing was all Horace was willing to handle—particularly after he took up with an army nurse, Clara Mae Tinsley, whose love for the bottle matched Horace's. This soon ripened into Horace's fourth marriage following his divorce from Mickey. Anna Dodge objected to this union since she had spent much of her life trying to wean Horace off of booze without much notable success. In any case, Anna didn't have to worry about the marriage because it, too, soon began to come apart.

Then he met the love of his life, platinum blond knockout, Gregg Sherwood, while attending a fashion show with his mother as part of a grand tour of Europe. Sherwood was a TV actress and John Powers model 27 years younger than Horace. This irritated Clara Mae because their divorce was still pending. Clara Mae's irritation was soothed by a $3 million settlement.

The $3 million may not have been well spent since Horace's love of his life turned on him. Their romance began to turn sour and strange. There were fights and things thrown and smashed. Soon, Gregg walked out on Horace and vowed not to return until he got off the booze. She didn't want a divorce because a million-dollar trust fund was set up for her by Horace when they got married and it had a clause that nullified the trust fund if she ever divorced him. In other words, she was a piece of Dodge property bought and paid for.

Indicative that all was not well in the Horace-Gregg Dodge paradise, he called the cops and had his true love arrested in hometown Detroit. The charge? He claimed she had stolen four cigarette lighters from him. Later, he apologized saying he only wanted to keep her from leaving town and deserting him.

She didn't want to desert him, particularly since she was pregnant and would soon deliver a son, John Frances Dodge, II. However, Gregg did get revenge by penning a series of embarrassing newspaper articles that were, for their day, sexy confession tales about life with Horace. Gregg did other things to keep up with the headlines such as slapping a lot of people, including policemen and musicians, who didn't like it and complained publicly.

In 1961, Horace finally filed for divorce claiming that Gregg had such a hot temper that he feared for his personal safety. He also feared for his bank account since Gregg was a notorious big spender running up bills that amounted to twice or more than Horace's annual allowance from his mother. There was talk of reconciliation and things dragged until Horace became ill and died of cirrhosis of the liver at Christmas time 1963 at the age of 63.

Horace's death was not only unexpected, but created an enormous problem for his mother, Anna. She tried to outfox the inheritance tax collector by putting much of her real estate in Horace's name figuring Horace would outlast her. When he didn't, Anna had to buy it all back. At the end, Horace left an estate of $2 million and he also left eleven wills.

Clara Tinsley promptly filed suit for the back alimony and creditors by the score lined up to get their claims on record. Even Horace's mother, Anna, filed a claim against his estate for the more than $10 million she had "loaned" him over the years. Horace's earlier wives, Lois Knowlson and Muriel Sisman, also filed claims against the estate.

Gregg, seeing that everybody's claims and lawyers' fees would eat up the estate and more, turned around and sued her mother-in-law for alienation of affection—estimated to be worth $11 million—and for the $1 million supposedly held in trust for Gregg when she married Horace. Gregg claimed that Anna, her mother-in-law, had guaranteed the trust.

To the surprise of many, the 92-year-old Anna

quickly settled with Gregg out of court for $9 million. Soon after, Gregg married a detective 12 years her junior who Horace had hired to follow Gregg and check up on rumors she was having affairs. The rumors apparently were true because she spent the last two years of her marriage to Horace having an affair with the detective.

By contrast to her children, Mrs. Anna Dodge, widow of Horace, Sr., married an ex-actor in 1926, Hugh Dillman, several years younger than herself. The two set up shop as high society leaders in Palm Beach in an estate whose $1,800,000 value was exceeded only by their $2 million yacht.

On John's side of the family, things were a little quieter except for John Duval Dodge. The other four children of John Dodge took their money and genteelly slipped away from most public notice. Not John Duval.

In the first place, John Duval had made his father furious by running away to Texas with his high school sweetheart bride and living the life of a simple mechanic, which incidentally his father had been before he became rich. John, Sr.'s attitude was that, damn it, he had worked hard to elevate the Dodge family's social stature and his idiot son was trying to revert to the bad old times.

It would not do and to make his point, John, Sr. cut John Duval off with nothing but $150 a month. John Duval's two brothers and two sisters each got a shade over $8 million. Newspaper headlines in January, 1920 trumpeted the death of John Dodge and also the fact that he had cut his son off with nothing but a pittance.

The apple didn't fall far from the tree in this

case and John Duval could also get furious. So, he became a bad boy in public getting into brawls and fights and vowing to carry that pugnaciousness into the courtroom with lawsuit after lawsuit to get his fair share of his father's estate.

One night he and a friend were cruising around town looking for some action when they picked up three Kalamazoo College coeds. They offered the girls whiskey and tried showing off by driving so recklessly that one of the girls jumped out of the speeding car in fear. She was picked up by another motorist and taken to the hospital.

The girl's mother filed charges and the two men were arrested with John Duval acting the arrogant punk. Even though he spent the weekend in jail, he lorded it over all the police and jailers, reminded them who he was and how they would be sorry about all this.

The newspapers were, of course, all over the story and John Duval played his arrogant asshole role up to the hilt, posing casually smoking a cigarette in the sheriff's office with his feet up on the desk. He ended up shoving coal for the county jail for five days. On a second charge, he got off with a stiff lecture from the judge.

Meanwhile, his sisters, Winifred and Isabelle, were trying to force their stepmother to stop spending any more money on the elaborate Grosse Pointe mansion begun by John, Sr., in a bid to be accepted into high society, but left several million dollars short of completion by his death.

Both John, Sr. and Matilda had come from ordinary backgrounds and were determined to buy their place among the aristocracy of their region by be-

ing part of Grosse Pointe society. The silly rule
that existed for acceptance and admiration in
Grosse Pointe society was that your social stature
was directly proportional to the size of your Grosse
Pointe mansion and to how little time you actually
lived there or anywhere else in Grosse Pointe.

Winifred and Isabelle knew that their father's
will allowed all the money necessary to complete
the Grosse Pointe mansion to be taken from the
general estate and not from Matilda's portion. That
meant the estate left for the stepchildren would be
smaller.

John Duval had sued to break the will and get
what he thought was his fair share. Matilda, his
stepmother, tried to avert the unpleasant publicity
that John Duval seemed intent upon generating for
the bereaved family. She wanted to have a quiet,
private settlement worked out. Unfortunately, the
law in Michigan didn't permit that.

The law said that the terms of a will could not
be altered by settlements and agreements among
the heirs. Matilda's ready solution to this law was
to have the law changed and changed it was.
Everybody involved then agreed to give John Duval
Dodge $1.6 million in exchange for his foregoing
any further claims against the estate. It seemed
pretty small considering what everyone else in the
family got, but John Duval grabbed it and took
off for a tour of Europe with his new wife, Marie
O'Connor. They ran through the money faster than
Mexican water through a Yankee tourist.

John Duval tried parlaying his $1.6 million into
more money in real estate, the car business—he
tried to market a new car called the Dodgeson—

and a nightclub venture, but nothing clicked.

The Dodgeson project was ripening in 1924 — three years after he got his $1.6 million settlement from the family and the same year that his half-sister, Anna Margaret Dodge, died on Palm Sunday of complications resulting from severe measles. The death devastated Matilda who was being comforted by her companion and soon-to-be husband, Alfred G. Wilson, a respected member of her church and one of Detroit's most eligible bachelors.

All of that aside, John Duval decided that he was entitled to one-fifth of his half-sister's estate and was soon in court demanding it. Besides he needed the money to go ahead with the introduction of his Dodgeson car.

It took until January 1926, for the court to rule on John Duval's claim on his half sister's estate and the ruling was to reject his claim. The judge said the $7.5 million estate of Anna Margaret should all go to her mother who was, incidentally, also John Duval's mother.

It made no difference to John Duval; he appealed the ruling and his two sisters Winifred and Isabelle also joined in the action to keep the money from all going to their mother. Their mother, Matilda, asked the court for a summary dismissal of their court actions by her children, but the judge said no and the game went on with the newspapers having another field day over the Dodge blood-money feuds. The mother finally won after three years of court battles and that killed John Duval's dream of launching the Dodgeson car.

He had another chance at getting money when his half-brother, Daniel, died in a freak accident.

Daniel was a quiet, outdoors type who spent a lot of time in the Ontario providence of Canada at his remote lodge, Gore Bay. There he met an equally quiet, outdoors woman, Laurine Mac-Donald, who was the local telephone operator. They courted for two years and married in 1938.

Eight days later, Daniel and some men friends were fiddling around with dynamite when it exploded prematurely injuring Daniel and several others including Laurine. Dan, cut and bleeding with a mangled arm and the other injured victims—Laurine's arm was broken—got into their speedboat and the group raced across a storm-whipped lake to the nearest medical facility.

Laurine was trying to steer with her one good arm, but was getting weaker. As one of the other injured men took the wheel from her, Daniel stood up in the boat and fell over the side. He was never seen alive again. Two fisherman found his mud-encased body weeks later.

It was a sad time for the Dodge family, but not so sad that they couldn't dredge up a lawsuit over dead Daniel's estate.

Laurine had signed an agreement during the few days after she and Daniel had married in which she agreed she would only get $250,000 and the Gore Bay lodge. After $175,000 to his siblings and chauffeur, Daniel wanted the rest of his eight or ten million estate to go to his mother, Matilda Dodge.

First came the inquest into Daniel's death in a Canadian court where testimony was given suggesting that Daniel's death was not accidental. It was shown that the dynamite explosion was not enough to have killed Daniel and that there had been life jackets in the boat. Even so, the jury ruled the death an accident.

When the court finally ruled on the claims against Daniel's estate, it was the government that won. His mother got $3.75 million, Laurine got $1.25 million, and the government got $6 million in inheritance taxes.

It was only one battle in the blood-money feud over the Dodge money. Daniel's half-sisters and sister registered appeals of the ruling saying that, if the money were to go to them, there would be no inheritance taxes.

The reasoning was that inheritance taxes had been paid on their father's estate when he died. And, according to their father's will, if any of his children died without children, that child's share of the father's estate was to be divided among John Dodge, Sr.'s remaining children with the exception of his disinherited son, John Duval Dodge.

Then, in typical fashion, John Duval jumped in to muddy the situation by filing a new lawsuit demanding that his father's original estate be divided as if he had died 18 years before without leaving a will.

The dispute was finally settled out of court when Daniel's mother, wife, half-sisters, and sister all agreed to split his estate. Half went to his mother and the other have was split among the other women. John Duval got nothing.

John Duval was a rich kid who repeatedly messed up his life and that of other people. He seemed to always be getting arrested for fighting or drunken driving and once ran down a child. If he sounded like a kid doomed to a bad end, he fulfilled that fate in a mysterious way. In early August 1942, he was dead from a concussion, but the cause was vague.

Earlier on the evening of August 11th, he ended up at the Tiger Bar in Detroit after a bout of pub crawling. Somebody sent him home in a cab, but, instead, he went next door to call on 33-year-old Mignon Fontaine who was alone at the time. She tried to get rid of him, but gave in to his demand for a drink, which she gave him in the kitchen.

At that point, John Duval's second wife, Dora, showed up and a fight followed with Dora hitting John with a bowl and John knocking Dora down. He left the house, Mignon washed the blood off Dora and sent her home with some friends who had come looking for her.

Then John returned to Mignon's house and tried to get into her bedroom by climbing in the window, but she fled from the house and hid in the bushes outside. The police arrived, arrested John and took him to jail where he behaved in his usual arrogant way and became unruly. In the process of the police subduing him at the station, John Duval hit his head on the floor. He didn't get proper medical treatment for several hours and, when he did, it was too late. John Duval's troubled life ended late on the night of August 12th on the floor of a jail.

John Duval's wife, Dora, died a couple years later by deliberately driving her car directly into a onrushing freight train in Florida.

Also in Florida, Anna Dodge Dillon's marriage to Hugh Dillman was not going well because of rumors of his infidelities and Anna's uncertainties about whether he would have married her if she hadn't been an heiress. The marriage dissolved in 1947 with Dillman getting a million-dollar settlement and Anna getting back her first married name, Dodge.

Anna would survive until she was 98 or 103, depending on which newspaper you read in June of 1970. She controlled millions of Dodge dollars until her death and when she left, the lawsuits arrived.

The way the inheritance was supposed to work at this point according to Horace, Sr.'s wishes was that the remainder of his estate, $48 million, was to be split between his two children, Horace, Jr. and Delphine. Since each of them was dead, Horace, Jr.'s half would be split five ways among his children, Delphine Dodge, Horace Dodge, III, David Dodge, Diana Dodge, and John Dodge. Delphine's half would be split between her two daughters, Christine and Yvonne.

Meanwhile, the $20 million of Anna's estate was to go in trust for Horace, Jr.'s oldest four children, with his oldest son by Gregg, John Dodge, getting virtually cut off with a piddling $25,000 similar to how his namesake, John Duval, had been treated by John Dodge, Sr. Anna left nothing to the children of her daughter, Delphine, apparently because they were getting much bigger shares of their grandfather's estate and were, thus, well taken care of financially.

While that may have seemed rational to Anna, Delphine's daughters, Christine and Yvonne, saw it much differently. Being Dodges who must have in-

herited the family's notorious litigious gene, they
wanted to share equally in Anna's $20 million with
their cousins and sued to break the will.

In fact, they had a special reason for concern
because they had borrowed heavily against their expected inheritance over the previous years — in
Christiana's case since 1944 — and there were some
700 creditors or claimants waiting in line behind
the two sisters.

Gregg's new husband, Dan Moran, was another
litigant, filing suit on behalf of his stepson, John
Dodge, for an equal share of the estate even
though Anna was very specific in her willing about
the $25,000 bequest "and no more."

Then, there were creditors of the late Horace,
Jr., who, not able to collect on his meager estate,
wanted to get what was due them from his
mother's or grandfather's estate.

The blood-money feuds over the Dodge millions
would drag on for years and enrich mostly the lawyers, but a respectable number of millions did finally trickle down to the next generation of
great-grandchildren.

At the end, the two Dodge brothers' wives ended
up intentionally isolated from the world and, most
importantly, their children.

Matilda spent her last years alone at her
Meadow Brook Hall estate refusing to communicate with most of her family because she was so
angry at what they had done and the way they had
lived. She died in 1967 at age 84 and was survived
by one daughter from John Dodge, Frances, and
two adopted children from Alfred Wilson, Richard
and Barbara.

Naturally, all three sued to break her will. They lost.

Horace's widow, Anna, also isolated herself in her mansion, Rose Terrace, refusing to see or talk to her family. She spent her days watching three TV sets all on at the same time in her turquoise bedroom and eating enormous meals.

Visitors, few and infrequent, were permitted to go into the bedroom and speak to her only for a few minutes during commercials. She died June 2, 1970, a lonely, embittered woman of 98 or 103.

The Dodge story seems typical of a family of pioneer men in a field who made a lot of money quickly and passed it on to their heirs who had no idea of how to deal with their sudden riches. None of them had worked for all that money and had no idea of what their fathers had done to earn it.

They all lived with the bewildering freedom their family wealth gave them while plagued with guilt about being undeservedly better off than others. Some felt the curse of their superachiever fathers whom they could not emulate. The fathers succeeded at everything and the sons and daughters failed at everything.

In the process they fell victim to hustlers, shattered the dreams of others, and were always insecure about whether they were accepted and loved for who they were rather than the family money they had.

In general, a pathetic and bewildered lot whose who existence was summarized by the 63-year-old Horace Dodge, Jr.'s dying words, "Where's Mommy?"

Three

How Money and Sex Twisted the Heirs of H.L. "Arizona Slim" Hunt—Gambler, Bigamist, Oil Man, Right-Wing Militant, Health-Food Faddist, and Genuine Texas Eccentric

The boy who became America's richest oil man suckled at his mother's breast until he was in his midteens.

The story of H.L. Hunt is more than the tale of a man who sought money vastly beyond what he needed. It is a story of a rich man who really wanted immortality and he tried to buy it with money by creating as many offspring to carry his seed as possible—with peculiar results.

He was convinced his loins harbored a genius gene that must be spread as far as possible. His conviction colored his life and the lives of those whom his seed produced.

Later, some would believe his suckling sustenance out of his mother for so long was symbolic of his life. Whether it was or not, it drove his father bonkers and ultimately forced Haroldson Lafayette Hunt out of his parents' Illinois home when he was only sixteen and set him on his way to making a fortune of $13 billion.

The observable basis of Haroldson Lafayette Hunt's fortune was a photographic memory, his ability to assess human nature, and his love of gambling. These made him rich and saved him from disaster on many occasions. It made him one of the best poker players in America in every sense of that phrase.

Beyond that, he womanized with a passion and regarded women primarily as a conduit for his genes to duplicate his image. He had three families, two at the same time, and sired 15 children, many of whom would battle over his money.

This supreme egotist who believed in greed as an essential quality became a right-wing nut and health-food faddist. He was a classic American eccentric. He turned to fundamentalist religions late in life—at age 70—when he felt his confrontation with God was near. Congenital gambler that he was in his lifetime, he didn't want to gamble on that last hand destiny would deal him.

In 1906, he left his Ramsey, Illinois, home, the youngest of eight children and headed west to seek his fortune taking life and work as it came. He drove sheep in Utah, washed dishes and harvested sugar beets in Colorado, repaired railroad tracks in Kansas, and planted trees on the Irvine Ranch in southern California.

In San Francisco he fell in with a drinking and gambling crowd and made the most important personal discovery of his life. He learned he could do well at poker because of his photographic memory and natural ability to read men's personalities. He loved the excitement and would have stayed in San Francisco, but a whore changed his mind.

She liked him because he paid well and was polite and, one night after she had serviced him, she warned him not to go back to his rooming house. Ship captains, desperate for seamen, hired press gangs to sweep rooming houses, brothels, and bars to shanghai sleeping and drunk men onto their ships. When the men woke up, they would be at sea on their way to China. A sweep was set, she told him, for his rooming house. He hid out and escaped, but it wouldn't be the last time he hid from men bent on harming him.

That experience and word of semipro baseball tryouts in Reno got Haroldson Lafayette out of town. He didn't make the cut in the baseball tryouts and drifted south to the logging camps of northern Arizona where his poker skills almost got him killed.

The camps were divided ethnically with Mexicans in one and whites in another. After a long day of sawing and hauling timber in the high plateau near the Grand Canyon, the loggers settled around the campfires to drink, tell tall tales, sing, and play cards.

One night Hunt and some others drifted over to the Mexican camp where a vigorous game of poker that was in progress gave the young Hunt a chance to show off his poker.

At first his skill was greeted with sighs of appreciation, but, as player after player was stripped of cash, the Mexicans grew silent. Apprehensive or bored, Hunt's fellow white loggers drifted back to their own camp.

The Mexicans did not like the gringo cleaning out all the cash in the camp and, reading their sullenness, Hunt cashed out, promised to give them a chance to get even the next night, and melted into the darkness.

He moved quickly through the tall pine trees toward the white camp some distance away afraid that the Mexicans would decide to kill him and reclaim the $4,000 he had won from them. Yet, when he came within sight of the white camp's fire, he hung back in the woods. He was safe from the Mexicans, but what would his fellow white loggers do to get his $4,000? Being a winner could be hazardous, so he decided to sleep alone hidden in the forest.

It was an uneasy night because the wind on the northern Arizona plateau tiptoes through the tree tops creating a *sshhhing* sound like distant surf and loud enough to cover a killer stalking in the darkness. Occasionally, it knocked loose a pine cone or rotten branch to drop to the forest floor a hundred yards away. The sound makes you positive someone is coming with a gleaming blade to slit your throat and let your life-blood gurgle out onto the dark brown earth.

Before that scary night was over he decided it was time to head on home to Ramsey and see his kin. He arrived there, but only stayed for a few months before he was off again, this time with his less worldly brother, Leonard, in tow. They hit the lumber camps around Flagstaff again and then on to California to visit their sister Florence.

Hunt never liked his given name and picked up the nickname "Arizona Slim" along the way. Some

friends called him that and some called him H.L.
We'll call him both, but mostly H.L., since that's
what most people called him.

From California, H.L. and Leonard moved into
the misty forests of Oregon to work the tall timber
camps and, then, to harvest wheat in the Dakotas.
Leonard, not the rugged soul Slim was, dropped
out and headed back home while Slim took off for
Canada.

He had been knocking around Western Canada
doing odd jobs during the day and sitting around
brightly lit card tables at night when his sister's
telegram caught up with him. Leonard had died of
an illness. Slim packed in the cards and headed
back to Ramsey.

They buried his brother and it left Slim sad. A
few months later, Hash, his father, died of cancer.
They buried his father and it left Slim relieved. He
had feared and hated the man as long as he was
old enough to know him. Now the man was dead
and Slim had a $5,000 inheritance in his pocket
and he hit the road south.

The inheritance was spent on 1,000 acres of what
the Confederate local sharpies around Lake Village,
Arkansas, told him was good farm land and Slim
planted cotton. The rains came and Slim's cotton
drowned under several feet of water and the Rebs
were laughing. The second year, Slim switched to
corn and the cutworms, probably also Confeder-
ates, did the crop and Slim in. He was 23 years old
and worse than broke. He was in the hole.

Not one to sit still in adversity, he wandered over
to nearby Greenville where he had heard there were
high-stake poker games at the Planters Club. Well,

hell, he was a planter—maybe not a harvester, but at least a planter—and so he went and his poker winnings soon got him out of the hole.

For H.L., 1914 was a bad and a good year. It was bad because the one human being that meant the most to him, his mother, Ella Rose Hunt, died and he went home to bury her and cry. After that, he came back to Lake Village and courted Mattie Bunker who toyed with him, but didn't take him seriously, so he married her sister, Lyda Bunker.

It was a turn of good luck. World War I began in Europe and that meant prosperity in the America that was supplying the Allies and land prices started jumping with gambler H.L. Hunt buying and selling and making good profits. He found a way to gamble in business and make money.

He also found something else that would be important to him for the rest of his life: a conduit for his genes. He was gone from home a lot, gambling on real estate and at poker, but he seemed to be home enough to get Lyda impregnated. They already had Margaret and November 1917, the first son was born, Haroldson Lafayette Hunt, Jr., who was promptly nicknamed, "Hassie."

He certainly did carry the H.L. Hunt genes and that proved not to be as fortunate as his father thought it would be. His life became a series of twisted heartbreaks.

Now, H.L.'s world had expanded into big-money deals and big-money games in New Orleans where he sat with confidence playing five-card stud. For him it was the one form of poker that involved the most skill and the least luck.

He wife stayed in Lake Village and fumed about

his gambling. Even though he made good money at the card table, Lyda hated that he gambled at places like the Gruneswald in an atmosphere of easy money, easy whiskey, and easy women. H.L. enjoyed all three.

The war boom ended and H.L. suddenly wasn't doing very well in his real estate deals. He had gobbled up land all over the Louisiana-Arkansas region figuring that cotton prices would drop with the lessening demand for uniforms and clothes at the end of the war. H.L. decided that land would skyrocket. That's what happened, but it happened too late for H.L.

It was 1920 and H.L. Hunt was broke again. Then, he took another gamble. He heard there was a minor oil boom going on in El Dorado about 100 miles west. Oil boom to H.L. meant oil field workers with lots of money and a need for fun at night.

He borrowed some money and showed up in El Dorado where nights saw swarms of money-heavy oil field workers flow through the bars and brothels, yelling and singing, and moving on. For those looking for a session of five-card stud, H.L. Hunt was their man.

Hunt kept winning money, but his most important winning was a one-acre oil lease that he won three months after showing up in El Dorado. He returned to Lake Village to say hello to the family and hustle $10,000 drilling money. He got it from friends, returned to El Dorado and hit oil.

Unfortunately, his equipment was antiquated and he couldn't exploit the well properly. So, it was back to the card tables for more operating money.

He got the money, the new equipment he needed and the oil started flowing.

Now it was January 1922, and H.L. had parlayed his poker winnings and first oil well into two wells on a twenty-acre lease pumping out 10,000 barrels a day. Springboarding off this success, he raised money for a third well and moved Lyda, Margaret, and Hassie to El Dorado and a nicer house.

Always dressed in a white suit, H.L. continued to move around. He worked the Arkansas-Louisiana border buying oil leases and started two gaming houses, which brought him into a working relationship with underworld characters who trusted him.

The fourth expression of his gene pool emerged briefly into the world, Lyda Bunker Hunt, only to break her parents' heart by dying a month later. H.L. decided he was doing well enough to afford it, so he took Lyda to New York City—first time for both of them—for a second honeymoon and so they could get over the loss of their daughter.

They both had a good time, particularly Lyda who didn't get to travel much, and loved the sights of this strange concrete wilderness on the island of Manhattan. But H.L. was H.L. and enjoy it as he did, he heard real estate was booming in Florida. So, he took Lyda back to El Dorado a week later, impregnated her once again and got on the train to Florida.

He thought he knew the woman with the well-turned figure and the cascade of long blond hair from somewhere the minute he walked into the real estate office in Tampa. Blue-eyed Frania Tye, knew him, too. She met him in El Dorado where he went by the name of Franklin Hunt and she was a waitress.

A hurricane threatened Florida and real estate values were slipping, but the romance between Frania and Franklin was blossoming and on November 11, 1925, they were married. H.L. was enjoying a second honeymoon with a second wife in the same year.

Honeymoon or no honeymoon, Franklin had to get back to El Dorado and he left Frania in Florida with instructions to wait for him. Then he rushed to the side of his other wife, Lyda, who was about to deliver another child. Their first two children, Margaret and Hassie, didn't know what to make of this father who came in and out of their lives and pretty much ignored them and their mother.

A few days later, February 22, 1926, Lyda produced Nelson Bunker Hunt and H.L. left town to rejoin Frania whom he moved to a rented house 60 miles from El Dorado so they could be together more often. After all, she had her duty to transmit genes, too, and H.L. set her right to it getting her pregnant a month before wife #1, Lyda, delivered Nelson Bunker. Howard Hunt, by wife #2, arrived October 25, 1926.

H.L.'s travels continued and ranged out to California, up to Chicago and back to New York. He dealt in cards and leases and was worth a few million with lots of business friends—some of whom the law might want to question. Yet, with all his traveling, he wasn't neglecting his gene-transfer program. He came back to Frania and Lyda frequently enough to keep them pregnant regularly. Frania delivered Haroldina on October 26, 1928 and Lyda came up with William Herbert on March 6, 1929.

Then H.L. heard about 60-year-old Columbus Marion Joiner who was appropriately named because he was about to open up an entirely new world. Joiner was poking around Rusk County in East Texas on the land of widow Daisy Bradford to whom Joiner had been paying romantic attention.

Joiner was part oil man and part con man—mostly con man. He got the widow Bradford to give him an oil lease on some of her property, bought some junky drilling equipment that barely worked and sent out fancy brochures and official-looking studies to a sucker list of investors. The investors sent their money and Joiner went ahead to drill a well he romantically named, Daisy Bradford No. 3.

The whole thing turned out to be a surprise. The mailing was so impressive that the Mid-Kansas Oil and Gas Company decided to cover itself by hiring one of the drilling crew, Ed Laster, as their spy. Laster secretly sent Mid-Kansas core samples and the people liked what they saw enough to secretly buy a lease adjacent to Joiner's lease. Then, to the astonishment of everybody, particularly Columbus Marion Joiner, oil began gushing out of Daisy Bradford No. 3 on September 5, 1930.

For Joiner, it was a disaster.

He had vastly oversold shares in the venture and that was fine as long as it turned out to be a dry hole. Everybody would write off a dry hole as a loss and Joiner would pocket most of the money.

But, with oil coming in, it would soon be public knowledge what the well was producing and all the investors could quickly figure out what their shares should be. However, with the project sold out several times over, there was going to be trouble.

H.L. Hunt came to Rusk County soon after he heard about the possibility of oil. About this time, Frania sent word that she was pregnant. Hunt moved her to Dallas, but kept busy making what would become the biggest oil deal of his life. It was a deal born of Columbus Marion Joiner's dishonesty.

The investors soon found out they had been duped and filed fraud charges against Joiner, who was in hiding. The process servers couldn't find Joiner, but H.L. Hunt did. With adequate supplies of strong whiskey and strong persuasion, Hunt got Joiner to sell his interests in Rusk County to him.

It was quite a deal. Hunt paid Joiner $1.3 million for all his oil leases and agreed to assume his liabilities and any legal claims against Joiner by his investors. For this package, H.L. had to come up with only $10,000 cash—less than 1 percent cash down.

H.L. was moving around faster than ever now. He had Frania in Dallas where she delivered another Hunt baby, Helen, October 28, 1930. He moved Lyda and family #1 to Tyler and got her pregnant again. Meanwhile he was gambling more than ever on cards, sports, and anything else that took his fancy.

At the same time, he had oil deals going everywhere in the fabulous East Texas fields and sank 900 wells in 1931 alone producing thousands of barrels of oil and millions of dollars for H.L. His deal with con man Joiner launched H.L. as a multimillionaire. And, of course, 1932 brought another Hunt when Lyda delivered Lamar in August.

The lawsuits that began against Joiner and shifted to H.L. were piling up to over 250, but H.L. kept fighting every one of them and won them all. Even when Joiner tried to sue H.L. for more money, H.L. outfoxed him — he continued to outcon the con man.

As wonderful as it was on the business front, there were cracks developing on the home front. Frania was becoming boring. His emotionally unstable son, Hassie, was becoming more and more of a problem.

Then Frania saw H.L.'s picture in the newspaper with his son, Hassie. At first she couldn't believe it. That was Franklin, her husband, and they didn't have any son named Hassie and they lived in Dallas, not Tyler, like the newspaper story said.

Frania was stunned, heartbroken, and angry all at the same time. The emotions flooded over her and she had been betrayed and wanted to move immediately to friends on Long Island. First, of course, there was the current pregnancy to see through and she did that a few weeks later with the birth of Hugh, the fourth child she'd had by Franklin Hunt — also known as H.L. Hunt.

Lyda found out her husband was an active bigamist about the same time, but she decided she didn't have any place to run to and, besides, the kids needed her. So, she stuck. She didn't like it, but she stuck.

Frania's leaving had the usual effect on H.L., he

didn't much care. She had served her purpose as a brood mare. Still, he was fearful she would forget her purpose in life and become a legal problem. So, he set up trust funds for Lyda and the five children to protect them from legal claims by Frania. He was anticipating the blood-money feuds that were coming.

Hassie became a serious problem. He was irrational and subject to violent rages without warning. A stint at military school only made things worse and H.L.'s continual neglect did nothing to reassure or comfort the boy.

Yet Hassie had one uncanny talent that no one could explain or dispute. He had an intuitive sense for oil. He could predict where pools of oil were in spite of contradiction by experts. His predictions were so right so often he should have been his father's dream. Instead, he was just another problem as far as H.L. was concerned. H.L. didn't like unsolved problems and, in time, he would solve the Hassie problem in a cruel and horrible way.

Frania had sense enough to put the past behind her for the time being and to get on with her life. She got a divorce from H.L. and married one of H.L.'s old friends, John Lee. The kids took Lee's name.

World War II arrived and Hassie was the only Hunt son old enough to go, but H.L. didn't want that. So, strings were pulled and Hassie became Lt. H.L. Hunt, Jr., United States Army, stationed in Washington, D.C., living at the Mayflower Hotel.

Soon Hassie got the army shaken up with his uncontrollable tantrums including one where he trashed his hotel suite. Lt. H.L. Hunt, Jr. was put on medical leave and transferred to the army hospital on Lake Ponchartrain near New Orleans.

Closer to home, H.L. Sr. was having some personal troubles of his own. Frania was gone and, for some inexplicable reason, Lyda refused to have more children by her bigamist husband. For H.L. there were all those raging hormones in his body clamoring to fulfill their biological mission by carrying the Hunt genes to exciting new places. H.L. found a new place right in his own office. Her name was Ruth Ray and a secretary 31 years his junior. Another perfect gene conduit. The impregnations began again.

Hassie was a trauma to both himself and H.L. and H.L. couldn't stand it. Something *had* to be done. That something brought Hassie to a mental institution in Andover, Massachusetts, where they gave him the latest treatments designed to set the mind right.

They strapped Hassie down on a table immobilizing his legs, arms, torso and head and clipping electrodes to his body from the head to his feet just like they do in Frankenstein movies. Then the healers sent electricity surging through his trapped body as he lurched and strained in torment against the imprisoning straps with each jolt. In time, his tormentors freed his body from the table without having freed his mind.

The prognosis on Hassie was not good and the healers recommended a new type of brain operation that would slice away the offending portion of Hassie's brain which made him act in ways that irritated his father.

H.L. agreed because, after all, something *had* to

be done. So it was that Hassie, the senior heir to the H.L. Hunt fortune, was given a frontal lobotomy that turned him into a suppressed, introspective, dazed creature.

The operation was certainly a success for H.L. Something *had* been done and a problem in his life eliminated. Some of the women in the family would never forgive H.L. for what he had done to Hassie.

He moved Hassie back home into the replica— but larger than the original—of Mount Vernon H.L. built next to White Rock Lake, in Dallas. There Hassie remained quietly while his every need was cared for including one that caught the doctors and H.L. by surprise.

Hassie suddenly had an insatiable appetite for sex with women. He wanted to have women sexually in ways that astonished his father and to have women service him sexually in ways that surprised everyone even more. As with everything else, H.L. saw to it that Hassie's voracious sexual drive was satisfied by having women there whenever he wanted them.

As for Hassie's mental and emotional condition, H.L. knew better than the doctors the cause of that. It was the Jews and the international communist conspiracy that was poisoning America's food supply that got Hassie. His oldest son was a victim of the red Jews.

Perhaps without realizing it, but as he got older H.L. fell into a classic pattern of the rich. They become Calvinist in the belief they are rich because they are blessed by God who finds them pleasing. This brings them to the conclusion that anything that enriched them or protected their wealth is divine.

Thus, the rich oppose any government interference with their private business unless, of course, such government actions protects their wealth.

No one in America was more against government interference with their private affairs than the Hunts, except when they needed it. H.L. wanted government interference in the early days of the East Texas oil boom when production was skyrocketing and the oversupply drove the price down just as it was supposed to under the terms of the rich's sacred icon — the free enterprise system. The rich didn't give a damn about free enterprise when it interfered with their profits.

And, when foreign governments interfered with Hunt oil interests, the Hunts wanted the U.S. Marines to land and protect them.

The other great danger seen to the serene enjoyment of their wealth by the rich was those damn Godless communists. To simplify matters, H.L. lumped all liberals, Jews, atheists, and communists together. His sons would add Eastern intellectuals and all members of the Phi Beta Kappa honor society as well.

So it was that H.L. and the rest of his brood got involved in fighting communism by hiring a devout fundamentalist, stiff-spined conservative, Sidney Latham, to spearhead their crusade against Godless communism, Jews, intellectuals, liberals, and assorted other left-wing vermin.

Latham brought in an ex-FBI agent, Dan Smoot, and together they began broadcasting, "Facts Forum," paid for by H.L. Hunt and his companies and publishing a magazine of the same name. For Latham and Smoot it was a gravy train going where they wanted to go and the fare being paid by the balding, squinty-eyed richest man in America, H.L. Hunt. The only curse was that Hunt buried them in memos about every trivial detail.

With age, H.L. also was taken by another obsession of the aging, health food. He founded the HRH company that produced the health foods to which he subscribed, most notably that named, "Gastro-Majic," which the old man promoted at every opportunity including a personal pitch from the stage during intermission at the Dallas opera.

With all this going on, H.L. was still paying attention to his domestic duties. He had moved Ruth Ray out of the office to an apartment in Shreveport and was keeping her busy as a bearer of his genes. In 1949, she produced their third child, Helen. A year later, she issued forth their fourth, Swanee.

But this wasn't enough. H.L. needed more and more children in spite of how some of them had turned out. His second oldest, Bunker, who assumed the senior male position among the children with the twilight of Hassie, was the constant butt of H.L.'s irritation. H.L. thought Bunker was among the dumbest creatures he had ever encountered in a long life of encountering dumb creatures. And, it was true that Bunker had run through $250 million of the family's money in a vain search for oil around the world. But Bunker would have his day.

Never mind, Bunker's father was still having his day and spreading his sperm was a major project.

He had already sired 15 children by three women, but that still wasn't enough.

He sent a secret emissary to the one place where they really understood this breeding stuff, Germany. His representative discreetly offered a million dollars to any woman who would agree to be a surrogate mother to continue expanding the Hunt gene pool. The aide returned after finding no takers.

But there was today as well as tomorrow that required H.L.'s attention and H.L.'s big chance to change Commie control of the American government into which it had fallen under Roosevelt and Truman.

Hunt arranged a secret meeting in May 1952 in his favorite suite at the Waldorf-Astoria with Dwight D. Eisenhower, Douglas MacArthur, Lucius Clay, and Herbert Hoover. The purpose was to convince Eisenhower to drop out of the race for the Republican presidential nomination in favor of MacArthur. There was much conversation, talk of heavy-duty money, but no commitments and the meeting broke up.

The Republican convention came to Chicago in July and Eisenhower was running hard for the nomination. H.L. Hunt was there running hard, too, to derail Eisenhower in favor of MacArthur. One of the keys was Senator Robert Taft and the delegates he controlled. H.L. scheduled a meeting with Taft before the first roll-call vote, but Taft canceled at the last minute and Hunt was unable to swing the convention to MacArthur.

Disappointed, H.L. went back to Dallas and his dealing and gambling until early 1955, when Lyda had a stroke and he chartered a plane to rush her to the Mayo Clinic where she died a few days later. H.L. waited a few months and then married Ruth Ray in November and officially adopted "her" four children.

Ruth Ray shared his intense concern over the Jewish communist conspiracy. His struggle against godless Commie Jews was taking more and more of H.L.'s time. So, when his continuous interference with Dan Smoot's "Facts Forum" led to a split, Ruth Ray connected H.L. with some fire-and-brimstone evangelicals including Rev. Wayne Poucher with whom he started a new radio program, "Life Line."

While Hunt refused to join with Robert Welch, a candy manufacturer from New England, in a meeting in an Indianapolis motel to form the John Birch Society, he agreed with Welch about the communist danger. Hunt, however, wanted to fight it in his own way.

The year 1960 brought another political convention and H.L.'s fear was that John F. Kennedy would be nominated—a New England liberal, Catholic from Harvard—unthinkable.

Before the convention, H.L. teamed up with Rev. Dr. W.A. Criswell, a Dallas minister who also feared a Kennedy presidency. Criswell preached a vicious anti-Kennedy sermon, which H.L. reprinted and distributed nationwide to great editorial backlash. Undaunted, H.L. went to the convention and worked hard to block the nomination with his money.

Instead of being feted and welcomed into the closed-door strategy meetings at Los Angeles' downtown Biltmore Hotel, one of the richest men in America came off as a pathetic, out-of-touch ideologue. Hunt could only wander alone down the hotel corridors slipping "Life Line" pamphlets under doors. It was an embittering experience for this powerful man and he wouldn't soon forget it.

Another of H.L.'s enterprises was the authorship of two novels, *Alpaca* and *Alpaca II*. The books took place in a mythical South American country with a government created according to H.L. Hunt's eccentric racist, anti-Jewish, health food-conscious ideas. Voting, for example, depended upon the amount of taxes one paid.

All the while, his hatred of Kennedy—now President Kennedy—grew. The man was obviously a communist tool because he spewed all that liberal nonsense and, worst of all, called for a cut in the oil depletion allowance that would severely erode the millions the Hunt family made from its oil wells.

It was to calm the rising disaffection with the Kennedy administration that inspired the President to schedule a speech in Dallas for November 22, 1963. The day before Kennedy flew into the Dallas-Fort Worth airport and spent the night in Fort Worth.

The next morning a full-page advertisement appeared in the conservative *Dallas Morning News* attacking Kennedy and his administration. One of the people who paid for that ad was Nelson Bunker Hunt, H.L.'s son. Kennedy gave a speech to workers in a Fort Worth parking lot and moved on to Dallas where he was assassinated.

Lee Harvey Oswald was arrested for the crime

and, as a white-hatted police officer was taking him out through the basement of the jail in Dallas, Jack Ruby stepped forward and shot Oswald dead before millions of television viewers. How a civilian like Ruby got into the heavily guarded basement without an official pass or without being searched has never been satisfactorily explained. Nor have the two "Life Line" scripts found in his pocket at the time of his visit to the Hunts' business offices a few days before.

Nelson was the focus of the old man's disappointments for a long time. H.L. called his second son stupid, but one has to wonder who was stupid if H.L. let Nelson run around the world punching holes in the earth's crust in a vain search for oil. How many fathers would let their stupid son squander that kind of money?

Libya was in turmoil and the king was looking for fast money by selling off oil leases in the desert. Nelson joined with British Petroleum and bought a lease in a remote desert location. He put up money and BP did the drilling.

The drilling crews dodged through old World War II mine fields and some of the BP equipment got blown up and some people were injured. Even so, the drilling went on, but soon became discouraging as every hole was dry.

Finally, on the last try, the crew figured they had another duster and they notified their bosses that they were going to quit. The drilling crew chief, just before he ordered the drill pulled up, did what he usually did. He drilled down another ten feet just for luck and punctured into one of the largest oil pools in the world—an estimated six billion barrels. Now, Nelson Bunker wasn't stupid anymore. His Libyan wells were pumping 100,000 barrels a day.

Some other things in the Hunt clan were not going nearly as well. Domestically, the children of his first family could not have been thrilled when H.L. married Ruth Ray and "adopted" her four children. They had to be even less happy when Ruth Ray publicly announced that her four children had been sired — not just adopted — by old H.L. himself. That they were blood kin just like those children of Lyda's and Frania's. That could dilute the old man's estate even more than anticipated.

In addition, there was the HLH company that made H.L.'s favorite health foods. It was losing money and that was against the Hunt philosophy. Bunker and Herbert thought they ought to look into HLH's affairs because they were sure somebody was stealing from their father.

Such an investigation would automatically involve H.L.'s right-hand man, Paul M. Rothermel, Jr. Paul took care of everything for H.L. even to the point of having his power of attorney and doing a lot of important things without clearing with the old man in advance — something even the boys were afraid to do.

Rothermel was not a favorite of Nelson or Herbert's anyhow since he had openly advised H.L. not to split his estate evenly among nine or ten heirs he would leave behind.

The way Rothermel saw it, the first five kids already had plenty of money in their own name and H.L. had given them more because they had been his kids for a lot longer. So, it seemed to Rothermel that H.L. ought to give something extra to Ruth Ray's four kids who were now H.L.'s "adopted" children.

Well, the three Hunt sons from family #1 were not about to accept that idea quietly and they did something about it. It was Mrs. Rothermel who first noticed the red car parked near their house. It had been there a number of times before and she knew it was not one of the neighbor's. So, suspecting something was wrong, she called the police.

When the police questioned the man in the red car, they discovered he had elaborate eavesdropping equipment. They decided he was illegally wiretapping the Rothermels and arrested him.

Now, the fat was in the fire.

The man in the red car turned state's evidence and said he had been hired by Bunker and Herbert to bug the Rothermels and their telephone. With that, the two Hunt brothers were indicted on a federal wiretapping charge.

The Hunt boys struck back with a million-dollar lawsuit against Rothermel charging he defrauded the Hunts and illegally meddled in family affairs although no one could find a law on the books covering this last charge.

The case against the Bunker boys dragged on for a couple of years with postponements while the Hunts tried back-channel maneuvering with the federal government to defang the charges. In spite of that, the case went to trial in mid-1975 in Lubbock. When it was over, it had cost the Hunts about $1 million and the boys were acquitted. The old man didn't live to see it. He died November 29,

1974.

Meanwhile, Bunker and Herbert were quietly buying up silver wherever they could find it and ultimately getting about 10 percent of all the known silver in the world. This would lead to more government investigations and legal hassles.

They were convinced that the CIA, the Trilateral Commission, and Eastern liberals such as Henry Kissinger, George Bush, and Jacob Javits along with the Rockefellers and all Phi Beta Kappas were dupes helping the international victory of Godless communism. They would ultimately nationalize corporations and all other wealth except for whatever one held personally.

The Hunts' plan was to corner the market on world silver and have the silver in their possession and safe from the Commies. They began buying it up at $2 an ounce in the mid-70s and then engaged in a variety of moves until they had pushed the price up to $35 an ounce by 1979 and brought the Chicago Commodity Exchange into crisis.

Then the system struck back; holders of silver began taking profits—just as it says they will do in the free enterprise system—and the price of silver dropped rapidly and on March 27, 1980 panic selling hit the market. This was followed by panic buying and utter confusion and a lot of financial pressure on the Hunts.

Finally, the federal government stepped in. Naturally, Congress held hearings. Naturally, the Federal Reserve chairman, Paul Volcker, had a plan. Naturally, the plan called for "restructuring the Hunts' debt load." Naturally, it cost the American taxpayer a bundle to bail out these multimillionaires.

From then until 1984 and into the future, William Herbert and Bunker Hunt were stripped of their fortune in a court-directed bankruptcy reorganization with creditors going nuts trying to collect and the Hunts shifting and transfering assets every which way but loose. Most commonly, they have moved property into children's, cousins, and the names of their 27 grandchildren to avoid paying anybody including their Numero Uno creditor, the IRS.

Meanwhile, Hassie stays in his room and watches the sun go down over White Rock Lake.

Four

Rich Fathers Who Ruled And Ruined Their Sons

The founding fathers of family fortunes use their wealth to force their families into doing things that the families don't want to do.

The story of the Guggenheims is typical.

The Guggenheim fortune began when Simon fell in love with Rachel. Meyer Guggenheim's father, Simon Guggenheim, lived in Lengnau, Switzerland's Jewish ghetto where he worked as a tailor. A widower with one son and five daughters, the 55-year-old Simon wanted to marry the 41-year-old widow, Rachel Weil Meyer, who had three sons and four daughters. However, the Christian Swiss authorities wouldn't permit it because the Guggenheims were too poor.

So, Simon and Rachel pooled resources and sailed with their children for Philadelphia arriving in 1848. Enroute, son Meyer Guggenheim fell in love with 15-year-old Barbara Meyer and they decided to marry as soon as they could afford it.

Simon became a peddler in Philadelphia and

Meyer a peddler in the coal mining communities of Pennsylvania. His most popular seller was stove polish that he sold for a penny profit. When he discovered the man who sold it to him was making seven cents profit, Meyer told his father and they learned how to make the stuff themselves. Simon stayed at home making it and Meyer went out peddling it for eight cents profit.

Next, they devised a cheap coffee-flavored substitute for real coffee and began making and selling it and made enough profit so that Meyer could marry Barbara. They had been in the United States four years. Two years later, Meyer opened up a grocery store and Barbara presented him with the first of ten children. He was always on the lookout for money-making opportunities because money to him meant safety and freedom more than anything else. As one of his biographers observed, Meyer was obsessed by money, more than anything else in the world.

The Guggenheims, like the Du Ponts, prospered from the Civil War by supplying food and clothing to the Union Army and that led Meyer into becoming a well-to-do spice merchant after the war. With his profits, he began to play with stocks. First, it was railroad stocks that made him $300,000 profit and, then, it was Swiss lace that had become all the rage for American ladies. Guggenheim went into the lace importing business. He made a deal to buy lace from one of Barbara's uncles who owned a lace factory back in Switzerland. By 1879, Guggenheim was nearly a millionaire, but his greatest days were still ahead.

In 1881, almost by accident, Guggenheim bought a one-third interest in two mines in Colorado. When he arrived in the town of Leadville to see his new mines, Guggenheim discovered they were flooded and couldn't be worked unless they were pumped out. Owners of the other two-thirds didn't have the money, so Guggenheim — with no assurance the mines would be profitable even if they were working — bought out the other owners. Then he gave his foreman the money for four water pumps and returned to Philadelphia. Telegram after telegram arrived in Philadelphia asking for more pumping money until finally a telegram arrived saying mining had resumed. Soon, a rich strike of silver was hit and Guggenheim was on his way to unimagined riches.

As usual, Meyer was on the lookout for making a bigger profit. As with the stove polish, he found out that somebody at another step in the process was making the big money. In the case of mining silver, it was the smelter who refined the ore into the precious metal. So, he sent one of his sons west to investigate and they ended up building their own smelter and refinery. This was the first step to the Guggenheims becoming dominant in the mining and smelting business.

The next step came when, after putting down labor unrest at their smelter and tightening up what had become a losing operation, the Guggenheims decided to circumvent a new import tax on the silver and lead ore they had been bringing in from Mexico, by buying mines and building a smelter in Mexico.

Son Daniel was sent to scout out the territory and ended up making a contract with Porfirio Diaz, the dictator of Mexico, on very favorable terms. Then it was son William's turn to go to Mexico and build the smelter. It took four years and William worked and played very hard on his assignment. The family business provided the work and the local senoritas provided the play for the rich man they called "Prince Billy" around the cantina known as "Peppersauce Bottoms." By 1895 the Guggenheim mining-smelter operations in Mexico were bringing the family $1 million a year in net profit.

By this time, the old man was semiretired from the business with his sons deeply involved in ownership and operations while Meyer explored new money-making possibilities in New York City to which he and Barbara had moved in the 1890s.

Socially, the Guggenheims were part of a new Jewish elite that was forming in New York in answer to the long closed Gentile elite in New York and other American cities. This new Jewish elite consisted of self-made wealthy Jews of German origin and would, in time, become known as "Our Crowd." They would hold sway for almost 100 years in New York Jewish circles until a new form of wealthy Jew appeared on Wall Street. But that is a story for another time.

Meyer and Barbara Guggenheim continued to live together happily until she died in March of 1900 leaving him to his music and occasional visits from children at his Upper West Side home.

Then trouble struck when, eight months after his mother's death, William suddenly married a divorced woman from California who was — horror of horrors — a Gentile. Her name was Grace Brown Herbert and the family, led by brother Daniel, immediately did a number on her.

William was ordered to Europe and Grace instructed to get a quick divorce and assured she would be handsomely paid. In Europe William promptly fell into bed with a baroness in Paris, and Grace got the divorce in Illinois along with a check of $150,000. Three years later, Meyer died, leaving behind a very rich family.

His seven sons were collectively worth $75 million and Meyer left most of his $2.25 million estate to his three daughters.

The sons stayed comfortably in their Manhattan offices and hired a swashbuckling adventurer mining engineer, John Hays Hammond, at an enormous salary ($250,000 — reputed to be the highest salary then being paid a corporate employee anywhere in the world). Hammond's job was to scour the earth for mineral wealth that the Guggenheims could exploit.

In 1907, Dan heard of a green mountain near Kennecott Creek in Alaska. It turned out to be almost pure copper and, for the Guggenheims and a new partner they brought in for this project, J.P. Morgan, it was pure gold.

Morgan was anti-Semitic, but that didn't keep him from doing business and making money with Jews. The project was hugely profitable and the Guggenheims went off on a buying spree scooping up everything that looked promising in Alaska. Conservationists sounded the alarm in Congress, but it was muted by a U.S. senator from Colorado by the name of Simon Guggenheim, one of the seven brothers.

Then came the development of the Belgian Congo where the Guggenheims' expertise and smelters brought King Leopold to them suggesting they form a joint venture to extract and refine ore from that African country.

Much as Meyer wanted the seven sons to stay in the business together, it wasn't to be. William's interest faded after his work in Mexico and Ben decided he had other things he wanted to do, so they both dropped out of active participation in the day-to-day operations in 1901. However, the family tradition held that each brother had to be given a chance to join in each new venture and had to sign off if he didn't want to.

William and Ben, apparently, signed off on many ventures routinely and never thought more about it. In April of 1912, Ben went down with the *Titanic* and that left six Guggenheim brothers including William whose money was beginning to run low. So, in 1916 when William found out that one of the deals he had casually signed off on had turned out to be a hugely profitable copper mine in Chile, he sued his other brothers.

Many people believe that William was strongly encouraged to do this by his second wife, Aimee, who didn't like the other brothers and was jealous of how they treated William. The publicity turned out to be unnerving to the other five brothers and, after a short court appearance by all parties, an out-of-court settlement of $5 million was quickly reached.

Of the remaining Guggenheim brothers, Isaac was the most sensitive, withdrawn, and conservative. He was battered emotionally by some of the vicissitudes of business and life, but his greatest disappointment was the lack of a son. It wasn't that he didn't love Beulah, Edyth, and Helene, his three daughters, it was just that they weren't sons.

In desperation for a son, he created an heir in a novel way. With the birth of a grandson, William Speigelberg, Jr. to his daughter Beulah and her husband, William, he made an audacious proposal. If William, Jr. would change his name to Isaac Guggenheim II, Isaac would leave him almost $5 million in his will. The parents were not entirely pleased with the idea, but greed triumphed and it was done.

When Isaac, Sr. died, he kept his word and Isaac, Jr. inherited approximately $5 million. Five years later, Isaac, Jr. went back on his word and changed his name back to William I. Speigelberg, Jr. Another heir had struck back.

Dan was the spark-plug brother who ran the Guggenheim brothers' operation, who was always for expansion, for taking chances and for working hard to get results. He rewarded himself by living well. His estate, Hempstead House on Long Island, was a feudal fiefdom of enormous luxury on 350 acres.

"Mr. Dan," as he was known by friends and associates, also rewarded the society that had allowed his family to do so well by their generosity in a number of areas, particularly aviation and space rocketry, as well as a wide range of charities and for the establishment of the first school of aeronautics ever established. When he died in 1930, he was widely hailed as the foster father of aviation for all the research and development that he had sponsored.

It was, for example, money from his estate that his son, Harry, used to finance the establishment of the Cal Tech Jet Propulsion Lab (JPL) in Pasadena that has been the brain center of our space exploration program.

Murray was the numbers cruncher, the conservative, the cautious brother who was always nervous about the expansive ideas of brother Dan. Sometimes his caution was proven right and sometimes it wasn't.

After Dan's death, Murray guided Guggenheim fortunes with the result that he almost lost much of it. He decided that the family should take a big plunge into nitrates in Chile. Initially this looked promising, but it soon turned out badly and the Guggenheims were on the verge of the biggest loss in the family's history only to be saved by Adolph Hitler and World War II when nitrates were needed for explosives. In the end, Murray's switch from metals to nitrates worked out and he died in 1939 worth about $30 million.

His two children married three times each, but no sons were produced so the Guggenheim name was not continued through this branch of Meyer and Barbara's children.

Solomon Guggenheim was the dapper fashion-plate brother who enjoyed his wealth, flaunted it and had fun hunting, collecting art, and chasing women. He had a dutiful wife, Irene, and three daughters. He not only enjoyed sex with a variety of beautiful women, he invested a good deal of time and money in gratifying his sexual appetite. Once he bought a yacht on which to have sexual liaisons more conveniently. Naturally, he kept the existence of the yacht a secret from his wife, but she ultimately found out about it.

In addition, he tutored his nephews on the subject of sex, carefully explaining the best time of day to have sex and how to leave a lover when you were bored. And Sol was often bored — rich, satiated, and bored.

That was before the baroness, of course.

Baroness Hilla Rebay von Ehrenwiesen was an unlikely seductress. She was a short, chunky artist who talked a lot and tended to take charge. The daughter of a German army general, she lived a Bohemian life and she totally captivated Sol. He paid her $9,000 to do his portrait and then began to travel around Europe with her.

Hilla got Sol interested in art and that got the press interested in Sol because he began to buy art and establish foundations for art and to create art museums. After having been in the shadow of his more dynamic business tycoon brother, Dan, Sol was beginning to become famous and that pleased him in public almost as much as Hilla pleased him in private—at least, until she began spending too much time talking about her favorite lover, an artist named Rudolf Bauer.

Oddly, Hilla convinced Sol of Bauer's genius as an artist—a view not shared by the critics—so that Sol bought everything Bauer painted and made the man rich. Bauer was not a nice man and was known to traffic in counterfeits and to cheat his patron.

In spite of this, when the erratic and unstable Bauer was arrested by the Nazis in 1941 and sentenced to the gas chamber, Sol secretly bought off a lot of people and got Bauer smuggled out of Germany to America where Sol bought him a house and gave him a monthly retainer. Hilla was delighted because she could visit him on weekends for fun and games. Hilla loved the arrangement, but Bauer tired of it and, with his usual ingratitude, married another woman.

Hilla drove Sol to plan and finance his art museum and to hire Frank Lloyd Wright to design it in the 1940s. By 1949 Sol had given $5 million to his art foundation and set aside another $5 million in his will. Hilla said she was happy with what he left her, but pushed him to increase the museum foundation legacy to $8 million. He did and died three months later at age 88 on November 3, 1949.

Sol's family hated Hilla for her long affair with their husband and father and they had the portrait of him that she had painted destroyed. Yet she had been the driving force behind his generosity to the world of art and his museum was built solely because of her.

The heirs were not happy with the will nor with Hilla. Sol's widow, daughters, nephew Harry, and his business colleagues were against her. Yet Sol had stuck by her. Most of his paintings went to his foundation. A sum of $2 million went for museum construction and $6 million into the permanent endowment.

Sol's nephew, Harry Guggenheim, the son of Dan, became the head of Sol's foundation that had the money with which to build the Guggenheim Museum. Harry and Hilla were doomed to work together to get the museum built and they hated each other every stinking inch of the way. She insulted him roundly with every anti-Semitic label she could think of and he retaliated by stripping her of her titles and jobs with the Guggenheim Foundation and she struck back by holding back the hundreds of paintings and artworks she had agreed to give the museum. These were originally given her by Sol who made her promise she would give them to his museum.

Harry and his curator, James Johnson Sweeney, put many of the paintings she had Sol buy into the cellar. Meanwhile, the building was stalled because the estate was not settled until 1952 and the money was not available until then. Also, the building permits were not issued because Wright's unusual design violated numerous regulations. The hearings on the building permits dragged on for another four years and were finally issued March 13, 1956. Wright died a few months before the museum opened in October of 1959. It was and still is one of most controversial buildings in the U.S.

Throughout the early '60s Hilla battled with Harry and the trustees to include her kind of art in Sol's museum. It was an emotional battle among Sol's heirs with Harry demanding she give back all the paintings Sol had given her and she stubbornly refusing.

Admittedly, Sol had written her before he died that, in return for the legacy he had left her, she had to give back the paintings he had given her and this was also in his will. Nevertheless, she refused and the heirs battled her over this until she died in September 1967 and her estate finally sold the paintings to the Solomon R. Guggenheim Foundation for a million dollars—a bargain. The $1 million Sol had left her in 1949 had grown to $5 million.

Ben was one of the younger Guggenheim brothers and always resented the dominance of his older brothers. In 1895 he married Florette Seligman of the Jewish banking family.

He didn't really like the family smelting and refining business to which he was assigned as much as he liked the pleasures of being a rich young man touring around Europe. So, six years after his marriage, he quit the first so he could enjoy the second.

He and Florette had three daughters, Benita, Marguerite (Peggy), and Barbara. Peggy would become famous in the years to come as a patroness of the arts and for her Venetian home, which was a mecca for the talented and titled of Europe and America.

The domestic arrangements of the home were unusual in that a beautiful redheaded nurse was hired to tend to the massages Florette needed to relieve her chronic neuralgia and to service the sexual needs of Ben, which Florette refused to do.

Florette didn't do things that many wives did and it drove Ben out of the house to openly consort with other women or to his apartment in Paris where he had numerous affairs.

The Seligmans, it turned out, were a real bunch of crazies. Florette's mother apparently constantly demanded that strangers speculate on the last time her husband had sex with her and Florette's aunt sang while walking up and down the street. Her brother did little else but gamble, drink whiskey, and eat charcoal. He finally shot himself.

All of the Guggenheim men discovered early that women were attracted to them and their money and all of them did some womanizing, but the champion was Benjamin. His friends said it was because he really liked women and needed their company that they were attracted to him. And, he to them. His involvement with other women was so blatant that he would sometimes bring them into his family's home.

On April 14, 1912, Ben was returning home from Europe on a grand new ship, the *Titanic,* when it hit an iceberg and began to sink. It soon was clear there weren't enough life jackets or lifeboats for everyone on board. So, Ben and his valet, Victor Giglio, changed into evening clothes, went up on deck, gave their life jackets to two women and declared that they were going to go down with the ship "like gentlemen." And they did.

The family was stunned by the tragic news and distressed by the tangled and debt-ridden estate Ben left behind. He apparently had run through $8 million and his heirs were left with relatively little. Of them all, Peggy did the most with hers. In time, she transformed her $250,000 annual income from a trust into a beautiful palazzo in Venice and $30 million worth of fine art.

The most elegant and the most Jewish-looking of the seven brothers was brother Simon who was short and dark with a fine taste for gracious living, fine wines, and beautiful women.

As with the other younger brothers, he felt looked down upon by his older brothers and exiled to the West to look after the many Guggenheim mining and smelting properties. To change that, he decided to run for the U.S. Senate from Colorado in 1907 while senators were still elected by the state legislature and not at large by the people.

He openly spent money with a free hand to buy the support of the members of the Colorado state legislature. Then, before election, he announced that, if he was not elected, he would publish the names of all the legislators he had paid. He was elected, served one term during which he did little and retired with honor and respect of his brothers.

He had two sons, John Simon and George Denver, and both met premature deaths. John Simon died at 17 of pneumonia. George, on the other hand, was highly sensitive, unpredictable and, after graduation from Harvard and a brief stint with the Guggenheim business, declared he was going to live off his trust fund and play.

His father was angry and disgusted and read him off in strong terms to no avail. George entered a life of parties, fun, drinking, and casual sex — usually with men since he was primarily homosexual. He became emotionally unstable, manic-depressive, and attempted to kill himself several times until his father employed a male nurse whose job it was to be with

George constantly and protect him from himself.

One morning in November of 1939, George slipped away from the nurse, went to Abercrombie and Fitch and bought a .300 hunting rifle. He went to the nearby Paramount Hotel, rented a room and shot himself.

As the second generation of Guggenheims was aging at the beginning of World War II, the family businesses were fading and there were only four males left in the third generation. Of these, only Harry, one of Dan's two sons, was cut from the same cloth as his father and grandfather.

Founder Meyer's seven sons collectively produced eleven daughters and four sons. Of the sons, one ended up a playboy, another died at age 17 and a third committed suicide. But grandson Harry tended to the family businesses, was ambassador to Cuba, and founded the Long Island newspaper, *Newsday,* for his wife, Alicia Patterson, to run.

And one of Meyer's great grandchildren, Roger W. Straus, Jr., help found the publishing house Farrar, Straus and Giroux.

The family still maintains extensive holdings in mining around the world through companies such as Yukon Gold, but is today mainly known for its support of artists, composers, writers, and scholars through various grant programs and the Guggenheim Museums in New York and Venice.

The Guggenheim fellowships given out at the rate of $4.5 million a year have in the past supported talents such as Aaron Copland, Robert Penn Warren, Paul Samuelson, and Henry Kissinger. Guggenheim money has been important in financing the schools of aeronautical engineering at MIT, Cal Tech, Harvard, and Stanford.

The Guggeheim Museum of Art in New York was initially the most controversial building in Manhattan and today has the works of Leger, Chagall, and Kandinsky plus a number of other modern artists whose work its founder, Solomon Guggenheim, collected.

The Peggy Guggenheim Museum in Italy houses the art collection of the Guggenheim who ran away to her own life in Venice, Peggy Guggenheim.

Peggy loved her reputation as the black sheep Guggenheim and, aside from World War II, she spent most of her adult life in Europe settling in Venice in 1947 where she became a notorious art collector and free love advocate bedding Samuel Beckett, Constantin Brancusi, Marcel Duchamp, John Cage, and Jackson Pollock. A friend of such diverse women as Emma Goldman, Gypsy Rose Lee, and Yoko Ono, Peggy Guggenheim was destined to end up in a Truman Capote book and she did: *Answered Prayers*.

Her friends characterized her variously as crazy, stupid, boring, ghastly, ridiculous, and insane, Her son labeled her a lousy mother and her neglect of daughter Pegeen was shameful and ended when Pegeen committed suicide in 1967. Peggy's self-assessment was simply that she had spun through life as through a dream.

Peggy died in 1979 and left her extraordinary 326-piece collection of Cubist, Surrealist, and modern art paintings to the museum she founded in Venice, the Peggy Guggenheim Museum in the Palazzo Veneir dei Leoni that had been her home and in the garden of which she is buried.

The Solomon R. Guggenheim Foundation, which runs the Guggenheim in Manhattan and the Peggy

Guggenheim in Venice, has become the source of controversy itself. Having spent $24 million renovating the Manhattan Guggenheim and planning on building branches in Salzburg, Austria, and Bilbao, Spain, it is under fire from Peggy's grandchildren, Nicholas and David Helion and Sandro Rumney for mismanagement of the Peggy Guggenheim collection and museum. Naturally, the foundation officials deny that allegation and another fight is on.

Much less savory has been the activities of Guggenheim descendents who moved to the Newport Beach area of California's Gold Coast. The most recent brush with the law was when Terri Ann McMullen, the stepdaughter of M. Robert Guggenheim, was arrested for selling cocaine in June of 1989.

She had been arrested the year before on the same charge and, when she was brought before Municipal Judge Calvin P. Schmidt, she was released and shown preferential treatment by authorities. Judge Schmidt himself has come under investigation for his political campaign practices and for accepting sex from women in exchange for easy sentences.

Probably more symbolic of the archetypal rich kid without a sense of direction is William Guggenheim III, 54, who lives in an average middle-class neighborhood of Altamonte Springs, Florida.

William lives on the interest from his trust fund, less alimony and child-support payments, and has been a stockbroker, stock analyst, retail store operator of Indispensable Disposables selling paper dresses. In 1971 he published something called, *Love Game,* the objective of which was to promote sexuality among the genders. Today, he is deeply into being a mystic counselor and focusing on the afterlife.

If he could ever make psychic contact with his

grandfather and founder of the family fortune, Meyer Guggenheim, it might make a very interesting conversation.

Five

Fashionable Blood-Money Feud—The Guccis

Guccio Gucci learned a secret in London that made him rich.

The Guccis are a macho male-dominated, emotional family in the classic Italian tradition. There was the strong, dictatorial, aloof father whose word was law in a family where women were respected and important, but secondary. No female Gucci, for example, could ever own a part of the Gucci businesses. No child could contradict his or her father—and it was a rite of manhood for a son to argue with his father, but always accede to his decisions.

Then there was the hair-trigger sensitive Italian male egos accustomed to playing the lordly role and theatrically outraged when "insulted" even though the "insult" might be incomprehensibly trivial in another culture.

The hot blood, the vendetta, the vengeance— even though often self-destructive—that was marbled through the Rome of the Caesars were still alive in the libido of the modern Italian male and, specifically, the Guccis.

Contrary to the Gucci myth, the family's history in fine leather goods did not go back five centuries. The truth is that it was born out of the clever mind and observations of a Savoy Hotel waiter in London who was in love.

Guccio Gucci ran away from his Italian home and an embittered father, Gabriello, whose straw-hat business had failed. Guccio soon found himself washing dishes at the posh Savoy Hotel in London where he eventually became a waiter and learned a secret that would enrich his family.

The secret was that the rich enjoyed and would pay premium prices for quality—quality service, quality goods. The rich wanted the best and often couldn't get it.

In addition, Guccio was fascinated by the luggage carried by the rich. Their lifestyle required many pieces of luggage and, because the rich traveled more than most, luggage was important to them.

Had it not been for Aida, Guccio would have probably stayed happily in London's cold foggy weather and become a prominent hotel manager some day. However, he did miss the warmth of his native Florence and, even more, he missed the warmth of his true love, Aida Calvelli.

She was the daughter of a tailor and, even though it was true that she had had an illicit affair with another man that produced a male child, Ugo, Guccio longed to be with her again. And so he was and on October 10, 1902, Guccio and Aida were married and Guccio adopted Ugo as his own.

His first work was in an antique shop where he

learned the retail business so well that by the time he was called to the army in World War I, Guccio had become the store manager. The war ended with the Italians on the winning side, Guccio returned home and switched focus by taking a job with one of the best leather manufacturers in Florence, which was noted for its leather artisan, Franzi.

That was in 1918 and Guccio was a good student while Aida was the ambitious one who pushed him to open his own leather goods shop while she was busy having babies. There were to be five in all by Guccio, the first being their daughter Grimalda who had arrived three months after the wedding. Then there was Enzio who died as an infant, and three more sons, Rodolfo, Vasco, and Aldo.

One Sunday in 1922, the Guccis spotted a store for rent on the via del Parione and Aida urged Guccio to take it and start his own business. Reluctantly he did with a 25,000 lira loan from a friend. He specialized in luggage of the finest quality and was always mindful of what he had learned at the Savoy watching the rich: the more expensive something was, the more highly prized it was by the rich.

During the next several years, Guccio learned and endured sad and happy things. The sad was that his adopted son, Ugo, had grown into a brawling, drinking bully who had no interest in the family business and whom Guccio convinced a friend to hire for his farm.

Also sad was that his friend who had lent him the money to start the business was a prying nuisance interfering with Guccio at every turn. Guccio determined to pay back the loan and get rid of the man, Signor Calzolari. To do that, Guccio made the mistake of turning to Ugo, whom he thought had some money saved. Ugo didn't, but his pride wouldn't let him admit it, so he stole it from his employer to give to his father.

Mortified, Guccio arranged to repay his friend, Ugo's employer, while Ugo became worse, joining the new fascist movement of Benito Mussolini and strutting around with a gun while he gambled, drank, and chased women.

Of course, in fairness it should be noted that all of the Gucci men chased women including Guccio.

In time, bejeweled American women tourists were stopping at the modest Gucci shop. Soon the word had spread that Gucci was the *only* place to get that leather opera bag or overnight makeup case. Soon, the interlocked Gs of the Gucci trademark could be found in the closet of most wealthy women in America and Europe. The ultimate sign of Gucci's stature was to know that when the first ladies of the two world superpowers met in Washington, D.C. in the closing years of the Reagan administration, both Nancy and Raisa were Gucci aficionados.

The growth of the little leather shop was not without problems. It was almost dealt a death blow in 1935 when the Italian dictator, Benito Mussolini, invaded Ethiopia, outraged the world community and brought down a boycott on Italy that cut Gucci off from his supply of prime leather. So, the ingenious Gucci switched to making luggage of canvas with the famous interlocking Gs trademark.

Gucci emphasized Florentine quality with modern snob appeal and tight family control of the business.

Gucci's three sons—Aldo, Rodolfo, and Vasco—

were destined to become heirs to his growing business and would also threaten to destroy it and the Gucci family with their jealousy and betrayal.

Aldo, Vasco, and Guccio all worked in the shop and were all subject to flirtations with the wealthy women who came and went through their door. But one day the handmaiden to a Rumanian princess came through that door with her employer and Aldo was a goner. She had the clean sparkle of a Welsh outdoors-woman which, in fact, she was.

Olwen Price was an unfamiliar sort of name to the Italian Guccis, but she was Aldo's choice and, in the tradition of the Gucci men, he quickly had her pregnant. A marriage proposal followed instantly after the news was secretly passed to him and a wedding in Wales that puzzled both families promptly ensued.

Olwen moved to the Gucci fiefdom in Florence, but never really joined the family and this also puzzled everyone. Her conception of marriage apparently consisted of bearing her husband's children and caring for them and him, but not getting involved in the extended family. In fact, she refused to learn Italian or to get involved with helping in the family business or to go on trips with Aldo. The marriage, conceived in heated romance, quickly transformed into cool imprisonment for both of them.

The psychological impact on their three sons, Paolo, Giorgio, and Roberto would tell in later years after they grew up seeing and hearing their parents at odds with each other and enduring the long absences of their father.

Perhaps a mark of the extent of the alienation was secretly demonstrated by Olwen during World

War II when she was a key part of an underground railroad to get downed Allied airmen smuggled out of Italy. The children all knew of the scores and scores of fliers hidden in their house much of the time.

For those on the Allied side, this may seem wonderful and heroic but consider this: Her brother-in-law, Ugo, was an officer in the elite SS guards and her husband's family all depended on the goodwill of the government to keep their business open and feeding the family. Olwen's underground role endangered the lives of her husband's entire family, but she did it anyhow.

From these experiences, Paolo grew up the rebel respecting neither his father nor his mother. It was he of the three Aldo sons who was the maverick who was willing to deny his mother and father if it needed to be done. His rebellion was disciplined by his father's hand or belt, but it was not quelled.

And Aldo followed in his own father's steps as the strong-willed patriarch who enjoys the good life of wine and women and refused to be kept down by a sullen, withdrawn wife or troublesome sons.

Aldo and Guccio differed in one major way and that was risk-taking. Aldo wanted to expand, expand, expand their thriving business and Guccio always was slow and cautious. It took enormous cajoling and arguing by Aldo before Guccio would consent to opening a second shop in Rome, but the gamble paid off handsomely.

Aldo and Olwen moved their family to behind the shop on the via Condotti near the Spanish Steps. A year later, World War II came, but the Allies declared Rome an open city and spared it the destruction of Allied bombing. They were safe, but business was terrible and it was a struggle to keep open until the nightmare ended.

Yet when the end came for Italy and Rome was occupied by the Allied troops, business instantly boomed. Dollars were plentiful and goods were not. Gifts for girlfriends and wives were snapped up and the Guccis began selling many smaller items to compensate for the shortage of materials and the blossoming market for goods—any kind of goods. The interlocking Gs were getting better known and the Rome store—resisted by Guccio— proved the salvation of the company.

As the war went away, Rodolfo came back to the family business. He had made 50 films but his movie career was stalled; he was broke, married to film actress Alessandra Winkelhausen and his father told him he was silly not to be in the family business with his brothers Aldo and Vasco. There was plenty to do for everybody even though Aldo was pretty much in charge.

Rodolfo quickly made a remarkable contribution to the Gucci business by designing a pair of moccasins that would become an essential in the Gucci line and so famous that the first pair made is now on display in the New York Metropolitan Museum of Modern Art.

It was the expansion of Gucci production that was inexorably transforming it from a small hands-on operation for the Guccis to a mass-production line producing thousands of handbags and shoes and other leather goods. In short, the nature of the Gucci business was changing from a small family business to a large manufacturing and marketing empire. The full impact of the change would take several decades, but it was happening.

Another happy discovery Gucci made was that the rich also needed a good and quick luggage repair service and this became an increasingly important part of the Gucci services that attracted new customers for new goods.

In addition, Gucci began making leather goods other than luggage and found a ready response to his wallets, belts, and other accessories.

Then also came another lesson about the rich: they do not pay on time while suppliers demanded their money promptly. As business got better, the Gucci finances got worse until, one day he literally called the staff together and announced he was closing the business. The only thing that saved the company at that moment was daughter Grimalda's fiance' instantly lending Guccio the money he had saved to wed Grimalda.

The business was saved and Aldo was restless as ever and as he would be all his life. He saw the post-war period in Europe as a slow recovery with the Guccis depending on revival of the American tourist trade. Why wait for the rich to come to Italy and Gucci? he asked his father. Why not bring Italy and Gucci to the rich of France, England, and America? His father had a fit.

Through good times and bad, Gucci had survived — just barely at times, but survived. Now his headstrong son Aldo wanted to risk it all with some harebrained scheme to expand — just not to another Italian city, but to a strange foreign place like France or England. Worse, this fool son of his wanted to cross the entire Atlantic Ocean and open up a store in New York City — one of the most expensive and toughest places in the world to do business. Guccio's motto was that the best vegetables come from your own garden.

They compromised, as usual, and did it Guccio's way. Aldo was sent to locate a place for a store in Milan.

Aldo did it, but kept thinking of the Rue de Rivoi, Bond Street, and Fifth Avenue. He talked— argued actually—with his father once more. Again, Guccio told Aldo he was crazy, but if the banks would back him, Guccio would reluctantly permit it. Besides, the Rome shop had been picking up more and more Hollywood movie personalities as customers, many of whom were friends of Rodolfo's and they encouraged both brothers to open in the United States.

It took until 1952 and the finding of a money connection in the U.S., attorney Frank Dugan, but Aldo finally got his store on Fifth Avenue. Rodolfo backed the move, Vasco thought it was dangerous, and Guccio was angry. All normal reactions for each member of this excitable family.

The three sons were variously involved in the operation of the business: Aldo, the driving majordomo; Rodolfo, the dreaming artist widower with an obsessive fear for the safety of his son; and, the naysaying Vasco who guided factory production, but preferred hunting and farming.

Guccio made one trip to see the new stores in New York, shook his head in disbelief, and returned to the comfort of his Florence to brag about his sons. One day in 1953, the grand padrone of the family, Guccio Gucci, died.

The death of Guccio was less an occasion of sorrow than it was of suspicion, hope, and disappointment for the children he left behind.

He left behind the bastard Ugo whom Guccio

thought he had bought out of the family years earlier with gifts of farm lands and his oldest child, Grimalda, whose fiancé and, later, husband, had saved the Guccis from ignoble bankruptcy with a loan made on a few minutes' notice and who would later design and build their Florence factory and shop without payment.

For Aldo, Guccio's death meant a new freedom to expand Gucci particularly in the United States where he spent most of his time. His cold separation from Olwen was made bearable by a string of willing nubile creatures, most notably a Gina Lollabridgida look-alike, Bruna Palumbo, who would become his constant companion for years and "Mrs. Gucci" to the uninformed in the United States.

For all three brothers, Guccio's death also meant a possible threat from Ugo who might claim to be entitled to part of the inheritance — Guccio owned 100 percent of Gucci when he died.

For Grimalda and her husband, Giovanni Vitale, the death meant the stunning revelation that her father had left her absolutely nothing of the ownership of Gucci. It was devastating and demoralizing. She went into a depression, but her husband went into court for her where she was dealt another blow.

Her brothers, Aldo, Vasco, and Rodolfo, each of whom got one-third of the business, all teamed up against her and tricked her into telling the court the four had come to an agreement outside of court. Grimalda thought the agreement was that she would share, but the three brothers betrayed her and she was left with nothing from them. It would be years before she recovered.

The three also took court action to insure that Ugo was frozen out as an illegitimate child.

Meanwhile the sons of Aldo and Rodolfo were making their way learning the business bit by bit. Paolo was still the rebellious maverick who increasingly thought his father and two uncles were stuck in a turn-of-the-century time warp, so what else is new about children? Rodolfo's only son, Maurizio, was working between school semesters and would become the most educated of the Guccis with a law degree from the University of Milan.

He was also the most rigidly controlled and disciplined of the third generation. His father was obsessed with his health and safety. Guards watched over him lest he be kidnapped and even his playtime was carefully monitored so that he would not hurt himself.

His companions were carefully monitored and he was not allowed the freedom and social life that his contemporaries had. He had tighter control on his time and freedom than had he been a virgin daughter of great price. In fact, he usually had to be home for an earlier curfew than the few girls he dated did.

This continued until he was 24 and fell in love with Patrizia Reggiani against his father's wishes. Finally, Maurizio rebelled and ran away from home with his love. They married 18 months later in spite of enormous pressure by Rodolfo on Maurizio, Patrizia's family, and the Church. Not a single Gucci attended Maurizio's wedding. It was not something he was going to forget. If they were hot-blooded, emotional Italians, so was he.

Meanwhile, Aldo was expanding around America with stories in key cities such as Beverly Hills,

Palm Beach, Philadelphia, and San Francisco. Gucci has become the symbol of those who have made it—the symbol of wealth and success even though the company was run, it seemed, largely by disorganized whim with each of the brothers making decisions and changes without consulting the other two.

Maurizio was estranged from his father. Paolo worked in the factory with Vasco in charge and still thought the operation was out of date. And Giorgio struck out on his own with a Gucci boutique appealing to the young market that couldn't afford major Gucci goods, but could afford the less expensive belts, wallets, scarfs, and so on.

Aldo was traveling here and there constantly in search of another deal or another store that would expand Gucci's while his estranged Olwen stayed in Italy with her children by Aldo and Bruna stayed in Palm Beach with her child by Aldo. Vasco focused on manufacturing to fill the growing orders while longing to retire childless with his Maria to their farm. And Rodolfo was becoming more and more withdrawn while producing a continuing film documentary about his own life.

Gucci shops were a golden empire, but that wasn't enough for Aldo and he asked his two brothers to meet with him to discuss a major change in the company's organization. Each of them held one-third of the company and the company was, as usual, cash poor for expansion. Although their father had established the principle that ownership of the company would always remain in the hands of male Guccis only, Aldo was proposing a reconsideration of that policy.

He proposed, and Guccio Gucci must have spun

in his grave at the thought, that the Guccis go public and sell 20 percent of their combined holdings on the Milan stock exchange. This would give the company the money it needed for expansion and a tidy profit to each of the brothers to boot. What did Rodolfo and Vasco think of that? asked Aldo.

He was really only asking what Rodolfo thought about it because he knew that Vasco was against anything new or different and always had been even though he had profited mightily over the years from Aldo's imagination and initiative.

What Rodolfo thought, seconded by Vasco, was to pass a resolution that banned the passing of Gucci stock to anyone's hands outside the family for another 100 years! That's what they thought.

So, the total ownership of the Gucci company enterprises remained in Gucci hands. However, within four years it was not in the same Gucci hands as it had been during the 1971 meeting.

In 1975, Vasco died and, his one-third passed to his widow, which was ironic. Vasco was the most conservative of the sons of Guccio and the most obedient to his wishes and it had been the oft-stated insistence of Guccio that Gucci ownership should never be in the hands of anyone not a Gucci, but, more specifically, not in the hands of anyone not a *male* Gucci. Now, Maria owned one-third of the company—a Gucci only by marriage and, for God's sake, a woman at that!

We were talking about major Italian macho crisis here. Had Maria not been a dutiful wife willing to follow what she understood from her brothers-in-law to be Vasco's real wishes, she might have been a problem. The original papers creating Guccio's company said, that, "any son who dies leaving no sons to inherit his share in the company must sell to the others." She turned the stock over to Aldo and Rudolfo, half to each. Her wifely devotion was rewarded with about a million-plus dollars. Maybe she wasn't so dumb after all.

So now Rodolfo owned 50 percent of the Gucci empire and so did Aldo. Except that Aldo, shrewd businessman that he was then did something stupid possibly in an attempt to do something smart. He split 10 percent three ways among his three sons, $3\frac{1}{3}$ percent each to Giorgio, Paolo, and Roberto. He might have done this to reduce the amount of taxes that would have to be paid when he died or because he trusted his sons never to turn on him. In any event, he had planted the seeds of an evil whirlwind that would devastate his later years.

Of course, the word of what Aldo had done quickly came to other Gucci ears and Maurizio had another reason, as if he needed any more, to hate his father. He was now the only third-generation Gucci not to own a piece of the company.

This was reemphasized when Maurizio suggested the company come out with a line of very fine, expensive perfume. Everybody agreed and a new company was formed called Gucci Parfums. The stock in the perfume company was split up with Aldo's three sons sharing 60 percent, 10 percent to the parent Guccio Gucci company and the parental brothers, Aldo and Rodolfo, splitting the rest. The third-generation son who launched the project, Maurizio, got nothing. As far as Rodolfo was concerned at that time, Maurizio did not exist.

Paolo continued to be a problem for both his father and his uncle, Rodolfo, and his uncle was much less patient about it. That may have been because Paolo and Rodolfo were together in Florence while Aldo and his other two sons and Rodolfo's disowned son were in New York.

In any case, Paolo, couldn't understand why the company was doing so much business and not making any profits. The two brothers, Aldo and Rodolfo, lived well and spent money on boats and real estate, but the kids were on relatively small salaries. Business had grown manyfold in the past decade and the New York operation had $48 million in sales, but no net profit.

Beyond that, Paolo wanted to launch new lines and make new deals, much as his father had done, but the parents wouldn't go along with him. He wanted to launch a line of jeans of his own design called Paolo Gucci and another line called Gucci Plus, but his uncle and father said "No."

Relationships were getting bad between Rodolfo and Paolo, so Aldo had Paolo come to New York for a while. In his absence, Rodolfo fired him from the Gucci European operation after 26 years on the job without even severance pay due him of $240,000. Paolo immediately sued, which embarrassed everybody.

Trouble in the Gucci family went public and the two parents, Aldo and Rodolfo, went bananas over the slur on the family name. A few months later, Rodolfo pushed Aldo to firing his troublemaker son, Paolo, from the Gucci operation in America.

Paolo then began making deals with suppliers, manufacturers, and distributors to bring out his Paolo Gucci line of goods. He had declared economic war on his own family and both parents were furious. The board of Gucci, his father, uncle, and cousins voted almost $2 million to fight Paolo's venture.

Everybody in the business of significance was contacted and warned that dealing with Paolo would mean being cut off from the established Gucci business and Gucci lawyers began flooding Paolo and his business contacts with legal papers, filings of court injunctions, etc. It severely hurt Paolo's ability to get his line started.

The only good thing that came out of it was that Maurizio and Rodolfo began to reconcile. And, in fact, his attitude was softening toward his only son as Rodolfo grew older. He was also perfecting his epic movie on his own life, which he intended to leave to his son as an instruction on how life was to be lived.

It is thought by some that Rodolfo planned to leave his entire 50 percent share of Gucci to his son as had been decreed by his own father, Guccio, years before. Further, it was thought he might do this before he died so as to avoid estate taxes. However, if these were his intentions at that time, he said nothing to Maurizio about it.

One can only guess that Rodolfo was grateful he didn't have a son as bad as Paolo. Only neither Rodolfo nor Aldo realized just how bad Paolo was going to be for them.

Ever since Paolo began wondering about the big sales and small profits, he quietly gathered all the financial papers he could find about the company. Before long he discovered what was happening. The profits were being siphoned off and diverted to paper companies in Panama and Hong Kong to avoid paying income taxes. Aldo and the company were involved in a giant income tax fraud.

The intra-family vendetta was growing hotter. There are some who believe that Paolo did not know what he was actually doing to his own father. Others believe he knew exactly what he was doing.

In any case, Paolo had amassed enough documents and letters from the confidential files of the company to put his father in jail or to cost him millions in fines. That is what Paolo threatened to do unless the Gucci companies settled with him and let him go on with his projects. Rarely had an Italian family vendetta been drawn in bolder letters. The proud, arrogant father in a face-off with the proud, arrogant son he had sired.

It was a family destroying itself while friends and strangers looked on in morbid fascination. Neither would back down.

Meanwhile, Rodolfo in Italy moved to gain greater control of the Gucci properties. Perhaps seeing Aldo unable to control his son emboldened Rodolfo or perhaps fear that what Paolo was doing would destroy their empire unless Rodolfo got things in hand was the motivation. Whatever it was, Rodolfo wanted to pull things together in a neat package. The perfume operation, for example, had become much more profitable than anyone had expected and Rodolfo wanted a bigger share of it and better control.

A board meeting was called in which Paolo was included and the family proposed a peace with Paolo that they said would meet all of his demands if he dropped all his lawsuits and withdrew all the incriminating documents. It turned out that the fine print still required Paolo to get a majority vote of the board for his projects and that he didn't have the total freedom of action he had demanded. The peace deal fell through.

That's when Paolo probed another way to cause trouble. He went to Maria, Vasco's widow, to probe details of her stock sale to the remaining brothers, Rodolfo and Aldo, after Vasco died.

Paolo said that there was stock in other companies owned by the Guccis and which they should have paid her for. She had been under the impression that Vasco only had stock in an Italian Gucci company, but there were English and American Gucci companies, too. Paolo suggested that she may have been defrauded and induced to sign a lot of papers transferring Vasco's stock in all Gucci companies, but was only paid for the Italian company stock.

Paolo couldn't prove his allegations and had to let them drop, but he had already done enough damage. His lawsuits became public knowledge, the press wolfpack seized upon them and the publicity robbed the judge of any empathy toward Aldo and it also unleashed the IRS bloodhounds. When this last pack got done pouring over the Gucci ledgers, they found more than even Paolo knew. For example, $18 million in income had not been reported.

The attempts to reconcile the split family — mostly to settle with Paolo — continued, but everybody wanted to cover themselves and protect their financial position and pride. Each time they failed primarily because of the hostility that centered between Rodolfo and Paolo.

Then came the fateful board meeting in July when another attempt was made. However, Paolo insisted on being provocative. He demanded to speak at the beginning of the meeting and that his questions and the others' answers be taken down by the secretary. He wanted to know who were the two mysterious Hong Kong stockholders in the Gucci companies. An uproar greeted his question. He was angrily told that was none of his business.

Paolo repeated his question and when his father and uncle refused to answer, Paolo whipped out a tape recorder to get his question and their non-answer on tape. That's when one of his brothers grabbed him and someone else got a hold on Paolo from behind and a gash appeared on Paolo's face.

He ran bleeding from the meeting through the staid Florence offices of Gucci screaming for the police and a doctor. His doctor arrived and took him off to a clinic for examination while the world press immediately held the Gucci feuds up for examination one more time. Naturally, Paolo sued for $13 million charging assault and other crimes.

Then the spring of 1983 brought a chance at peace again. Rodolfo died of cancer and Maurizio inherited his 50 percent, which obstensibily had been secretly transferred to Maurizio without his knowledge before Rodolfo died. Now Maurizio, who had never owned a share of Gucci before, was the largest single stockholder with 50 percent and he assumed control of the company.

Maurizio had been trained in the law and held a doctorate and had a worldview of the Gucci business. He felt it was too fractured, too disorganized, and too limited. It should be a true multi-national company and tap countries such as Germany and Japan, which they had barely touched. He felt, too, that family differences needed to be healed.

After Maurizio assumed control and still remembering what he had endured at the hands of his father, he came to his aunt, Grimalda, to do what was right. He put her on the payroll as a senior designer with no duties and saw to it that she was paid five million lira a year for life. Giovanni dropped his lawsuits against the family.

In addition, Maurizio dealt with Paolo and agreed to a deal that would reorganize Gucci, give Paolo $20 million for his 3$\frac{1}{3}$ percent and let him be free to market his line of goods under his own name, but under the Gucci corporate umbrella. Paolo agreed and the papers and money were to be exchanged in the offices of the Credit Suisse in Switzerland. At the last minute, the papers presented to him were not the agreement he had previously made with Maurizio and the $20 million was not delivered. The deal was off and the family feud was on again, but with another "betrayal" to fuel it.

In November 1984, Maurizio was named the chairman of Gucci Shops, Inc. and replaced Aldo who was under increasing pressure as the IRS people continued to probe deeper and deeper into Gucci affairs. Paolo was sanguine. He was sorry that his documents were endangering his own father, but it was the old bastard's own fault. If he had given in to Paolo, Aldo wouldn't be in this trouble now.

And Paolo wasn't done yet. In an odd combination at that moment in their lives, Paolo and his father, Aldo, were challenging Maurizio's control of the company. They were alleging that the signature transferring Rodolfo's 50 percent to Maurizio was a back-dated forgery made after Rodolfo's death to evade estate taxes.

The significance is that, if true, Maurizio would

have to pay enormous taxes — probably a third of a billion dollars. Since he didn't have that kind of money, he would have to sell some of his stock and that would probably restore Aldo to being the major single stockholder and give him back control of the company.

In fact, it is claimed that Aldo and Paolo had several witnesses from Rodolfo's old staff prepared to swear that the signature was a forgery.

In January of 1986, Aldo stood up in an American federal court and pled guilty to tax evasion. Eight months later, he was sentenced to serve one year in jail to be served at the federal prison at Elgin Air Force base in Florida near Aldo's home. In addition, he was to repay over $7 million in evaded taxes and to pay a fine of $30 thousand, which seemed rather trivial to some people. So Paolo had gotten his revenge by putting his 82-year-old father into jail.

The courts in Florence and Milan charged Maurizio with exporting capital and evading taxes. An arrest warrant was issued and Maurizio took refuge in Switzerland. Maurizio was removed from office at Gucci and, in 1987 Milan's Attorney General appointed a receiver to run things until the whole mess was sorted out, which happened when Aldo got out of prison and resumed control of operations.

In 1988, the Guccis sold 50 percent of their company to Investcorp, an Arab Bahrain-based investment bank headed by Nemir Kirdar for $170 million. Soon thereafter, on January 19, 1990, things changed when Aldo died at age 84 and Maurizio assumed control.

Gucci had been doing very good business up

until that time with its trademarked name and symbol on 23,000 different products available in some 1,000 retail outlets.

And the blood-money conflict continued when Maurizio won another court battle against his cousin, Paolo, now a 59-year-old man balding with a ponytail. In October 1990, a High Court in London ruled that Paolo could not use the Gucci trademark on his merchandise in the United Kingdom. This battle has raged for 12 years with Paolo winning in the U.S. courts and losing in France, Italy, Belgium, Switzerland, and Liechtenstein.

The London Times characterized the blood-money feud, "Running beneath the dry legal arguments [are] the strains of a family war that makes television soap operas look tame. In 12 years it has laid bare the domestic, business and even sexual lives of the most famous fashion family of all. The male-dominated Gucci Clan is not silent by nature and for years members have been screaming their accusations at each other in the media."

To Paolo, it is a matter of honor and he believes he has been cheated out of his inheritance by the forgery Maurizio made years before. His surprising ally in litigation is Olwen, the widow of Aldo, who left his estate to his mistress Bruna Palumbo and their child.

Maurizio was now in charge and decided to make a major change in Gucci's merchandizing strategy and bring Gucci's back to the upscale, luxury level it used to be. Unfortunately, it was the wholesale and less-expensive canvas Gucci lines that were the big money makers. He brought Dawn Mello, former president of Bergdorf Goodman, on board to help with his revitalization plan. This included moving company headquarters to Milan and spending $6 million on remodeling its new digs with antiques and exotic art and paneling plus the purchase of an expensive 18th-century villa.

Some of the moves Mello has made raised questions among the merchandizing community such as stripping Gucci products out of department and speciality stores and closing a lot of Gucci's own stores. The result has been to slash the number of places where Gucci products are sold from 1,000 or more to only 180. This is to make Gucci more exclusive again, but it also meant losing millions of dollars in sales.

She has also dumped a lot of tourist items from the Gucci line of products reducing the number from 22,000 to 7,000 and brought back the classic hand-stitched Gucci loafer for $295 and the A-frame handbag for $795 to $995.

Many in the industry don't think this is the time to go upscale and note that, as a result of swimming upstream, Gucci is now heavily in debt — between $80 and $100 million — and now suffers from some $30 million in losses.

Maurizio claims the problems are transformational as he improves the company and works through the recession. However, Investcorp chairman Nemir Kirdar, who doesn't like Maurizio, seems to be getting restless and wants a third partner and new management. On July 26, 1993, Maurizio issued a challenge to Kirdar: buy out the Gucci 50 percent or sell the Investcorp 50 percent. Kirdar said he would buy out the Gucci 50 percent for $50 million or sell the Investcorp 50 percent for $250 million.

Finally, on September 27th, 1993, Maurizio

threw in the tassled loafer or, perhaps, the towel, and sold out his 50 percent to Kirdar for $170 million. Investcorp also owns pieces of Saks Fifth Avenue.

Why did the Guccis do what they did and why did they persist in their intra-family blood-money feuds? To outsiders, it made no sense. To insiders, it was normal.

One is reminded of the folk tale about the scorpion and the fox who stood on the riverbank. The scorpion asked the fox for a ride to the other side and the fox refused saying,

"I am afraid you will sting me and kill me."

"Don't be ridiculous," said the scorpion. "If I sting you and you die while we are crossing the river, I will drown and die, too."

It seemed to make sense so the fox started swimming across the river with the scorpion riding on its back. Halfway across, the scorpion stung the fox. The fox was dying and sinking into the river and the scorpion was clearly doomed as well.

Bewildered, the fox's dying question to the scorpion was, "Why did you do that? Now we will both die."

The scorpion said, "I couldn't help it. It's just my nature."

Six

Rockefeller Heiress
In Chalk-White Mask

He was the most hated man in America.

John D. Rockefeller made a fortune for his family and his heirs by creating what would become Standard Oil and, later, Exxon. In the process, his narrow, skull-like face and rail-thin body topped with a black silk hat became the stereotype of the heartless miser insensitive to the hardships of ordinary people.

Much has been written about some of the Rockefeller heirs descended from old John D. There were his sons, Nelson, John, Laurence, Winthrop, and David informally known in the family as, "The Brothers" and the family association of heirs, The Rockefeller Cousins, all of whom had their squabbles.

Yet little has been said about the Rockefeller heiress with the white mask, old John D. Rockefeller's favorite granddaughter, Margaret Strong who was also a Spanish marquesa.

Margaret Strong was born in 1897 and grew

up as one of John D. Rockefeller's most coddled and protected grandchildren. She was the only child of her mother and father, Mr. and Mrs. Charles A. Strong. Her early years were spent mostly at the family villa in Florence, Italy, and she was left with $25 million when her grandfather died in 1937.

As an adult, she wore red lipstick and heavy white paste and powder makeup on the front of her face with heavily blackened eyes and lids leaving the back of the cheeks, neck, and ears untouched, which gave her a bizarre, kabuki-dancer look. She eloped to Paris in 1927 to marry a highly theatrical ballet master, the 8th Marquis de Piedrablanca de Guana de Cuevas of Chile.

George de Cuevas, as he was ordinarily known, was identified by friends as a swishy bisexual who carried his two white Pekingese with him everywhere and sported a black velvet cape with red satin lining. The marriage stunned Margaret's grandfather who is seen in pictures with the married couple starring in confused disbelief at his grandson-in-law.

Their separate-bedroom life together in New York City was, however, sexual enough that two children arrived in rapid fashion in 1929 and 1930. These children, Elizabeth and John, were brought up in the Rockefeller tradition of nannies and boarding schools.

The marquis and marquesa lived for the first few years in either New York City or Paris, but when the Nazis invaded France, they moved to New York where their odd bisexual relationship was the inspiration for a scandal novel, *The Double Door,* published in 1950.

In time, the children saw less and less of their mother and father while their father used Rockefeller money to create a distinguished ballet company called the International Ballet in New York and, after World War II, the Grand Ballet de Monte Carlo in Paris. This last became a notable success.

It was during this period that another Chilean appeared on the de Cuevas scene, 18-year-old Raymundo de Larrain, who came to Paris to study ballet under de Cuevas. Before long, de Larrain become more important in the management of the ballet and as an assistant to the marquis. By the time the marquis died in early 1961, de Larrain was vital to the ballet and virtually a member of the family.

With the death of de Cueva, the blood-money feud began. Clearly, Margaret knew of her husband's primary sexual preference and it had not bothered her enough to do anything about it until he publicly slapped her in the face from the grave. He left all his estate to Horacio Jorge Guerrico, his male secretary and longtime collaborator, and nullified a previous will that left his estate to Margaret.

Margaret immediately sued in Manhattan court charging that her husband had been mentally incompetent and under the influence of drugs when he signed his second will cutting her off. Guerrico backed away from the fight and gave up all claims to the marquis's estate.

It seemed only logical that Margaret appoint

de Larrain director of the ballet company and she did and then withdrew to her Palm Beach home where de Larrain followed to attend her. Her life was quiet and lonely. She had little contact with her grown children and heard from the Rockefellers only in connection with her fortune. Over the next few years, she gave her two children gifts of over $4 million and, on June 11, 1968, signed a new will leaving almost everything to them.

Everything was relatively calm until suddenly the relatives became very uncalm at the outrageous news that quiet, withdrawn Margaret had married her young protegé, Raymundo de Larrain, a man 38 years her junior, on April 25, 1977, at the Palm Beach home of friends.

All of a sudden daughter and son broke their long estrangement from Momma and came calling to find out what was going on. The first meeting of mother and daughter, Elizabeth, after her mother became Mrs. de Larrain, took place in a suite at the Madison Hotel on 15th and M Streets in Washington, D.C., where Margaret was dressed tastefully, but confined to bed.

Present were a doctor and several of de Larrain's relatives and his good friend and financial adviser William Lucom at whose home the de Larrains were married. Elizabeth's mother had trouble speaking and the doctor said that she had suffered a brain spasm, but would be all right with some medication and rest.

De Larrain gave this assessment of the marriage and his stepchildren at the time,

"We became inseparable and our relationship quite naturally evolved into marriage . . . I totally devoted my life to her, giving up all my other work . . . Elizabeth and John only really knew their mother in the abstract and from a self-imposed distance. They made no effort to reach out to her or to her world except when they read or were told of our marriage, and then only to feign love and shock, which was in reality a transparent mask to cover their avarice and greed, which their mother quite properly rejected."

Elizabeth was troubled by her mother's condition and returned to New York the next day to set the alarms off with her other Rockefeller relatives and her Harvard-faculty member brother, John.

In the immediate months that followed, Margaret ordered the transfer of her business papers, money, and securities, including 193,620 shares of Exxon from New York and the family-run Chase Manhattan bank to her personal control in Palm Beach.

Her cousin, David Rockefeller, persuaded her to donate two of her New York City town houses to the Center for Inter-American Relations. Once that had been done, David, who had considerable influence with the center, got the center to *sell* the property for $1.6 million to the Council on Foreign Affairs.

Margaret was angry at this shell game and demanded, without success, that David get her property back. It was reported she wrote to David saying, "Since this is completely contrary to our understanding, I want you to see that they [the two town houses] are returned to me." Nothing happened and this convinced both Margaret and her new husband that the Chase Manhattan trustees and the rest of her family could not be trusted.

In February 1985, she signed her last will specifically cutting off her children and grandchildren without a cent. Nine months later, the Marquesa Margaret Strong de Cuevas de Larrain died in the Palace Hotel in Madrid. All of a sudden the family became intensely interested in Margaret and the blood-money feud went public in August of 1986.

Margaret's estate was valued at about $30 million including the Exxon stock, which disappeared. Armies of lawyers were marshaled to break the will on the grounds, "Every indication points to a massive fraud on an aging, physically ill, trusting lady," by de Larrain.

De Larrain's lawyers responded by saying Margaret was an old lady almost abandoned by her family to whom de Larrain gave complete attention, love, kindness, warmth, and companionship and she rewarded him for his devotion.

The lawyers for the Chase Manhattan Bank and the heirs respond that Raymundo kept Margaret boozed up or doped up and exercised undue influence on her and forced her to change her will so as to leave her Rockefeller relatives out in the cold.

Naturally, the blood-money feud ended up in

court and in the courtroom of the bizarre surrogate judge, Marie Lambert, whose behavior was the focus of bemused gossip in legal circles for years particularly in the Johnson vs. Johnson case and the Goldman case, both of which are detailed in this book.

The trial between Margaret's children and her second husband came to court in September 1987. The basic issue was which will was Margaret's "official" will. Was it the one made in 1968 before her second marriage leaving most of the $16 million to $60 million estate (no one was exactly sure how much it was worth) to her neglectful children or was it the last will, made after her marriage to Raymundo de Larrain leaving everything to him?

The kids said Raymundo was a shameless gigolo who had screwed their 80-year-old mother while she was alive just to get her money and was now trying to screw them to get the money they claimed was theirs.

In a hearing a year previously, Raymundo's lawyer, Thomas A. Dubbs, had waved a mangy and mangled document before the judge. It was the torn and retaped 1968 will that Dubbs claimed had been torn up by Margaret in front of three witnesses in 1978. It was the main evidence in the September 1987, trial deciding which will should be probated.

After four weeks, both sides were ready to talk settlement. On the morning of September 23, both sides sat down and, by that afternoon, a deal was struck. Raymundo would give the kids the Palm Beach house worth about $4 million along with $400,000 worth of jewelry and a promissory note for $500,000 payable on his death.

Even so, it left Raymundo a very rich man and left the blood heirs to reflect on the relationship between themselves and their now-deceased mother.

Seven

Behind Every Great Fortune: Du Ponts

Balzac said that behind every great fortune there lies a crime. In many cases, he is right and most of us are unwilling to take the chance of committing a crime on the chance of gaining a great fortune.

Astor made his fortune by importing opium and selling whiskey to Indians in exchange for furs. The Manhattan real estate he bought became tenements, sweatshops, and slums.

The railroad barons such as Stanford, Huntington, Harriman, Crocker, and others bribed and bullied their way to their fortunes. Helen Clay Frick, the only surviving child of the 19th-century steel tycoon went to court in Pennsylvania to keep a history of the family from being published that held the family responsible for un-Christian practices of exploiting workers and the bloody Homestead strike of 1892.

And the founders of the great Du Pont family fortune did it by swindling their own family to gain control of the company.

The members of the Du Pont family were renegades from their homeland just as many other immigrants had been. Except they were noble refugees fleeing the common people who had seized their country in the French Revolution. Had the Du Ponts stayed in France, many of them would have been beheaded.

Beyond that, they were different in other ways from ordinary immigrants in that they didn't trickle in to America, a few at a time. They did a carefully planned and executed migration involving the entire family arriving New Year's Day 1800 off Newport led by the patriarch, Pierre Du Pont.

It was the plan, in fact, of the senior members of the family to come to America and create a colony for other refugee French noblemen. However, the guillotine got most of the other French noblemen first.

In the 190-plus years that the Du Ponts have been in America, they have established themselves as a family of manufacturing noblemen who have turned much of the state of Delaware into a Du Pont barony.

They are probably the greatest industrial family in the country living in their own distinctive way. The explosive and chemical industry they founded is still tightly held within the family and they tend to marry among themselves—cousins with cousins.

In the early days while they tried farming and other endeavors, the Du Pont men noticed that no reliable source of good gunpowder existed in the colonies. Gunpowder was essential for most Americans who fed their families by hunting and had to protect against Indian attack.

The Du Ponts began making the best gunpowder in the colonies and their business thrived, but it was the War of 1812 and the Civil War that made the family rich.

However, by 1872 there were many powder makers and the market became glutted, so Du Ponts organized the Gunpowder Trade Association. Even so, by 1902 wars were scarce and business was off, and some of the Du Ponts wanted to sell the company to outsiders.

Alfred Irenee Du Pont, the eldest son of the eldest son of the company's founder, a 38-year-old "black powder man" who had been working in the mill, offered to buy it for $12 million. The family gave him a week to raise the money.

Alfred knew the technical side of the business, but not the financial side, so he took in two Du Pont cousins. They were from the Kentucky branch of the family, 6'4," 220-pound Thomas Coleman — an organizer and promoter, and Pierre Du Pont — a good conservative manager.

Here's how they raised the money under Coleman's guidance: They had the business appraised and the value was set at $24 million instead of the $12 million they had offered the family. So they revised their offer to $15,360,000 if the family would take 4 percent notes and a loan. The deal was made, Coleman ended up the largest stockholder of the new company, as well as president with Pierre treasurer and Alfred production chief.

The three men actually put up only $2,100 in cash for the deal. The rest was in the 4 percent notes or stock. So these three Du Ponts made $8,640,000 profit off their relatives on a cash investment of only $2,100.

In time, the two young cousins finessed Alfred out of the business and, the cleverer Pierre then pushed

T. Coleman out in the cold. As replacements, Pierre brought in his two brothers, Lammot and Irenee. Angry, Alfred sued Pierre, but lost—the first of a number of Du Pont blood-money feuds.

Following a merger strategy begun by T. Coleman, the remaining Du Pont brothers absorbed 64 rival companies in four years and got absolute control of the explosive business in the U.S.

This brought charges of violation of the Sherman Anti-Trust Act, which hung around for five years before Alfred I., coming to the rescue again, convinced the court that Du Pont's monopoly of the gunpowder industry was essential to the national security. With war threatening in Europe, this was an argument that was accepted by the court.

The fact that the U.S. Attorney General at the time, George W. Wickersham, had been the Du Pont's attorney at the time of all the questionable mergers didn't hurt either.

World War I came and made the expanded Du Pont businesses very wealthy just as the War of 1812 had done a century before. The company grossed $1 billion from the war and that was when a billion dollars was a lot of money.

Heavy with cash, Du Pont looked for ways of diversifying and decided to buy into a new company that was the combination of 21 small automobile companies. It bought control of General Motors. It also bought into various chemical companies while individual Du Ponts made heavy investments into aviation companies and U.S. Steel.

Domestic strife hit the family with the second-only divorce in the history of the Du Ponts. Alfred decided to dump his Bostonian wife, Bessie, and marry his cousin Alicia Bradford. Coleman said this was outrageous and advised Alfred to sell out and move from Delaware. Instead of that, Alfred remained true to his stubborn character and ended up ostracized by Coleman and Pierre. The lid really blew when Alfred's daughter was divorced by her husband who charged her with adultery on their honeymoon.

Alfred and Alicia withdrew to their magnificent new estate, Nemours, and refused to see any of their hundreds of relatives except for two. Meanwhile, Coleman and Pierre worked to get Alfred divorced from the Du Pont business. Pierre succeeded to complete control of the company and, in 1911, he finally got Alfred removed from the company after working a secret stock deal with Coleman.

The deal benefited Alfred financially, but pushed him out of management in the family business and left him even more bitter than before.

The next guns in the Du Pont blood-money feud were fired in court with Alfred and some other Du Pont family members suing Pierre for breach of trust. The case failed even after repeated appeals including one to the U.S. Supreme Court. Then Alfred turned to the media for revenge.

Alfred owned the *Wilmington Daily News* in the Du Pont's hometown plus a chain of smaller newspapers. Alfred used them to attack the political ambitions of Coleman who had his eyes fixed on Washington and, maybe, the White House.

Alfred successfully smeared Coleman to the point that Alfred ended up as a delegate to the Republican National Convention instead of Coleman. Alfred's wife and children died, he remarried and moved to Florida while cousin Pierre became president of General Motors for a time.

To date, the most explosive substance the Du

Ponts have manufactured over the years was their own blood-money feuds.

Eight

It's Not About Money, It's About Revenge

Are the rich different? Yes. There are many humiliating things they do not have to endure in life. They are more free of fear than ordinary men. Often, they don't know what it is *not* to be rich.

Beyond that, as John Tebbel says in his book, *The Inheritors—A study of America's Great Fortunes and What Happened To Them,* "The gulf that separates the rich from all the others is not only a matter of income. Wealth is also a state of mind."

Psychologists say that the obsession with money is really a yearning for love. Money becomes a substitute for a loving personal relationship or, for some heirs, it becomes a way to get revenge for the love they sought and lost as in the strange court case of the Johnson brood versus the opportunistic art student.

For Barbara "Basia" Pisecka, a young Polish refugee, those three years were a fairy tale too fantastic for even Cinderella to dream.

She arrived in America in 1968 hardly speaking

English with only a degree in art history and $100 in her purse. To support herself, she went to work as a maid on the New Jersey estate of a wealthy family. A year later, she was the mistress of her rich, married employer. Her lover, 42 years her senior, set her up in a condo on Manhattan's posh Sutton Place with a $12,000-a-year allowance. Two years later she was his wife and the heiress to half-a-billion dollars.

It is easier to understand J. Seward Johnson after you know about his family and how he was raised. Domineering people surrounded him as a child and into his early adulthood. His no-nonsense, workaholic father dominated family life with his obsession about the constant danger of germs lurking everywhere ready to strike.

Seward's older brother and father's namesake, Robert Wood Johnson, emerged strong, determined, and a cookie-cutter duplicate of the father. In later years, after he took over Johnson and Johnson following their father's death, Robert told Seward to leave and sent him home with no work, no self-respect, but lots of money.

For his mother, Evangeline Armstrong Johnson, Seward became the focus of her need for love and being a nurturing mother. Seward almost became a doll who she continued to dress in fancy velvet suits and keep in long, golden curls until well into his teens.

The mother's protectiveness increased when Seward began to show signs of feeblemindedness. In fact, he had dyslexia and it took him such a long time to read anything that he avoided reading whenever possible. Even though others didn't know he had dyslexia, Seward obviously knew it and it undermined his self-esteem even more and made him more of a recluse.

To protect him from unpleasantness, Evangeline had Seward tutored at home away from the rumble-and-tumble socializing process of school. His tutors discovered Seward's difficulty in reading and his odd spelling that is characteristic of the dyslexic. For example, he would write "word" as "wd" and "boat" as "bod" because that's how the words looked to him.

So, he was a young boy isolated from normal society and one of the most common windows on the world, reading, being brought up pampered and rich on a huge country estate by a lonely mother yearning for someone to love.

Then came the milestone year of 1909. Seward turned fourteen. His father died leaving most of his estate to his two sons, Robert and Seward, and Mother made two decisions: one about housing and one about sex. The housing was that she preferred that the family live in New York City and so they moved.

The second was that it was time for Seward to learn about sex. Normal boys learn about sex from other boys and their fathers and older male relatives. The mysteries are transformed into nervous curiosity and, then, experimentation with one's self and, ultimately, with a willing, and possibly equally curious, female. Evangeline had a more direct approach.

Evangeline arranged for a close woman friend of hers to keep Seward "prisoner" for ten days. He was forced to stay with this woman his mother's age while she kissed and caressed him to sexual excitement and then guided him through the various ways of relieving that excitement and tension with a female or of having a female relieve it for him.

Ten days later, Seward was released from his sexual

captivity a wiser but bewildered young man for whom the experience would be etched in his mind and personality. It may account for his constant fears of being kidnapped and for his uncontrollable sexual appetites.

Having fulfilled what she regarded as her last important duty to at least one son, the widow Evangeline left. She went off to England, leaving the kids behind, and married a member of Parliament.

Seward thus grew up as a self-centered recluse who wanted for nothing and understood little of the outside world beyond his personal experiences. The things that mattered in his life were women and boats. He did like farming and cows, but women and boats were the main focus most of the time.

He sailed well and enjoyed being at sea, which has a monastic appeal since one sees only a limited number of people and doesn't have to speak much to any of them. That suited his personality.

His main obsession was women and he often combined them with his love of sailing. He was totally indiscriminate about females, pursuing any and every woman that came within range regardless of her position or status. Because of his upbringing it is not a surprise that women were disposable commodities in his life.

His boat was used for frequent seductions of secretaries, heiresses, stewardesses, daughters of diplomats—any form of human female. He also boasted that he had sailed with his brother to seaports around the world to make use of the local brothels and how their favorite sport was to both have the same woman satisfy their sexual needs.

There were no sexual barriers for Seward. His sexual hunts and conquests were an endless embarrassment to the family and his brother, Robert, who nurtured the family business that financed Seward's escapades.

Seward didn't care what he did because he knew that Robert and the family would bail him out and his enormous wealth made people tolerate his irrational and unconscionable behavior.

Seward first married Ruth Dill whom he met in Bermuda where her father served as attorney general. He chased Ruth using his money and gifts of Cartier jewelry as bait and it worked. They had a luxurious wedding, European honeymoon and returned to the estate he had built for her in Highland Park, New Jersey, and the baby-making began.

Starting in 1926 she bore four children, Mary Lea, Elaine, J. Seward, Jr., and Diana. Then Seward said no more babies and Ruth had abortions instead of children.

Then Seward announced to his wife that he wanted a divorce. The reason? Seward was in love with his wife's 14-year-old sister, Fannie, and wanted to marry her instead. Fannie said "No" and Seward took off in his boat. Two years later, he and Ruth divorced with a settlement that gave each child $6,000 a year and Ruth $12,000 a year. At the time, Seward was worth $9 million.

Aside from everything else, Seward left a lasting mark on his eight-year-old daughter, Mary Lea, when he slipped into her bed and initiated her into sex. The regular nightly sex sessions continued until she was 14. Bewildered, Mary Lea first told her mother who either didn't believe her or refused to accept the truth for fear it would jeopardize the marriage and all that money.

Psychologists say incestuous fathers are sexually

unsure of themselves and their helpless daughters give them confidence because the daughters cannot reject them. As the daughters get older, the fathers became strict authoritarians about these daughters dating. For one thing, they don't like to compete for their daughter's sexual favors with other, younger men and, for another, they are afraid the daughters will tell what happened.

Rejected by his sister-in-law, Seward began trolling for other women and he met one at a dance in 1938. She was Lucinda Ballard, a costume designer in the theater, a pleasant woman, but unwilling to let Seward bed her or marry her.

Seward seduced any woman willing to be seduced, but when they caught his fancy and would not trot off to bed, he pursued them relentlessly, constantly proposing marriage. A proposal, in some ways, was just another device for having his way with a woman.

Lucinda continued to reject his proposals until one day he showed her a Johnson and Johnson document proving that he got $368,000 a year in company stock dividends. That day she accepted his proposal.

Later, she met his children and thought it was scandalous that they were so poorly dressed and badly cared for, as well as largely ignored by the father whose acceptance they desperately wanted. At that point, Lucinda Ballard realized that J. Seward Johnson, Sr., was not a very nice man and she had been seduced—not by his charm—but by his money. She called off the engagement and returned to her former life.

The next summer, Nina Underwood McAlpin, who was recently divorced, made a play for Seward and he responded immediately by marrying her sister, Esther "Essie" Underwood. She was a plain New Englander and they settled into a transplanted New England farm Seward bought in New Jersey. He kept busy with the farm and with sailing and they began to breed a great herd of milk cows.

They also did some breeding of their own and produced Jennifer Johnson in 1941 and James Loring Johnson in 1945.

They had been married thirty years when Essie hired Barbara Pisecka as a chambermaid at their Oldwick, New Jersey place. Barbara worked for ten months and then quit to take English at New York University. She had saved $400 a month from her wages and was anxious to learn better English so she could do something with her degree in art history.

Whether there had been any romancing behind the stairs with the master or not is unclear. What is known is that, soon after she left the Johnsons' household, Seward, Sr. began telephoning her. After several calls, he asked Basia to visit him in his office to evaluate some paintings. At the time, Basia's romantic interest was a sailor named Peter Eastmont.

Johnson said he wanted to hire her to evaluate art for him and would pay her $12,000 a year plus a place to live. Also, he invited her to go on a sailing trip with him, but wanted her to take scuba diving lessons at his expense first. Basia sensed this all involved more than appeared on the surface, but played along with it anyhow.

Seward, Sr. had already announced to Seward, Jr. in late 1968 that he was going to get a new mistress. Essie clearly knew about it and decided to wait it out as a closing phase in the life of a senile man.

A year later, in November 1969, Basia sailed with

Seward, Sr. to the Bahamas and then to Rome, Paris, London, and Ireland. Basia became his constant companion and Seward, Sr. seemed rejuvenated and in January 1970, he moved in with Basia at his Sutton Place apartment. A month later, in Sao Paulo, Brazil, Seward, Sr. proposed to Basia. She quickly said yes.

In the meanwhile Essie bitterly bided her time assuming he would come back, but who finally came to her door one day was not Seward but the lawyer with the divorce papers. She had been sick and this depressed her further as it did when Seward, Sr. and Basia married just eight days after the divorce.

Friends and children witnessed Seward, Sr. turn back the clock and become a love-stricken teenager. Some thought the energetic and willful Basia a wonderful tonic for the old man and others thought him a fool. It didn't matter because Basia and Seward, Sr. didn't give a damn what others thought. They didn't have to—that's one of the perks of being rich.

In her early years Basia knew hard times, homelessness, and oppression by the Nazis. Some relatives had been shot and others, including her father, fought in the Polish underground resistance. The safe and limitlessly rich world of Seward, Sr. was a fairyland that she had never dared dream of. Now it was hers and she was determined to enjoy it and to rejuvenate her man to enjoy it, too.

Fine art, luxurious cars, an island in the Bahamas, two homes in Italy and one in Florida were purchased and on 140 acres near Princeton, New Jersey, a $30 million estate was constructed in 1982. "Jasna Polana,"—Bright Meadow—was the most expensive private home in America.

In the four years it took to build Jasna Polana,

Basia supervised the scores of imported Polish work-men and she complained constantly about the mate-rials or workmanship. Entire sections of the project had to be torn down and rebuilt and torn down again and rebuilt again before she was satisfied.

The amenities included a 72-foot swimming pool, an orchid house, air-conditioned doghouse, heated marble floors, a twelve-foot-square bathtub, a nu-clear bomb shelter and chapel, the latter presumably in case the bomb shelter didn't work out.

The house had $100 million in art treasures and the most sophisticated security system and guard force available.

Basia, having achieved this incredible dream in America in such a short time, made sure she kept it. There had been the usual prenuptial agreement. Had she balked at signing such a document before the wedding there might not have been any wedding.

However, she soon put the pressure on the old man to renounce the prenuptial agreement. She withdrew her sexual favors and her company saying the pre-nuptial agreement made her feel like a slave. Ulti-mately, sex won over rationality and he tore up the agreement so she would return to his bed.

Then came the attorney, Nina Zagat. Starting back in 1971, soon after they were married, Nina played a bigger and bigger role in the Johnsons' lives first in legal work and, then, socially. Before long, Nina was a member of the household.

Basia also tried to soothe things between Seward, Sr. and his children, particularly Seward, Jr., whom she helped get control of the Harbor Branch Insti-tute plus a million-dollar contribution from the father for Seward, Jr.'s sculpture atelier. Still, Basia made the children uneasy.

In October 1980 Seward, Sr. checked himself into Boston's Peter Bent Brigham Hospital to get medical help in getting an erection, which was becoming more troublesome. Basia was traveling in Europe and Nina was with Seward, Sr., and he swore her to secrecy, but she quietly called Basia anyhow. He was sent home declared perfectly normal.

In May of 1981, Seward, Sr.'s health began to fail in spite of his daily vitamin doses, massages, and even an English faith healer. In May, he went into the Medical Center at Princeton for a prostate cancer operation and the doctors cut out all his testicular tissue.

During the next two years, Seward, Sr. got worse and an atmosphere of suspicion and tension grew stemming from the old man's impending death and the gigantic estate he would leave behind. Nina had been there much of the time and had drawn a number of changes in Seward, Sr.'s will and the children—particularly, Seward, Jr.—were increasingly anxious about the will. Talk of a fight over the will surfaced in family conversation in the months before Seward, Sr. died.

The marriage lasted 12 years and, when 87-year-old J. Seward Johnson died, he left his third wife, Basia, an estate of $500 million while disinheriting his six children and his favorite charity.

Naturally, the children tried to break the will and, in the process, waged one of the bitterest, oddest, most revealing blood-money feuds in the history of the American courts with murder threats, mental illness, odd sex, drugs, bribery, incest, suicide, a scandalous divorce, and a riot thrown in for effect. It was a merry old time for the tabloid newspapers.

The players were the six Johnson children and

Harbor Branch, an oceanographic institute that was his favorite charity. The attempt to break their father's will was spearheaded by Johnson's son and, by then, a well-known sculptor, J. Seward Johnson, Jr.

Others included the incest victim, Mary Lea Johnson Richards married to the distinguished-looking Martin Richards with whom she has created a Broadway theatrical production company that enjoyed great successes. Its productions included such hits as *Sweeney Todd* and *La Cage aux Folles* and the Pulitzer-prize winning *Crimes of the Heart*.

She has been sorely bruised emotionally by her early years and a low sense of self-worth and displayed the same ability to withdraw into her shell and lock out the world that her father had.

Her first husband did not help her emotionally. She and her devout Catholic husband, William Ryan, started a chicken farm. They also had six children and one miscarriage about as fast as they can be had over eight years. She secretly got a diaphragm, which her outraged husband found and branded a tool of the devil and he refused to have sex with her thereafter.

The marriage was crumbling while her trust account was growing and had reached $30 million. During the early 1970s Mary Lea got to know Dr. Victor D'Arc, her son Seward's drug therapist. Sex starved, she became an easy seduction for the doctor and there followed four months of great sex for Mary Lea and ultimately marriage. Then John Fino showed up.

John came into the relationship by Victor's invitation and Mary Lea's function became satisfying both men sexually and having sex with John alone while

Victor watched. She complied, but John didn't like it too much until she finally refused to let Victor watch. This led to a bizarre scene with Mary Lea and John in the bedroom having sex and her husband Victor outside pounding on the door and screaming to be let in.

Then Victor brought more men around for Mary Lea to service sexually while he watched. In the next phase, Victor used Mary Lea as bait to attract men that Victor wanted to have sexually.

Through John Fino, Mary Lea met theatrical producer Martin Richards who was in search of an angel to finance a film script he was trying to produce. Mary Lea liked the script and Martin and ended up financing the film, *Fort Apache, The Bronx,* starring Paul Newman.

Her life was tumbling down around her with Victor demanding that she get him more men for both homosexual and bisexual parties, three of her kids involved in drugs, and an indifferent family that was no support.

She turned to Martin. They had moved in together when John Fino warned her that Victor had put out a contract to have her killed. He played a tape of Victor making the arrangements, but when Mary Lea went to the authorities for protection, John refused to testify to a grand jury and went to jail for contempt of court. Victor went free and, even today, Mary Lea has a bodyguard with her everywhere.

The incident got a lot of press but, instead of rushing to his daughter's side to comfort her as most normal fathers would have done, J. Seward Johnson, Sr. ended all contact with her and refused to see her or speak with her. She had become an incon-

venience, and Johnson refused to deal with in-
conveniences.

J. Seward Johnson, Jr., 56, had an interesting marriage, too. It went back to the time that his uncle,
Robert, wanted to raise a lot of money and got his
brother, Seward, Sr., to create several trusts in 1944.

The trusts were a business device in which Robert
manipulated matters for his own benefit. The benefit
of the children was an incidental excuse to keep the
tax man quiet.

Here's the way they worked: Seward, Sr. transferred 90,000 shares of Johnson and Johnson stock
to six trusts, one for each of his children. The trustees were Robert Johnson and two of his cronies. In
this way, Robert controlled the voting power of those
shares at the moment that he was taking the Johnson
and Johnson company public and raising a lot of
money.

So a great deal of money was raised with a public
stock sale, while leaving Robert in control and, essentially pushing his brother, Seward, Sr., out the
door to become a playboy and gentleman farmer.

Seward, Jr. became the trustee of these trusts when
he was 33. He was angry at how his uncle Robert
had emotionally castrated Seward, Sr. and decided to
go to work at Johnson and Johnson and regain control. Uncle Robert, used to running things with an
iron hand, wasn't happy. He also wasn't the type
who tolerated challenges to his position without doing something about it.

For Seward, Jr. the quest to regain honor for the
males on his side of the family suffered a serious setback when he met an exotic German brunette
woman, Barbara Eisenfuhr Kline Bailey Maxwell.
Uncle Robert spoted her as the chink in Seward, Jr.'s

armor and he put private detectives on the job to find out everything about this woman. Whatever else they did, the detectives stirred up so much trouble back in Germany that Barbara's father almost lost his job at a Frankfurt bank.

Seward, Jr. complained to his father and demanded that the investigations stop. His father, not wanting to confront his brother, Robert, nor deal with any unpleasantness simply lied to his son and said the investigations had stopped. When Seward, Jr. discovered the lie, he became enraged and threatened to shoot his father. Instead, he and Barbara eloped to Virginia City, Nevada, September 16, 1956.

Whatever Barbara's motives in marrying Seward, Jr., money certainly was one of them. She began putting the squeeze on Seward, Jr. for more and more money and pressuring him to cash out the balance in his trust account. The pressure began to tell on Seward, Jr. and his married life turned into a hell.

His wife accused him of things that he had not done, but in an attempt to prove himself to her he volunteered to have truth serum, sodium pentothal, administered to himself. In 1957 they went on a Christmas cruise to the Bahamas with his father only to have his stepmother, who had stayed behind, accuse Seward, Sr. of sleeping with Barbara.

The next week, Seward, Jr., back home in Princeton, went into the garage with a gun and connected a hose from the tailpipe of his car and put the other end inside the car. He got in, put the gun and a suicide note on the seat and turned on the engine in the enclosed garage. He couldn't even do that right and was discovered before it was too late and rushed to a hospital in critical condition.

The suicide note professed his love for Barbara and said that he was dying a happy man.

Soon afterward Barbara came to the hospital and checked him out because Seward, Sr. was threatening to have his son committed to an insane asylum. Again, the old man did not want confrontation and he wanted the unpleasantnesses taken care of by someone else.

More pressures began pushing in on Seward, Jr. Barbara still wanted more and more money. She chastised him for bumbling his suicide and urged him to try again, but to do it right. Barbara had a lover moved into the house with whom she lived and had sex openly in front of Seward, Jr., who was invited to join in. She demanded he cook for them and serve her and her lover in bed. He meekly complied.

Seward at least was man enough to see that he had to be free of this woman and so turned for help to his father and his uncle. His father didn't even acknowledge his pleas for assistance. His uncle convinced him that he would have to pay Barbara off to get rid of her in spite of her open adulterous behavior. This was the same uncle who told him to take some time off after the suicide attempt and then fired him for absenteeism.

As usual, Uncle Robert had a solution and, as usual, it was one that benefitted Uncle Robert more than anybody else. He said he would approve releasing money from Seward, Jr.'s trust so he could be free of the bitch, Barbara, in exchange for Seward, Jr.'s resignation as trustee, thus returning all the voting power to Uncle Robert.

Instead, Seward, Jr. first tried to get proof of what Barbara and her lover were doing by hiring private detectives to raid his own house while Barbara was having sex with her lover. The raid went off like it had been orchestrated by the Keystone Kops and it generated lots of tabloid headlines and no evidence.

The detectives with cameras at the ready crashed through the door in a shower of splinters. Panicked, Barbara grabbed a pistol from under the bed and shot one of them and dived out the bedroom window in the finest tradition of Hollywood stunt people. Hitting the ground with a roll, but bruised and terrified, she sprinted next door where the neighbors answered her frantic pleas for help by taking her in and calling 911 immediately.

Charges and countercharges were filed and the tabloids had a holiday with stories that would resurface, as they always do, 21 years later in the case against Basia Johnson, Seward, Jr.'s second stepmother.

Bitterly, Seward, Jr. then turned to what he regarded as a Faustian bargain with his uncle trading his trusteeship and the lucrative pay plus his birthright, for his freedom from the bitch Barbara. He spent the next eight years putting his life back together.

Ultimately, he found himself as a realism sculptor whose bronzes have become popular on the urban landscape and through his marriage to author Joyce Johnson and, finally, his involvement with Harbor Branch. He had been pushed out of Johnson and Johnson entirely, but is probably better for it.

For Seward, Jr., the battle over his father's estate was the final step in his therapy and it was important for him to take the lead among the other Johnson children in seeing it through.

The divorce of his mother, Ruth Dill, from his father, Seward, Sr., affected Seward, Jr.'s life deeply.

He felt his father had abandoned him and, later when left to the care of nannies, that his mother had, too.

He was desperate for his father's love, but his father drifted in and out of Seward, Jr.'s life without rhyme or reason and it left the boy bewildered and rejected. As a boy he would often hide in a closet away from everybody for hours and hours. He, too, developed the Johnson trait of withdrawing into himself.

Seward Johnson, Sr.'s two children by his second marriage were Jennifer Johnson Duke, 45, and James Loring Johnson, 41.

Jennifer had a different relationship with her father than Mary Lea did. Jennifer's memory of him was as an easygoing guy who preferred that other people took care of the unpleasant things for him. She went through a messy divorce and what her father objected to was her giving her race-car driver ex-husband, $800,000. He then remarried immediately and committed suicide leaving the money to his new wife. Then Jennifer married a furniture designer and opened a New York gallery to display and sell his work.

James Loring Johnson, at 41 the kid of the family, is an artist and farmer whose father ignored him and, ultimately cut him off emotionally. At one time, Seward, Sr. had named James as the executor of his will, but the old man later removed him, but never explained why. In fact, the two rarely communicated at all. He became taciturn and withdrawn much like his father.

This was the group of heirs who gathered around to break their father's will and keep his third and last wife from getting all the Johnson money.

The grounds for breaking the will reminds one of that famous Claude Rains's line in the movie, *Casablanca,* when he, as police captain, instructs his men, "Round up the usual suspects." The children's lawyer, Alexander Forger, of Milbank, Tweed, Hadley and McCloy, rounded up the usual reasons for breaking a will and charged that Basia was a gold digger who used her feminine wiles to entrap a senile old man, destroy his marriage, and cut him off from his children so she could dominate him.

The "children" it should be noted for proper prospective ranged at the time from 41 to 60 years of age and had personal fortunes ranging from $23 million to $100 million each.

In attacking a will, it is also occasionally appropriate to attack the person chosen as executor and, in fact, many challenges to a will consist of suing the executor. In this case the executrix was Nina Zagat who, with her husband, publishes a popular guide to restaurants in cities around the country.

Attorney Forger said that attorney Zagat was a tool of Basia who helped the third wife manipulate the old man through 22 changes in his will each leaving more to Basia. Zagat's reward for helping Basia "grab" all of the old man's money? A fee of $8 million plus a lifetime annual retainer of $900,000. That certainly beat what she was making on the restaurant guide.

Naturally, Basia could hire some pretty good lawyers, too, and they also rounded up the usual defenses. Old man Johnson was desperately in love with Basia and, in addition to screwing her, also wanted to screw the tax man plus he was irritated because he thought his kids had screwed him.

Her lawyers were Donald Christ and Robert Os-

good of the firm of Sullivan and Cromwell. Christ
and Osgood said J. Seward, Sr. cut off the Harbor
Branch Institute because he had already given the
place $130 million.

As for the kids, they disgusted him, Basia's lawyers said. After all, he established a big trust fund
for all the kids back in 1944. If they had left it alone
and used the money the fund was paying them with
any sense, the fund would now be worth $660 mil-
lion. Instead, they led wild, irresponsible lives and
kept drawing against capital in the trust fund. Their
father neither felt sorry for them nor thought he
should bail them out anymore.

The witnesses for the challengers claimed that
their father was mentally and physically sick beyond
belief. They claimed he had 24 illnesses or impair-
ments and was kept away from his friends and family
and totally under control of the Polish witch. It was
not an eight-on-the-Richter scale surprise that Basia's witnesses took the opposite view and testified
that Seward, Sr. and Basia loved and cared for each
other throughout those 12 years of blissful marriage.

The court conflict between Basia and her stepchildren over the estate of the dead Seward Johnson, Sr.
was a classic form of blood-money feud. A vast
amount of money was involved. However, the central
issue was not money since everyone involved had
more than they would ever use — collectively about a
billion dollars among seven people. The issue was
love and hate and the weapon used by both love and
hate, revenge.

And as is so typical of such cases, the lawyers got
rich dealing with issues having nothing to do with
the issues and, in spite of their fees, were often incompetent. Soap opera scriptwriters would get fired

if they wrote a script that paralleled the true story of the case.

The children of Seward Johnson, Sr. had desperately and vainly sought his love in life and, having been denied that, demanded it in death. As we saw, the last will and amendments signed by Johnson, Sr. cut all of his children and favorite charity (run by his eldest son) off without a cent. That was an open denial of his love. His son, Seward, Jr., then led the children in an attack against that will to reverse the public denial and to prove that they mattered and that he loved them.

To do that, they hired attorneys whose theme of attack was that the written public denial of his love for them could only have been due to the evil stepmother.

That theme was aired publicly by the children themselves. Seward, Jr. said the children were bitter that their father had been mistakenly influenced to leave his money to a bunch of Polish people nobody ever heard of. In fact, Basia Johnson, did hire a number of Poles for her staff and she was one of the many financial supporters of the Solidarity Movement in Poland.

Jennifer Johnson Duke set the tone of the children's attack on Basia Johnson, when she publicly said, "I don't need the money. I want to see that woman (Basia) publicly humiliated."

That was echoed by Joyce Johnson, wife of Seward, Jr., who said of her stepmother-in-law, "We'd like to see Basia suffer a little the way we have. She has such contempt for the Johnsons."

How had the children suffered? They had been left out of Daddy's will. A daddy who had largely ignored most of them most of their lives except for daughter Mary Lea whom he forced into an incestuous affair. A daddy who had given all of them collectively close to a half-billion dollars in trust funds and, speaking of contempt of a Johnson, a daddy who had treated his namesake son with contempt for much of his life.

At one point in the trial, May 23rd, Basia appeared dressed in black to mark the third anniversary of her husband's death. Seward, Jr. responded by going into the courthouse corridor and mockingly hawked "anniversary Kleenex tissues" to the press.

One of the most telling facts about this blood-money feud case is that, during the twelve years she was married to Seward Johnson, Sr., Basia tried to bridge the gap between him and his children. She made a number of efforts at reconciliation between her husband and his children. The professed hatred that the children had for Basia after their father died blossomed *only after they found out they had been cut out of the will.*

In court, Basia was represented by a set of attorneys who, relying on the ironclad will drawn by attorney Nina Zagat, felt it was a simple, open-and-shut case and the will couldn't be contested successfully. One of their main points was that Seward, Sr. had set up trust funds for his children long before he died and he had cut them out of an inheritance in every one of the last 30 wills that he had made.

This overconfidence didn't reckon with the somewhat bizarre surrogate judge, Marie Lambert, who would preside over the case, described by Barbara Goldsmith, the author of one of the books on the trial *Johnson vs. Johnson,* as part Portia and part Tugboat Annie. Surrogate Lambert quickly and obviously sided with the attorneys for the children to the extent that the attorneys for Basia filed a 79-page motion for mistrial citing over 100 instances of alleged judicial misconduct by Lambert.

Basia's attorneys' overconfidence also ignored one of the oldest and corniest truths about how lawyers conduct a case in court. Namely, if the law is on your side, you cite the law a lot; if justice is on your side, you cite justice a lot; and, if neither the law nor justice is on your side, you pound the table and shout a lot.

From the outset, the attorneys for the children ignored the law or justice and pounded the table a lot over the evil sorceress from another land who had stealthily invaded the lovely and benign Johnson household and taken possession of the soul of their sweet, warm, caring but senile daddy. The tale had a Snow White quality about it with attorney Nina Zagat playing a major supporting role as the evil stepmother's dastardly accomplice.

So, February 27, 1983, three years after Seward, Sr. died, the conflict came to the New York courts as did all the participants arriving in their stretch limos and Rolls-Royces. The jury selected to decide about all the money and, most importantly, about an old man's love for his children and much younger wife were an amalgam of urban society with a sanitation worker, a financial analyst for an oil company, a secretary, a travel agent, a business consultant, and a housewife and mother.

During the trial, attorneys for the children depicted Basia as a scheming shrew and Zagat, technically her husband's attorney, but really a family intimate who was very close to Basia. She traveled with Basia, shopped with her and took care of minute family business having nothing to do with the law.

For this, Nina Zagat was paid well and, after Seward, Sr.'s death would be paid even better. To the children's attorneys this was proof of unethical behavior on Zagat's part and collusion with Basia to cheat the old man and his children.

Belatedly realizing that they had a serious problem, the attorneys for Basia, after having been shouted at and cursed by Basia for their incompetence, tried to attack the personal lives of the children in retaliation for personal attacks on Basia. Surrogate Lambert refused to permit evidence of the children's squandering of their trust money; unusual marriages and sexual arrangements; sexual preferences; and other amusements to be admitted in court.

However, what Lambert's court wouldn't do, the news media would. Stories about incest, homosexuality, strange marriages, and wasted money flooded the newspapers. This was, after all, the biggest case of its kind in American history involving about a billion dollars, with testimony that would ultimately go to 400,000 pages and consume scores of witnesses and attorneys.

Basia had begun by trying to get the children to settle the matter out of court *before* the hearings began. She sensed it would not serve the family well to have a lot of secrets pulled out of the closet and she was perfectly willing to spend part of the half-billion dollars Seward, Sr. had left her to see that they weren't.

The children, led by Seward, Jr., would have none of it. Basia was talking money. They were talking pride, longings for love from a dead man, and revenge. There had to be revenge first. Then they would talk about money.

Basia's side was badly damaged by the many witnesses — servants, nurses, and the like — who came to
the stand and said she was loud, tyrannical, auto-
cratic with them and with her husband. Two servants, a maid and a handyman, produced tape
recordings they had made on identical tape recorders
of Basia shouting insults in Polish, allegedly at
Seward, Sr.

Why these recordings had been made at the time,
was never made clear, but Basia immediately charged
that they had been done at the direction of the KGB,
which was trying to discredit her because of her
strong support of Solidarity in Poland.

On April 16th, when the handyman was leaving
the stand after the playing of his recording, a crowd
in the audience rose up and began screaming names
at him, accusing him of being a KGB agent, a communist spy, and worse.

Surrogate Lambert lost her temper and shouted
that she would not permit this in her courtroom. She
immediately ordered the courtroom sealed and the
jury hustled out. Then she demanded that everyone
in the courtroom be identified and questioned. Thirteen of the demonstrators were employees of Basia's
estate and one was sent to jail for the night and
others were fined.

Lambert was clearly shaken by what some called a
courtroom riot and she warned everyone that she
would not be intimidated and that if anything happened to anyone on the jury or connected with the
trial, there would be hell to pay. During the next few
days, she claimed that she received several telephoned death threats at home.

At this point the outcome of the trial became academic. Everybody wanted it over with and over with quickly. Some of the children had gotten ill through the long weeks that had been consumed already and were also upset about the family secrets headlined in tabloids around the country.

Whether she was ready to admit it or not, it seemed that Surrogate Lambert was shaken by the courtroom uproar and the death threats plus the serious implications for her career when Basia's lawyers filed their motion for mistrial based on a long list of Lambert's alleged judicial misconduct.

Basia had never wanted the trial in the first place feeling at a disadvantage as a foreigner and angry at the incompetence of her legal team.

And everyone had, by this time, become aware of the fact that no matter how this trial came out the unpleasantness in court could go on for another five or six years with appeals from whatever verdict came down.

So, both sides and Surrogate Lambert sat down in marathon sessions to work out a settlement. In the end, each child got $6.2 million net of taxes with Seward, Jr. getting an extra $8 million. Seward, Sr.'s favorite charity, Harbor Branch, run by Seward, Jr. got $20 million; all the lawyers (including Zagat) split $25.6 million; and Uncle Sam's tax man got $86 million. All charges against everybody on both sides and Surrogate Lambert were dropped and Basia was left with $350 million.

Afterward, in what appeared to be unseemly for those involved, the children treated Surrogate Lambert, the jury and some of the press to drinks at a celebration party.

So, it was over. Who won? Everyone won something by getting part of what they wanted to get or avoiding what they wanted to avoid. Was anybody guilty of anything? Officially not since the matter never went to the jury. The chronicler of the trial, Barbara Goldsmith, rendered her own private verdict.

Goldsmith labeled Seward Johnson the villain who foisted his psychological hang-ups on those around him without regard for what it did to them. He did what he damn pleased such as dumping his first wife so he could lust after her fourteen-year-old sister or spending a small fortune on a jet plane exclusively to fly his dogs around the globe. He gave a favorite dog, Princey, a luxurious funeral in a special chapel on his estate.

In Goldsmith's eyes, Seward's seduction of his daughter, Mary Lea, was one of the most despicable things the man ever did in a lifetime of doing despicable things.

In 1993, David Margolick's book, *Undue Influence: The Epic Battle For The Johnson and Johnson Fortune,* savaged Judge Lambert and the lawyers involved in the case as a horde of greedy, incompetent cretins bumbling their way through conflicts of interest and stupidities in the case while amassing $25 million in fees. *The Houston Chronicle* reviewer of the Margolick book, David Johnston, summarized it by saying, "If you hate lawyers, you will absolutely love this book."

Nine

Rich Fathers and Reclusive Sons

The sons of the fortune founders tend to be uncertain who they are and who they should be. Typically, they divide roughly into three classes: those who spend the family fortune, those who try to conserve it, and those who give it away as an apology for the way it was accumulated.

For heirs, their wealth and role is not as easy as the rest of us think.

First, the fortune founder often wanted them to think and feel as he did and do what he did. This can stifle children who are not clones and want to be independent.

There are perverse twists to this. Some founders want their heirs to fail and prove that no one can take the founder's place. And there are heirs embarrassed at how the family became rich and want to cleanse the family name or distance themselves from it.

In most cases, there is a chasm between the fortune founder and his children. Parent and children are often alienated from each other. W. Clement Stone, Charles Tex Thornton, Joseph Hirschhorn, Averell Harriman, William Randolph Hearst, Howard Hughes, Barbara Hutton, Peggy Guggenheim, and Eleanor Medill (Cissy) Patterson were all examples.

Part of this is due to the way they are raised. Rich children are usually raised in three ways: One, they are lavished with money, luxury, and no responsibilities. Two, the parents use money to control the children. Three, the parents ignore them and leave the child-rearing to schools and hired help.

For many, the business of making money left little time for a caring relationship with the family. What the fortune founders want are heirs who perpetuate the name and don't interfere with business.

The wives of the rich usually did not marry great wealth so they could change diapers, attend PTA meetings, and play nanny. A rich wife sees her role as having to produce children and be a symbol of her husband's status. Having children is part of the bargain—raising them is not.

Although it must be said, in fairness, that a number of wives of rich men raised their children even when the husband was aloof or absent. These tended to be the women who were those men's wives *before* they got rich. The wives of the Dodge brothers are an example.

The story of the Marshall Field family is typical of the father who couldn't be bothered with child-rearing.

The Chicago store bearing his name was the consuming interest of Field's life and left no time for the family so his wife, ironically named Nannie, spent most of her time in Europe after delivering the required son and daughter, Marshall II and Ethel.

Marshall Field did not have much formal education, but the small-town New England boy had two things that made him a multimillionaire.

First, Marshall Field had an incredible memory and knew every item of merchandise in a store. Second, he had a diffident, courteous way of dealing with people that made them feel special. These two traits made him a natural retailer.

And, in his five years clerking in a small store in Pittsfield, Massachusetts, he proved his mettle to the point that he was offered a partnership in the store. To the astonishment of the owner, the 22-year-old clerk turned him down with the news that he had decided to go out west and seek his fortune.

Out west at that time meant Chicago and that's where Marshall went. Again, he took a job clerking in a retail store, worked hard, treated the customers well, and saved his money. In four years he was able to buy a junior partnership in the store just at a time when the Civil War began—meaning a shortage of goods and substantial profits for retailers.

When the owner of a competing store made it known he wanted to sell out soon and retire, Marshall joined forces with Levi Leiter to buy him out. Marshall brought in his two brothers, Joseph and Henry, and then devised a scheme to trick Leiter out of his share.

First, Field went around to the key employees of the growing store and sounded them out about what they would do if the partnership split. He convinced many of them to go with him if that happened.

Then he told his partner Leiter that he wanted out of the partnership and proposed what seemed to be a cleverly honest solution. He said he would name a price for 50 percent of the value of the store. Then Leiter could decide to buy out Field's half or sell out his own half at that price. It was like the ancient Arab method of dividing an inheritance between two surviving sons. One son draws the dividing line between the two halves and the other son gets first choice of which half he wants.

The price Field named for 50 percent was a lowball price, but Leiter thought it sounded fair not knowing that Field had rigged the deal. So Leiter said he would sleep on it and then he quickly checked with the key employees to see if they would stay with him if he bought Field out. Of course, they said they wouldn't and, so, Leiter let Field buy him out for what was really a bargain price.

The store became Marshall Field and grew as Chicago grew in the late 19th century and soon had 3,000 employees in a facility that covered an entire block.

Ignored by his father and raised by women, Marshall II seemed an heir adrift at sea with absolutely no interest in his father's business or much of anything else. He did what was required or expected of him and that wasn't much either. He went to Harvard mostly to do something and then got married to Albertine Huck presumably because his sister had married. When his sister married an Englishman and moved to England, Marshall and his bride did, too, so he could be close to Ethel.

One of the things expected of Marshall II, naturally, was to produce Marshall III. He did this twice. When the first one, Marshall III, died as an infant, he and Albertine dutifully produced a replacement who became the second Marshall III. In addition,

Marshall II and Albertine had Henry and Gwendolin.

By this time, the senior Marshall's wife had died in France and he only saw his son and grandchildren sporadically even when they were in Chicago, so at 75, he married Delia Caton, a widow of 50, who, along with her late husband, had been Marshall's friends for years.

He had been a lonely man completely absorbed in his business for so many years. After his marriage, he helped found the University of Chicago and began work on city wide projects. His marriage to Delia and his new interests could have marked a bright and wonderful close to his life. But they didn't. Soon afterward, rudderless Marshall II committed suicide.

The family tried to hush it up and pretend it was an accident, but the press was all over the story to the added dismay of his bewildered and haunted father.

Marshall II's widow emerged from her mourning long enough to observe to the world press, "American wealth is too often a curse." She then moved to England to raise her children.

The grief took its toll of all involved and Marshall soon fell ill and, on January 17, 1906, he died making Delia a widow for the second time in 14 months.

Marshall's will was tough and supposedly airtight, but had not been altered to account for the recent death of Marshall II. It left most of the estate to Marshall's grandsons Marshall III and Henry.

However, it put it in trust and didn't give them full possession of their money until they were fifty, which was the age Marshall thought would make them mature enough to cope with the approximately $40 million each was allotted. A number of unsuccessful attempts were made to break the will or to have it modified.

For example, there was the possibility unforeseen by Marshall that neither of his grandsons would reach age fifty. Remote? No, because eleven years later, Henry died and the question arose. Was Marshall III entitled to part of his late brother's share of the trust? It was off to court to find out.

The court said Marshall III was entitled to get the income from both his own and his late brother's share of the trust. So, again, the heirs were able to modify the wishes of their benefactor parent.

By the time Marshall III came into his full inheritance he had wisely been through analysis and tried to make sense of his life. Being raised in England away from the scene of family tragedies and influence had helped. As he grew older, he got involved, not in retailing, but in some of the playboy things rich young men focused on. He got into investment banking because that seemed appropriate, but his real enthusiasm was newspapers.

When one of the founders of *TIME* magazine, Ralph Ingersoll, came to him in 1940 with the idea of *PM,* an honestly liberal—almost too liberal—daily newspaper for New York City, Marshall III put up the money. Then, he started the *Chicago Sun.*

PM didn't work and finally closed down five million dollars later, but the *Sun* did work, became the *Chicago Sun-Times,* and is around today although the current heirs of Marshall III dislike one another so much that they refused to own anything jointly, so they sold off much of the old family business including the *Sun-Times.*

Along the way, Marshall III produced Marshall IV

who was the reincarnation of the personality and business acumen of his great-grandfather. When Marshall III died in 1956, Marshall IV took over control of the *Sun-Times,* the *Chicago Daily News, World Book Encyclopedia,* four radio stations, and a variety of other interests with a sure hand.

Later, the blood-money feud resumed with the two sons who followed, Marshall V and Frederick, known as Ted, born of different wives. The two half-brothers couldn't have been more different than if they had been born on different planets. Marshall V, eleven years older than Ted, was brought up on the East Coast through the usual strain of prep schools and lifestyle. Predictably, he is the conservative financial mind content with following the family tradition and family home base of Chicago.

Frederick, child of Marshall Field IV's second wife, Kay Woodruff, was brought up in Alaska in a middle-class home drenched in the teachings of Mary Baker Eddy and Christian Science. Kay had loaded her belongings and her son and two daughters into a station wagon when her marriage collapsed and drove to Anchorage. In time, she became a reporter for the *Anchorage Daily News* and in even more time, she bought the paper. It was never a financial success and she finally sold it and became the editor of the prestigious *Christian Science Monitor.*

When the elder Marshall Field died, Marshall V took over the family operation while the younger brother came back from Anchorage and enrolled in Northwestern University. It was the first of a number of colleges the shy, brooding, awkward Ted would drift in and out of in the next few years. He admired his brother, but wasn't comfortable around him ever since the day they were kids and he had to watch Marshall V chop the heads off turtles for fun.

Technically, the two brothers legally came into their father's estate on June l, 1977, with each brother's share worth about $100 million. Unhappily, for the next seven years, the two fought each other over the family inheritance all the while Ted was regarded as the odd, self-indulgent brother. He had a beard, lived in California, and raced cars—hardly a Chicago Field.

After seven years things got so hairy that the only possible solution was to split the estate. They did that, forcing the public sale of the *Chicago Sun-Times* to the dreadful Rupert Murdoch who was not only not from Chicago or the Midwest—the man wasn't even an American! The sale was severely criticized by leaders in Chicago and it precipitated a feud between the brothers that would last for years.

Marshall remained in Chicago shaking his head in disbelief, tending to investments, and following the social life of the town.

Ted fled to Hollywood to live on the old Harold Lloyd estate and soon leveraged his millions into an important stake in Hollywood's movie and music industry. Along the way his car racing had the tragic result of crippling his left hand in a freak accident.

A serious race-car driver, he was at the Riverside, California, track when his race car died and a tow truck crew came out on the track to pull it off. The truck driver gave him a line to hold, lost control of his truck and dragged the car and Ted entangled in the line with his hand jammed between the roll bar and the pavement of the track for almost a hundred yards—the length of a football field.

"When I was pried apart from the car and taken to

the hospital, I finally got over my shock enough to look at my hand. It looked like raw liver with pencils sticking out. The pencils were my finger bones."

Disabled with his crippled hand, he was warned that he would never drive anything again much less a race car, but he defied that prediction and was soon back at the track. Still, it has to be scary to take your right hand off the steering wheel to shift gears while going over 200 miles an hour steadying the wheel with only your left thumb.

A restless man with troubling blue eyes, he has gone through three wives, is heavily into Hollywood liberal causes, and has launched a new record label as an adjunct to his movie production company, Interscope (*Three Men and A Little Lady, Cocktail, Bird On A Wire,* and *Revenge of the Nerds*).

His restless nature has extended to relations with the opposite gender and a king-size reputation of having an endless string of affairs that caused him some trouble with each of three wives. However, being the wife of Ted Field has its rewards.

The first wife, Judy, produced two daughters and, after the divorce, was set up in a $3.5 million home in the tony Bel-Air district near Beverly Hills. The second wife, Barbara, didn't produce any children but adopted a daughter, and failed to overturn the mandatory prenuptial agreement on the grounds of his constant infidelities. "He had been having affairs throughout the marriage and constantly told me about them. In fact, at times, he went so far as to bring them into our home." Barbara lost and now resides in a $5 million house also in Bel-Air.

The third wife, Susie, formerly involved with Rod Stewart, produced three daughters—all in the first three years of their marriage—left Ted because of his

running around with other women and settled into a
$14 million house. Each successive wife seems to get
a more expensive payout.

Susie and Ted reconciled once and had their third
daughter. Susie said she was determined to try for
two more in the hopes of getting a much needed boy.
That plan was sidetracked because Ted and Susie got
divorced. He now hangs around with a drop-dead
gorgeous blue-eyed blond actress, Tracy Tweed, who
may someday be invited to sign one of Ted's complicated and highly detailed prenuptial agreements that
has protected the bulk of his money from the ravages
of three failed marriages.

Naturally, everybody in Chicago expected that he-
donistic Ted would squander his half of the $520 mil-
lion estate and solid, straight, buttoned-down
Marshall would make the right investments and do
well. In fact, Ted has more than doubled what he
walked out of the family businesses with, while Marshall V has not done nearly as well.

Before he came into his inheritance in 1965 at age
24, this great-great-grandson of the original Marshall
Field had been a Harvard art history graduate living
with his mother, as they say in Chicago, Back East.
He came to Chicago and took over running the family newspaper, the *Sun-Times* and quickly got bored
with that and turned the day-to-day operations over
to editor Jim Hoge, who would later go on to be editor of the *New York Daily News*.

Marshall turned his attentions to real estate deals
working through the family investment company,
Cabot, Cabot and Forbes (CC&F). When he and Ted
fought over the inheritance, they ended up selling the
Sun-Times to Rupert Murdoch for $100 million and
hating each other in the process. It didn't matter.

They sold anyhow and went their separate ways.

Marshall bought out Ted's interest in CC&F, formed another company, Field Corporation, and began wheeling and dealing including buying Funk & Wagnalls, Muzak, and the *Weekly Reader* newspaper.

When the real estate market started going into the porcelain, Marshall's enterprises suffered and he began dumping holdings. *Forbe's* magazine claims that CC&F now has a negligible net worth, but that Marshall is a totally liquid "passive investor" these days with a mere $300 million to his name.

The plus side is that it now leaves Marshall with lots of time for doing what he really wants to do, charitable work. "I have a ton of friends who died with a lot of money and nobody remembered them 24 hours later. My overall goal is for people to say when I drop dead, 'Marshall did something for the city. He didn't just go through it.' "

So, he does pro bono work for the Rush-Presbyterian-St. Luke's medical institutes and the Chicago Art Institute. Meanwhile, his eccentric brother works at figuring out his own life.

Restive Ted is in search of something, but nobody is quite sure what—maybe not even Ted. Some say this is a common phenomenon of rich kids: searching for their own identity and purpose.

When Ted decided that he wanted to sell the old Harold Lloyd estate, Greenacres, that he had bought in 1986, and move to another Beverly Hills house, he felt that the 31 Old Italian Masters he owned weren't right for the new digs. So, in May of 1991, he had Christies put them up for auction at $10 million plus. Everybody can understand what it's like to have to redecorate a new place.

He is aware of the mystique that surrounds him because of the great wealth he had at birth and the unconventional life he insists on leading. He, in fact, revels in being known as the Black Sheep Field, but would like to dispel anything intimidating about that. "I've realized that one of the things I need to do is try to make clear I'm not this scary, mysterious figure everyone speculates about."

Even so, when *Premiere* magazine ranked Ted the 38th most powerful person in Hollywood, it described him as having a "Bizarre Trumpesque lifestyle with a big inner-darkness problem." Dennis Hamill of the *New York Daily News* who has worked for Ted thinks that's bull and that Hollywood doesn't connect with Ted because he cuts through all the Hollywood pretense, pomp and palaver like a hot machete through chocolate.

He has met and mixed with a wide variety of people while getting involved in a number of causes and projects. Along the way, he met and became good friends with the late Jerzy Kosinski; studied kick boxing from the technical director of *Batman;* and became a world-class chess player and patron underwriting international matches between Kasparov and Karpov.

Among other things, Ted is a largely unknown, but powerful, supporter of liberal political causes, mostly Democratic—he is one of the top five contributors to the Democratic party. He influences political events largely through what is called in Hollywood, his "Big Pen." He personally bankrolled the drive to defeat Judge Robert Bork's nomination for the U.S. Supreme Court working through his then-political aide, Robert L. Burkett,

"I felt that [Bork] was a superauthoritarian,

completely insensitive to human concerns and to personal freedoms. I thought he was a true monster—the most dangerous kind of monster, because he was a very smart monster."

In September of 1992, he hosted a glamorous $2,500-a-head party for Bill Clinton and raised $1.3 million for the presidential candidate. While the *Legal Times* calls Ted, "A flaming, unabashed liberal," he is a curious contributor to the Democratic party in that he asks no favors or ambassadorships or other perks in return for his money.

An obsession with Ted, who is described by Robert W. Cort, a long-time ex-CIA operative and business colleague of Field's as "a very intense man and a very internal man," is the fundamentalist religious right of the Republican party.

It is possible that the religious right wing of the conservatives isn't terribly thrilled with Ted either since his record company has put out albums by the Thrill Kill Kult whose repertoire includes, "Leather Sex" and "Devil Bunnies."

And, he took heat in the Clinton campaign when Dan Quayle picked Ted as his #2 Hollywood target because Ted's record company had released a record album by Sister Souljah and one by rapper Tupac Amuru Shakur with cop killer lyrics on it.

It was an uncomfortable irony since the vice-presidential candidate's wife, Tipper Gore, had earlier led a campaign to censor vulgar and violent record lyrics. Linda Davidson, the widow of a Texas Highway Trooper, Bill Davidson, killed by a teenager, Ronald Ray Howard, who said he was urged to do it by the song on the album, has sued Ted's Interscope Records over the killing.

Ronald Ray Howard was sentenced to death by an

Austin, Texas, jury July 14, 1993 and, with that state's pro-death penalty record, he will probably be executed by lethal injection within the next two years. Linda Davidson's suit against Interscope will probably go to trial at the end of 1993 or beginning of 1994. The 19-year-old Howard who sold drugs and stole hundreds of cars for a living, as well as siring six children with four women says he might testify on behalf of his victim's widow to establish blame for the killing on the Interscope record album.

Beyond all this, everyone in Chicago and California is watching and waiting for a Marshall VI to be born. So far, only daughters have appeared and, while Ted scoffs at the inheritance question, no one believes him. He is still a peripatetic dilettante searching for meaning and fulfillment.

As for the blood-money feud between the two half-brothers, they have not spoken since Ted forced the sale of the *Chicago Sun-Times* until just recently. That was when Marshall called to get Ted to share the living expenses of their former nanny. The nanny who raised them since their father and mother were too busy to be bothered.

Ten

Blood Money Murder

Of course, for the heirs to live the way they want, they usually must first get their hands on the family money. That often has meant vicious fights in the courts or against other claimants or against other relatives.

For example, the lawsuit contesting Cornelius Vanderbilt's $100 million will by his relatives was launched on the grounds that the old guy was wacko because he claimed to be able to communicate with the dead through spiritualists.

But there has always been a simple and direct way: *Murder.*

Colonel Thomas Swope was one of the more successful businessmen who founded Kansas City and amassed millions, but that didn't save him from being murdered. In fact, that's *why* he was murdered.

A local physician, Dr. Bennett Clarke Hyde, married into the wealthy Swope family when he courted and wed Swope's daughter, Frances Swope.

Even though Dr. Hyde's medical practice was doing well, one of the attractions of Frances Swope was the wealth of her family. He fully expected to have access to that wealth himself.

Even though the considerable fortune of Thomas Swope was large, a number of people were slated to share it upon Swope's death. This was a huge disappointment to Hyde. The millions were to be split among the immediate heirs plus a goodly number of nieces and nephews, which reduced Frances's share to a few hundred thousand when it should have been, in Hyde's view, several million dollars.

Unfortunately, Thomas Swope had created an ancient tontine where, as each heir died, his or her share of the Swope inheritance reverted to the other Swope heirs. It was a tempting invitation to murder and Dr. Hyde accepted the invitation and the challenge.

In short, Dr. Hyde set off to correct the "mistake" in Thomas Swope's will so the doctor's wife would get all the millions Dr. Hyde felt were rightfully hers — and his. Dr. Hyde set off to murder all the other heirs. He bumbled through his lethal project, and the only redeeming aspect of his murderous odyssey was that it worked.

First, there was the not-too-difficult problem of getting rid of the old man, Thomas Swope, who was already 82 and in poor condition. Hyde, of course, was in the perfect position for murder because he was the family's physician, the son-in-law doctor, and saw to the medical needs of those in the Swope family.

Even so, poor Tom Swope was not number one

on the doctor's list of victims. Number one was James Hunton who was Swope's long-term friend and colleague and who Swope had named the administrator of his will. Hyde wanted to kill Hunton first in the hope that his father-in-law would then name him, Dr. Hyde, as administrator of the estate. That would make manipulation of the Swope millions easier.

Hyde's chance came when Hunton wasn't feeling well in September 1909 and called Dr. Hyde to help him. Hyde said it was a sad case of apoplexy and recommended an old medical treatment from Colonial days that modern medicine had long abandoned. However, in this instance, said Dr. Hyde, it was just the thing.

It consisted of bleeding the patient to draw off "bad blood." This was what killed many patients a hundred years before and was the cause of George Washington's death. So, Dr. Hyde bled James Hunton until the poor fellow died. Everyone was sad, but what could you do? That's the breaks.

The death of James Hunton came as a shock to many people, particularly his old friend, Thomas Swope, but not as big a shock as the next step in Dr. Hyde's plan.

Swope was, as we said, not in good health anyhow and the death of his friend depressed him. Dr. Hyde suggested that he get some rest under Dr. Hyde's care and, of course, Swope agreed with Hyde. He was, after all, a doctor. Before long, the old man's body turned icy cold and he went into convulsions. A nurse was present when this happened and Dr. Hyde ordered her out of the room to do something for him. When she came back, the old man was dead.

Dr. Hyde pretended to be stunned and depressed and with a mock heavy heart made out the death certificate for his father-in-law noting the cause of death was apoplexy. That was also what he claimed was the reason for Hunton's death. Now the redistribution of the Swope millions began, but not in the right way. It was going to all the heirs instead of going to Mrs. Hyde as the doctor wanted.

Earlier that same year, Dr. Hyde had approached a colleague, Dr. L. Stewart, who was doing some research into the deathly typhoid microbe and got him to give him some typhoid cultures supposedly for some research of his own. What Stewart didn't know was that Hyde had intended to use the typhoid on some of the Swope heirs.

A few weeks later, four of the other heirs, all nieces and nephews of Tom Swope, were stricken by typhoid. Again Dr. Hyde, along with a family nurse, were in attendance on the sick relatives. By the end of November 1909, Chrisman Swope went into convulsions and died as the other sick heirs clung tenaciously to life.

One of the stupid things that Dr. Hyde did at this point was to greet another heir, a niece arriving home from Europe, at the train station. He warned her of the illness that had afflicted the others and gave her something to drink, which he convinced her would protect her from the disease. She drank it and came down with typhoid within hours.

At this point the nurse, who didn't like what was going on and didn't want to be a part of it, quit. As she gave her notice, she told Mrs. Hyde that her husband was murdering people and she, the nurse, wanted out. Oddly, Mrs. Hyde, who would remain unwaveringly loyal to her husband and, who knows, may have been in on the plan herself, told the family lawyer what the nurse had said.

The red lights and alarm bells went off in the attorney's mind and he immediately demanded that a second doctor be brought in. This was done. Even though Dr. Hyde was upset about this, he could hardly refuse. The second doctor examined the patients and the circumstances and decided the typhoid infections could not have reasonably occurred naturally.

For one thing, these cases were unique in the area and only Swope relatives were getting typhoid. Normally, typhoid is an infection resulting from contaminated food or water so that lots of people would contract it. In this case, that wasn't so. Beyond that, the most commonly suspected source would have been the Swope family water supply, but when tested, there was no sign of typhoid.

Dr. Hyde was made to leave the care of the ill Swope heirs to the second doctor, and they all recovered quickly. Then it was discovered that Dr. Hyde had tried to dispose of a deadly poison, potassium cyanide, for which there was no legitimate medical use.

This was enough to arouse suspicions among the other heirs, but no vital connection was made until the other heirs insisted on autopsies of James Hunton and Thomas Swope. And, guess what? A connection was immediately made. The two dead men were loaded with potassium cyanide, the deadly poison. So, Hyde must have given poison to Hunton, as well as bleeding him. Well, it pays to be sure.

Up to this point, Dr. Hyde's plan to murder all the other heirs to his father-in-law's fortune was amateurishly handled. Yet that was not as strange as what happened next.

First, the doctor was arrested on February 9, 1910, and charged with murdering Hunton and Swope. Even though charged with murder, he was out on $100,000 bail and the sensational murder trial began. Witness after witness testified to the details of the murders and Dr. Hyde's behavior that clearly pinpointed him as the murderer.

The druggist he bought the poison from identified him and testified against him. The nurse testified about his strange behavior and the sudden death of Thomas Swope. Dr. Stewart told the court about giving Hyde the typhoid germs for "research" and, then, having second thoughts and trying to get them back from Hyde. However, Hyde told Stewart he couldn't return the typhoid microbes because he had thrown them out.

It would seem like a fairly open and shut case, but it took a month for the prosecution to present its case and the defense to refute it. Then it took the jury sixty hours to agree on a verdict. Finally, they filed back into the courtroom and pronounced Dr. Bennett Clarke Hyde guilty of murder in the first degree and off he went to jail.

Upset, but determined to stand by her husband, Frances Swope Hyde then invoked one of the ironies of this story. She used the considerable money left by her father to fight the conviction of the murderer of her father.

She poured her money into creating an imposing legion of lawyers who examined every minute detail of the case and the trial and began flooding the courts with writs and petitions and motions. Publicly, Frances Hyde declared that her husband was the innocent scapegoat of a plot by the other members of the family. Naturally, this didn't endear her with the other heirs and they became estranged as she fought the battle for her husband's freedom.

Finally, some of the torrent of legal moves produced an order by the Kansas Supreme Court in 1911 for a new trial. The basis of the Supreme Court's order was that there had been a number of judicial errors in the first trial and it was possible that Dr. Hyde had been unfairly convicted.

With the best lawyers that money could buy on his side, the tide began to turn for Bennett Clarke Hyde. A juror became sick during the second trial and the judge declared a mistrial. Doggedly pushing ahead, the public prosecutor filed the charges all over again and went on with a third trial. This trial was completed, but the jurors could not agree and the trial ended in a hung jury.

Persistent about this blatant and amateurish murder plot, the prosecutor filed charges a fourth time and went to trial again. It was now seven years since the first trial and conviction and the prosecutor was determined to see Dr. Hyde punished, but it was not to be. In midtrial the work of the defense team's researchers turned up a Kansas law that forbid trying a man more than three times on the same charge. Astonishingly, the bungling murderer had to be released with the issue of his guilt or innocence never resolved.

Since the notoriety of his murder trials shattered public confidence in his healing talents, Dr. Hyde retired and lived with Frances on the inheritance left her by her father.

Chapter Nine

Since the history of the murder trials featured
quite convincing in its medical talents. Dr. H...
will continue with the eyes on the Intelligence

Eleven

Parents' and Children's Blood-Money Battles

Even after the children and heirs of the rich succeed in seizing the long-awaited prize of the inheritance, there is often another struggle among the children and their heirs for the second-generation inheritance.

A classic case of mother against children and children against mother, is the Goldmans of New York.

It was crazy. Here was the biggest landlord in New York City hooked up to a dialysis machine that washed his 67-year-old blood while he went through a bitter divorce that ravaged the family he loved. What did he need this for?

Sol Goldman, a secretive and harsh man at times, started with a grocery store on Brooklyn's Union Street and spent his life building an unrivaled urban real estate empire while being denounced as being a cheap son of a bitch by tenants and competitors.

Now, as his life was slipping away, his wife of

many years, Lillian, and their kids were fighting him and one another. Lillian accused him of cheating her out of her inheritance and Sol counterattacked with charges that she was insane and three of their four children swore their mother needed psychiatric care.

Typical of this odd relationship was the 30th birthday party at the Carlyle Hotel for their middle daughter, Amy, on April 19, 1984. Even though they were all at each other's throats, much of the family was there trying to act civilized. Naturally, Amy attended with her fiancé, as did daughter, Jane, with her husband and Lillian. Everybody was polite and the pending divorce between Lillian and Sol was not mentioned. It was one of those uncomfortable gatherings that people endure in the name of family.

The only discordant note came with the raucous arrival of the beautiful, petite manic-depressive daughter, Didi, who entered amid much noise and confusion in the sedate Carlyle dining room followed by her ever-present nurse. She fluttered in, kissed everybody and was led out by the nurse as the group reset its flustered feathers. It was as if a summer squall had passed through a serene meadow.

After dinner, Sol took advantage of the circumstances to try working things out with Lillian. Sol never missed a chance to make a deal. Even while he was on the dialysis machine, he had the phone to his ear wheeling and dealing. Bargaining was part of his psyche.

Now, Lillian and Sol faced the prospect of ending their long marriage in a bitter courtroom drama that would be embarrassing for everyone. Sol and Lillian talked as they had talked their way through problems for years. The post-dinner talk ended with their agreeing to agree. They decided to meet in four days, along with their lawyers, to work things out without a trial.

Four days later they met with lawyers in tow. They came to an informal agreement of the issues between them. However, instead of settling things, this meeting and informal agreement triggered one of the biggest private lawsuits and blood-money feuds in American history.

There was no doubt that Sol loved Lillian, but their children knew Lillian had a history of not standing by her man at critical times of his life. In some senses, the lawsuits were a repetition of that pattern.

Sol, born Usher Selig Goldman in 1917 to Fannie and Charles Goldman, began his rise to great wealth when he bought his father's Brooklyn grocery store with $5,000. Both his father and the business had been ailing and Sol turned it into a profitable business using the earnings to buy up foreclosed real estate.

His parents were a sad couple who kept several hundred canaries in their basement and Sol's mother was almost miserly. Lillian would later say that her mother-in-law could hear the sound of a dollar bill hitting the floor.

Sol's mother thought he should stay in the grocery business, but in 1941 Sol met a beautiful 19-year-old girl, Lillian, whose rich, brown hair and alabaster skin drove him crazy and she liked the idea that he was a real estate investor. She didn't want to be married to a grocer. She wanted to be married to a real estate tycoon and seven months after they met, it happened—the marriage, not the tycoon-hood.

A few weeks after the wedding came the first test of whether Lillian would stand by her man and she flunked. World War II was on and young men were being swept up in the draft and sent overseas to get killed. Sol didn't want any part of that program, so he asked his wife to say that she was pregnant so he wouldn't be drafted. She refused and into the army went the budding young real estate tycoon.

He was sent initially to Fort Monmouth, New Jersey, and ironically got his wife pregnant during one of his visits home. Lillian miscarried and lost that baby and later lost a second one.

When Sol got out of the army, he went into business with a long-time friend, Alex Di Lorenzo, Jr., and the two began to pyramid mortgages and properties. They would use the income from the properties they owned to finance buying new properties. They also used an old system of pyramiding real estate by getting bigger mortgages on the properties they owned to raise money to buy more properties on which they got bigger mortgages to raise money to buy more properties and so on. The two young partners did so well in the next few years that, by 1960, they were able to buy the landmark Chrysler building from another real estate tycoon, William Zeckendorf.

All this time Lillian demonstrated an instinctive sense about Manhattan properties. She and Sol would tour around the town and she had a native sense of what was a good property and what wasn't. She had a nose for profitable real estate. It was analogous to H.L. Hunt's oldest son in Texas, Hassie, who was not good in a lot of things, but who could sniff great pools of oil where others said they didn't exist.

An oddity about Lillian in this sense was that she was agoraphobic and afraid to go out alone and mix with strangers. She had to have somebody she knew and trusted at home with her all the time and she had to stay with Sol as they drove around Manhattan.

The partners, Sol and Alex, also followed the standard rule of the rich by being incredibly cheap; paying bills slowly; skimping on services to tenants; and bargaining creditors down at the last minute. Sol even steamed uncanceled stamps off and reused them. He was obsessed with making deals and making money.

In 1956, the Goldmans moved from Brooklyn to a nice five-bedroom house in Kings Point, Long Island, where they would live for 12 years before moving into Manhattan and a suite at the Stanhope Hotel. From then on, the family stayed mostly in hotels, which embarrassed the children because it marked them as rich and different from other kids. Most kids had a mother who fixed their meals, but the Goldman children had room service.

In raising the children, Sol loved them all and catered to his daughters, but was demanding of his son, Allen, so he would grow up to be a man capable of taking over the family business.

In 1969, the year after they had moved to the Stanhope, troubles began. The city demanded that Sol and Alex pay $4.7 million in back taxes and the news media jumped on the story, emphasizing that they were the biggest landlords of massage parlors, sex shops, and whorehouses in New York.

As this was going on, Allen got married and Sol brought him into the business, which soon caused friction between Allen and Alex. Di Lorenzo complained to Sol that Allen didn't do the work properly and lost profits for the company. Things got to the point that Alex fired Allen and Sol couldn't object, but tried to smooth things over with his partner and get Allen back on the payroll. Allen ended up being hired and fired repeatedly.

As if this wasn't enough, Allen couldn't keep his own family under control. His wife, Lorraine, sued him for divorce and got custody of their two kids so Allen retaliated by trying to evict her from the family residence. Her lawyer summoned up not the law, but the specter of the press by threatening to take the story of a man who wanted to evict his own kids to the newspapers. The eviction bit the dust.

Later Lorraine struck again. Allen, following the routine used in the family business of stalling creditors, tried to stall paying Lorraine the alimony she had been awarded. Lorraine didn't fiddle around, she had Allen arrested and sent to the Queens House of Detention for a time in 1973.

Meanwhile, Allen's sister Didi had a daughter by the name of Robin in 1974 and, then Didi became a manic-depressive. The other sister, Jane, married Ben Lewis, a Harvard fellow in cardiology. However, instead of living in Cambridge with him, Jane stayed in New York to help her father with his increasingly troubled business. The two became very close during this period.

As if all the personal problems in the family weren't enough, Sol and Alex's business was being squeezed. Interest rates and operating costs were skyrocketing and too often income was frozen under the terms of some long-term leases and profit was getting pinched in between. It got so bad that Sol and Alex lost the Chrysler building through foreclosure in 1975.

It may have been the humiliation of that setback or the cumulation of all the other business pressures, but a few days later, Alex Di Lorenzo dropped dead at his desk in the office. It stunned Sol and everybody else in the company at the time. What stunned them more was the vicious battle that followed when De Lorenzo's heirs came riding in demanding their separate share of everything. Another blood-money feud had erupted and Sol was in the middle of it.

This all put Sol into a state of deep depression and Lillian decided to come into the office to help because Sol could hardly function. Jane didn't like this development and wished Lillian would stay out of the business and let her and Allen run things.

The dispute with Alex's heirs continued and it looked as if it was going to be messy and expensive. In order to split all the properties that the partnership owned would require expensive appraisals and big attorneys' fees for the paperwork. So, to cut right through the Gordian Knot, Sol came up with a solution that was typical of the deal maker. It also would help Sol by relieving the emotional trauma of the heir battle.

Sol proposed that all the properties owned by the

partners be split between him and Alex's heirs by the toss of a coin. Surprisingly, Alex's heirs agreed and it was done—another deal made. It was the biggest deal of Sol's life with the ownership of hundreds of millions of dollars of prime Manhattan real estate being decided by a flip of the coin. Still, considering the price of lawyers, it was probably a sensible idea.

In spite of this and Sol's penny-pincher reputation, he and his wife lived in a Waldorf Towers suite that cost $18,000 a month and spent weekends at their 20-room Oyster Bay home with its tennis court and 26 acres. When they tired of New York and Oyster Bay, there was always the Palm Beach condo.

Lillian spent $300,000 a year on her clothes and another $120,000 on odds-and-ends expenses. Just so she wouldn't look like a poor shop girl, she had a million dollars' worth of jewelry to flaunt including a remarkable 200-carat diamond bracelet and 40-carat diamond ring. These were not poor people worrying about the next car payment. As for cars, there were two Rolls-Royces, a Mercedes, and a Cadillac so they didn't have to take a taxi cab to get around town.

But other things were going wrong in Sol's life. In 1978, Sol's kidneys gave out and he had to go on dialysis that washed his blood for sometimes as long as five hours in one day. While he was handicapped in this way, the deal-making pressures exploded as New York's latest real estate boom began.

Sol loved that part of his life. He was doing deals while daughter Jane ran the office. Sol knew the real estate of Manhattan block by block so well that he never left the office. He bought and sold over the phone and loved it. In one deal he bought the Manufacturers Hanover Trust building on East 57th Street and sold it the next day for $11 million profit.

Not that all was perfect. As a result of a lawsuit ending in 1985, he had to repay tenants $3 million for overcharges he had made earlier. Then came the divorce.

Lillian charged that the marriage breakup was partly the fault of her daughter, Jane, and her son-in-law, Ben, who had returned from Harvard. Lillian said that Jane had taken charge of Sol's business and Ben had taken charge of Sol's health. Besides that, Lillian said that Sol was having sex in lieu of rent with some of his female movie star tenants and that she found love letters from a former receptionist in the office.

Then, of course, there was the time Sol tried to kill her. That really got her to thinking about divorce. Son-in-law Ben had put Sol into the hospital for a time and when he came home, Lillian complained of severe shortness of breath one night. She asked Sol to call an ambulance, but, instead, he pushed her head out the window of the 34th floor suite so she could get some fresh air.

She was terrified (her lawyer would later charge that Sol dangled her out the 34th-floor window by her ankles), but they stayed together. Then Lillian collapsed from pneumonia while at their Long Island estate and, again, Sol refused to call an ambulance. That's when she moved out and filed for divorce on the grounds of cruelty.

Sol didn't want a divorce and he hired one of the hottest lawyers in town, Raoul Felder, to stop it. For one thing a divorce meant Lillian would get half the property and it meant breaking up some terrific sites. He had been through that already with Alex's heirs. In fact, a Goldman divorce involved so much property in New York, it literally could have seriously affected Manhattan real estate values.

No matter, Lillian did want the divorce and hired Roy Cohen to get it for her. Another blood-money battle was beginning and it was vicious. Lillian filed for temporary alimony and Sol responded by getting their daughters to file an affidavit saying Lillian was crazy and needed psychiatric care. Allen didn't join with his sisters. He knew how rough divorce could be and didn't want to side with either parent.

Sol kept trying to reconcile, but he couldn't get over the lifelong habit of negotiating—making the deal no matter what was involved. Once he took her to dinner so they could make up, things went well until he balked when she wanted raspberries for dessert. He said no, she should settle for cookies because they came with the dinner.

She got $700,000 a year temporary alimony, but the case was dragging. She worried that her case might be weakened by the fact that she had been married to Sol for 42 years and only now she was complaining about cruelty. She said she refused to charge him with adultery because she wouldn't give any man the satisfaction of looking that macho. Felder said the adultery was bogus since Sol was impotent from the dialysis anyhow.

Miss Marion DuPont
and two friends.
(*Archive Photos/Edwin Levick*)

U.S. industrialist
Pierre S. DuPont.
(*Archive Photos/Camera Press*)

Harry F. Guggenheim (1963), President and Publisher of
Newsday, with Mark Ethridge (right) who was
then editor. (*Archive/Pictorial Parade*)

John Dodge (left) died worth $12 million, but left his
oldest son Horace (right) only $150 a month and
specified in his will who would get his 109 shirts and
10 overcoats. *(Chrysler Historical Foundation)*

Howard Hughes with Ginger Rogers. (*Archive Photos*)

Howard Hughes. (*Archive Photos*)

Walt Disney indicates the Sleeping Beauty Castle which will be the entrance to Fantasyland in Disneyland, not yet built at the time of this photo (1955). (*Archive Photos*)

Harry F. Guggenheim (second from left) accepts the Laura Taber Barbour Award from the Flight Safety Foundation. (*Archive Photos*)

Oil Tycoon H.L. Hunt, 68, weds stenographer
Mrs. Ruth Ray Wright in Dallas (1957). (*Archive Photos*)

Gloria Vanderbilt as a girl. (*Archive Photos*)

Gloria Vanderbilt
with Pearl Bailey
and Truman
Capote.
(*Archive Photos*)

Gloria Vanderbilt
and Bill Blass
attend the
preview of Erte's
exhibit at the
Dyanson gallery
(1982). (*Archive
Photos/Tom Gates*)

Jacqueline Kennedy
becomes Mrs.
Onassis in the tiny
chapel of the church
on Skorpios Island
(1968).
(*Archive Photos*)

Jacqueline Onassis
strolls with her sister
Lee Radziwill in
Mayfair, London
(1970). (*Archive/
London Daily Express*)

Marshall Field V.
(*Crain's Chicago Business*)

John Crosby, the father of Atlantic City gambling casinos. (*The Press of Atlantic City/Mike Blizzard*)

Lynn and Oscar Wyatt. (*Betty Tichich/Houston Chronicle*)

Doug Wyatt. (*Houston Chronicle*)

Robert and his wife Laura Sakowitz. (*Houston Chronicle*)

Jett Williams, daughter of legendary Country music
singer Hank Williams, posing with her book "Ain't Nothing
as Sweet as My Baby: The Story of
Hank Williams' Lost Daughter."
(*The Atlanta Journal-Constitution/Peter Schumacher*)

Then came the birthday party at the Carlyle. Sol and Lillian talked reconciliation and settlement. That was April 19, 1984. Four days later and just two days before the divorce action was to go to court, Sol and his lawyer, Raoul Felder, came to Lillian's suite at the Carlyle. Attorney Roy Cohn joined them representing Lillian. Felder made notes on his yellow legal pad.

After several hours of negotiation, a settlement was agreed upon with a hand-written agreement down on the yellow legal pad, read aloud, amended, read again and finally signed by Sol and Lillian. This hand-written agreement said that both of them anticipated that a more formal agreement would be written up later and signed, but that the yellow legal pad agreement would be binding even if that didn't happen.

This was basically a covenant of reconciliation and not divorce—in fact, it required Lillian to drop her divorce action—because it didn't talk about alimony or support for Lillian and it contemplated that both of them would resume living together, but it also said that the agreement held even if they later separated or divorced.

The deal worked out was this: Lillian would drop the divorce and waive an equal split of property. Sol and Lillian would try to reconcile. Whether they did or not, Lillian would get one-third of Sol's estate "outright" when he died. To give Lillian some spending money, Sol would give her $1 million by the end of the week plus another $5 million in installments at $1 million a year. Sol would also buy and furnish an apartment for Lillian on the Upper East Side for a maximum of $4

million. The temporary alimony would stop and
Sol would give Lillian her $1 million worth of jew-
elry he had been keeping.

Three nights later they had a celebration dinner
at the "21" and Lillian moved back in with Sol.
They began to shop for apartments in the multimillion-dollar class. Lillian received a typed copy of
the yellow legal-pad agreement on April 30, a week
after the meeting. By this time she was already
beginning to have some doubts. Then she called
her ex-son-in-law lawyer, Kenneth Kemper, who had
been married to Didi and had stayed close even
after their divorce.

Kemper reviewed the yellow legal-pad agreement
and hit the ceiling. It was a real screwing. It didn't
let her have a 50-50 split on the property if she did
go ahead with the divorce. It made no provision
for alimony and it never mentioned their homes in
Palm Beach and Long Island.

Lillian realized she had been had and cursed Roy
Cohen when he called. She fired him and filed a
legal malpractice suit against him for $1.5 billion.
She said, about Cohen, that he was, "The biggest
waste of protoplasm that ever lived."

Kemper became Lillian's chief adviser even
though he got her another divorce lawyer, Norman
Sheresky. She now owed Kemper $1 million in legal
fees. Sol's side claimed Kemper had been having an
affair with Lillian, but Lillian and Kemper denied
it.

Back to April 30th, the day Lillian got a typed
copy of the yellow legal-pad agreement. There was
an envelope with Sol's lawyer's return address on it
in one of Sol's jacket pockets and she opened it

thinking, she said, they were some theater tickets he had promised them.

Instead it was a handwritten note from Roy Cohn who was supposed to be her attorney. It was to Raoul Felder saying he was disappointed that Sol was only going to pay Cohn $100,000 when he had saved Sol $300 to $400 million by getting Lillian to waive an even split on the property.

Outraged, Lillian hid the note and kept silent while she and Sol continued to look for apartments. Meanwhile she was avoiding a messenger who was trying to deliver the first $1 million check to her fearful if she accepted the payment it would seal the yellow legal-pad deal.

Finally, a week and a half later, Lillian confronted Sol and they had such a terrible fight the police were called. Sol moved out and Lillian tried to refile for divorce, but a judge said "no." First, she would have to sue to overturn the yellow legal-pad agreement. She did. She started trying to get out of what was now variously called the Yellow Legal-Pad Agreement or the Carlyle Agreement.

She filed suit to invalidate the Yellow Legal-Pad Agreement on March 1985 in New York County Supreme Court claiming a wide variety of misconduct by Sol.

Lillian charged Sol with fraud, unconscionability, overreacting, undue influence, duress and coercion, incompleteness and ambiguity. Golly! One is surprised she left out dyspepsia, dandruff, and diarrhea.

The case opened in July 1986 with State Supreme Court Justice Kirstin Booth Glen. The two lawyers said the note was simply over legal fees, not a conspiracy to defraud Lillian.

Jane appeared and testified against her mother. Furious and humiliated, Lillian went over to Sol during a recess and screamed at him while kicking him as hard as she could.

A year later, September 21, 1987, the court ruled against Lillian saying the Yellow Legal-Pad Agreement was valid. Judge Glen said that it was a valid agreement because it protected Sol from having his holdings arbitrarily broken up while he lived and it protected Lillian if she outlived Sol by giving her more of the estate than she might have ordinarily inherited.

However, the judge didn't rule on the technicality of whether or not the agreement could be enforced since Lillian had repudiated it. So, they had one of those stupid legal rulings that created more problems than it solved. It said that the agreement was valid, but so what?

Besides what did it matter to Sol? On the verge of death then, he would die from complications arising out of hip surgery at Lennox Hill Hospital less than a month later and the blood-money feud resumed in earnest with everyone fighting everyone else and even contradicting themselves.

Sol's will left Lillian one-third of his estate *in trust* with her getting only the income from it during her lifetime. That could amount to about $33 million a year, but no matter, that wasn't the issue. She also got the Palm Beach and Long Island property. Her reaction was that this bequest was a "paltry fart."

One-sixth went to charity, $2 million in trust for each of the three grandchildren and the rest split among the four kids. Jane and Allen were trustees, which put them in charge of their mother's money.

Now came the twist. A few weeks after Sol's death, with the mother on one side and the children on the other side, both sides switched positions.

Now, the mother [Lillian] wanted the Yellow Legal-Pad Agreement enforced. It gave her one-third of Sol's estate *outright* — not in trust.

The kids, who had supported their father's claim that the Yellow Legal-Pad Agreement was valid, now rejected that idea and, beyond that, charged that their mother was trying to divorce their father when he died and, therefore, wasn't his surviving spouse entitled to anything even though she was still his surviving spouse.

Lillian filed suit demanding that Judge Glen's ruling be enforced while the kids countersued demanding the judge's decision be "clarified" now that Sol was dead and everybody's position had reversed. The Appellate Court upheld Judge Glen's ruling, but now the action shifted to the Surrogate Court since the issue involved the estate of a dead person.

Lillian now wanted the Yellow Legal-Pad Agreement enforced, but the kids testified that she had broken the deal while their father was alive by not seriously reconciling with him, by not living with him, by not accepting the benefits under the agreement that Sol had offered her, and by going to court to nullify the deal.

What the kids wanted to apply now was Sol's will that gave Lillian a share of the estate *in trust,* which meant she would get the interest from that share during her lifetime and the kids would get it all when she died. The children's lawyers also filed a motion claiming that Lillian was entitled to nothing under the will because she had abandoned her husband. Lillian's lawyer, of course, filed countermotions.

The lawyers were: Norman Roy Grutman with a retainer of $300,000 a year representing Lillian—her eighth lawyer after $2 million in legal fees. For the Goldman children, Thomas J. McGrath of Simpson, Thacher, which was handling the probate of Sol's will and would get something like $20 million in fees for that. And in the background was Raoul Felder as adviser to the Goldman kids and defense attorney for them in 200-plus lawsuits by tenants, banks, and brokerage houses.

Both sides knew guilt was as important a part of their blood-money feuds as was greed. Lillian said her children were tormented with guilt for filing the affidavits saying she was crazy. Allen, who was running the business, said his mother was guilty for walking out on Sol when he really needed her.

In another twist, Allen asked the court to release enough money to fund the trust funds for the grandchildren. The reason Allen wanted this done, he admitted, was so he could get the trust funds to repay him the $82,000 he claimed to have spent on his daughters, Stephanie and Cindy, for college education.

In keeping with the family mode of operation, the two daughters countersued saying Allen was dutybound to provide them with a college education and he should get nothing from their trust funds.

This was a blood-money feud that involved some of the best real estate on the island of Manhattan including the Dorset Hotel, the land under the Stanhope, Gotham and Gramercy Park hotels, and the Olympic Towers plus some 600 properties all over midtown Manhattan and the Upper East Side.

Finally, on July 20, 1991, a Manhattan court handed down a ruling saying Lillian was entitled to the one-third of the estate that she had been seeking and which had been promised her in the Yellow Legal-Pad Agreement and which she had wanted, not wanted and, finally, wanted. Thus, Lillian had won a battle against her children who had challenged the agreement and said their mother was a nut case.

What made this decision particularly significant was the court allowed Lillian to pick and choose what properties she wanted in her $300 million share and this would have a severe effect on the value of what was left, as well as Manhattan real estate values in general since there was so much of it.

Because of that, Lillian asked the court to seal the files of the case because the financial information involved was highly confidential and if it got out it might frighten creditors into demanding payment of loans and bankrupt the estate. Also, this confidential information could put the Goldman family at a disadvantage in future real estate deals. The judge said "no." The judge felt public policy called for open trials except in very unusual circumstances and this wasn't one.

Even though the court ruled in favor of Lillian on July 23, 1991, months passed and nothing significant happened and Surrogate Judge Eve Preminger was not happy. In a ruling couched in judge talk on January 2, 1992, she said,

> With respect to Mrs. Goldman's application
> for partial payment, it is undisputed that she
> has a valid and enforceable claim against the
> estate. By decision dated July 23, 1991, this
> court found that Mrs. Goldman was entitled
> to an outright one-third share of the estate
> pursuant to the terms of a reconciliation
> agreement executed by her and the decedent
> prior to his death. (She means the Yellow Le-
> gal-Pad Agreement between Lillian and Sol
> was a deal.)
>
> It might have been expected that this deci-
> sion would finally resolve the dispute over the
> agreement which began in 1985 and has been
> the subject, in one court or another, of
> lengthy and costly legal proceedings ever since.
> Unfortunately, this has not been the case.
>
> For reasons best known to themselves, the
> lawyers have agreed to postpone entering an
> order on the July 31, 1991 decision. Instead,
> an astonishing amount of time has been spent
> in fruitless conferences, letters, accusations,
> and counteraccusations, followed by vague as-
> surances of imminent settlement proposals and
> other legal maneuvering which has not ad-
> vanced resolution. It is a misuse of the
> strained resources of this court to countenance
> further delay. (She means there had been too
> much foot-dragging and she wanted it
> stopped.)

What happened July 31, 1991, was both sides

got in a long wrangle over paying Lillian some of the money due her. The executors of the estate were willing to pay her $3 million cash and $22 million in real estate then. She agreed and got the $3 million, but for the next five months the executors twiddled, twaddled, and fiddled over the value of the real estate, how it should be given to her and so on.

Back in court on January 2, 1992, the executors admitted that the estate had $44 million in cash and stocks, but they didn't want to pay out to Lillian claiming they needed that money to meet mortgage payments. Besides, they claimed that Lillian didn't really *need* the money just yet. Wrong, said Judge Preminger,

> Mrs. Goldman has a valid claim against the estate that has been vigorously litigated in two courts and innumerable proceedings. She is 70 years old and it has been over four years since decedent's [Sol's] death ended their 40-year marriage. She is entitled to receive her share of her late husband's estate promptly.

So, the judge ordered that Lillian get $25 million cash immediately and the rest due her within 60 days.

Two curious sidebars involving lawyers came out of this convoluted feud over blood-money. In one, ten months later Lillian announced the biggest single gift ever made to legal education in this country. She donated $20 million to the Yale Law School Library for a new law library in the memory of Sol, but bearing Lillian's name. The money

will also be used to help women attending the law
school, especially those studying women's rights.

The second came in September of 1991 and involved a judge and two of Lillian's attorneys. Surrogate Judge Marie Lambert was originally on the
Goldman cases, but, when she retired, Surrogate
Eve Preminger took over. Likewise, Norman Roy
Grutman was Lillian's attorney originally in these
cases, but was replaced by attorney Richard Emery.

Judge Marie Lambert was a colorful, but somewhat eccentric character. You may recall she was
the presiding judge in the largest contested inheritance case in New York history, Johnson vs. Johnson. At that time, she was described by Barbara
Goldsmith, the author of one of the books on the
trial *Johnson vs. Johnson,* as part Portia and part
Tugboat Annie. She has also presided over other
more famous blood-money feuds such as the case
of Ake Fredriksson who tried to overturn Greta
Garbo's will in 1990 on the grounds that he was
her nephew and she had illegally disinherited him.

It turned out that the U.S. Attorney for the
Southern District of New York was investigating
the behavior of Judge Lambert in the Goldman
case and 49 others because it was alleged that she
was handing out lucrative guardianships to personal
friends. In fact, one such friend, Vincent Catalfo,
had already copped a plea and admitted guilt in a
fraud and income-tax evasion case. For sure, Lambert had appointed Bronx Civil Court Judge Lorraine Backal as guardian for one of the Goldman
grandchildren.

Grutman, who stopped being Lillian's attorney
partway through the proceedings, had filed a peti-

tion with the court for an extra $5 million in bonus fees from Lillian and Emery countered by filing a misconduct complaint against Grutman with the court. Grutman countered, of course, with a cross compliant charging that Emery had leaked his complaint to the press, which is a violation of disciplinary rules.

In the case of Grutman, Emery charged he tried to bribe Judge Lambert on behalf of Lillian which, if discovered, could have meant jail for Lillian. There was a lawsuit between Marie Lambert and her former law partner Herbert Katz that had nothing to do with the Goldmans. Lambert went on the bench and was hearing the Goldman case while Katz joined the Grutman law firm.

When Grutman was brought on board to represent Lillian in April of 1988, he had a meeting with Lillian and her ex-son-in-law, Ken Kemper, at which Grutman suggested Lillian pay Grutman's firm $3 million. This $3 million, said Grutman, would be used to pay Lambert in settlement of her lawsuit with Katz. Are you following this?

In a sworn affidavit by Grutman and filed May 4, 1989, Grutman said that Lambert's friend, Bronx Civil Court Judge Lorraine Backal telephoned him and said she was interested in helping to settle the Goldman lawsuits. Grutman's affidavit relates, "Towards the end of this discussion, Mrs. Backal mentioned that she thought it would be a good idea if Katz settled the pending case with Judge Lambert."

Recalling that conversation in August 1991, Judge Backal put her own interpretation on what was happening: "We did discuss a proposed settlement in the Goldman case, but I categorically deny ever discussing the Katz-Lambert case with him [Grutman]. I also deny placing any conditions or pressure upon Mrs. Goldman concerning the settlement of the Goldman estate."

Whew! makes one wonder, doesn't it.

As the end seems to draw near in this blood-money legal endurance contest, one observer summed it up nicely: "The Goldman family is the best thing to happen to lawyers since the Magna Carta."

Twelve

Like Grandfather,
Like Granddaughter

James Irvine arrived in the West as a poor Protestant Scottish immigrant in 1846 and died as one of the two greatest land barons in California. Today, 150 years later his California empire is still intact and the focus of a bitter blood-money feud that has gone on for over 30 years.

Three years after Irvine landed in New York, the 22-year-old joined the Gold Rush to California, but instead of breaking his back panning for gold, he went into the grocery business in San Francisco and sold provisions to those who did.

About ten years later, California was devastated by a bad drought and many of the southern ranchero owners became desperate for money. Irvine seized the opportunity and bought acreage in southern California south of the sleepy pueblo of La Cuidad de la Reina de Los Angeles—the City of our Lady, Queen of the Angels.

He threw in with three friends and, together, the four bought Rancho Lomas de Santiago, Rancho

San Joaquin, and a section of Rancho Santiago de Santa Ana—roughly 120,000 acres including 13 miles of Pacific Ocean beaches and coastline for $50,000. The three friends had experience raising sheep and that's what the partners ran on their new ranch.

In little more than a decade, James Irvine's fortune increased in many ways. He had owned half of the ranch at the beginning, but soon bought out his partners giving them six times what they had paid. The sheep herd had grown to 50,000 head with each earning a net of approximately a dollar a head each year. Irvine's personal herd also increased as he married Nettie Rice and they produced James Irvine, Jr. or J.I. as he would be called—their only child. J.I. inherited the ranch when his father died.

J.I. grew up to be a lean and mean man, marbled through with contradictions. A tough dictator to work for, he ruled with an iron and sure hand to be sure the ranch prospered. Coarse and unrefined, J.I. didn't care for the company of most people, but excelled at charcoal drawings, poetry, and the piano. He also liked to chase women.

In some ways, he was a bit of a boor, but a rich boor and, thus, indulged by those around him who wanted his favor or his money. He was popular as the eligible bachelor even though his habit of bringing some or all of his twelve unhousebroken dogs with him when he came calling was disconcerting to hostesses who didn't enjoy having dogs urinating on their furniture.

His other amusement as a guest in people's homes was to throw lit firecrackers into the blazing fireplace. The dogs would rush after the tossed ob-

ject only to leap yelping from the fireplace when
the cracker exploded scattering ashes, sparks, cin-
ders, and canines in all directions to the roaring
laughter of J.I. and restrained consternation of his
hosts.

The land held the center of J.I.'s life with its
seemingly endless expanse from the rolling inland
mountains of the Santa Ana range to the breaking
surf of the Pacific Ocean. It encompassed 138
square miles and he ran it either from his inland
mansion when he was there or from his home in
San Francisco when he was there.

In 1892, J.I. followed the example of his father
and married a woman from Cleveland, Frances
Anita Plum, who produced three children in quick
succession, James III (Jase), Kathryn, and Myford
(Mike) to fill their San Francisco home.

Six years after the marriage, hard times returned
with the same kind of big drought that had given
his father the chance to buy the land in the first
place. Once again the drought turned out to be
good fortune for the Irvines because it moved them
out of sheep herding (their herd had been cut from
50,000 to 12,000 head by the lack of water) into
more stable and diversified crop and orchard farming of grains, grapes, walnuts, and oranges.

Another disaster, the 1906 San Francisco earth-
quake and fire, convinced the family to leave the
Bay City and move to the ranch permanently.
There, tragedy struck three years later when his
beloved Anita died of pneumonia plunging J.I. into
a deep depression that would last for years even
though he traveled the world attempting to overcome his grief.

Ten years later another tragedy hit when his only

daughter, Kathryn, died in childbirth after he refused to take her to the hospital. He thought it more appropriate for his grandchild to be born at home. Guilt-stricken and depressed once again, J.I. soon lost all his body hair for reasons that are not certain.

In 1922, son Myford (Mike) married Thelma Romery from Australia and they lived initially in San Francisco where Mike ran the Irvine business office.

In 1931, J.I. got remarried and his bride, Katherine Brown White, was a very buxom San Francisco divorcee whose laugh and fun-loving nature made her friends characterize her as a Diamond 'Lil kind of woman. She knew how to handle men, J.I. included, and he loved it. She brought him great happiness for four years until tragedy struck the family again with the tubercular death at 42 of J.I.'s oldest son, Jase.

Jase and his second wife, Athalie, and daughter Athalie Anita Irvine, had lived with grandfather, J.I., and Athalie Anita grew up as the apple of J.I.'s eye. She spent most of her time with him, becoming a tomboy who could surf, snorkel, sail, ride, and fly airplanes.

Three years after her father's death, she decided she liked the name, Joan, better than the one her parents gave her and that's what she was known as from that time on. Now she had the same initials as her beloved grandfather. Raised on the Irvine ranch, Joan was used to driving, riding, and hunting all over it with her grandfather. The ranch became a psychic part of her. The land became as much a part of her as it had of J.I.

Mike and Thelma moved down from San Francisco to help during J.I.'s depression again. He drew up a new will leaving much of the stock in the ranch to his Irvine Foundation under the supervision of four trustees who were old friends, Loyall McLaren, Robert Gerdes, Arthus McFadden, and James G. Scarborough.

Life improved with little Joan, Mike, and Thelma around to add to the joy of Kate and time seemed to be healing J.I.'s sorrows until the summer of 1947. Then J.I. went on a fishing trip to his ranch in Montana with a real estate broker buddy of his, Walter Tubach and his ranch foreman, William Bradford Hellis. J.I. mysteriously drowned on that trip. It was a death that didn't make sense since J.I. was in good health, an experienced outdoorsman, and knew the terrain at his Montana ranch well. It wouldn't be the last mysterious death in the Irvine family.

Mike Irvine, a city kid who was a frustrated musician, now became the president of the Irvine Ranch, but he left the day-to-day operation to Brad Hellis, the foreman. In fact, Mike and Thelma lived for a time in Pasadena, nearly 80 miles north and Mike would drive down daily instead of living on the ranch.

Even so, Mike did a number of important things for the ranch in developing its coastline property and setting the stage for the massive land development due to come a few years later by bringing a good, steady supply of water in from the Colorado River project.

Three years later, Mike stunned his wife of 28 years, Thelma, by asking for a divorce. He had fallen in love with Gloria Wood White, a friend of Thelma's and Mike's stepmother's former daughter-in-law who had been married to Kate's son from a previous marriage. Mike got his divorce and married Gloria who would play a key role in a fatal mystery later.

About this same time, Joan Irvine had emerged from her cocoon of private schools and college and began a merry-go-round of failed marriages, most of which seemed to last about two years.

First, she married a Laguna Beach lifeguard, Charles Swinden, and produced a son. Next came Russell Penniman III, a navy pilot, and that also produced a son. Richard Burt, a building contractor, followed without producing children. Finally, she married Morton Smith, one of the landed gentry from the Virginia horse-country around Middleburg, Virginia, west of Washington, D.C.

Early in this matrimonial tour, Joan came into her inheritance from her grandfather, J.I. She turned 24 in 1957 and got control of her grandfather's bequest to her, 22 percent of the Irvine Ranch. The Irvine Foundation controlled the ranch with 54 percent but Joan stood as the largest single stockholder and, as the trustees soon found out, a terror to contemplate.

Joan knew there had been an old-boy game going on with the ranch and the four trustees had reaped many undeserved benefits as had the real estate broker friend of J.I., Walter Tubach and the ranch foreman, Brad Hellis.

At her first meeting of the trustees, she trotted out a series of tough questions those present couldn't or didn't want to answer. She also detailed several conflict-of-interest deals involving Hellis.

This embarrassed her uncle, Mike Irvine, who remained technically in charge and she didn't want to hurt him, but he obviously hadn't been minding the store. Joan just wanted the double-dealing to stop. She notified the board of trustees, whom she regarded as a bunch of senile bozos, that she had filed a stockholder's suit against the ranch management.

Very soon afterward, Hellis decided it was time to resign and Joan dropped the suit, but she had set the tone that would escalate into one of the two most acrimonious business relationships and blood-money conflicts in California ranching history for the next third of a century.

The loss of Brad Hellis hurt Mike and put a lot more pressures on him as did the cantankerous personality of his niece, Joan. Mike seemed a man of endurance, but sensitive and easygoing. Joan was tough, driving and demanding. In short, Joan had J.I.'s genes. Two years later, this would contribute to another tragedy and unsolved mystery.

Sunday morning, the eleventh of January 1959, started as a relaxed day. It didn't stay that way.

About 1 o'clock, Mike told his wife Gloria that he was going over to the office, next to the house, to do some work. Mike had rarely done that before, but Gloria said she and their five-year-old, Jimmy, would take a nap. Aside from Mike going to the office about 100 feet away from the house, it promised to be a sleepy, routine Sunday.

A few hours later, Gloria and son Jimmy woke up and wandered over to the office to see Daddy. The next hour would be filled with unexplained oddities.

Gloria and Jimmy got in the car and *drove* to the office 100 feet away. They didn't find Mike and returned home. Gloria parked the car and Jimmy pointed to a light burning in the basement of the house that seemed out of place.

Gloria and Jimmy went down to the basement to get an explanation of the light being on and found their husband and father, Mike Irvine, dead.

The gory scene stunned them both and Gloria screamed as she pulled wide-eyed, frightened Jimmy up the stairs. She ran to the telephone and called her family doctor, Thomas Rhone, and sobbed to him that her husband had shot himself. The doctor raced out to the house and called the coroner. Less than half an hour had lapsed since Mike's body had been discovered by his wife and son.

It was unpleasant inspecting the body and it raised some serious questions right away. An automatic 16-gauge shotgun lay at the left side of Mike's body with his lifeless hand resting on the barrel. Two rounds had been fired into Mike's stomach. A spent cartridge rested in the chamber and a second spent cartridge had ejected nearby on the floor.

Mike had been shot in the right temple and laying next to him was a .22 pistol with a spent cartridge in one chamber and a live round in another chamber. The index and middle fingers of his left hand were singed with powder burns.

After examining the scene and the evidence, the coroner ruled that it had been suicide committed at approximately 2 o'clock in the afternoon while Gloria and Jimmy were sleeping upstairs.

An even darker shadow hovered over this tragedy, however, because of the disturbing and unexplained facts about Mike's death unanswered by the coroner's ruling.

1. Why two shots in the stomach? The coroner assumed that Mike pulled the trigger the first time, and the second shot came when the butt of the gun recoiled against the wall and fired by itself. That seems to violate the basic safety construction of the gun and if the recoil was strong enough to do that, how come his hand was resting on the barrel?

2. After being shot twice in the stomach with a 16-gauge shotgun, how could he then pick up a .22-caliber pistol and shoot himself in the head?

3. Powder burns on his left hand show he apparently held the pistol in his left hand to fire the shot. Mike was right-handed.

4. Beyond that, even if he did hold the pistol in his left hand, how could he have shot himself in the right temple?

5. Why didn't Gloria and Jimmy hear the shots upstairs? It was not an unusually well-insulated house and sound normally traveled readily.

6. Why was there no suicide note? This is the norm with people committing suicide.

7. Mike's casual behavior earlier in the day did not betray the depression or introspective mood that is common before suicide.

8. Why didn't the cook and the maid in the kitchen on the first floor hear the shots?

None of these questions were ever satisfactorily answered.

On the previous Friday, he had told a few close relatives and associates that he was sitting on a keg of dynamite and had to raise $5 million in cash in the next few days. What this meant never has been explained.

Ed Reid, in his book about the underworld, said Mike was heavily involved with the Mafia because of big gambling debts at Caesars Palace in Las Vegas, but no one knew the cautious and financially conservative Mike ever to gamble.

His first wife, Thelma, is still convinced Mike was murdered some place else and brought to the basement. The official verdict still stands as suicide, but many don't believe it.

The death of the last adult male Irvine marked the beginning of change for the huge ranch against the wills of the conservative board of J.I.'s old buddies. For one thing, the next thirty-three years riveted on the raucous, running battle between Joan and the good ol' boy trustees.

Joan saw the future of the ranch in the development of new cities with houses and stores and a branch of the University of California. The trustees saw the future of the ranch in the past—farming. They didn't know anything about urban development, weren't city people and were suspicious of those who were. No, things were just fine as they were so let's not go making a fuss.

Joan lived to make a fuss. Worse than that, she liked doing it in public.

Her first fuss focused on the ranch being undervalued and her share not paying enough. The trustees snapped back that Joan didn't care about the tradition of the ranch and the memory of her generous and kind grandfather, but only cared about money.

As the battle got worse between Joan and the other trustees, she hired public relations people to carry her crusade of modernization and urbanization to the public and she hired lawyers to carry it to the courts.

One of her lawyers struck litigation gold. For

some odd reason that no one could ever figure out,
Grandfather J.I. had incorporated the Irvine Ranch
as a West Virginia corporation. In West Virginia,
the law said that anyone owning at least 20 percent
of the shares of a West Virginia corporation (Joan
owned 22 percent of the Irvine Company) could
force the company to be liquidated — sold off to the
public — if there was "sufficient cause."

No one knew what "sufficient cause" meant
other than it meant a long expensive lawsuit that
would put the whole ranch in jeopardy. The trustees suddenly transformed from irritated men to
scared men and they caved in to Joan partway.
They brought on board a celebrated architect, William Pereira, to plan conversion of the sprawling
ranch into a new city.

Meanwhile, Joan's lawyers were busy in Washington and got a provision slipped into the Tax Re-
form Act of 1969 that said a foundation could own
only 2 percent of the stock of any single company.
This meant that the Irvine Foundation, the majority stockholder in the Irvine Company, had to sell
off most of its stock. Joan assumed this would
happen right away and it would be sold to the
general public and leave her as the controlling
stockholder.

She figured wrong on both counts. The other
trustees had lawyers, too. These lawyers convinced
the Feds that selling off of the foundation's shares
of the Irvine Company should be delayed until
1983. Otherwise, it would drive down the value of
the shares and hurt the foundation and all the
good causes it supported. The Feds agreed.

Then, in contradiction to what they told the federal government, the other trustees decided against

selling the stock to the general public. Rather they went looking for a single, mega-bucks buyer who could buy them out and still leave Joan as the minority stockholder.

They found that kind of buyer in the Mobil Oil Corporation with whom they began negotiating in secret. Of course, Joan found out about the secret negotiations and, of course, Joan immediately filed a lawsuit to queer the deal.

She charged that the $110 million Mobil was going to pay was unreasonably low. In addition to the lawyers, Joan's public relations team spread the story that Mobil was only fronting for the Arabs — this was during the 1974 oil shortages — and it was an environmental polluter.

The State Attorney General killed the deal for sure when he jumped into the lawsuit on behalf of the charities supported by the Irvine Foundation. He agreed with Joan about the price being much too low and, on behalf of the beneficiaries of the foundation, he objected to the sale.

Meanwhile, Joan looked for her own mega-bucks partner to counter the Mobil bid. She found hers in a company owned by the department store millionaire, Herbert Taubman and the Wall Street banker who had long been involved in the movie studio business in Hollywood, Herbert Allen.

This group combined with Joan and bid $337,400,000 and Mobil dropped out. This new company got the ranch and Joan got $72 million, 10 percent of the stock in the new company and a seat on the executive committee. And, so Joan lived happily ever after.

Wrong.

Soon, she began waging a guerrilla war against

the new management. She flooded them with memos. She harangued the board on how the ranch should be developed and, when she lost her arguments in the boardroom, she took them to the newspapers and the courtroom to sue both the company and other directors personally.

In the time since 1977 when she engineered the Taubman-Allen deal, she has become bitter, reclusive, and so difficult that her fourth husband divorced her, her family — including her own mother — rejected her and her old friends gave up on her.

In the mind of some relatives, Joan has become obsessed with the ranch and has always wanted to be the only one in control just as her late grandfather J.I. had been. That can never happen now, but don't try to convince Joan Irvine of that.

Ten years ago Donald Bren, a risk-taker by nature, took the biggest risk of his business career when he put together a group to buy the Irvine Ranch. He didn't realize then that the biggest risk involved dealing with the heir of J.I. Irvine, Mrs. Joan Irvine Smith.

Bren, an active skier (he got through the University of Washington on a skiing scholarship) and helicopter pilot who was an ex-Marine captain, grew up in Beverly Hills. When he got out of the service in 1957, he went into home building and, just like he used to catch the crest of the wave surfing off Newport Beach, he caught the crest of the real estate boom in southern California and did very well — well enough to sell his real estate company to International Paper for $34 million. He later bought it back from them for $23 million.

Smart enough to associate with politicians and

the rich, he has been a major contributor to Republican politicians in California. He envisioned huge profits by buying what is now the 65,000-acre Irvine Ranch and the many ground leases it owns under homes and commercial buildings in Orange County. He got it for $337 million and immediately streamlined the company and pushed ahead on a go-go plan to develop, develop, develop.

Just as a surfer can pick a deceptive wave that flips him instead of speeding him into a beautiful shoreward glide, Bren picked a time when Irvine residents and environmentalists were balking at further developments and when the real estate market was about to nosedive.

Add to this the seemingly omnipresent hornet of the ranch, Joan Irvine Smith, who was, as usual, suing. Joan charged that, when Bren bought out Joan and her mother, Athalie, in 1983, to get control of the Irvine Company, he agreed to pay $114 million. However, Joan later decided the shares she and her mother had were actually worth $300 million and that's what she now demands. As usual, it will be decided in court.

So the blood-money feud over James Irvine's old ranch continues.

Thirteen

Blood Feud Over Mouse Money

Dramatic battles over inheritances are not limited to the business tycoon's family. They can take place among the inventors of cartoon mice and the painters of ethereal desert flowers.

Walt and Roy Disney used to joke about how Walt had been pissing on Roy all their lives.

When they were boys back in Kansas City, the brothers had to share a bed and Walt was an incorrigible bed wetter getting his brother soaked almost every night. That story was true and it defined their relationship until Walt died and it was rumored his family had him quick frozen to be resurrected some day in the future. Roy wasn't frozen when he died and he's probably happy to be at some place where Walt isn't pissing on him anymore.

Walt and his other brothers, Herbert and Raymond, came to Los Angeles from Kansas City, Missouri. Roy was already there when 21-year-old Walt arrived in 1923.

In Kansas City, Walt had some success creating short, primitive, black-and-white silent and animated films for movie houses. He decided to come to Hollywood where the movie industry had begun and see if he could expand his horizons. His brother, Roy, the conservative, business-minded half of the duo threw in with him and they started doing business as the Disney Brothers.

They had a number of false starts until Walter hit on the idea of two mice characters, Mickey and Minnie Mouse. The concept came to him as he traveled across the America he was soon to enchant on a train trip from New York to Los Angeles. Some dispute that version and say Mickey was actually the invention of a colleague of Walt's. Nevertheless, Walt and Roy worked very closely with a division of labor that continued all their lives: Walt did the creative side and Roy handled the business side.

The first big score the Disney Brothers had was in 1928 with the first talking animated movie. It was called *Steamboat Willie* and starred Mickey and Minnie playing on other animals as if they were musical instruments. Walt and Roy both married women who went to work at their embryo studios and their lives became, as it did for many who got involved with them later, immersed in the life of the studio.

The families of the four brothers were very close although Walt and Roy were the closest because they worked together daily. The four families got together for dinners, croquet games, backyard barbecues, and all the other typical American family weekends almost every Sunday.

However, a rift began to open between Walt and Roy. Their business Siamese-twin existence and success forced them to stay together, but Walt's ego was growing and nurturing another side of him.

It is not unlike the creative talent to feel that he is doing all the work and getting only part of the credit. This seems to happen in most enterprises involving a creative side. Walt was the most outgoing and the most outspoken of the team and got most of the public spotlight. Roy, sometimes begrudgingly let it happen that way because it was best, he thought, for the business.

Finally, Walt insisted that the public recognized him as the heart of the Disney Brothers and the name of the studio must be changed to Walt Disney Studios. It hurt and bewildered Roy, but once again, he bit his tongue and accepted the humiliation for the good of the company and the families depending on it.

The studio was now making smashing movies such as *Snow White, Pinocchio, Fantasia* and *Bambi*. These had started out with Walt's "crazy idea," as Roy regarded it, of doing a full-length animated movie, *Snow White*. In spite of Roy's objections, the project went ahead and was a huge success.

Then the studio got into true life nature films, against the advice of Roy, beginning with *Seal Island* in 1949 and that won the studio an Oscar. From there, Walt's crazy ideas led the studio to do action-adventure films such as *Treasure Island, Rob Roy,* and *Davy Crockett*.

All this time, the studio grew through the combined talents of Walt and Roy with Walt's crazy creative ideas delighting the public and Roy's careful management keeping film costs down and revenues up delighting the bankers.

Beyond the movies, came the new medium that terrified the movie studios—television. Instead of being intimidated and holding back as Roy was inclined to do, Walt plunged right in and scored another success with a weekly television program. Also enormously successful, but not of real concern to Walt, was the licensing of the Disney name for spin-off products such as toys, clothing, books and gimmicks. It was very lucrative and something that Roy saw to in order to fatten up the bottom line.

Then came the early 1950s and Walt's craziest idea of all—a theme park. Now, said Roy, we're getting out of what we know—the movie business—and going into what we don't know—the real estate business. This time, Roy snapped shut the Walt Disney Studio purse after allowing $10,000 to be spent for preliminary work on the theme park project.

Part of the problem was the Disney empire had grown rich and the brothers' differences had ripened to a white heat. In 1953, Walt did something that outraged Roy, but again, he chose to swallow his pride and let it happen. It would create a lasting chasm between Walt and Roy and between their families. It is the Rubicon of the dissention that would be passed on to their heirs and why a blood-money feud erupted later on.

Walt formed a new company that he, not too cleverly, named Retlaw Enterprises. Retlaw is, of course, Walter spelled backward. Walter gave Retlaw Enterprises the exclusive right to the use of his own name, Walt Disney. Thereafter, Retlaw demanded, and got, a royalty from anybody that used the name, Walt Disney. Absurdly, this included Walt Disney Studios, Walt Disney movies, Walt Disney spinoff products that were being licensed by the Walt Disney Company, and so on.

To Roy, this was a blatant and unwarranted move to skim off profits for the Walt Disney side of the family including Walt's two daughters. It was to the detriment of Roy's side of the family and his son, Roy E. Disney. Roy felt his own brother had knifed him in the back and stolen for Walt's family alone what the two families had built together. It would never be forgotten by Roy or by the heirs of Walt and Roy. For the next ten years, neither brother spoke to the other.

On his grandiose plan for a theme park, Walt refused to be deterred. Angry at being stymied by his brother on one of his great dreams, Walt pushed ahead anyhow. He went to banks to borrow the money projecting that one million paying visitors would go through the turnstiles at Disneyland in the first year. The bankers told him he was crazy. Walt knew that, but what about the money? The bankers said "no."

So, Walt put it all on the line. He scraped up all the money he personally could raise including borrowing on his life insurance and went ahead.

As one device to finance Disneyland, he offered exclusive rights to various companies to sell their products or services inside Disneyland. For example, only one brand of soft drink could be sold, one brand of film, and so on. For these rights, the companies had to pay Walt a fee up front even before the theme park was built. These fees, of course, made building the park possible.

Again, Walt's crazy idea worked out because, not only did one million people pay to visit Disneyland the first year it opened, but several million people came. So much for the faith of bankers. At the end of the park's second year, 1956, it produced one-third of the gross income the Disney organization made.

By this time, the Disney studio was split between the creative side and the business side. Employees of the first were called "Walt's men" and employees of the second were called "Roy's men." There was strong rivalry and dislike — perhaps even hatred — between the two sides, each of whom felt it was primarily responsible for success of the Disney enterprise and was not adequately appreciated by those fools on the other side.

With the smashing success of Disneyland, Walt decided he would duplicate the theme park in Florida. However, this time he would buy enough land so that sleazy motels and hamburger joints couldn't mar the setting. He put Disneyland — an exact duplicate of the one in southern California — in the middle of 30,000 acres near Orlando and called it Disneyworld.

In addition to Disneyworld, he had another crazy idea and that was the city of the future. A city built the way Walt thought a city should be built and occupied by the kind of people Walt thought should exist living the kind of life Walt thought should be lived. It would be called EPCOT, an awkward acronym standing for, Experimental Prototype City of Tomorrow. It would have, for example, a giant plastic dome over the entire city with a carefully controlled climate for those living within and an enormous underground vacuum-tube system to carry away trash from each of the 50,000 homes planned.

When finally completed the grandiose plan had to be trimmed back considerably including scrapping the dome and even so, it cost $1 billion to construct—many times more than anticipated.

It was Walt's last hurrah. In an ironic twist of fate, Walt learned that he had inoperable, incurable cancer in late 1966 and he died a few weeks later. The Disney empire was now Roy's. Except, he really didn't want it.

What Roy wanted to do in 1966 was retire. However, with Walt dead, he stayed on to run the company and finish building Disneyworld. Financially, he did well as always. In the six years after Walter died, Roy doubled the gross income, but creatively the company was in the doldrums. That was too bad because Roy was tired and didn't care that much. In 1972, he died.

Left behind as heirs were two widows, two of Walt's daughters, and Roy's son, Roy E. Disney. Young Roy was the largest single stockholder in the company and had spent much of the years his uncle and father were alive producing Disney true life nature films. A quiet, taciturn man much like his father, Roy was referred to by people on the Disney lot as, "The Idiot Nephew," behind his back. And, of course, some in-laws were in the mix of heirs, most notably Ron Miller, the husband of Walt's daughter, Diane.

During the older Roy Disney's last years, he was assisted in running the world of Disney by Donn B. Tatum, who had been director of administration and E. Cardon "Card" Walker, who had run the marketing operation. Tatum was a Roy man and Card was a Walt man and each soon assumed the personalities of their dead mentors.

Card soon took on to himself the title of Chief Executive Officer and made it clear that he was going to be in charge. Tatum apparently let him do it. To clinch his position, Walker kept very close to Walt's widow and her daughter Diane and Diane's husband, Ron Miller, a former pro football player who was on the Disney payroll working his way through various jobs to learn the business. Card made Ron chief of production.

The 1960s and 1970s Disney film production devoted itself to family comedies: *The Love Bug* and *The Absent-Minded Professor* featuring wholesome actors such as Fred MacMurray. It also produced the most profitable film in Disney history, *Mary Poppins,* but Young Roy felt the studio was out of touch and wanted it to do more contemporary films.

Tatum and Walker's response was to recycle the old plots and to make sequels. It became a joke around Disney that the test of every decision to be made was Walker asking out loud, "What would Walt have done?"

Roy was concerned about the way the Disney company was being run and had shown his displeasure by resigning as a vice-president and employee in 1977, but that didn't have much effect even though Young Roy was the largest single stockholder and a member of the board.

Things did not improve. By 1983, Tatum had retired and Walker was ready to do the same. It was logical that Ron Miller be put in charge, but everybody knew that he couldn't handle it by himself. Walker fiddled around until he finally got Ray Watson, an architect from Irvine, California, who had been deeply involved with the planned urbanization of the Irvine Ranch for several years, to come on board part-time to act as chamberlain to the inexperienced Ron Miller.

Watson came on board, Walker flew to Tokyo to open Tokyo Disneyland and moved up to chairman so Watson could become vice-chairman even if he was only working two days a week. Predictably, there were a series of disastrous movies such as *Tron* and *Something Wicked This Way Comes,* and earnings continued to drop.

Beyond his resignation as an officer, Roy had not decided if he wanted to do anything more about the management situation and he didn't like dealing with Walt's people anyhow. However, in 1984 Roy's stock in Disney had dropped some $40 million in value to $50 million and he decided it was time to do something about it. Buttressed with knowledgeable lawyers and advisers, he decided he would make a hostile buyout and oust Walt's people.

Unbeknown to Young Roy and others at Disney, a corporate raider whose name struck fear into corporate executive's hearts around America, Saul Steinberg, made the same decision two weeks before in a New York restaurant.

Roy felt it was a conflict of interest for him to

do this as a member of the board, so on March 8, 1984, he resigned from the board.

For the next four months, Card Walker and Ron Miller, representing the Walt side of the family, engaged in a corporate and ego life-and-death struggle for which they were ill-prepared by experience or temperament as they tried to stave off the company being swallowed alive by the Saul Steinberg python.

The elements of the struggle were mainly three: First, there was Walker, Watson, Miller and the Walt side of the family who wanted to keep control of the company at any cost, but were totally unsophisticated in the nuances and ways of corporate raiders. Its naïveté was enhanced by the ghost of Walt Disney that hovered over their decisions and the myth that the fathers, mothers, and little children of America wouldn't let anything bad happen to Walt Disney. The only problem with this delightful fairy illusion was that the fathers, mothers, and little children of America didn't own a lot of stock in the Walt Disney company, but Ivan Boesky and Saul Steinberg did.

This element hired conflicting professionals for guidance and then got involved with the Bass Brothers of Texas to help fight off Steinberg.

Second, there was Saul Steinberg, a professional corporate raider who knew more angles and more tricks than a Mississippi riverboat gambler when it came to raping, ruining, and running from a corporation. He knew what moves to make and how and when.

Significantly, the news that Steinberg had bought a lot of stock in a company panicked executives and board members so much so often that one of the things they often did was to pay Steinberg an exorbitant profit on the shares he had already bought just to get him to go away and leave their company alone. This is called "greenmail" on Wall Street and Saul Steinberg had gotten more greenmail from more companies than anyone in the history of America.

The third element was the Roy side of the family led by Roy Disney and his group of advisers who decided to make their own hostile takeover of the company, but weren't as aggressive or clever as Steinberg.

During those fateful months in the spring of 1984, there were constant meetings, lies, confessions, phone calls, sudden trips, crazy negotiations, bluffs, hand-wringings, threats, sleepless nights, moments of fear and exhilaration among the parties involved.

Because of its lack of will, principally on Roy's part personally, the Roy side seemed unable to mount its own viable takeover attack and, instead, flirted with each of the other sides and acted like it was willing to heal the rift between Walt and Roy Disney's heirs and bring the family back together running the company together. In the end, Roy's side wound up on neither side. Roy's side became irrelevant because of its failure of will.

In the end, the Walt side of the family, in control of the company and faced with several alternatives, none of which it liked, made a last-ditch decision. They decided to give Steinberg the alternative of taking greenmail and leaving them alone or they, the Walt side of the family, would effectively destroy the Disney Company in such a way that Steinberg would pay hundreds of millions of dollars for a ravaged company. It was Disney's scorched earth defense versus greenmail.

The Walt side hated the idea of greenmail because it smacked of blackmail to them, it did violence to the Walt Disney image, and it was grossly unfair to the other stockholders. But if it had to be done to save "their" company, it had to be done.

And it was done.

Saul Steinberg was greenmailed once again. This time he made a net profit of almost $32 million. Editorial writers, politicians, and moralists cried out in anguish, called the whole process reprehensible and evil. A few weeks later, most people had forgotten about it. Most except Roy Disney who was now more determined than ever to mount an old-fashioned proxy fight for control of the company.

Ray Watson, the architect arbitrator, tried to reconcile everybody and hold the Walt and Roy sides from destroying the company while fighting off the raiders and, just incidentally, keep the company functioning.

Watson continued to feel that it was vital for the public image and the private peace of the company that Roy Disney return to the board so that both sides of the family would be represented. Roy wanted to return, but on his terms. Ray wanted to avoid a proxy fight and worked to cut a deal with Roy through his effusive and temperamental lawyer, Stanley Gold.

Gold told Watson what Roy's terms were for not continuing the blood-money feud with a proxy fight: 1) Roy and his nominees were to get three seats on the board of directors; 2) that Frank Wells, an executive favored by Roy, be brought in at a top management position; and 3) Cardin Walker and Donn Tatum be replaced on the company's executive committee by Roy Disney. This last was revenge for all the slights the two had visited upon Roy when he was a vice-president.

Even though the Walt side of the family owned more shares of stock than Roy did, it had only one seat on the board of directors. Nevertheless, the board gave Roy two out of the three things he wanted. He got three seats and Walter and Tatum were dumped from the executive committee.

Moving in Frank Wells, who was at that time working at Warner, wasn't do-able because it would threaten Ron Killer, Diane Disney Miller's husband. That, of course, is exactly what Roy Disney and Stanley Gold intended. They were very unhappy with Ron Miller's childish management and knew someone stronger was needed. Miller's position had become shakier because he had separated from his wife, Diane, and that weakened the backing he had from Walt's widow, Lillian Disney. Still, Roy Disney and Stan Gold had to suffer Ron for a time longer.

In the process of fighting off Steinberg, Disney management had invited Sid Bass of Texas in as a white knight. It turned out that Bass wasn't needed, but now he had already become a major stockholder in the company. So, Gold turned to Bass as an ally in revamping the management at Disney. The problem was that Roy Disney and Stan Gold thought Disney needed creative management because that was what had made the company famous and rich over the years. Unfortunately, Bass and his advisers were "hard asset" men and suspicious of "creative talent." They wanted to be able to kick the tires and measure the acres.

From July to September 1984, Roy's side and Sid Bass and some other stockholders made three big achievements that resulted in getting Disney back on the track to success. Each required an enormous amount of negotiations, horse-trading, and reevaluation. Ray Watson was the soother, the go-between and the mediator in many instances, but it was primarily in response to pressure from Roy's side. He had three major tasks ahead of him.

One was to kill a previously made deal for Disney to merge with Gibson Greeting Card Company controlled by Bill Simon. On the surface, it appeared like an innocuous deal that might even make sense. However, the hidden agenda was Bill Simon, who had once been Richard Nixon's unloved Secretary of the Treasury and who had a reputation for an overly aggressive and abrasive personality to the point that nobody wanted him on their board of directors. Certainly Roy Disney and Sid Bass didn't want him on Disney's board.

Yet the traditional American sense of honor, "my word is my bond" mind-set, clouded the issue for Disney executives such as Ray Watson and some others. A deal is a deal, they said, and we can't go back on our agreement to merge with Gibson.

However, the feeling against Bill Simon was so strong that the Disney board would be facing a rash of lawsuits and a proxy fight for control of the board just at a time when it was trying to overcome the bad greenmail publicity from the Steinberg affair. So, old-fashioned honor flew out the window as the new business reality walked in the door and the Gibson deal was killed because of one man's personality.

Second was to replace Ron Miller with a better management team. The team Roy Disney wanted was Frank Wells from Warner and Michael Eisner from Paramount. Wells for the business side and Eisner for the creative side. Both had proven track records of great success in the movie business, but lacked hard, financial experience of the type Wall Street likes.

With a vigorous campaign focusing on each of the 13 Disney directors one-on-one and on the major stockholders, particularly Sid Bass, the Roy Disney-Stan Gold team sold a majority of the board on pushing a tearful and betrayed Ron Miller out the door and inviting Frank Wells and Michael Eisner in. Sid Bass later became so enthusiastic about the Wells-Eisner team that he bought more and more Disney stock until Bass owned 24 percent of the company.

Ironically, the key vote that made this last achievement came from the man who Roy Disney sought revenge upon, Card Walker. It was his support and the three votes he controlled on the board that put the Wells-Eisner management team in place.

That may be because Card once again applied his constant test when making a decision, "What would Walt have done?"

The Burbank Mouse Studio has done well under Eisner with the possible exception of its involvement with the Shakey French Euro-Disneyland. The main current irritation for the Disney heirs is a new book published by Birch Lane Press in July of 1993. Written by Mark Eliot and entitled, *Walt Disney: Hollywood's Dark Prince,* the author claims Walt was a right-wing ideologue and secret informant for the FBI.

Walt's widow, Lillian Disney, and his surviving daughter, Diane Disney Miller, immediately issued a rebuttal calling the charges untrue and castigating Eliot for libeling a good, decent man. The documents Eliot got from the FBI seem inconclusive and could be used to show Disney as being anything from an informer to simply a citizen sympathetic to the FBI. Both the recently deposed director, William Sessions, and the Los Angeles agent in charge from 1960 to 1964 say Disney was not a secret, paid informer.

Author Eliot supports his charge by saying that Walt was always uncertain about who his real mother and father were and this led him to cooperate or work for the FBI in exchange for the FBI helping him determine his heritage. Eliot claims Walt was the bastard son of Elias Disney and Isabelle Zamora, a woman from Majacar, Spain, whom Elias met and mated with in California in 1890.

Eliot's claim goes on to say that Elias brought Zamora into his household as a domestic servant for 35 years and when Elias died, Zamora was moved into Walt's household. Mrs. Miller and Mr. Eliot contradict each other on this point with Diane saying they never had a Spanish servant and Eliot saying they did.

Well, if Roy were still alive, two things about this latest controversy would please him. First, the controversy has hyped the book sales and that's good business. Birch Lane ran an initial printing of 35,000, but the flap over Walt has promoted enough demand to justify a second printing of 30,000 more.

The second thing that would have pleased Roy is hearing Walt publicly called a bastard.

Fourteen

Art and Blood-Money Feuds

She was famous for her irreverent lifestyle, bold art, and unconventional sex.

When Georgia O'Keeffe died two years short of 100 near Santa Fe, New Mexico, in 1986, she triggered still another controversy as she had done all her life. This one swirled around her unusual intimate relationship with a man 57 years her junior and the $70 million estate she left behind.

When she was a young woman and a teacher at a small college in Canyon, Texas, she met and charmed the famous photographer, Alfred Stieglitz, who was the unhappy husband of a brewery heiress and 24 years older than Georgia. That was in the year 1917 in New York City.

They became lovers immediately, which was followed several days later by a passionate affair between Georgia and Stieglitz's most brilliant student, Paul Strand. A year after that, Georgia moved in and, for the next eleven years, became Stieglitz's most famous female photo subject. When he gave an exhibit of his nude photos of Georgia, all of New York was shocked, and, somehow overcoming its shock, jammed the Stieglitz gallery. Some of his photos of Georgia are said to be so sexually explicit that they have yet to be exhibited three-quarters of a century later.

The year after the exhibit, Paul Strand married Rebecca "Beck" Salsbury, who idolized Georgia and tried to turn herself into Georgia's twin in hairstyle, black dresses, and a face without makeup. Tempestuous Georgia and Alfred were having problems and Georgia left for the summer of 1923, so Beck took her place in Stieglitz's bed. That clarified things for Georgia and she returned and married Alfred the next year, but the tension remained.

Accepting the invitation of a friend, Mabel Dodge Luhan, who was developing Taos, New Mexico, as an artists' colony along with her fourth husband, a full-blooded Pueblo Indian, Tony Luhan, Georgia took a trip west in 1929.

Alfred didn't like the idea, but agreed provided Beck went along to keep an eye on Georgia and keep her from crawling into some man's bed. The two women became enthralled with Taos, Mabel, Tony, and, more importantly, each other. Beck kept Georgia from crawling into some man's bed by having her crawl into Beck's bed. She bragged joyously about the freedom and pleasure she and Georgia reveled in so lushly.

Then Mabel had to go to Buffalo, New York, for an operation and long recovery. During her absence, Georgia indulged herself with the strong, primitive, and very male, Tony. Georgia took a sadistic delight in writing to both Mabel and Alfred strongly implying she was having a passionate affair with Tony. Which, incidentally, she was. Both Mabel and Alfred reacted with intense jealousy. Yet amazingly everybody got back together with their original partners within a year, Mabel with Tony and Georgia with Alfred even though Alfred continued to have affairs with other women.

Georgia continued to paint and spend her summers in New Mexico and her winters in New York with Alfred. During this time, she had a nervous breakdown that friends attributed to Stieglitz's refusal to have a child, which Georgia desperately wanted.

She loved New Mexico for its lifestyle and the light of its skies both day and night. It was New Mexico that inspired the bold, dramatic paintings that assured her stature as a major American painter. By the time Stieglitz died at age 82 in 1946, Georgia was far more famous than he was partially because he constantly promoted her work. Their relationship had been loving, intense, and very sexual.

It was also very private because, O'Keeffe in particular, was a very private person. She shunned people even in Santa Fe and thus it surprised those who knew her when she took in a young man, John Bruce Hamilton, 14 years before she died.

Called Juan, the Spanish version of his name, by O'Keeffe and most others, he literally showed up on her doorstep in New Mexico, uninvited and unannounced in 1973 when he was 27. A tall, handsome man with regular features, a square face, full head of hair and bushy mustache, he said he was looking for work. She gave him a job crating a painting. He never left after that.

Juan was a sculptor of no great renown as yet,

but spent the next 14 years as O'Keeffe's intimate companion in a relationship that many called curious and all whispered about wondering just how intimate it was.

Hamilton took over the running of O'Keeffe's ordinary life acting in the multirole of agent, friend, secretary, majordomo, and general manager of all things O'Keeffe.

A quiet, intense woman known to have had passionate needs in earlier years, her relationship with Juan quickly led to basic speculations about their sexual connection. Neither of them enlightened the gossips during her lifetime and he seems not inclined to do so now, but the conjecture is that their relationship included the bedroom.

All Juan will say is that those who claim she was "in love" with him are not exactly accurate because there are nuances in that phrase that did not apply, but that she loved him and he loved her. He suggested that any criticism of their relationship is sexist since it has been historically common for male artists to have very much younger female lovers and cites Picasso as an example. Why can't the reverse also be acceptable, he wonders, particularly when he and Georgia were closer and more supportive of each other than Picasso and any of his woman lovers were.

None of this was sufficiently disturbing to her family to cause any great hoo-ha until she died and great quantities of money presented themselves. It seems that all of O'Keeffe's estate including a number of her paintings and the works and memorabilia of her late husband valued at a total of $70 million were bequeathed to Hamilton.

When the money appeared, naturally, the family

heirs became outraged by the relationship and immediately sued to nullify the will and freeze Hamilton out.

The trail of legal documents demonstrating O'Keeffe's trust in Hamilton began in 1978 when she gave him her power of attorney permitting him essentially to run her business affairs as he saw fit. The following year, she made a will appointing him executor of her estate and giving him a New Mexico ranch and 21 of her paintings as compensation.

In 1983 and 1984, O'Keeffe added amendments or "codicils" in the jargon of lawyers, that were even more generous to Hamilton and leaving him almost all of her estate.

The news of this after her death, brought her heirs, June O'Keeffe Sebring, the artist's niece and Catherine Klenert, the artist's sister, running with lawyers in tow. The theme of their lawsuit is that Hamilton and O'Keeffe had a "curious relationship" in which he was the Svengali controlling everything O'Keeffe did and using "undue influence" to grab all the goodies for himself.

The sister, Klenert, just wanted the last two amendments [codicils] set aside, which would still leave Hamilton with a goodly amount in the ranch and 21 paintings. The niece was tougher about it and wanted Hamilton cut out of the will entirely.

The curious part of this particular blood-money feud is that the law in New Mexico seems to favor the sister and the niece. That's because the law in New Mexico says that, if the person left the most in a will had a relationship of trust with the person who made the will, it is assumed that there was "undue influence." So, the burden of proof was not on the heirs who challenged the will, but on Hamilton to prove that he didn't pressure O'Keeffe into leaving him almost everything.

Was O'Keeffe a nearly blind and senile woman who didn't know what she was doing or was she a mature, loving woman showing affection to a man she loved? Unless the two sides were willing to settle this blood-money feud before they got into the courtroom, the answer to those questions would be decided by a jury of Georgia O'Keeffe neighbors from the remote Rio Arriba County in the New Mexico made famous by her brushes and canvas.

Finally, on July 25, 1987, the warring heirs agreed on a settlement and it was approved by New Mexico District Court Judge Patricio Serna after going through 13 drafts.

Forty-two of O'Keeffe's oil paintings worth almost $20 million at the time, were donated to eight U.S. museums. Heirs Sebring and Klenert each got $1 million in art and cash while Hamilton got 22 artworks, O'Keeffe's Ghost Ranch, and all of her writings, papers, and personal property.

In addition, a foundation was created for the purpose of continuing O'Keeffe's "artistic legacy" by distributing some 100 of her artworks and 300 of her late husband's, Alfred Stieglitz, photographs. The foundation will be run by five trustees with the fighting heirs, Sebring, Klenert, and Hamilton being three of them.

It was a quiet peace pipe-treaty ending to a vicious blood-money feud.

Fifteen

Media Blood-Money Feuds

One of the greatest newspapers in America — one most people have never heard of — was almost sabotaged by the bullheadedness of its heirs.

The newspaper is the *St. Petersburg Times* in the Florida town of that name and, while not well known outside its territory, it is sort of a farm team for all the newspaper giants in the East.

The St. Pete *Times* has been for half a century one of the most admired and progressive operations in the arcane world of newspapers. It had the color and TV era eye appeal of *USA Today* years before Gannett's Al Neuharth ever got the idea for *USA Today.* Many of the best editors and reporters peopling the *Washington Post* and the *New York Times,* as well as key press jobs in Washington are alumni of the St. Pete *Times,* which also publishes a journal of record of the U.S. Congress, Congressional Quarterly which, oddly for a quarterly, is published every week.

The greatness of the St. Pete *Times* can be attributed directly to one man, Nelson Poynter, who was a flaming liberal about how everybody else ran their businesses, but a mossback, tightfisted, uncompromising right-wing tyrant in running the St. Pete *Times*.

He came from a newspapering family in Indianapolis. His family owned the St. Pete *Times* in 1938 when Nelson, age 32, was sent to the west coast of Florida to rejuvenate the faltering daily.

A type-A compulsive driver, Nelson told his father he would go only if his father would ultimately turn over complete control to him. A natural dictator, Nelson thought of his own father as a doddering, weak-willed wurst and Nelson's credo was "Only one Poynter can run a great newspaper. Two can ruin it."

Nelson may have been right about his father's lack of spine because he agreed to Nelson's terms and nine years later, his father sold Nelson all the voting stock in the St. Pete *Times* for $50,000.

While father Paul Poynter may have been ineffective, Mamma or "Minno" definitely was not. After all, those type-A genes of Nelson's had to come from somewhere. And, Minno was a mother who knew, as most mothers do, that it is fatal to family cohesiveness to favor one child over another.

So, when husband Paul sold all the voting stock in the St. Pete *Times* to son Nelson, Minno instantly stepped up to the plate and demanded that these two males recognize there was another side to the gender equation. She put the squeeze on Nelson to sell 40 percent of his voting stock to his older sister, Eleanor. Of course, this was a violation of his ironclad credo about two Poynters, but nobody disobeyed Minno.

Even so, Nelson retained a scrap of his manhood

by politely asking and politely getting the option to buy back Eleanor's stock at "a fair price." Which as all lawyers and businessmen know, is a phrase that guarantees a deal now and a lawsuit later because not all of Mimmo's tough genes went to Nelson. Some of them found their way to Eleanor and she was running the family newspapers in Indiana while festering about the way Nelson was running things in Florida.

Two Rubicons were crossed in Nelson and Eleanor's relationship that changed it forever. One, when their father died in 1950, Nelson gobbled up his parents' nonvoting preferred stock and used his 60 percent share of the voting stock to force Eleanor to sell him her preferred shares. Then he made "a fair price" offer for her 40 percent voting stock. It was an offer that was laughably low and confirmed her aggrieved view that her kid brother was trying to screw her out of her inheritance.

Second, when Eleanor's marriage was in trouble because her banker husband's bank failed and he desperately needed a job, Nelson turned him down. His stiff-necked explanation was that nepotism diluted a newspaper's strength. It was the final straw and the opening shot in the Poynter's blood-money feud.

Admittedly, Nelson was building a great newspaper that was light years ahead of the sleepy Deep South mentality of the community when he arrived. He crusaded for civil rights, labor unions, the environment, ran color photos and maps and led the newspapers of the country in innovation and experimentation.

Something else was happening to insure the success of his newspaper that had nothing to do with

Nelson's genius or drive. It was the swelling migration of the elderly snow birds from the frozen Northeast flocking and nesting permanently in the Tampa Bay region served by the St. Pete *Times*. This population surge of retirees from up north would make the Tampa area one of the hottest markets in the country economically. It would also swell the advertising linage and number of digits in the St. Pete *Times's* bottom line figure.

At the same time, Nelson fretted that his success would tempt his sister to meddle in what he was doing.

Worry turned to reality when Nelson got this great idea of creating a commercial journal of record that would report on Congress, on how each congressman voted, did vote and would vote on the critical issues of the day. Eleanor didn't like the idea of this new *Congressional Quarterly*.

Eleanor immediately charged that profits from the St. Pete *Times* that should rightly have gone to its two stockholders [her and Nelson] had been illegally diverted to found and support this new publication. It didn't help that Nelson's unyielding rule against nepotism didn't seem to apply to his second wife, Henrietta, who was working at the *Congressional Quarterly*. The difference, some cynics might say, is that Nelson was screwing both women, but each in a different sense.

Anyhow, the auditors swarmed into the St. Pete *Times* armed with legal documents allowing them to scrutinize the books. Minno tried to mediate, but understood her daughter's feelings and still wanted to protect her other child, Nelson, from harm and assured him that she would do everything possible to keep him out of prison, which did not reassure Nelson one bit. His own mother obviously thought he was a crook!

Now the blood-money feud began to assume serious, heavy-duty proportions. At the end of 1955 Nelson notified Eleanor that he was exercising his option to buy her 40 percent of the voting stock and said they should let a neutral arbitrator set the price. Eleanor, imitating a besieged general at the Battle of the Bulge, said, "Nuts" and filed suit to cancel his option. Nelson fired back with a breach of contract suit in early 1956 and the battle was on.

Or, maybe, the battle was off.

Later in 1956, the two combative kids settled and Eleanor won. She got $38,000 which is what she was cheated out of when St. Pete *Times* money was diverted to the start-up of the *Congressional Quarterly,* she kept her stock, and Nelson lost his option.

Was this a triumph of sweet, rational reason? No. It was a triumph of Minno's explosive outrage that her two kids were dragging the family name through the courts and,—gasp! shock! horrors!—*the press*. One cardinal rule about the American media is that it is horrified if it is treated publicly in the press the way it treats everyone else publicly in the press.

Another unpleasant truth about many liberal press barons who espouse a wide range of publicly funded programs to make this a better world, is that they hate paying the taxes necessary to pay for all the wonderfulness.

So, looking toward his own mortality, Nelson fished around to find a way to save his estate from paying taxes when he died. He didn't want to leave his empire to his heirs because he thought the inheritance taxes would be so high they would have to sell his beloved press dominion to pay them.

Fishing around, he came up with the idea of leaving it all to an education institution because such establishments can own newspapers and not pay any taxes — inheritance or income. So, Nelson created the Modern Media Institute (since renamed, the Poynter Institute for Media Studies).

With that in place, Nelson designated as his professional heir to be the new absolute dictator at the St. Pete *Times,* a stocky ex-managing editor of the *Washington Post* and World War II tank commander with a George C. Patton complex by the name of Gene Patterson. Then, with everything in place, Nelson died. It was 1978.

Patterson, like a good soldier and not-so-smart diplomat, continued the war with Eleanor at every chance he got. Getting back her stock was his number-one mission, journalistically, economically and, in reality, militarily. He got a chance to poison the relationship early when he reenacted the dead Nelson's insensitivity and refused to hire Eleanor's grandson.

Nelson was right about one thing in terms of what would happen if the heirs inherited stock as proven when Eleanor died in 1987 and left her stock to her two daughters. They had to sell their stock to pay the inheritance taxes. It was a golden opportunity for a smart diplomat to fulfill the mission of getting back the 40 percent of the voting stock. Unfortunately, a smart diplomat wasn't in command at St. Pete headquarters. It was a pompous, bully soldier.

Eleanor Poynter's daughters lived in the Tampa

Bay area and it would have been easy for a tactful person to schmooze them, show them some sensitive courtesy and work out a deal. Not Tank Patterson.

The St. Pete *Times* by this time was worth around $500 million and the two sisters hired a New York specialist in brokering newspapers to find them a buyer. The specialist, Henry Ansbacher, first took a swing at Patterson and asked if he wanted to buy the sisters' stock. Sure, he said, for $2.4 million. Certain that Patterson had been driving around too much in the sun with his hat off, Ansbacher said the fair price would be more like $120 million.

Patterson scoffed, Ansbacher frowned, and the two sisters exploded! They told Ansbacher to sell to whomever would pay a decent price. Ansbacher shopped other newspapers and found they had closed ranks behind the admired or feared Patterson and nobody was bidding. When the word got back to Patterson, he guffawed that he was in the cat bird seat and those two broads across Tampa Bay had no one to deal with but him. So, the too-long-in-the-sun-without-a-hat analogy proved accurate.

Patterson's incredibly stupid assessment of his battle situation was that only newspapers bought newspapers. So, he thought, it was a closed market and he was the only merchant in the square. That was when the Tank Commander's successor, Andy Barnes, got a wake-up call from Reality Central. It was two weeks before Patterson was due to retire and turn his command over to Barnes who was thought an ineffectual intellectual by many.

The caller said, "Hello. I'm Robert Bass. I've

purchased the minority stock from the Jamison daughters and I wanted you to hear it from me first."

Bam! Incoming Round!

Bass bought the sisters out for $28 million and planned to force a stock restructuring of the company that would give him a net cash flow of $1.7 million a year while strengthening his ownership and weakening that of the Poynter Institute.

Barnes, a classic hand-wringer and whiner, was ill equipped emotionally to weather the battle that had begun. The best he could do was mutter platitudes about the journalistic virgins grappling with capitalistic rapists. Patterson added his bombastic rhetoric and media connections to the struggle so Bass was portrayed in the newspapers around the country as a mindless minotaur despoiling the purity of the First Amendment with — ugh! — money.

Meanwhile, Bass was making bone-rattling points where it counted in front of the eternal courts of law instead of the ephemeral courts of public opinion including a serious challenge to the pristine Poynter Institute's non-profit status.

In the end, there was the end.

Both sides tired after 20 months of catapulting mud, money, and mental mayhem at each other and settled. The St. Pete *Times* got all the stock and regained complete control of itself. Bass and the sisters got the money they wanted. It cost the St. Pete *Times* about $75 million to get what Bass bought a couple of years before for $28 million. At the end the remaining heirs of Eleanor got their $28 million and, in the final settlement, another $15 million to boot.

Another blood-money feud ended as a monu-

ment to revenge, hatred, greed, parsimony, hurt,
insensitivity and all those other great family values
touted by that other media person from Indiana,
Dan Quayle.

Coincidentally, Henry Ansbacher, the man who
played a central role in settling the Poynter blood-
money war, played a similar role in breaking up
family control of one of the other great newspaper
blood-money feuds involving the *Louisville Cou-
rier-Journal* and *Louisville Times*.

Nelson Poynter and Barry Bingham, Sr., the
publisher of the Louisville newspapers, were good
friends, but they disagreed on heirs.

Poynter, as we have seen, didn't want to trust his
heirs to safeguard and nurture the publishing empire he had built. Bingham felt that the heirs were
the only ones who could be trusted to protect the
family's dominion. He was wrong.

To Sallie Bingham, her brother Worth was worth-
less. He was a womanizing drunk egomaniac who
had charmed their parents into thinking he was the
most amicable, articulate companion possible and
they let him get away with things they wouldn't
even let Sallie talk about. Sallie voiced her bitterness at the unfairness of her upbringing in her
book, *Passion and Prejudice,* over the fact that
Worth was the heir to the family empire and she
was not. It was the real cause of the blood-money
feud that ripped the Binghams apart.

When 34-year-old Worth was killed in 1966, the
control of the empire did not pass to Sallie, but to
the second son, Barry Bingham, Jr., which enraged
feminist Sallie who railed against how females were

undervalued and ignored. (There would have been another brother, Jonathan, in her way, but he died in 1964 at age 21). To say that Sallie was livid over the sequence of inheritance would be like saying the Civil War was a minor misunderstanding. She had returned to Louisville at age 40 in 1977, a bitter woman from two failed marriages and an unsuccessful attempt at a literary career.

Sallie owned stock in the family companies and sat on the board of directors. When she began to accuse her brother Barry, Jr. of being a sexist incompetent, he asked her to simplify his life by resigning from the board. Of course, she refused.

Sallie, along with her mother and sister, were put on the board by her late father toward the end of the 1970s. The other women did needlepoint, but Sallie kept asking awkward questions at board meetings. Clearly, this lady was a problem in the male-dominated southern society of Louisville because she, just like Scarlett, didn't know her proper Southern place.

"Women have often been silenced in history. I chose to speak," Sallie said.

Apparently, some of the rebellious genes of Sallie's grandmother, Mary Lily Flagler, were surfacing. Mary Lily was a high-spirited woman and wealthy widow of a former Standard Oil executive turned Florida real estate developer and builder of the famous Florida railroad that once stretched to Key West.

Mary Lily brought $5 million to her marriage with Robert Worth Bingham, a relatively obscure lawyer turned judge, in 1916. She was, at the time, regarded as one of the richest women in America. She died eight months later under mysterious circumstances and amid whispers of murder, syphilis, and drug addiction. She had changed her will a few weeks before her death leaving her husband a very rich man. From this base, the Bingham family fortune was built with the judge buying the *Courier-Journal* a few days after getting his inheritance and launching himself into Louisville society, which had been previously closed to him.

It was a fortune, Sallie claimed, built on "primogeniture, misogyny, and racism."

The family disputes assumed volcanic dimensions with the inevitable result that reporters from outside newspapers such as the *New York Times* began writing stories. Before long, things had escalated enough to inspire four books about the family—all at about the same time in the late 1980s.

As usual, media families who have no qualms about broadcasting other people's dirty linen to the world, are paranoid about anybody doing the same to them. One book, *The Binghams of Louisville* by David Leon Chandler, was canceled by Macmillan in 1987 under pressure from the Bingham family. It was later brought out by Crown Publishers.

Immediately after this incident, Barry Bingham, Sr., took the unusual step of copyrighting all the public material he had made available to researchers including an interview he had given to Mr. Chandler.

Four members of the family, including Sallie's mother, brother, and sister, sent letters to book reviewers around the country condemning Sallie's book saying her views, "rest on unsupported assertions, erroneous suppositions, leaps of logic and, in some cases, outright fabrications."

Mindy Fetterman, reviewing all the Bingham biographies for *USA Today,* made this assessment of the central theme of all four books:

> Greed and sibling rivalry, jealousy, and a stilted, stiff-upper-lip upbringing left a family frozen in an emotional tundra—and a great family legacy lost. What a shame.

The battle of the heirs, precipitated by Sallie and vigorously engaged in by other family heirs, had finally so alienated the family that everyone was sick of it and wanted it over. So, under the emotional trauma that infested their lives, the Binghams relented and in May of 1986, sold the two newspapers to the Gannett Company for $300 million. The television stations and other properties brought in another $150 million or so.

In the end, they were all richer, but it's doubtful if they will ever be happy again in each other's company as a family.

The same is true of the Hoiles family and their Freedom Newspapers. Most people haven't heard of the Freedom Newspapers, but the name suggests an ultraconservative bent and that's accurate.

They are the fourteenth largest newspaper chain in the country having been around since the 1930s when R.C. Hoiles had a fight with his brother over the family newspaper in Ohio and went off to start his own paper.

Fighting among the family and heirs seems to be a Hoiles tradition and today R.C.'s children are hard at it quarreling over control.

R.C. had two sons and a daughter and 70-year-old Harry H. Hoiles, the last surviving son, has been going hammer and tongs with his sister and brother-in-law for years. At stake is money. The closely held chain of 29 daily newspapers and five television stations based in conservative Orange County, California, has done very well financially and everybody wanted a piece of the billion-dollar empire that old R.C. left.

In some ways, Harry has been the outsider of the three children for most of three decades. He kept many of his thoughts to himself and bordered on taciturn even though he staunchly maintains the ultraconservative philosophy that marked his father's views.

These views include abolishing taxes, unions, public schools, and all other government agencies that interfere with people's lives. He would substitute "voluntaryism" where each person acts as an independent, but socially responsible, member of society. It was an early forerunner of George Bush's 1000 points of light. Harry thinks of himself as the spiritual heir of his father saying that his sister and other relatives have become too liberal.

While Harry was in college, his father, anxious to have both his sons in the newspaper business with him, got Harry to drop out and come to work at the family newspaper. Eleven years later, in 1948, R.C. bought a newspaper in Colorado Springs, the *Gazette Telegraph,* and put Harry in charge. Harry stayed there for almost thirty years before coming home to Santa Ana to help his brother Clarence run the family's flagship paper, the *Santa Ana Register.* The name would later be broadened to the

Orange County Register.

Harry assumed when he returned home to Orange County, the vast agricultural domain south of Los Angeles and the home of the California Angels baseball team and Disneyland, that he was the heir to his brother's position as the chief operating executive of the family communications conglomerate.

It was not to be and, when Clarence died in 1981, the rest of the family denied a bitterly disappointed Harry the number-one position. Control of the Hoiles fortune was equally split among the families of each of R.C.'s heirs and Clarence's family and Harry and their sister, Mary Jane Hoiles Hardie, each hold a third.

There were advance warnings of hostility among the siblings even when the old man, R.C., died in 1970, but they didn't escalate into open warfare as long as Harry stayed in Colorado Springs and Mary Jane was busy with her marriage and Clarence ran things in Santa Ana.

Clarence was essentially the linchpin that held things together, but his health began to fail and that's when the "what ifs" began quietly among the various family segments—"what if Clarence steps down or dies?," "what if Harry thinks he should become the boss?," "what if Mary Jane's husband, also a newspaperman, wants to be boss?"

As it happened, all those "what ifs" came to pass. Clarence died, Harry assumed he would be boss, and Robert Hardie, Mary Jane's husband, wanted to be boss. The family blood-money feuds had begun in earnest.

The situation started getting dicey when Clarence retired early from active management because of his poor health and Harry was not immediately voted in to succeed him. In March of 1981, Clarence and his sister voted to create a three-person executive committee to run things after Clarence.

The committee consisted of Clarence, Robert Hardie, and Harry. That delivered a strong negative message to Harry and he didn't like it and began to think of alternative arrangements that didn't involve his family. Harry began talking of pulling out of the family business and, so, the day after Christmas 1981, the other family members offered him $74.1 million or $120 a share for his stock. He refused and five days later, Clarence died.

Things got worse when Clarence died because Harry seized the moment to try taking over control of the papers. In a very painful confrontation, Mary Jane told Harry right to his face that she couldn't back him for the top job. Beyond that, she said, Clarence's family wouldn't support him either. This humiliating rejection decided Harry on splitting up the company and going his own way. Or, at least, the rest of the family could buy out his third and free him to do other things. The family refused to either split or buy Harry out at the price he wanted.

Harry responded by three times offering to buy the others out with his latest bid being over $1 billion, but nobody would accept it. Some believe the issue was no longer money, but pride and stubbornness among the members of a naturally proud and stubborn family.

Harry made his move in April 1982 when he turned to the courts for resolution of the conflict even if it would take time. The next five years passed in arguing and fighting over Harry's plan or Harry's price without anything being settled. Going to court to settle the dispute was distasteful to both sides. For Clarence and Mary Jane's family it meant airing a lot of family dirty linen in their hometown and revealing financial information they would rather be secret.

For Harry it was a violation of his conservative libertarian philosophy that the government should not interfere in people's lives.

Harry did it because, he said, it was the only way in the real world that he could get what was coming to him. Clarence and Mary Jane's families were both willing to give Harry what was coming to him, but the two sides disagreed on exactly what that was.

While all this was going on, the flagship paper of the 29-newspaper chain, the *Orange County Register,* was locked in mortal struggle with the giant of California newspapers, *The Los Angeles Times,* and was decisively trouncing the *Times*.

In 1984, when the Freedom Newspapers wanted to buy two television stations, build a new head-quarters building and expand the facilities of the *Register* so it could continue to compete against the *Times* effectively, Harry said they were wasting his money and tried to get a court order stopping the expansion. A few weeks later, the court ruled against Harry.

In April of 1987, the family feud came to the courtroom of Orange County Superior Court Judge Leonard Goldstein. Harry's lawsuit, filed in April of 1982, contended that the rest of the family froze him out of a key management position, pushed him off the executive committee [February 1982], and had taken actions that damaged the value of his stock, so he sought a court order to force the dissolution of the corporation and dividing of its assets.

Harry and his lawyers spent eight weeks offering testimony and proof of their position while Mary Jane and the heirs of Clarence claimed they only did what was necessary to protect the company from Harry's threats to sell his stock to outsiders.

On June 2, 1987, Judge Goldstein ruled that Harry had failed to prove his case. Beyond the ruling, the language of the judge's opinion was hurtful to the aggrieved Harry. Goldstein said there was no pervasive and persistent abuse of power against Harry by his family and that, when they kicked Harry off the company's executive committee, the family was "motivated by sound business judgment."

The ruling was a stunner to the 71-year-old Harry and his wife, Barbara, and they were visibly shaken as they heard it. They left the courtroom quickly. Although Harry was, as a result, liable for the other side's court costs, everyone assumed that he would appeal and continue the fight.

David Threshie and Richard Wallace, both sons-in-law of Clarence and key executives in the Hoiles organization, said they were relieved that the seven-year-long ordeal with Harry might be over. They wanted to get on with the business of running their billion-dollar dominion, but Hardie was pretty sure that Harry wasn't going to roll over and surrender that easily.

Naturally, Harry filed an appeal to Judge Goldstein's ruling, thus insuring the feud would continue.

In 1990, the battle took a tougher turn when

Harry hired Fort Worth lawyer, E. Glen Johnson, who is an associate of Robert Bass. Coincidentally, at the time Bass was involved in an attempted takeover of the *St. Petersburg Times* from heirs of the Poynter family. This sounded the alarm that Bass might join forces with Harry to take over the Hoile's properties.

In May 1990, the other side of the family, led by Harry's brother-in-law, Robert C. Hardie, countered by hiring Martin Lipton, a lawyer who specialized in fighting off hostile corporate takeovers. As a defense against Harry, Clarence and Mary Jane's family have pledged to sell their shares only to one another and to vote in a block. This agreement is to last five years until 1994. Following the expiration of the agreement, it can be renewed among the family members for one year at a time.

At the time, Hardie said the mutual sale agreement was designed to "signal anybody who is thinking of making a raid on the company that we're determined to remain a privately held, closely held, family company."

On July 13, 1990, the California Supreme Court cast out Harry's appeal of Judge Goldstein's ruling. It was another bitter blow, but it didn't foreclose still another appeal to the U.S. federal courts.

Hardie wished Harry and his lawsuits would go away, but didn't think they would, "We think they have an agenda to still do what it is they want to do. That seems to be the drift we get from them. They seem to be in a very hostile posture most of the time."

Harry's son, Timothy Hoiles, shot back that whatever hostility there was came from the rest of the family's refusal to let Harry participate in management and in reneging on the promises they made to him. He was a bitter and vengeful man poisoned by the betrayals of his own brother, sister, and their heirs.

Still, time was having an effect, as it often does in these matters of family blood wars, and Harry and Barbara had moved to Arizona sorrowfully realizing that they weren't going to win against Harry's sister and the heirs of his brother so, at age 77, they began focusing on other things.

Clarence and Mary Jane's side of the family were *trying* to cool things down. They dropped a counterlawsuit against Harry that charged him with malicious prosecution and put his son, Timothy, on the board of directors. And, 40-year-old Tim was mellowing out a bit, too. In a statement in October, 1992, he said, "There's still some animosity, but we're trying to put that behind us. We all have to do what's best for the business."

And, son-in-law Bob Hardie, who had been rigidly defending the family fortress two years ago with his, "we're determined to remain a privately held, closely held, family company" statement had now chilled down to saying, "Anything is for sale if the price is right."

Maybe the Hoileses, after a vicious blood war, learned what Dallas columnist Molly Ivins calls the First Rule of Holes: "When you're in one, stop digging."

Sixteen

Texas Gothic Blood-Money Feuds

There must be something to explain the bigger-than-life excesses of relations among Texans. Maybe it's the water or the climate or, as someone suggested, the imaginary Texan personality that is transformed from the inventiveness of the mind to the reality of life.

Whatever the reason, the effect of big money on personalities and upon the heirs of the Texas merchant king, Bernie Sakowitz, was spectacular. When Bernie cashed in his chips in 1981, it was the end of a retail success story and the beginning of a bitter blood-money fight among Bernie's heirs.

It took until 1987 for the heirs in the family to get heated up enough to drag the filial name into the public arena of a courtroom but when they did, their barbs about each other were on the front pages of the *Houston Chronicle* and *Houston Post* every morning.

Two of the central characters in this Byzantine soap opera are freebooter oil-and-gas man Oscar Wyatt (The Beast), and his to-die-for gorgeous fourth wife, jet-set socialite Lynn Sakowitz Wyatt (The Beauty). On the Wyatt side, there were also her two sons, Douglas and Steven, by a previous marriage to the scion of a Manhattan real estate family, Robert Lipson.

That union began in the '50s, when the beautiful and carefully cared for Lynn dropped out of Bennington to marry Lipson. They moved to Houston and Lipson took advantage of the marriage to maneuver a job at her father Bernie's small upscale department store chain, Sakowitz's. It wasn't much of an advantage because the old man started his new son-in-law out in lowly jobs with the intent that the boy work his way up. That wasn't Robert's plan. His plan was to start at the top and go on from there. After all, he had wedded and bedded the daughter and bred the two grandsons—didn't that entitle him? Bernie's short answer was "no."

From there on, the marriage went from worse to worse. Robert began drinking heavily and decided he, Lynn, Steven, and Douglas would move to Florida. They moved, but didn't find the Holy Grail of marital happiness there, either, and in 1960 Lynn returned to Texas with the boys, and without Robert.

Robert went on to find sex and drugs in London and the high point in his voyage of discovery came in the Chelsea district with the murder of an 18-year-old French student in her flat. The weapon of choice he employed was either the pillowcase with which he smothered the breath out of her or the LSD that he claimed had made him do it. At 37, he went into a British prison for six years after which he moved to Austria where he died suddenly. Lynn's story is that he was hit by a streetcar, but others suggest the death was much more ominous. No matter. Robert Lipson was dead.

Meanwhile, Lynn returned to the watering holes, gala parties, and matrimonial hunting grounds of the Houston rich. Like the women of her class, she was on the prowl for another husband, but one who could afford her. She found a man who could afford her and a lot of other women, but it was one of the most unlikely matches Houston society could envision.

He was the coarse, tough, big-time womanizer, Oscar Wyatt, a man who clawed his way out of poverty in a pimple on the map of East Texas named Navasota to found Coast States Company and become a very rich man. The only child sired by a happy town drunk and a rigid Southern Baptist mother who still worked as a bookkeeper at her son's company when she was 90 years old, Oscar made no secret that he lusted after money, power, and women and took all and any of them at every opportunity.

By the time Lynn met him at a party in Corpus Christi in 1962, Oscar had been through — literally — three wives and countless affairs. He was not accepted then, nor has he ever been, by "polite Texas society" such as the manicured River Oaks Country Club set of James Baker, John Connally, or George Bush. It is a rejection he is proud of since he regards men like Baker, Connally, and Bush as born with silver spoons in their something and never having had to prove their manhood mano-y-mano with the rough-and-tough real world.

Lynn liked him immediately because of what he was: a no bullshit, brass-balls man. He wasn't one of those prissy, pompous goody-goodies who graduated from the correct prep school and college and was guaranteed a vice presidency in Daddy's mega-bucks company upon graduation from school. Here was a

tough, take-no-prisoners, red-blooded specimen of
the species Homo Masculino Texacanus who reeked
maleness and danger and he was one steer that
creamy smooth Lynn Sakowitz was going to rope all
the while Oscar thought he was the one doing the
branding.

The proposal was symbolic. Oscar was flying Lynn
in his private plane and the talk turned to marriage
with Lynn complaining that Oscar had not yet proposed to her. Oscar roared that it was Lynn who had
to propose to him and she damn well better do it right
then. When she playfully refused, sensing she was
about to throw that doggie to the ground and get him
for her own, Oscar put the plane into a steep dive.
Lynn, without much more urging, threw herself on
top of Oscar and mockingly begged, "Marry me!
Marry me!" He said "yes" instantly and that began
their Beauty and the Beast marriage that has lasted
almost 30 years and produced two more sons, Oscar
III — called Trey — and Brad.

Before Lynn's father, Bernard Sakowitz, would approve the marriage, he insisted that Oscar give Lynn a
million dollars in Coastal States stock as protection
against Oscar's infidelities and a possible divorce. For
Bernard, that was a lot of money, because while the
Sakowitzes were very highly regarded in the Houston
community and thought to be rich, they were actually
millionaires on a very modest, Un-Texan scale.
Bernard's estate amounted to only $3 million when he
died.

After the marriage and Robert Lipson's death, Oscar insisted on adopting his two stepsons, Steven and
Douglas. Steven would run Oscar's London office
from which he became a tabloid item for his close
friendship with Sarah "Fergie" Ferguson, the Duchess

of York.

Oscar Wyatt is regarded as an amoral fixer and deal maker. He was the last American businessman to do business with Saddam Hussein before the Gulf War and he probably still trades with the tyrant. He does deals all over the world and his connections with the CIA were close under the administration of Ronald Reagan, but frozen under the administration of George Bush. His private intelligence network is regarded as one of the best in the world—information is how he makes his money.

Oscar vehemently opposed the Gulf War claiming American soldiers would be killed just to protect the oil investments that George Bush's son, George Bush, Jr., and the wealthy Dallas Bass family had in nearby Bahrain. After the war began, Hussein took hostage a bunch of Americans unlucky enough to be in Iraq at the time including some of Oscar's employees of Coastal States. Oscar flew his personal jet into Baghdad, met with Saddam and flew back to Texas with his people on board plus a man from A&W Restaurants who got trapped when his plane made a refueling stop in Kuwait just as the Iraqis seized the airport.

On the other side of the family dispute was the Sakowitz family. The key people on that side were the late Bernard's son, Robert Sakowitz (Lynn Sakowitz Wyatt's brother), and Ann Sakowitz, Bernard's widow and the mother of both Robert and Lynn.

Bernard left his estate to his wife, children, and grandchildren in a trust that was administered by Robert Sakowitz. Robert was also working his way up the corporate ladder of Sakowitz Department Stores from which came the income that supported the trust and, in turn, was supporting some of the heirs such as Ann. By 1975, the board of directors, which included his mother and sister, made him president of the stores.

Soon after Robert took over the small six-store chain and when Texas was basking in the glow of money from the 1970s oil boom, Robert decided to expand the chain dramatically. Neiman-Marcus, Saks Fifth Avenue, and Lord & Taylor had invaded the Houston market and Robert decided Sakowitz had to grow or die. Under his tutelage it would do both. He enlarged the chain to 16 stores and, even when the oil boom fizzled in 1982, he kept building.

Besides living a flamboyant lifestyle, attending Paris fashion shows in boots and a Stetson, and chasing after Laura Howell, a blond bookkeeper in the company who was 19 years younger, Robert was doing a lot of things that some might find questionable and others would say was a conflict of interest. Oscar Wyatt, when he learned about what Robert was doing and not doing, had a shorter, earthier way of describing it.

For openers, Robert was paid $100,000 a year as an outside consultant *to another department store!* In a number of cases, he was part-owner of the development and construction companies that built and leased stores to Sakowitz—he was, in effect, both landlord and tenant. He also had the company pay for his cars, club memberships, personal servants, and a lot of other expenses including his romancing of Laura, which culminated in marriage in 1984. They moved into a fancy River Oaks home near his sister and brother-in-law's place just three-months after Sakowitz, Inc. bit the bullet and filed bankruptcy. It would lurch on from crisis to crisis for another five years before it went Gucci toes up and closed.

The money that was supposed to go into the trust

for Ann, Lynn, and the grandchildren had swirled away as fast and ephemerally as a West Texas dust storm. To Oscar, it was all Robert's fault and this was not an abstract, considered opinion because Oscar had guaranteed a $2.5 million loan of the Sakowitz family back in 1974. Now that the family business was kaput, three guesses who was on the hook for the two point five mil? Right! It was old not-good-enough-for-the-Houston-elite-or-for-a-Sakowitz-daughter, loud, fat and gross Oscar. Mr. Oscar was not a happy camper.

When Oscar is unhappy, he doesn't call his shrink (doesn't have one)—he calls his lawyer, Tom McDade. It was at this point that Robert made a semifatal business mistake for which there was no excuse. An explanation, yes, but excuse, no. He certainly knew the kind of bull Oscar was and surely had heard of his obsession with avenging himself on anyone who crossed him by suing, pouring money into political connections, by making deals and by fixing things. Only the stupid and the foolhardy would cross Oscar Wyatt and hope to emerge unscathed.

But Robert must have assumed that his sister, Lynn, would protect him. Everybody knew that she went ballistic when Oscar ordered his lawyer to file suit. She argued, pleaded, fought, cajoled, and used every wile she had—some of which we will never know—but nothing would deter rhino stubborn Oscar once he put his head down and charged.

What Robert should have done is gone to Oscar, apologize for sticking him with the loan guarantee and work out a way to pay the man back. Instead, Robert thumbed his nose at that uncomfortable, but honorable approach.

What was particularly irritating about Robert's

lofty attitude was that Oscar hated him from the beginning of knowing him. In his eyes, Robert was born to wealth and security and never did a goddamn honest day's work in his entire life. Robert didn't have the brains to apologize to the crusty, crude old bastard. Aristocracy doesn't bow to peasants.

But in the end, Robert had to do that. His mistake was not doing it in the beginning. That was a big-time business mistake, because, by stalling around and putting off the inevitable, Robert gave time to the lawyer, McDade, to do a lot of sniffing around into Robert's private business deals. These were deals that could not pass the smell test.

Among them McDade found that Robert was stealing from the stores, shifting money around improperly, and lining his own pocket at the expense of the stores and the trust and the heirs of long dead, but probably still spinning, Bernard. He "borrowed" money from the store's account to make personal investments in oil deals. He finagled property rights in his own name using the store's money and, then, sold those rights to the store at a huge profit to himself.

When Oscar got the skinny on these shenanigans he went bonkers and ranted at Lynn about her goddamn, tight-assed, prissy thieving brother continuously until Lynn threw up her hands and, in July of 1987, assigned all her shares in the company to her son, Douglas, and told him to do whatever he thought proper. For one diddley sure thing, Lynn was not going to get involved between her brother and her husband.

After Douglas reviewed what his uncle Robert had done and, mindful of the rage of his adopted father, Doug, with Trey tagging along, filed the lawsuit from hell to recover the money Robert had dissipated and stolen. It soon had all of Houston and Texas and New York talking because of the incredibly vicious tone to which the rhetoric escalated almost overnight. One of the surprising twists would be that Lynn, the glamorous and lovely princess of both families, became the Evil Witch of the South.

The issue of the lawsuit pretended to be a simple, straightforward accusation that a set of accountants ought to be able to settle in a downhome minute. Ah, but that would ignore the hot and bitter blood racing through the veins of the families involved. It was hot and bitter blood that blanched the common sense out of people's brains faster than a Panhandle sunstroke.

John Taylor, writing in that down-the-nose way that Manhattanites have toward the South in general and Texas in particular characterized the suit this way for readers of *New York* Magazine:

> The suit, bristling with charges of fraud and betrayal, cult influence and manipulation, envy and family rivalry, was so wild, so quintessentially Texan in its narrative of greed and revenge, that it had mesmerized the entire state all summer.

In response to Doug's challenge, Robert Sakowitz drew his verbal Colt from its holster and fired back at the Wyatts: his sister, his brother-in-law, and his nephews. First, his lawyer, David Berg, targeted sister Lynn, a director on the board of Sakowitz, Inc., as an empty-headed blonde and shattered her during depositions and trial testimony.

Berg asserted that her brother, Robert, had patiently tried to explain to her what was going on in the business, but that Lynn had spent too much time under the hair dryer to understand. "She is always on her way to a party. She lights the fuse and then steps back into her vast wealth."

So, Berg claimed, Lynn was more negligent as an official of the company than Robert had been. Berg might have easily said the same thing of Ann Sakowitz, Robert and Lynn's mother, except that Ann was testifying on Robert's side.

As for Doug, Berg delighted in unleashing the bugaboo of mystique religious cult rituals on him giving the fascinated public audience something to suck breath in about at this circus of the rich and their foibles.

Berg exposed Doug's involvement with the late Frederick von Mierers, who started his career as an interior decorator and kissed up to wealthy patrons and suddenly discovered he was the reincarnation of the Biblical prophet Jeremiah with his own psychic powers and a divine mission to found a New York cult know as Eternal Values. As part of this spiritual awakening, von Mierers cast astrological charts and sold "jewels" to followers, the wearing of which protected one from evil forces.

Doug believed that von Mierers had brought happiness and serenity to many lives and was a prophet without honor among unbelievers. It turned out that von Mierers was interested in *making* a profit even more than in being a prophet. Some of these Eternal Value "jewels" were sold through Doug to his friends who later discovered that they were cheap costume junk and not worth the tens of thousands of dollars paid for them. This made Doug some enemies on the side.

The grotesque tenets of the von Mierers cult philosophy also alienated people from Doug. Von Mierers was viciously anti-Semitic and preached that "all women are selfish cunts and all Jews are evil." Cynics might suggest that von Mierers's theories were spawned of his Nordic, Aryan background and gay gender preference. In any event, he sermonized that the lowest form of life was a Jewish woman.

Inconveniently, Mother Lynn happened to be Jewish. However, that was explained away by a unique theory of reincarnation. Von Mierers held that Doug was really not a Jew only a incarnated Jew brought back to life to fulfill a mission uncompleted in a previous life, namely, to destroy his uncle, Robert Sakowitz, who was a Jew. That was what von Mierers peddled and what Doug bought into. Besides, Doug converted to Christianity and was poking around some Eastern religions, too.

Of course, it all didn't matter, said von Mierers, because, during a visit to the planet Arcturus, he had learned that Earth would be destroyed in 1999 and the people von Mierers had trained and prepared for the New Age would return to restore what was once an earthly paradise.

The one place that would not be caught up in the wholesale destruction of all evil on earth including women and Jews was the town of Lake Lure, North Carolina, where the cult had prepared a haven stocked with a cache of weapons.

Robert's attorney, David Berg, believed that there was some kind of celestial confluence in all this because Doug bought a place in Lure Lake, got a lifetime astrological reading from von Mierers, began wearing Eternal Values jewelry, and filed the lawsuit against Robert all in the year 1987. Berg suggested this was a maneuver by von Mierers to alienate Doug from his family and to generate great gobs of money for von Mierers. So, in other words, the invisible hand in the trial was that of von Mierers and not Oscar Wyatt as Robert has believed. Whew!

The judge, Pat Gregory, who presided over the case may have said "Whew!" to himself, too. Whether he did or not, he did ban any testimony about von Mierers.

Meanwhile, the suit clanked onward like a mindless Tiger tank intent on destroying anything that got in the way while the intra-family face-off was getting jalopeña hot even though the actual amount of money involved was ridiculously small. It was probably less than Oscar's phone bill for a month, but, as Lynn would testify, "it was the principle." Experienced watchers of the rich know that when any of them starts mouthing the word "principle" you should read it as "revenge." That was true, for example, in the lawsuit of the Seward Johnson heirs against their stepmother, Basia.

There definitely were some strange principals involved in this case. Even though Momma Ann was on Robert's side, she would visit Arlington, the Wyatts' luxurious home on River Oaks Road, to see her daughter and grandchildren, but only if "he" wasn't home. "He" being Oscar. Ann never thought Oscar was worthy of her daughter anyhow and Ann is convinced "he" is the one behind Doug's lawsuit. That is Robert's contention, as well, claiming that the invisible hand of Oscar is evident in every move Doug makes.

At the beginning, Oscar had wanted to explain the lawsuit to Ann, but she was having none of it then and she's having none of it now. She is only bewildered that her own grandson would do this to their family. The flip side is that Lynn and her brother

Robert are no longer speaking.

Observers who have followed these families through their legal self-emolations have, naturally, developed a set of theories to explain the unusual happenings. One explanation is the cult one. Doug is completing the work of destroying a Jew that von Mierers prophesied was Doug's mission in life. Von Mierers died in 1990 and so we have nothing more from him on that point, unless of course, he has been reincarnated, but has not revealed himself yet.

Another theory is that Doug, among all the four sons of Oscar Wyatt, wants to succeed to the throne of the Wyatt empire and needs to prove himself a loyal and effective spear carrier. He may have a stronger need to prove himself than Trey or Brad because Doug is one of Oscar's adopted sons and doesn't have the blood tie. This need for dutiful bonding may explain why both adopted sons would double-date with Oscar and his assorted girlfriends as he was cheating on Lynne.

At the trial, there was the uncomfortable spectacle of Lynn Sakowitz Wyatt testifying against her brother and for her son. This was compounded by Ann, who sometimes wears an Eternal Values jeweled ring she bought from von Mierers, testifying against her daughter and for her son. This was sure to make the seating at the Thanksgiving table a bit dicey.

In October, 1991, a jury said that Robert Sakowitz was a nice man and didn't do anything wrong. Simple as that sounds, nothing was simple in this case, and Robert Wyatt got the judge, Pat Gregory, to set the jury's verdict aside and allow a new trial.

So, Robert won, but Robert lost. This ratcheted up Robert's temper and he accused the judge of misconduct because the judge had written a book about the case. Robert said the judge's actions were less designed to serve justice than they were to hype the sales of his book.

Well, actually Robert won, but Robert lost. And, then, Robert won. He appealed to the federal courts to stop any new trial temporarily. This let things cool off for a time so that the two sides could chill out and calmer heads could try negotiating a settlement. Finally, in February 1993, a settlement was reached.

As a footnote mentioned earlier in this book, the judge in this case was the one who awarded the Howard Hughes billions to heirs whom he admitted were probably the wrong people. Unrelated to either case, you will recall that this same judge, Pat Gregory, was indicted for fraud in January 1993, pled guilty in a plea bargain deal and faces jail time and a $250,000 fine.

Soon after the lawyers' pontifications and the principals' hand-wringing was over, Little, Brown and Company of Boston and New York rushed a book into print about the feud, *BLOOD RICH: When Oil Billions, High Fashion and Royal Intimacies Are Not Enough,* by the ex-fashion editor of the *Dallas Morning News.* Largely covering previously plowed ground, the book did add one curious note. It implied that, amid the tangled Sakowitz-Wyatt affair, there was a whiff of murder. Then having raised the scent, the book inexplicably dropped it.

The settlement of the Wyatt-Sakowitz case essentially was that everybody would go home and forget it. All lawsuits were dropped and nobody admitted doing anything wrong.

Seventeen

Unwanted Children and Heirs

The marriage of Jackie Kennedy and Aristotle "Ari" Onassis stunned many people. It seemed like such an unlikely, no—unseemly—match. Here was the pristine, poised princess of Camelot marrying a Levantine oil tanker merchant even if his millions had earned him the nickname, "The Golden Greek."

Ari's son summarized the mutual motivations. "It's a perfect match. Our father loves names and Jackie loves money." C. David Heymann, author of the unauthorized biography of Jackie entitled, *Jackie O,* said that "She was drawn to the opulence and security Ari offered." But the marriage was doomed from the start because they came from two different gene pools and cultures. One was greedy, cold, indifferent, and arrogant, the other was conspiratorial, passionate, caring, and arrogant. Arrogance is all they shared and the effect of all that money distorted their lives and the lives of their children.

It was an odd arrangement from the start in any case. Christina Onassis, Ari's star-crossed daughter, knew that her father had been seeing Jackie and her sister, Princess Lee Radziwill and, in fact, had made several recent trips to the United States in spite of his dislike for the country, but she did not suspect that marriage was in the offing. As far as Christina knew, Maria Callas was still her father's woman.

This didn't mean that Christina loved Maria or even liked her. In fact, she hated Maria for having broken up her mother and father's marriage that ended in a 1959 New York divorce on grounds of adultery.

Christina had personal problems of her own that filled her mind, as well. She was the result of a surprise and unwanted pregnancy of her father's first wife, Athina "Tina" Livanos. Her mother's doctor warned Tina her health was in danger if she didn't abort the fetus that would become Christina. Her father, Ari, 30 years older than her mother, demanded the abortion and beat his pregnant wife bloody when she failed to do it. Christina was hardly being welcomed into the world by loving parents.

When the unwanted Christina was born, it was immediately noted that she was dark and Arabic-looking, which offended her blond mother. She and her brother were left largely to tutors and servants while their mother and father each actively and enthusiastically spent the next ten years being adulteress and adulterer. The children rarely had friends of their own and were watched closely for fear of kidnapping.

When she was with her mother, Christina was subjected to continual criticism over her weight and her looks. Her mother, Tina, kept pushing Christina to get plastic surgery for the dark circles under her eyes and her hooked nose.

For Christina, her childhood years were a life of "living among so many hurts." She would never escape that melancholy truth.

Desperate to please her rejecting parents, Christina gave in and had plastic surgery in Paris and, as she was recovering, learned from the newspapers that her father was going to marry Jackie Kennedy. The ceremony took place on Onassis's island of Skorpios on October 20, 1968.

If there was ever a miscast character in this drama it was Teddy Kennedy in the role of concerned surrogate father, razor-sharp negotiator, and urbane protector of the princess Jackie. On two major occasions, he had to deal with Onassis on behalf of Jackie and in both instances he was vastly outclassed.

The first was in August 1968 when he and Jackie went to Onassis's island of Skorpios to discuss the prenuptial agreement. This, traditionally, involved the family of the bride arranging for a dowry, but with tightfisted Jackie and her in-laws, Ari knew he could forget that pipedream.

Instead, Teddy was there to find out how good a deal he could get for Jackie who was off on her favorite activity, shopping.

The deal as set by Onassis — not by Kennedy — was this: Jackie got a $3 million signing fee up front for simply marrying Ari — almost as good as major league baseball. Her children would get the interest on a $1 million trust fund until they turned 21. If she and Ari divorced or Ari died, Jackie would get $200,000 a year for life. Period.

For her part, Jackie agreed to marry Ari and give

up any other claims she had on him or his estate. Also, period. As for her normal "needs," Ari simply said she would be taken care of and that was that.

The marriage was a blow to Christina who desperately yearned for her father's love and attention. When she got it and her father was calling her, "Chryso Mou," his Golden One, she was happy. That became less frequent now that he had snared one of the most glamorous women in the world for his wife even though it seemed up close to be an uncharacteristically formal relationship for the passionate Onassis. Nevertheless, Jackie was a jewel and trophy wife Ari used to flaunt his success to the world.

After the Kennedy marriage, Christina embarked on a search for love elsewhere. She had affairs with Danny Marentette and Luis Basualdo, an abortion and a humiliating public pursuit of Mercedes-Benz heir, Mick Flick. Brother Alexander believed all the chasing was her cry for attention from her father. She didn't get it and she hated Jackie for coming between her father and herself.

Christina's pattern was to find a man who interested her and, when she connected with one, began fantasizing almost immediately about sex with him. If it was not forthcoming, she made increasingly more open advances and, ultimately, demands for sex. "Why don't you screw me? Rich girls need it, too," was a common approach. Sex led her to anticipate and then insist on marriage and resort to jealousy games, attempted suicides, and other pressures to achieve it.

When she had worked in New York for her father's airline, Olympic Airways, in 1969, she had an adolescent romance with Peter Goulandris and it worried her that he didn't try to seduce her.

She was 19 and a virgin and not feeling very good about herself because no man seemed that anxious to bed her. His reluctance may have been natural shyness, but more likely it was the private talks he had with Christina's father, who had decided Peter was suitable husband material and was planning on the match. It would also mean the merger of Onassis with the Goulandris family and its 135 ships, which pleased Ari.

However, Christina didn't give a flying ostrich about ships. She was worried about her sexiness and it was in that frame of mind that she flew to St. Moritz for vacation at the villa of her uncle, George Livanos. Bingo! She met a well-to-do, playboy who dealt in racehorses, Danny Marentette, with whom she began to ski and spend her time. He quickly brought the rich brat under his control and his male dominance was obvious to everyone around them as was her pleasure to have a male that cared enough to want to dominate her.

What Christina didn't know is that her father kept close tabs on his Chryso Mou and had detectives check out every man she spent time with such as Danny. What Christina did know is that Danny wasn't shy about seducing her. He became her first lover and relieved her of the burden of her virginity, which she quickly learned she had traded for the burden of her father's wrath. Ari was determined to announce her engagement to Peter Goulandris anyhow even if she had turned out to be a whore.

Christina reacted by screaming at her father and fleeing back to New York with Danny. Ari reacted by screaming at his daughter and sending his wife, Jackie, to New York after her. When Jackie caught up with Christina, who was living with Danny, she learned that Christina, the newly deflowered virgin had flowered in another way—she was pregnant, proud of it and determined to keep the baby as a way of keeping her new man.

A few months later, family pressure from her mother and father, along with an advanced case of cold feet in Danny, moved Christina to part with forty pounds sterling in medical fees at a London clinic and who knows how many pounds of unborn child. She saw Danny once after that in a poignant accidental meeting at the Ascot races. They never saw each other again.

The sad weeks dragged by and, then, she met Luis Sosa Basualdo, an Argentine polo player, at St. Moritz where she was again. He had a girlfriend who he would be joining in a few days, but Christina, following her normal pattern, put the make on him in a relentless and determined campaign that succeeded. Luis left to join his girlfriend, but was back a few days later both in St. Moritz and in Christina's bed.

He, too, began dominating her and ordering her around in public and she loved it. When the St. Moritz season was over in March, however, Luis was off to Argentina—-alone.

That was when she immediately began her pursuit of Mick Slick. For Mick, who preferred blondes, she became a blonde even including her pubic hair, but it was no good, Mick didn't go for the overly eager and overly easy Onassis heiress. They had sex, yes, but he openly disdained the idea of marriage.

That wasn't good enough, they parted and she was at loose ends, uncertain what she wanted or where she wanted to go and ended up on her father's yacht, *Christina,* anchored off Monte Carlo.

Wandering around the town she met a friend who introduced her to a mature American from California who was pleasant and quiet and left the next day. Over the next few weeks they met in various cities in Europe as she quickly pressed her sexual availability upon him and they began enjoying weekends in out-of-the-way hotels.

Soon, he returned to Los Angeles and that was the end of the affair except for Christina who wrote him and telephoned him daily. When he tried to cool things off, it only made her more eager until she turned up at his doorstep in Los Angeles, unannounced and uninvited in July 1971.

He immediately called her mother who demanded that she come home instantly or that they get married. She refused to do the first and he didn't want to do the second. That sparked an outburst from Christina demanding to know why she wasn't good enough or sexy enough or rich enough or pretty enough for him. Then she slammed the bedroom door and stayed in there by herself. After a time, he gingerly investigated and found that she had tried to commit suicide by overdosing on pills.

A doctor was called, the stomach pumped and she recovered, but grimly swore she would continue to try suicide until he married her. Christina became the third Mrs. Joseph Bolker in Las Vegas on July 27th. The bride was 20 and the groom was 48.

Her father was outraged and refused to speak a word to her during the entire term of her marriage to Joe. Fortunately that was only seven months. She decided she had made a mistake and, with the decisiveness she had learned from her father, she called it quits much to Joe's relief.

Then she was off to Buenos Aires to see Luis Basualdo, but before they could connect, she stopped off to visit the Carnival in Rio and met a Brazilian polo player, Paolo Fernando Marcondes-Ferraz and had ten days of hungry, exciting lovemaking with him. Then of course, on to Buenos Aires and Luis.

When she found Luis, he was in bed with another woman, but Christina returned the next day and they went off for the weekend. It was a weekend of sex and confession, more sex and more confession. Christina had a compulsion to reveal every graphic detail of her sexual encounters with her first husband and others including Mick Flick who loved only blondes and her pathetic efforts to become a blonde in spirit as well as hair and even about Paolo en route to Luis's arms.

Luis enjoyed the weekend, but knew he could never marry her. Christina, in trying to demonstrate how sexually attractive she was so as to entice Luis, didn't understand that Luis didn't want to be sticking his cock where she had told him many others had stuck theirs.

In an odd parallel of behavior to Christina's, the opera star Maria Callas, who deeply loved Christina's father, continued to chase after Ari even though he had broken her heart by marrying that American slut, Jackie Bouvier Kennedy. Ari and Jackie had married in October 1968 and, now in early 1970, the marriage was turning sour.

Within a year after marrying Jackie, Onassis began seeing Maria again. Once when Maria had been photographed on Ari's arm coming out of Maxim's in Paris, Jackie rushed to Paris and insisted on being photographed exactly the same way. Maria struck back by taking an overdose of pills just as Christina did when she couldn't get her man. Soon after, Ari was photographed kissing Maria passionately on the mouth. Jackie began to deny Ari sexual privileges.

Jackie did not understand that to be Ari's wife one had to be where he was — not always in New York, which she preferred. To be Ari's wife she had to sleep with him not exile him to a separate bedroom or, when he came to New York, to a hotel away from her apartment. To be Ari's wife she had to share his passion, share his work, share his life. Jackie refused.

For example, Jackie was an obsessive shopper who would be in and out of a store in ten minutes having bought scores of blouses or dresses or whatever and run up a bill for $100,000. Each month Jackie's maid would bring a shopping bag of bills to Ari's office to be paid and Ari would go crazy. He couldn't understand, for example, why she had to buy 100 pairs of shoes at one time or why she would go to an international fashion show and buy out the entire collection. Ari's bank account could handle it easily, but his poor childhood and his mind couldn't.

By this time, Christina was back in the swirl of aristocratic London going from man to man. She still was unhappy that Mick Flick didn't want to have sex with her, but she made up for the irritation by having it with as many other men as struck her fancy. Then a happy phone call from her father came. It was the end of 1972 and he was going to divorce Jackie. It pleased Christina immensely who despised Jackie for her intrusion into Christina's life and because Jackie was such a cold, calculating, money-greedy bitch.

Weeks later, January 23, 1973, a tragedy struck the Onassis family that would radically change Christina's life. Her brother, Alexander, died in a small

plane crash in Athens. Ari was devastated and positive his son had been murdered by his enemies. For a
year, he had the "accident" investigated and everything he learned sustained his suspicion.

For Christina, the tragedy meant that she was now
the sole heir to Ari's fortune and business and she
was totally unprepared. She had become instantly, as
her father told her, his future, his destiny. It was a
heavy burden for a young woman alone. She needed
not to be alone anymore, but a happy connection
with a man continued to elude her.

The men in her circle didn't seem to be right for
her even though she fantasized with each that he
would be the one. Thierry Roussel, the French younger brother of her sister-in-law, was attractive though
three years younger, but he was enamored of someone else. Peter Goulandris drifted in and out of her
thoughts. Peter was the match that Ari wanted for
his daughter as noted before because it would merge
two great shipping companies. Ari had promised his
daughter he was divorcing the hated shopping queen,
Jackie, but he extracted Christina's matching promise that she would marry Peter. He did and she
didn't.

Jackie was totally out of synch with Ari and the
family in its grief over the loss of Alexander. Ari was
depressed and emotionally ravished by his son's
death and Jackie didn't seem to understand or sym-
pathize or, for that matter, care very much. She
seemed to have that same cold indifference ten
months later when Ari was diagnosed as having my-
asthenia gravis — an illness of the muscles.

In spite of his illness, Ari took Jackie to Acapulco
for New Year's, but had a bad time because his mind
was filled with business problems — tough times in

the shipping trade and a much-wanted refinery deal in New Hampshire going sour.

Jackie's total obsession with the pleasure-and-shopping principle made him angry particularly when she pressed him to buy her a home there, a resort where she and Jack Kennedy had often gone. On the flight back in his private jet they quarreled and he sat down and handwrote his last will and testament. In it, he stuck to the deal he had struck with Teddy Kennedy two months before the marriage. This meant that most of his $1 billion estate would go to Christina.

He left income of $200,000 a year to Jackie. Her children, Caroline and John, got $25,000 a year until they were 21. If Jackie contested the will, she forfeited everything and executors were instructed to fight her "through all possible legal means." The foundation of a blood-money war was laid.

For the next few months, Ari was in and out of hospitals and Jackie was in and out of expensive shops continuing her Olympic-class shopping.

Christina continued to blame Jackie for her father's ill health and business misfortunes. Her hatred focused so much on Jackie that she even began to like Maria Callas, who still openly proclaimed her love for Ari as when she was on the "Barbara Walters Show" talking about her new romance with Ari, "the greatest love of my life."

Christina became so depressed by everything that, early in August she and her maid, Eleni, withdrew from view and holed up in her London Reeves Mews house alone for 12 days instead of going to Skorpios with Peter as she had originally planned. She was so dangerously unhappy that she refused to clean her teeth — a common sign of suicidal depression with her. Finally, on August 16, Eleni called an ambulance because Christina was almost comatose and she was rushed to Middlesex Hospital. Her stomach was pumped and the doctors said it was a massive overdose of sleeping pills.

Her mother, Tina, was summoned from the south of France and Christina told her, "Peter says he can never marry me. I don't want to live." Tina and Christina agreed not to tell Ari until later when she was recovered.

Tina was particularly upset with this stunt of Christina's coming after the death of Alexander. She superstitiously thought retribution was at work. Her marriage to Stavros Niarchos was not happy. Niarchos was having other women and Tina began seriously thinking about divorce, as well as drinking and using drugs heavily.

Her husband made her get a medical checkup on September 21st and on October 10th, she was found dead in the Niarchos's Paris mansion. Stavros Niarchos was asleep in another room. The stories were confused: her secretary said it was a heart attack or acute edema of the lung; a Niarchos spokesman in London said it was a blood clot in the leg that moved to the heart; and the press speculated suicide from a drug overdose.

Christina flew to Paris and immediately demanded an autopsy. Ari and Stavros hated each other, but agreed on this to remove all suspicion. On October 13, two pathologists reported that Tina died from acute edema of the lung (too much fluid in the lung).

Christina returned to the New York office. About the only good thing that had happened was that Peter, shaken by the suicide attempt, came back to her. Stavros meantime was angry at her meddling in the death of her mother and his wife and, on October 14, issued a public statement revealing Christina's attempted suicide. He claimed that this aggravated her mother's weakened condition from Alexander's death and implied that Christina's suicide was a selfish act that killed her mother.

Ari's health deteriorated after Tina's death and the drugs the doctors were giving him weren't controlling his disease. It was during this time that Christina and her father became very close and he desperately tried to wrap up the details of his succession. January 15, 1975 was Ari's 75th birthday and he tried to arrange for how things should be after he died. Again, he got Christina to promise she would marry Peter in exchange for which Ari promised he would divorce Jackie.

A little over two weeks later, on February 3rd, he collapsed in Athens with sharp stomach pains. He was immediately moved to Paris for treatment. His condition was listed as critical and everyone understood that this was the end.

During Ari's last days, he was at the American Hospital at Neuilly-sur-Seine near Paris attended constantly by Christina and Ari's sister, Artemis, with daily visits by Jackie. Christina and Jackie avoided each other completely. In spite of her husband's grave condition, Jackie continued her regular round of shopping and social occasions.

After a time, Jackie got restive and decided to return to New York in spite of the advice of close friends. She flew back to New York and promptly left on a ski trip to New Hampshire. The day her husband died in Paris, March 15, 1975, Jackie was in New York. When she got word that Ari had died, Jackie made preparations to fly to Europe for the funeral after first calling the courtier, Valento, to design an appropriate dress for her to wear to the funeral. There are, after all, priorities.

Ari was buried on the island of Skorpios near his son as Jackie looked on stoically and Christina sobbed. In the funeral possession to the grave side a strange incident happened that puzzled many who were there. The limousine following the hearse had Jackie, Ted Kennedy, and Christina in it. Suddenly that limo stopped, Christina leaped out and moved to the next limo.

Ted Kennedy had chosen that moment to bring up renegotiation of what Jackie would get from the estate. Revolted and horrified at Teddy's insensitivity, Christina ordered the limo to stop so she could get out. The first shot of the post-Ari blood-money war had been fired.

Shortly afterward, Jackie hired attorney Simon Rifkind to break Ari's will and he raised some innovative questions in that quest. Rifkind argued that Greek law required a holographic will to be written all at one time without interruption and in one place. Among other things, Rifkind claimed that, since it was written on a moving airplane speeding over Mexico and the United States, it was—technically—written in many places and, therefore, invalid. He might also have suggested that the plane passed through several time zones and, therefore, the will was not written all at one time, but fortunately for legal rationality, he let that pass.

The heirs, Christina and Jackie, warred about the estate for 18 months after Ari was in his final resting place. Christina finally agreed to pay Jackie $26 million if Jackie signed off on any other claims forever. It was a 15-minute meeting in New York City and

Jackie grabbed the money and ran. That blood-money war was over, but the bitterness would last forever.

Christina ran, too. She ran all over the world looking for love and happiness. She tried to find it again in marriage. She married three more times, but was mainly caught up in running the vast Onassis empire and did rather well at it. She was smart, decisive, and imaginative as her father had been and it impressed the cousins and cronies who ran things.

She didn't do as well in her worldwide search for love and happiness. She tried to find it again in marriage. She tried to make the engagement to Peter work, but the Goulandris family regarded her and her late father as outsiders, come latelies and thought it was terrible that she was a divorcée. Peter was also getting cold feet again. After Easter in the Bahamas, she called the engagement off.

The first marriage after her father's death was to Alexander Andreadis, the son of a wealthy Greek family whom she met in Alexander's father's hotel in Athens. He was overweight, average height, and had Elvis sideburns. She bought him a coffee, "my heart skipped a beat," she said, and eight days later they were engaged. They married in Prince Peter of Greece's summer chapel at Glyfada and, curiously given their mutual hatred, Jackie was present with her son John. Ari had been dead three months.

It was not a marriage that started auspiciously because Alexander and his father immediately thereafter faced trial for destroying property as charged by the new military junta in Greece. Also, in all the rush of romance and wedding, Alexander forgot to tell his regular girlfriend, Denise Sioris of Washington, D.C., about the marriage.

By September, Christina and Alexander were quarreling openly in public including minor physical assaults such as throwing backgammon boards and dragging Christina into elevators. Finally, she held a press conference to say the Onassis fortune was separate from the now troubled Andreadis fortune. By November, Christina was reported to be pregnant but she denied it and apparently had an abortion. Six months into the marriage, she wanted out. Alexander was pushed into a corner, Peter reappeared on the scene, and Christina began dating Mick Flick again.

Christmas of 1976 she went to St. Moritz alone feeling good with the divorce set for March on grounds that her husband was, "despotic, foul-mouthed, blindly jealous and yet a womanizer, and fanatically self-centered." He responded in kind and the divorce finally came in July.

Maria Callas died of a heart attack in Paris in September and four days later, the *New York Times* published details of the heir war settlement between Christina and Jackie. That was okay with Christina who detested Jackie and thought the story displayed how money grubbing the former First Lady actually was.

Besides, she had other things to deal with in her busy life. One thing that was becoming a problem for the employees of her father's empire was the reality that, as one biographer described it, "Christina fell in love easily and her passion was both boundless and brief. She turned away from lovers and husbands, and turned toward others, with a capriciousness that was beginning to worry the Olympic hierarchy."

Christina continued to be an emotional mess and tried to stabilize her mood swings with an impressive array of drugs—prescription, as well as illegal. She had become a drug junky dependent on chemicals to get herself through every day, every crisis, every challenge, every depression and every exhilaration. If she had been a poor kid, she couldn't have afforded what she was doing to herself or she would have been in the slammer for dealing.

Symbolic of the out-of-control Christina was the Sergei Kauzov affair which could only be characterized as totally crazy even if it was the second marriage after her father's death.

She was in Moscow with her executive aide, Costa Gratsos, to lease some ships to the Russians. The Russian negotiator was a man named Sergei Kauzov to whom she took an instant liking probably not knowing at the start that he was a KGB agent. The talks required several meetings during which he was transferred to Paris and their meetings soon became social, as well as business, and in November, 1977 they began an affair.

Sergei was slim with brown hair, with a gold tooth and one eye that did not move as the result of a boyhood accident. He was married with a nine-year-old daughter, but none of that mattered and the affair went on for several months around Paris. He said they had to keep it secret or he would be hauled back to Moscow. In February, they got away to Rio for Carnival and in that exotic setting filled with sexual energy, one of the richest female capitalists in the world asked a $175-a-week Russian KGB agent to marry her.

French intelligence knew about the affair and, soon, so did CIA and British intelligence and a lot of top government officials were concerned. Christina had valuable information she could give Sergei, but CIA dismissed the idea that it was a KGB setup. Even so, everyone figured that, setup or not, the KGB would exploit the relationship.

Fearful that he might defect, the Russians called Kausov home to Moscow without warning leaving Christina in her usual romantic, lustfully frantic state. With enormous effort, she got his home number, but could not call him from Paris without going through an operator and that bothered her. So, little miss rich girl simply flew to London to dial direct to Moscow whenever she wanted to reach her lover.

She connected with him and learned that he was not only alright, but had asked his wife for a divorce so he could marry Christina. The downside is that the Russian authorities insisted they live in Moscow. That was all right with lovesick Christina and, while they were apart, she continued to fly to London three times a week just to be able to telephone him.

A time was set for Christina to come to Moscow and, excitedly, she jetted to the Russian capital to meet her lover who stood her up without an explanation. Rejected and dejected, she returned to Paris and went into immediate seclusion for a week, during which she played music from *Doctor Zhivago* constantly. Nursing her aching heart, but desperate to talk to her Russian, she flew to London and tried telephoning. Wonders! She reached him, he apologized for missing their date and, then, delightedly announced he was getting the divorce and would marry Christina.

Christina forgave all and was brimming with happiness unlike other people who were spinning conspiracy theories. The international press focused on her going to Moscow while some gossips theorized that the CIA leaked her marriage plans to embarrass her and force her to change her mind.

As the man said, "Just because I'm paranoid, doesn't mean they aren't following me." And just because gossips were making up conspiracy stories didn't mean that Western intelligence wasn't worried about the Onassis tanker fleet under control of the Russians.

Her executive aide, Costa Gratsos, warned her of the consequences of marriage to the Russian and told her that Kauzov was definitely KGB. Unconvinced, Christina was in a high-octane emotional state and determined to go ahead even though the Western world was aghast and her family appalled.

On July 27th, Christina announced the wedding would be August 1st, but close friends saw that the unpredictable Onassis princess had become disenchanted with Moscow. A few days before the wedding, she told her close friend, Florence Grinda, that she no longer loved Kauzov, but didn't want to humiliate him by backing out.

The strangest wedding any Onassis ever had was held in a former Russian prince's mansion with eight people present—none from Christina's side—and a string quartet. The total cost? $2.15. Four days later the bride flew to Greece alone.

After a relaxing breather on Skorpios, she went to a lunch with British Petroleum directors and customers in Britannia House, BP's headquarters in London. There she was quietly told that the Saudis were convinced the KGB now controlled her shipping fleet and the vehemently anticommunist Arabs weren't going to renew her charters. Eighty-five percent of the oil her fleet carried was for the Saudis.

Intelligence agencies, to help things along, leaked proof that Kauzov was back sleeping with his old wife. That aggravated her, but the Saudi attitude alarmed her. She understood what it meant: the Onassis empire was threatened by her impulsive marriage.

She returned to Moscow on August 13th, nearly two weeks after her wedding, and she knew what she had to do (which was what she *wanted* to do, as well), but didn't want to appear foolish. Before she left for the Russian capital, she secretly notified the Saudis that the problem would be taken care of soon. They agreed to give her a little time.

Christina and her Russian/KGB bridegroom were installed in a seven-room luxury apartment and she tried to play it cool by pretending to be the good wife for the next nine weeks. Then at the right moment, she told Kauzov it was over. He took it surprisingly calm and laid down his simple terms, namely, he wanted to get out of Russia with his mother. Christina agreed and promised to keep the charade of a marriage going until Kauzov and his mother were safely out of Russia.

Christina helped get Kauzov and his mother safely out of Russia to England and gave Kauzov two tankers worth $7.5 million as a goodbye present. On November 5th, 1979, the press said she was getting a Greek divorce, she strongly denied it, and a month later it was done. She was in her 30th year.

For Christina, it was back to the party circuit with a variety of escorts except for Yvon Coty, the heir to the perfume fortune, with whom she was angry because, "All he likes from me is a blow-job." She was seen with Philippe Junot, estranged from Prince Caroline of Monaco; polo player, Jean-Jacques Cornet-Epinet; and, her ex-lover, Luis Basualdo.

At Christmas she announced a moratorium on sex, but that lasted only a few weeks and, by February, she was aggressively on the prowl again when Nicky Mavroleon came into view: tall, dark, slim, dark curly hair, 21, well educated, but poor. The hormones clicked in and Christina was desperately in love again. At some point, Nicky got $50,000 from Christina, but that didn't hold him to her.

Christina told friends she was "almost suicidal" because Nicky was slipping away from her and even her three-times-a-week Paris psychiatrist was worried. He had her flown to the Lenox Hill Hospital in New York City for a rest and Christina went along with it because she knew she was losing it over Nicky.

To add to the tension, Luis came in from Buenos Aires with a friend, Marina Dodero, who dumped a tale of woe on Christina about Marina's father tottering on the verge of financial ruin. Christina didn't want to hear about it and lent her $4 million interest free for four years just to get her out of her life.

Then, in June, Christina flew to La Jolla, California, to be with Kauzov and make Nicky jealous. As much of her playacting turned out, this didn't work and she returned to Paris more depressed than ever at the thought of losing Nicky—if she ever had him. Her shrink turned her around immediately and put her back on the plane to New York and Lenox Hill Hospital. Once again, she accidentally ran into Luis and his English girlfriend, Clare Lawman, and he complained about being low on money. Christina invited them both to Skorpios for the entire summer.

Her father's island was now her island and, as it had been ruled by his idiosyncrasies, it was now ruled by her idiosyncrasies and after a few weeks of adjusting to Christina's wildly swinging moods, Luis got fed up and said he and Clare were leaving. Luis had been one of the loyalest of Christina's male friends, but he was leaving.

Christina broke down crying saying her doctor said she needed a companion and she begged Luis to stay with her forever and Clare, too. She said she would pay him well, but Luis indignantly rejected the offer of pay. What kind of friend wants to be paid for friendship? he demanded to know.

Then he asked her how much she had in mind and, in that way, answered his own mock-indignant question. They settled on $30,000 a month with a dress allowance for Clare and we all knew what kind of friend asked to be paid.

Summer was over and the trio of "friends" adjourned to the Onassis Avenue Foch apartment in Paris with Christina still seething about Nicky not dancing to her tune. He chose to be in England training to be a copter pilot instead of whirling her around.

Desperate and obsessed by Nicky's rejection, she resorted to another childish maneuver and announced she was pregnant with Nicky's child. Angered, Nicky flew to Paris on October 10th to confront and tell her he would repay the $50,000 she had given him and that there was absolutely no possibility of marriage. She admitted the pregnancy was a hoax and she was devastated that he rejected her.

What was worst of all for Christina is that Nicky's rejection was reported all over the world in the gossip press, as well as the lie about the pregnancy. She was depicted as a desperate woman who had millions, but couldn't get a man. Humiliated and confused, she let herself go, no tooth brushing, no hair washing, and getting fat again.

Luis worried about her heavy dependence on mood-altering drugs, strong amphetamines — black blacks "mavro mavro" and milder black whites "mavro aspro" — and he dreaded what he came to call "mavro mavro time."

When Christina got high, she wanted to dance all night so Luis and Clare took turns dancing with her on those mavro mavro nights in Paris nightclubs. Hours later at bedtime the heiress took handfuls of barbiturates. Predictably, the behavior of this young woman who controlled a vast shipping empire became disoriented, bizarre, and erratic.

In retrospect, it might be said that Luis was earning his money particularly since his imperial employer forbade he and Clare making love under her roof and had the maids inspect their sheets every morning for signs of sexual romps.

The drill was that Luis and Clare made love every day in places other than their own bed and that Luis serviced the sex needs of Christina as well so as to keep her mollified. To some men it might sound like a dream job, making love to two young women all the time for a shade over $1,000 a day, but it was wearing on Luis after a time.

In some ways, Christina's life had settled into a routine of St. Moritz from Christmas until Easter; the Avenue Foch apartment in Paris from Easter until the beginning of summer; off to La Jolla, California, for June; the island of Skorpios for July and August; and, finally, back to Avenue Foch and Paris for the fall.

The affair with Nicky finally worked itself out of her system and she went back to an occasional rendezvous for a few weeks at a time with Kauzov.

As her father had been, she reigned as absolute monarch on Skorpios and would give Luis names of those who displeased her in some minor way and they were off the island within hours or minutes. She often slept together with Clare and Luis or would summon him from his bed with Clare to come to her bed.

By this time, Luis was becoming addicted—addicted to the money and the power he enjoyed as majordomo, wet nurse, valet, adjutant, and ever-ready stud to the richest woman in the world. As his addiction with the lifestyle grew, so did his fear of being squeezed out of Christina's life by some unexpected interloper.

There were the usual torrid affairs mostly initiated by Christina, but that didn't bother Luis unless they lasted too long and, in a way, they relieved him of the daily need to service Christiana sexually. Besides, the lifestyle pandered to greed and Luis was charging her extra for everything he did. After a time, Christina, aching for someone who loved her and not just her money, finally ejected Luis from the Avenue Foch quarters, but, always insecure, kept him on the payroll just in case.

Christina's low self-esteem and insecurity made her a lightning rod for emotional pain and the next thunderbolt of pain came with the news that Nicky had married Barbara Carbare, who appeared with Sean Connery in *Never Say Never Again*. Christina's response was to balloon up to 180 pounds and go back for a short affair with Kauzov in La Jolla.

One observer pinpointed what was bedeviling Christina: "The frequency of her divorces and affairs strengthen Christina's conviction that she would never be happily in love for very long."

It was 1983, a few days before her 33rd birthday, that Christina ran into Henri Roussel, father of Thierry Roussel. The father said his son often talked about Christina and that, along with her memory of the seduction on Skorpios ten years before, prompted her to telephone Thierry in Kenya.

Miraculously, he was unattached and sounded interested again and, from that day on, they talked on the telephone every other day. She thought they should meet, but said she had gained weight and was afraid he might not like her. He gave her the name of a spa in Marbella where Paris models went and promised to marry her if she would lose 80 pounds. She couldn't get to Marbella fast enough and began losing weight to please him and he sent flowers and phoned daily to please her.

The amazing and unexpected was about to happen. They met in early February after she had lost weight—not 80 pounds—but enough to look good. The two connected and she and Thierry moved into Avenue Foch together with Christina rhapsodizing that she wanted to marry and have children.

Astonishing to her, Thierry said he did, too. They announced their engagement February 23, 1984, and were married three weeks later followed by a dinner for 150 at Maxim's. It was the fulfillment of a dream for Christina, for which she had waited twenty years.

She gave Thierry $10 million and he didn't sign a prenuptial agreement. He was about to be initiated into the world of wealth beyond his wildest fantasy while also seeing changes were needed.

To begin with, he was intrigued to learn that the interest on her savings accounts was over $1 million a week while her annual expenses were only $6 million. He set about changing that by ordering a new jet, calling for new luxurious quarters in Paris, and doubling the number of servants. Thierry believed that, if you were disgustingly rich, you ought to live that way.

In July, she learned she was pregnant and withdrew from drugs and their whirligig social life to give her baby the best possible chance. She said she knew it was a girl and it would be called Athina after her dead mother. January 29, 1985, in American Hospital in Paris where her father died 10 years before, Christina gave birth to Athina, six pounds two ounces. This was an Onassis girl baby different from its mother in that it was loved and wanted from the start.

Baby or not, the Onassis lifestyle continued at a fast pace. Christina lived on Diet Coke, which was not available in France and so, naturally, her personal jet plane picked up 100 bottles from New York each week. No more because she didn't want "stale" Diet Coke. For the mathematically inclined, this works out to about $300 per bottle.

The newlyweds spent a lot of time apart. Christina said Thierry came and went and that was good for the marriage, but she changed her mind when she found out that Thierry had begun seeing his old girlfriend, Gaby Landhage, again. Gaby had become famous with her nude modeling and soon became pregnant with Thierry's child!

What further humiliations could be visited on the insecure Christina? She ordered him out, crying she had given him money, marriage, and a child and he had betrayed her. But, like so many men in Christina's life, Thierry knew what buttons to push and he began seeing another girlfriend, Kirsten Gille. He knew it would inflame Christina's sexual jealousy even more and make her ache to be accepted into his arms again. It did and she humbly took him back in spite of the fact that Luis strongly advised her against it.

On July 31st, Gaby gave birth to Thierry's son in Malmo just six months after Christina had given birth to his daughter. Continuing his flaunting of power over Christina, he used his wife's plane to fly to Sweden for the baptism of his son, Erik Christoffe Francois.

This so depressed Christina that she called off the baptism of her daughter, which upset Thierry, who either truly didn't understand or truly didn't care why Christina didn't behave like the proper European wife who accepted her husband's affairs. Finally, the baptism was rescheduled for the benefit of the baby, but Christina said she could not have a marriage just for public occasions. She had come to loathe Thierry for the embarrassment he had heaped upon her and they fought constantly. She knew when the fighting stopped the marriage was over. A close friend summed it up: "She despised Roussel in many ways, but she also had this sentimental and sexual fixation about him being the father of her child. Athina was Roussel's strength, she was his grip on Christina, the leverage that no other man in the world had on her."

Although Thierry had banished Luis from Christina's circle because Thierry didn't want another man around to give her support, Christina had kept in touch with Luis regularly and continued to keep him on the payroll.

At last, Thierry told the press he couldn't continue the marriage and he wanted out. His family felt he should get a $50 million settlement for all his trouble. After all, he had to endure the bodyguards and being called, Mr. Onassis. There are limits to the indignities one can put up with, after all!

The marriage was gone and the pills were back.

So was Luis in the summer of 1985, but this time he had a plan to up the ante from that piddling $30,000 a month subsistence on which he was forced to scrape by. He used the former stepbrother of Christina, James Blandford, and a banking scam to swindle Christina out of several million dollars. This ticked Christina and she got the cops after him until he called and raised hell, when she backed off. How dare she object to his stealing a few million from her?

Even more aggravating for Christina was word that Gaby was pregnant again by Thierry. By mid-1987, Christina had divorced him. Then she became obsessed with winning him back again. She tried to cozy up to Gaby. She became an occasional lover for Thierry and told him that she wanted another child with him as the father. He agreed and performed as desired and required, which resulted in two pregnancies and two miscarriages for Christina.

About this time, Christina shifted her attention to Argentina where there were friends, men to love her, wonderful stores, sunshine, and nightlife. Thierry didn't like it because it was out of his territory and she didn't care because she had roots there. Her father had lived in Argentina 65 years before, so Christina looked upon it as a new beginning in an old place.

Her friends, the Doderos, were her hosts and showed her property to buy, while her buddy Marina Doderos was daydreaming about Christina marrying

Marina's brother: Jorge Tchomickdjoglou, who she regarded as controllable. In any case, Christina, still the amateur at the game of love, hoped that the stories of her and Jorge would be seen by Thierry and make him jealous.

She now traveled back and forth between Argentina and Europe with Thierry as the occasional lover while she talked about his fathering another child. In fact, friends reported that she had offered Thierry $10 million on the birth of another child. However, he candidly told her that she wasn't sexually attractive to him and he couldn't screw a woman who couldn't give him an erection.

However, to be decent about it in his unbearably arrogant way, he accepted her suggestion that he simply make his sperm available to her for artificial insemination. So, in one of those weird deals to which the very rich seem attracted, he agreed to the idea and got $160,000 for his deposits into Christina's personal sperm bank from which she made a withdrawal each month at the right time. In the romantically infantile mind of the woman-child, having another child by Thierry would prove to the world that he was still her man.

In Buenos Aires she continued to party and on the night of November 17th she dined with Jorges and the Doderos and they were up most of the night. The next night she was out again but complaining about the cold weather. She talked to her baby daughter on the telephone and ended the evening with a stroll around the grounds of her villa with Jorge. They kissed good night at 1:30.

At 8:30 the next morning, Marina went looking for her houseguest and found her naked and dead in the bathtub.

What happened next was cause of much speculation. Marina ran out calling for help and a Dr. Arthuro Granadillos Fuentes was the first medical help to arrive. He found Christina, not in the bathtub where Marina found her, but on the bed with her hair wet. When he tried to go into the bathroom where she was supposed to have been found to see if there was any evidence of why or how she died, he was kept out by members of the Doderos family. As a result, he refused to sign the death certificate saying there was reason to require an autopsy. He said he had been ordered out when he started asking too many questions.

The body was taken to the clinic of the Miraculous Virgin where three doctors examined it and also refused to sign a death certificate because they thought an autopsy necessary. At noon, Judge Juan Carlos Cardinali was notified of a "doubtful" death and signed an order for an autopsy at 3 P.M. on Saturday.

A sobbing Thierry arrived the next morning with Paul Ionnadis, one of the key executives of the Onassis organization. Thierry dismissed rumors of suicide out of hand and the authorities said her body could not be removed from the country without permission. Naturally, press speculation was rampant with gossip and rumor.

Finally, on Monday, the coroner reported that Christina Onassis had died of acute pulmonary edema — just as her mother had 14 years before — and had not had sexual intercourse during the previous 24 hours.

In a dark wooden casket with a red rose in her hand, Christina was laid out in the Orthodox church, where Thierry came to sit alone with her for an hour. She was the woman he had known for almost half her life who had loved him, enriched him and been too foolish, too romantic and too loving for her own good. She actually probably died of her own broken heart. It happens to many of the children in the blood-money wars. What kind of life would Christina Onassis have had if it weren't for the money?

On November 23rd, her remains were returned to Greece for a funeral in the Fotini Cathedral, which was mobbed by 1,000 reporters and photographers who cared only about her money and notoriety. Later, Christina was laid to rest in a simple coffin made from the wood grown on Skorpios in a hillside grave beside her father and her brother.

At age four, Athina Onassis became the richest heiress in the world. Either a great blessing or a great curse.

Eighteen

The Lives and Times
of The Vanderbilts

His family would become the richest in the United States, but Jan Aertsen Van Der Bilt didn't know that when he arrived in New Jersey before the American Revolution as an indentured servant.

It really began when Jan Aertsen's great-great-great-grandson, Cornelius Vanderbilt, dropped out of school and began working on his father's small boat at the age of 11. The family made a living ferrying passengers and, more important, fresh vegetables to busy Manhattan from rural Staten Island soon after the Thirteen Colonies became the United States of America.

In a few years, Cornelius asked his father to lend him the money for his own boat, but the old man refused. He continued to ask and finally his father said if Cornelius would clear three acres of the land the father owned of stones in three days, he would lend Cornelius the money. Promising friends he would give them a free boat ride to Manhattan if they helped, Cornelius cleared the land, got the money, and his boat.

Then in classic Cornelius style, he loaded the boat with his friends and set sail for Manhattan. Halfway across the river, Cornelius informed his guests the trip to Manhattan was free, but, if they wanted to return, it would cost them.

So, Cornelius was launched into his own transportation business where he adopted the strategy of cutting rates to the bone to drive out the competition. This brought the law down on him, but he successfully eluded the police, the courts, and jail until he became so rich and powerful that the authorities decided he was a respectable citizen beyond their concern.

One of his most imaginative ventures was triggered by the California Gold Rush in 1849. While others were carrying passengers from the East Coast around the Cape Horn or by ship-and-wagon across Panama, Vanderbilt figured out another way.

Vanderbilt took his passengers across Nicaragua on badly patched-up ships with insufficient food or lifeboats. His way was a week shorter than the Panama route and cost $50 instead of $500. He handled 2,000 gold hungry Forty-Niners a month.

In time, he turned the operation over to two partners who immediately double-crossed him. They hired a freebooter by the name of Walker who ousted the Nicaraguan government with a platoon of 50 renegades, seized Vanderbilt's ships, and took over the business.

This prompted the most famous letter that Cornelius Vanderbilt ever wrote because it distilled the man into his essence and forecast the tone of life for his heirs.

He wrote, "Gentlemen, You have undertaken to

cheat me. I will not sue you because the law takes too long. I will ruin you." And, a few months later, he did.

Commodore, as he liked to be called, Vanderbilt lived long and ended up the richest man in America, but his family was terrified of him because he treated them as badly as his worse adversaries. All he really cared about was money and power, which was his lifelong passion. Not that he spent a lot of it on himself because, most of the time, he worked out of a bare little office with only a small table and a chair, with cigars and whist his only indulgences.

When his wife died, he became painfully lonely and turned to spiritualism and a vigorous new sex life focusing for a while on the notorious Victoria Woodhull. She practiced occultism; openly advocated free love, feminism, and socialism; and became a stockbroker, using Vanderbilt's money. She also became the first woman candidate for President of the United States with the great black leader, Booker T. Washington, as her vice-president.

Following his sojourn with Ms. Woodhull, the Commodore stunned his family and outraged society by marrying the granddaughter of his aunt, a woman notable for three things: she was 50 years younger than Cornelius, she had the odd first name of Frank, and she reformed the old reprobate. She drove the spiritualists away, curbed his foul language and coarse behavior, got him to found Vanderbilt University.

At the end, of course, he reverted to himself. When the 83-year-old man lay dying in his bedroom at #10 Washington Place in May of 1876 attended by various doctors and his 37-year-old wife, a mob of reporters gathered downstairs. Suddenly they were shaken by a roar from the old man. First, came a string of obscenities and then the Commodore's announcement: "I am not dying!" followed by his threat to kill the lying bastards.

His oldest son, William, was the only child allowed to enter the Commodore's bedroom during those final days. When told his son Cornelius II was waiting downstairs to visit him, the old man bristled, "He has no business here. I don't want to see him. Go down and tell him not to come in here again while I am living or after I am dead."

It was the tenor of the old man's relationship with almost everyone including his children and it distorted their lives. One historian of the Vanderbilts, Clarice Stasz, characterized the Commodore as being "as brutal toward his wife and children as he was toward his competitors." He despised his children.

When he died, Commodore Cornelius Vanderbilt was the richest man in the United States, which was not bad for an uneducated man who was almost illiterate. The acerbic patriarch left most of his money to his son William Henry because he was the only one of the many Vanderbilt children who had remained patiently docile and respectful throughout Cornelius's life in spite of constantly being cursed and insulted by the old man.

The many children his wife, Sophia, had borne the Commodore were largely a disappointment to him. The first three Cornelius essentially dismissed out of hand because they were girls and no girls could carry on his name. Then came William, who ended up with the family fortune, but infuriated his father with his submissive behavior. Following William came another four damn daughters!

On the ninth try, a second son finally emerged and was christened Cornelius II. However, while William was a frustration for his father, Cornelius II was a mortification because he turned out to be epileptic, which was regarded as unsuitable for a Vanderbilt!

Initially, the oldest son, William Henry, had been summarily rejected by the Commodore as his successor. He was not an adventurer and was afraid of taking risks. Begrudgingly, the Commodore lent William Henry some money to buy a farm and then totally ignored him for the next 20 years. William Henry grew to become a middle-aged man denied the love and support that his father never gave him. Yet, when the old man was near death, he turned the family fortune over to William Henry.

Naturally, the other children, led by son Cornelius Jeremiah Vanderbilt, immediately sued and tried to break the will. Their claim was that William Henry had filled the old man's mind with lies about his other children and thus manipulated the Commodore into leaving his money in the hands of William Henry. Part of William Henry's efforts to discredit his brothers and sisters in the eyes of their father included having his brother, Cornelius Jeremiah, arrested in an attempt to get him committed to an insane asylum.

The prize was $70 million, which was *real* money in 1877, and the trial produced a panorama of children, experts, detectives, prostitutes, racketeers, mediums, and psychics. This array of witnesses was on hand to prove that Cornelius Jeremiah was deeply in debt to assorted gamblers; was a regular customer at brothels and psychics; and generally unsuited to be a rich man although those were all things that rich men did.

It was later proven that much of this testimony was bought and paid for perjury by William Henry, but it was too late. Even the revelation that the Commodore's marriage to Frank was bigamous since she had never divorced her first husband didn't change the judge's ruling in favor of William Henry.

They all lost and William Henry won. William Henry won using the same tactics his father used all his life proving that some of the key genes had been passed on to the next generation. The Commodore was actually wise in his bequest because the 50-year-old William Henry was the only one of the kids who was financially competent. William Henry proved that by more than doubling the family fortune to $200 million before he died eight years later while sitting in front of the fireplace talking business with a colleague.

The impact of the Vanderbilt fortune and the battle among the children for the money was a venomous inheritance that distorted normal human relationships and affections for generations to come pitting children, parents, spouses, lovers, and friends all against one another in an ever-changing motif of hatred, greed, and revenge.

Most of the dissident children ran through their money and ended up strapped. Cornelius Jeremiah, who fought his brother William Henry over the family fortune, ended up a suicide by shooting himself while in the vestibule of the Glenham Hotel on April 2, 1882—three years after the end of the Great Family Feud.

During the years following the Commodore's death, the Vanderbilt women tried desperately to bankrupt the family with their wanton spending on clothes, parties, and the building of mansions in the northern suburbs of Manhattan along what is now Fifth Avenue and 52nd Street—in those days, 39th Street was the upper limit of fashionable addresses on Fifth Avenue. Curiously, none of the great, luxurious Vanderbilt mansions—some of which covered an entire block and required over 100 servants to function—survive to this day.

In fact, the only significant building erected by a Vanderbilt in Manhattan that remains today was built by the Commodore and it is certainly significant. It's Grand Central Station.

The goal of the Vanderbilt women was to be accepted by New York's elite society and, specifically, the queen of that society, Mrs. John Jacob Astor. In time it happened, but at enormous cost.

Typical of the Vanderbilts' social-climbing women was Alva, the wife of William Henry's second son, William Kismet. The daughter of a rich Southern cotton family that had been ruined by the Civil War, Alva could have been the real life model for Scarlett O'Hara—beautiful, unpredictable, and spunky. The family moved to New York and the daughters of the family set out to catch "suitable husbands." Alva found that William Kismet Vanderbilt, "Willie K.," fit the bill, married him and launched her spending spree.

One of her main strategies was to barter her daughter for social respectability since the Vanderbilts were regarded as trashy, new rich by the established elite who had also been trashy, new rich, but a generation earlier.

So, Alva forced her daughter, Consuelo, to break her engagement to Winthrop Rutherford, whom Consuelo loved with an abiding passion. Alva didn't care. Her only goal in life was to surpass Mrs. Astor as the queen of New York society at whatever cost to the family fortune or feelings and Consuelo was a bargaining chip. To that end, she would have had Consuelo's palpitating heart ripped from her chest on an Aztec sacrificial altar if necessary. It is an apt analogy since that is what Alva did to Consuelo emotionally in her lust for a royal title in the family.

Alva literally kept her daughter a prisoner in the family mansions; intercepted all her mail and destroyed any communication from Winthrop; isolated Consuelo from supportive friends; and ordered Consuelo to marry Alva's choice for a husband, the impoverished Charles Richard John Spencer-Churchill, the ninth duke of Marlborough.

The ceremony was performed on November 6, 1895 in St. Thomas Episcopal Church. A nuptial contract was signed giving the duke $2.5 million in railroad stock with a guaranteed 4 percent yield a year for life. The bride was very late appearing for the marriage ceremony, but finally showed and reluctantly became the ninth duchess of Marlborough, princess of the Holy Roman Empire and princess of Mindelheim. Try to top that, Mrs. Astor!

As the couple left the church, the duke, whom everyone suddenly noticed was a head shorter than his new bride, sourly informed Consuelo of several realities of their new life together: l) He did not love her and had given up a woman he *did* love only to save the family estate with Vanderbilt money; 2) Consuelo would be required to immediately memorize the family trees and social status of 200 related royal families; 3) he intended to immediately take up with a mistress; and 4) they were never again to set foot in America, a country whose people he despised.

Aside from that, it was a lovely honeymoon.

Before long, both became sexually involved with a variety of partners in the British upper-crust social set and ultimately they separated. In many ways, her life in England would mirror that of her mother's in America including later involvement in the women's suffrage movement. She also got a divorce after 12 years of separation from the ninth duke and, more important, she convinced the Vatican to grant an annulment so she could marry her French Catholic lover, Jacques. She convinced the Church that she had been forced into marriage by a mother who held her prisoner, faked a heart attack, and threatened to murder the man she really loved and to whom she had been secretly engaged at the time. It was a curious ritual since the wedding ceremony had been conducted in a Protestant church, but that's how it happened anyhow.

Part of Alva's problem in getting accepted into the elite of New York society was her unconventional behavior. Marrying off Consuela for her own money in exchange for a royal title wasn't too bad and, in fact, became quite fashionable in time. However, she engaged in other scandalous behavior. For example, in an era when it *just wasn't done* she not only got a divorce from Willie, but did so blatantly, revealing the details of her husband's infidelities, which weren't as bad as those of John Jacob Astor who regularly held orgies. However, Mrs. As-

tor and her ladies who lunched had the good taste
not to publicly admit her husband's infidelities.

No matter to Alva who didn't believe women
should live in matrimonial bondage to be publicly
humiliated and privately threatened by the epidemic
of the day, syphilis.

Her own lawyer fought against her and tried to
talk her out of the divorce without success. Afterward, when Alva entered a room full of New York
society matrons, a hush fell on the women who
scooped up their skirts and left the room. Con-
versely, the men remained and had a wonderful
time chatting with this liberated woman to whom
they were all glad they weren't married. Almost
none of her friends spoke to her for months.

In later years, Alva became even more unconventional and rescued the women's suffrage movement,
which was on the verge of extinction until she
came to its deliverance with her enthusiasm and
money. By the time of World War I, Alva had
made the drive for the women's vote a fashionable
crusade. Eleven years later, in 1920, women got the
vote, over half a century after black, male ex-slaves
did. It can be fairly said that Alva Vanderbilt was
largely responsible for American women getting the
right to vote when they did.

The Vanderbilt fortune was so huge that, in
1885, when William Henry died, the stock markets
of the world closed down for several days until his
will was read.

The Commodore gene seemed to falter and the
running of the Vanderbilt family fortune quietly
passed to professional managers while the heirs
frittered away their time in the pursuits of the idle
rich. With the exception of Alva, none of the Van-

derbilts seemed to aspire to great public service as did the Rockefellers or promote science and the arts as did the Guggenheims. And, after William Henry, none of them seemed to have a clue about how money was made. They just became contented and extravagant consumers.

The ultimate example came from William Henry's grandson, Reginald "Reggie" Vanderbilt, born in 1880. A rotund man with a mustache, he later became the inspiration for comedian Jackie Gleason's caricature, Reggie Van Gleason III. He had been a colossal disappointment to his mother, Alice, all his life and she did nothing to keep that a secret.

He never worked a day in his life, arrogantly flaunted decency and the law and did whatever he damn pleased including being a drunken public menace. For example, he killed two people and maimed a small boy with his reckless driving, but never was taken into custody and never paid a penny in fines or spent a day in jail. The only punishment he ever had for his behavior was when a Newport, Rhode Island, man trashed him severely for flirting with the man's wife. When that didn't make the point, the man shot him.

One of Reggie's relatives, Arthur Vanderbilt II, described Reggie as a "self-indulgent, lazy, lackadaisical man who had absolutely no sense of responsibility or purpose other than to keep himself from being bored."

One day in 1912, while touring Europe with his wife of nine years and his eight-year-old daughter, he got bored with them and with marriage and parenting and returned to America. He left without explanation, without leaving a note, and without

leaving them any money. They were divorced in
1922. When his longtime mistress learned that Reggie wasn't planning on marrying her, she tried to
commit suicide with opium and Veronal pills.

For Reggie, life was an endless round of drinking, horse racing, drinking, women, drinking, gambling and, of course, drinking. Brandy milk
punches were his greatest weakness.

The irony of history is that, when Reggie's
brother, Alfred, went down with the *Lusitania* on
May 7, 1915, Reggie became the head of the Vanderbilt family. It was unexpected and, also, symbolic of how far the family had fallen in the
generation since the death of William Henry. Reggie was a Vanderbilt with nothing more than a
modest income of $775,000 a year for living ex-
penses. The rest of his $13.5 million inheritance
was gone—spent on women, gambling, brandy milk
punches, and assorted excesses.

It was snowing outside the Café des Beaux Arts
in New York one night in January 1922, but things
were about to heat up inside. Bachelor Reggie met
Gloria Morgan—a drop-dead gorgeous 17-year-old
identical twin—at a party in the café and instantly
Reggie's heart was aflame with passion. Gloria and
her twin sister, Thelma, the daughters of a minor
American diplomat, had become the rage of New
York's fun-loving speakeasy-and-café society. Four
days later he proposed and four seconds later she
accepted. She was a year younger than Reggie's
daughter.

He confessed that, if they married, she would be
a Vanderbilt woman without money and she said it
didn't matter. She loved him and wanted to marry
him. Besides, partying was the only really impor-

tant thing and that was something both of them excelled at doing.

After getting a chilly reception from the matriarch of the family, Alice Claypool Vanderbilt, because Mrs. Vanderbilt thought Gloria was a woman with a questionable past, Gloria took a bold step. She called upon Mrs. Vanderbilt one day at home without advance warning or an invitation and asked the name of her doctor. A few days later the dowager received a letter from her doctor assuring her that Gloria was a virgin—a fact that was duly reported in the newspapers. From their earliest years the Morgan twins figured out that their being virgins was important to men—particularly rich men—and they were going to bring that great gift to the marriage bed. Unfortunately, neither of them brought it to the marriage bed of the right men.

In any case, Gloria's ploy worked and melted away the apprehensions of Reggie's mother. Soon, Gloria received a formal invitation to come visiting again. This time, the invitation announced the purpose was for her to meet her future relatives.

On March 6, 1923, Gloria Morgan, suffering from a 104-degree fever, a severe case of walking diphtheria and barely able to walk, insisted on going through with the ceremony. She married Reginald Vanderbilt and was immediately confined to her bed and couldn't walk for three months.

However, walking was not the most important function to be achieved at that point and 11 months after the wedding on February 24, 1924, she delivered a child through a difficult cesarean while also suffering from phlebitis.

Almost immediately, Reggie took big Gloria off

to Europe leaving the newborn little Gloria with Grandmother Morgan and a new nurse hired for the occasion, Emma Keislich. Mother and kid would not see each other for the next six months, but little Gloria slept every night for the next eight or more years with nurse Keislich or Dodo as little Gloria called her.

The child was supposed to be Reginald Vanderbilt, Jr. Instead it was little Gloria Vanderbilt. Reggie was disappointed not knowing that this Gloria Vanderbilt would turn out to be the only special Vanderbilt in America since World War I.

Reggie and Gloria continued to live high with the partying and heavy drinking beginning about four in the afternoon and going on all night until dawn, with big Gloria loving every fun-filled minute until one day she found Reggie bleeding from the mouth.

She insisted a doctor check him out and was told he had an advanced case of sclerosis of the liver and must stop drinking entirely if he was to live. Gloria pressed a nonalcohol regimen on Reggie, which obviously didn't take since he continued to get drunk on a regular basis.

One evening when they were invited to dinner at the Breakers estate of Alice Vanderbilt, he showed up late and looped. A few days later Gloria took the train to New York City and when she called home, a strange voice answered identifying herself as Mr. Vanderbilt's nurse and refusing to explain why she was there.

Panicked, Gloria took the midnight train back to their Sandy Point Farm home and, when she rushed into the house, found her frail mother-in-law there. The butler announced that Mr. Vanderbilt had died two minutes before and 80-year-old Alice tried in vain to keep Gloria from going into the bedroom to see her dead husband.

It was a shocking sight. The walls of the room were splattered with Reggie's blood from the sudden rupture of the vessels in his throat as he died of a stroke. It was as if a hand grenade had exploded inside his neck. He was 43.

Overnight Gloria Vanderbilt was the penniless widow with a small child to care for in what had once been the richest family in America. She was 20 years old and unable to sign any of the necessary legal papers concerning her husband's estate by herself. This was only one of the odd twists about her situation. Another was that her small child would actually begin supporting her. The ways of money were taking their bizarre twists again.

Reggie left nothing to big Gloria, but a mountain of unpaid bills. Everything was sold to satisfy creditors, the homes in Sandy Point and Newport, furniture, clothing—everything down to little Gloria's pram, which brought $1.50.

Under the terms of Reggie's will there was no money left to his wife, but little Gloria was the beneficiary of a $4.3 million trust fund set up by her grandfather, Cornelius, which the creditors couldn't touch and which she would get control of when she turned 21. The trustee of the trust fund was Surrogate Judge James Aloysius Foley who agreed that the older Gloria should be given $4,000 a month for the support of the younger Gloria. That amount was twice the average *yearly* income of Americans at the time.

With this, the older Gloria immediately revived

her life of overindulgence going to Europe a dozen times a year and getting caught up in the swirl of the international high society party circuit that centered around the Prince of Wales, the heir to the British throne. Her twin sister, Thelma, was in the midst of this social maelstrom having, at age 21, divorced her first husband and remarried the Duke of Furness.

Big Gloria was soon involved with His Serene Highness, Prince Gottfried Hohenlohe-Langenburg, an impoverished Bavarian royal who would some day inherit a fortune, in an affair that would ultimately doom her to more pain than she could ever imagine.

He proposed and she accepted, but they decided to wait because Surrogate Foley would have cut the $4,000 allowance if she married a prince and, in fact, both she and the prince were living off the money that was supposed to be the support of little Gloria.

Meanwhile, little Gloria was shunted aside and left mostly in the care of her nurse, Dodo, and big Gloria's mother, Laura Morgan, known as "Grandmother Morgan." These two fawned over little Gloria and were critical of big Gloria's lifestyle including casual affairs with both men and women, all-night drunks and dusk-to-dawn orgies.

Soon, there were battles over big Gloria's partying, irresponsible companions, and her general neglect of little Gloria. Both Grandmother Morgan and Nurse Keislich began to believe Prince Gottfried was plotting to murder the child so he could marry the older Gloria and have that $4,000 a month. This wasn't rational, but that's what Nurse Keislich and Grandmother Morgan thought.

Horrifyingly, they filled the child's mind with fears of being kidnapped and abandoned in a dark Bavarian forest and left for wild animals to devour. It didn't take long for the child to be terrified of the prince and unable to sleep because of hellish nightmares. In time, little Gloria became terrified of being alone with her own mother and would throw tantrums and threaten to jump out of windows to get away from her.

In time, the acrimony grew immense with Nurse Keislich and Grandmother Morgan on one side and big Gloria and Prince Gottfried on the other side. In the middle was the impressionable and bewildered little Gloria. Ultimately, Grandmother got Surrogate Foley to make big Gloria bring the child back to America where Grandmother had forged an alliance with a rich branch of the family, Gertrude Vanderbilt Whitney, who was the late Reggie's aunt.

Aunt Ger, as she was called, was a fascinating, artistic woman who was an accomplished sculptress and whose lasting legacy was the Whitney Museum of American Art. She was an acknowledged bisexual who dallied in numerous heterosexual and lesbian affairs—particularly with an architect's daughter, Esther Hunt, and a stockbroker friend of her husband, William Stackpole.

She spent much time in the artistic community of Greenwich Village where she posed nude, seduced and was seduced, and ultimately wrote a novel about her secret erotic life entitled, *White Voices*. She would become a major player in the money-driven manipulation of the Vanderbilts and the two Glorias.

In 1934, big Gloria belatedly went to court to

have herself declared the guardian of young Gloria's trust property. It was a routine and overdue procedure that suddenly took on an astounding twist. The petition was challenged by big Gloria's own mother.

Thus began one of the most savage custody cases in American history with big Gloria's mother and aunt on one side battling against big Gloria herself for the custody of little Gloria. The grounds were that big Gloria was an unfit mother who rarely tended to little Gloria and was immersed in a Bohemian lifestyle of free love, endless orgies, and constant drunkenness.

One interesting sidebar of this incredible custody battle was that big Gloria's sister, Thelma, came over from Europe to be beside her sister during this moment of trial. In keeping with the sisters' lifestyles, Thelma was having an affair with the Prince of Wales whom she complained was an inadequate lover because of his constant premature ejaculations. When she left to be with big Gloria, Thelma asked her best friend to take care of the prince and to see that he didn't get into any mischief. The best friend was a divorcée from Baltimore by the name of Wallis Simpson for whom the Prince would later give up the throne of Great Britain and marry.

After a long and vicious battle, the courts awarded custody of little Gloria to Aunt Gertrude Vanderbilt Whitney with big Gloria getting her on weekends and in July. In that gloriously Kafka like world of our judicial system, big Gloria was an unfit mother except on weekends and in July. One other provision of the court was that Nurse Dodo had to be fired and never see the child again because she was too much of an influence on little Gloria.

So, big Gloria lost her daughter and her source of income. Grandmother Morgan lost her daughter and her granddaughter. Little Gloria lost Dodo, the most trusted and precious adult in her life while gaining little else because Aunt Whitney was a rich maternal type—in fact the richest woman in America—who turned the raising of children over to servants, tutors, and assorted others. She rarely saw little Gloria and the child meant so little to her that, when Aunt Ger died leaving a $78 million fortune, all little Gloria got was a modest bracelet.

Little Gloria was another victim of enormous money without ending up with much of it for herself. That would have to wait until little Gloria reached age 21. That seems to have been the fate of most of the Vanderbilts.

In fact, when 120 of the Vanderbilts showed up at Vanderbilt University in 1973 for the family's first reunion ever, there wasn't a millionaire among them. It is a curious state of affairs for the family that was acknowledged to be the richest in the country at the turn of this century.

After the custody struggle over little Gloria was ended, she was nationally famous, fawned over, and guarded around the clock by six servants because the Lindbergh baby kidnapping and murder struck fear in the hearts of every wealthy family around. Little Gloria herself had instilled in her a bone-chilling fear of her own mother, death, and kidnapping. Even so, as time went on Gloria developed into a dazzling young woman who would socialize in the same party circuit as her mother did.

Meanwhile, her mother fell on hard times and

survived only through the help her twin sister,
Thelma, gave her. When Thelma's ex-husband, the
Duke of Furness died, Thelma successfully sued to
get $6 million for the son she had borne by the
Duke. Then, just as her sister had done with little
Gloria's money, she and big Gloria lived off her
son's inheritance.

Big Gloria moved to a rented home on North
Maple Drive in Beverly Hills, California, and little
Gloria went there for the prescribed July with her
mother and found herself thrust into the fast lane
of the Hollywood glamour scene.

Soon she was appearing at filmland parties in
designer dresses, spike heels, and net stockings always leaving to go home with older men. The thing
that stunned Gloria in retrospect is that no one—
particularly, not her mother—cared that she had
left the party or what happened to her afterward.
Once more her mother wasn't there and, yet, little
Gloria was intoxicated by the excitement and allure
of the party life. So much so that she got her
mother to call Aunt Ger and get permission to stay
the whole summer. Frankly, Aunt Ger was relieved
because she had her own parties to attend.

Finally, one of the oddest and most sexually
predatory moguls in Hollywood moved in and
swept her up in his mysterious world of limos, secret trysts, yachts, private planes, and serious
money. His name was Howard Hughes and she became his love toy.

Gloria was 17.

Little Gloria was reliving the life of her mother
at the same age. Cast adrift by the emotional
abandonment of both her mother and her aunt,
Gloria clung to Hughes trying to define herself in

terms of her man. It didn't work. Her man wasn't there when she needed him and her only function was to be there when he needed her. Even so, she was convinced that Hughes was going to marry her, but he had a confidential telephone conversation with Aunt Ger and that put an end to it. There was a young Connecticut man, Geoff Jones, longing to marry little Gloria, but he was a boy to a girl who was entranced by the men she had dated in Hollywood. Aunt Ger was horrified at what little Gloria did next.

Hurt and disappointed that Hughes wouldn't marry her, Gloria rushed into a stupid quick marriage to a small-time Hollywood type named Pasquale "Pat" De Cicco, who worked for Howard Hughes and played gin rummy with his cronies Zeppo Marx and Joe Schenck constantly, including on his and Gloria's wedding night. They were married in Santa Barbara with her friend Carol Marcus as a bridesmaid and Errol Flynn as an usher and thousands of spectators including her beaming mother and Dodo who had reappeared in little Gloria's life. Almost immediately, he began berating her with insults and knocking her around.

It was an unhappy marriage from the start and she began desperately looking around for some way to escape from her abusive husband. There was little help from her mother or aunt.

On a visit to New York, Pat beat her up so badly that she was unconscious. She begged for help from Aunt Ger who turned her down because she was ill and her brother Neily was dying. Aunt Ger would die a few months later on April 18, 1942. She left little Gloria a Cartier pearl and dia-

mond bracelet and enraged Dodo by leaving her
nothing.

Escaping for a time to New York, she went to a
dinner party on December 13, 1944, given by her
friend Carol Marcus who had married writer William Saroyan. There she met the legendary Leopold
Stokowski whom she described as a man, "so tall,
a tree rooted in beauty, stretching up into the sky
above me with white clouds in a halo around his
head."

The chemistry was instant and overwhelmed
them both. The two fell passionately in love and
she became dreamily poetic at the thought of him,
"He touches my face, my eyes and I am no longer
blind, my flesh is clay, his hands on my breasts
and my nipples rise to meet his lips as he calls my
name." She had met the great love of her life and
she only prayed that she could be worthy of him.
Nothing else mattered.

She learned that her current husband had become seriously ill, but it didn't matter. A higher
duty called her. She had to be free of Pasquale to
worship at the shrine of her sacred love.

She fretted when her lawyers said she would have
to wait six Reno weeks to divorce Pat so she could
legally spend her nights in the arms of Leopold,
but she did. Along the way Leopold failed to men-
tion he had one career in shambles, two ex-wives
and three daughters. He was as attracted by the
Vanderbilt name, which promised renewed recogni-
tion and success, as he was by the beautiful young
woman who shared his love bed.

To Gloria, it didn't matter what she didn't know
about him. What mattered was what she did know,
namely, that he was a musical genius on the po-

dium and a sensual genius in bed as one of the most fervent and proficient lovers she had ever known.

About that time, she came into her inheritance, so she sent De Cicco $200,000 and divorced him. The day after her divorce in 1945, she married the famed conductor. She was 21 and he was 63.

Stokowski was a machiavellian egomaniac who took advantage of little Gloria's insecurities and guilelessness by encouraging her growth as an artist, only as long as he could keep her isolated. Genius he may have been, but he was also a jealous old man fearful that Gloria might leave him for a younger man. In the end, she didn't leave to go to a younger man. She left to get away from an old man.

Big Gloria and little Gloria were totally estranged during most of the late '40s and the '50s while little Gloria was trying to be the submissive child-wife to her world-esteemed husband. She had two sons and began drifting back into the emotional hell of nightmares and uncontrollable fears that had robbed her of her childhood with fears of kidnapping and murder. She began to stutter badly. In spite of it all, she began what was a modestly successful career acting on the stage to which Stokowski objected since he felt there was only room for one star in the family.

Finally, on New Year's Eve, 1954, after ten years of marriage, she left Stokowski who had previously warned, "If Gloria leaves me there will be a custody fight for our boys that will make the court battle her mother and aunt waged look like a picnic."

Threat was overcome by reality and she got a divorce and custody of the boys in 1956, the same year her Grandmother Morgan died, big Gloria went completely blind, and little Gloria had a brief affair with Frank Sinatra and, then, married director Sidney Lumet to whom she was attracted by their mutual love of the theater. It was a busy year.

In 1958, little Gloria's mother and aunt wrote a book, *Double Exposure,* about their amazing lives and foreclosed any early reconciliation with little Gloria. It would have been enough for big Gloria to express her frustration and anger at losing the custody battle, but instead she insisted on ridiculing her daughter and describing how much she hated the times she came visiting. It would have angered even the most serene and stoic of daughters.

The next year came a painful replay of the 1934 custody trial as Stokowski sued to gain custody of their two sons whom he had lost in 1956. It was the 1934 trial all over again with the same issues, but different actors. Stokowski charged he should have sole custody of their two sons on the grounds that little Gloria was an unfit mother. He claimed that she partied too much and neglected their sons.

Pained by the memories this evoked, she nevertheless had the strength to countercharge that Leopold was spending much of his time in the company of Natasha and Feodora, two sexually loose camp followers of the great man who also conducted a lesbian relationship with each other. Again, Stokowski lost.

Meanwhile, little Gloria acted professionally, wrote poetry, appeared in TV dramas and began painting and designing clothing. In August 1963 she divorced Lumet who subsequently married

Lena Horne's daughter, Gail Jones, while little Gloria went on to have an affair with Nelson Rockefeller, which didn't last long, but which could have had dizzying social implications had it matured.

On Christmas eve, 1963, little Gloria married Southern writer Wyatt Emory Cooper from a family of Mississippi eccentrics and whom one of her friends told her was going to make her a very happy woman. He did. He was handsome, thoughtful, devoted to family, well educated, and a modern man who wanted his woman to be liberated and free to be who and whatever she wanted to be. Under his influence her attitude toward her mother softened a little just in time for her mother's death of cancer at age 60 in the same year little Gloria and Cooper married.

After meeting big Gloria and Thelma, Cooper told little Gloria that the twin sisters who were her mother and aunt never grasped what their lives were all about and they just stumbled from party and affair to party and affair. The money made it possible for them to have passed through life as brilliant comets whose passage was impressive and memories quickly forgotten.

Throughout her grown-up life, which seemed to begin at age 15 or so, little Gloria has been close friends with Oona O'Neil, daughter of the playwright, and Carol Marcus. Oona married Charlie Chaplin; Carol married William Saroyan and, later, Walter Matthau; and, little Gloria married Stokowski. All had lacked strong, dependable fathers and pop psychology would say that they spent their lives searching for one. In Gloria's case she had been robbed of a father by the Vanderbilt fortune, which allowed Reggie to destroy himself.

Under Cooper's encouragement, little Gloria began to expand her design work particularly in collages and other decorative expressions. Soon, the press was noticing her exquisite fashion taste and in 1969 Hallmark Cards commissioned her to produce a wide variety of paper materials for them.

By 1977 she had matured remarkably as a designer and as an astute businesswoman and she made a deal with Murjani International to license her name on a line of clothing beginning with Gloria Vanderbilt blouses followed by the incredibly successful jeans. In three years the sales of Gloria Vanderbilt jeans went from zero to a ballistic $300 million.

In 1980, one of many books about the Vanderbilts, this time about little Gloria, came out. It was titled, *Little Gloria . . . Happy At Last*. Gloria refused the author, Barbara Goldsmith, an interview saying she was saving her material for her own book. After *Little Gloria . . . Happy At Last* appeared and became a best-seller, Gloria decided to publish her autobiographical diaries, *Once Upon A Time* and *Black Knight, White Knight*.

In the years since then, little Gloria has carved out a career as a designer and become the constant companion of Bobby Short, the black society pianist who has entertained at the New York Carlyle for as long as anyone can remember.

Symbolic of the decline of the Vanderbilt family's power and money, little Gloria was rejected by a New York coop board as being unsuitable to live in an East Side Manhattan building.

But the worst tragedy to befall Little Gloria was with Carter Cooper, one of her four sons—two by

Stokowski and two by Cooper. A Princeton under-graduate and aspiring writer, he was subject to de-pressions and disturbed about breaking up with his girlfriend. On July 22, 1988, he climbed out on the balcony ledge of his mother's 14th-floor apartment. Terrified, Gloria tried to talked him back onto the terrace, begging him to come inside. She had her hand outstretched to him and he had his out-stretched to her when he slipped and plunged to his death with his mother watching in disbelieving horror.

Another troubling episode came to an end in a New York court in the autumn of 1993. In 1978, Gloria took the advice of her psychiatrist, a man with the unusual name of Dr. Christ L. Zois, and got a new lawyer who was a close friend of Dr. Zois's. Gloria needed someone to give her legal ad-vice and manage her business affairs because she was too busy reliving the life her mother had lived traveling to Europe constantly, giving and attending parties and, most of all, shopping. She rivaled Jackie Kennedy Onassis as a world-class shopper. Like Jackie, she can move through a chic boutique like Sherman moved through Georgia and drop thousands of dollars in minutes.

Unbeknownst to Gloria, her new lawyer, Thomas A. Andrews and her psychiatrist, Dr. Christ L. Zois formed a secret partnership, A to Z Associ-ates, to exploit and market the Gloria Vanderbilt name and designs.

According to Andrews and Zois, "The two of us took an alcoholic, pill-addicted, insolvent failure and turned her into the queen of jeans and made her rich." In the process, A and Z were looting Gloria's accounts of money that they controlled on her behalf and to which they weren't entitled.

One day in 1986, a woman friend of Gloria's spread out all the canceled checks and statements on the kitchen floor and told Gloria she was being cheated. Designer Bill Blass recommended a new accountant and the accountant confirmed it and Gloria got a new attorney, Jerome Walsh.

Foolishly, A to Z sued Gloria. She countersued and Walsh also filed a complaint against Andrews with the bar association.

The judge ruled in the fall of 1993 that the two men had stolen money from Gloria and preyed on her wealth and emotional vulnerability. It didn't make any difference to lawyer Andrews who had been disbarred in December of 1992 and died in January of 1993. The court awarded Gloria $1.5 million.

Gloria was raised in one of the richest families in America. In her first years, others preyed on her wealth and emotional vulnerability because she was a Vanderbilt. Now, other people are still doing the same thing because she is a Vanderbilt even though she is 70.

Nineteen

Crosby Heirs Gamble
On Gambling

Day after day, throughout the fall of 1985, James Morris Crosby could feel himself weakening, his lungs disintegrating, leaving him a virtual prisoner in his emphysema-ridden frame.

By early winter, the once-robust chairman of Resorts International was spending much of his time in an Amigo cart, sucking bottled oxygen, puttering feebly around his beachfront suite on the ninth floor of the grand old Haddon Hall Hotel on the boardwalk, which Jim had bought in 1976 and transformed into Atlantic City's first casino.

Consumed as always by schemes, deals, and projects — building the $525 million Taj Mahal Hotel, buying a blimp for Resorts, dreaming of expanding into Europe — Jim Crosby conferred here with his company's officers, but he was growing increasingly frustrated by his alarming decline.

So he entered the New York University Medical

Center for radical lung surgery and in early April accepted the fifty-fifty odds the doctors had given him, because the alternative — long, agonizing decay — was too awful to contemplate.

Jim Crosby was well aware of the dangers. Indeed, before his operation, the unmarried, childless chairman sat down with Resorts's attorney Charles Murphy, his closest confidant (and the brother of Crosby's brother-in-law Thomas Murphy, chairman of the board of Capital Cities/ ABC) and reviewed his last will and testament.

Crosby intended to keep control of his $800 million casino-hotel-transportation empire firmly within the hands of the close-knit Murphy/ Crosby family in the event of his death. At the same time, he wanted to enrich the devoted mistress who had suffered with him throughout his long decline: Baroness Marianne Brandstetter.

A man big on family values, Jim always did whatever he could to hold together the family clan that included his two brothers, John, a former plastic surgeon, and William, a Florida real estate broker, as well as his brother-in-law, Henry Murphy, a Trenton undertaker and Henry's cousin, Charlie Murphy, who had been general legal counsel for 25 years.

And, importantly, there was the German blond bombshell, Marianne Brandstetter who was the uncontested love of Jim's life. A woman who loved the rich life and who had always attached herself to rich men who enjoyed her plunging décolletage and flirting ways, Marianne was just a gold digger in the eyes of some of Crosby's family and friends.

Marianne had been married to Frank Brandstetter, who managed the chic Las Brisas beach resort in Acapulco when she met Crosby at Monte Carlo. Hearts fluttered and soon there was a divorce and she moved in with Jim in the Resorts Hotel in Atlantic City. Whatever family and friends thought, Jim loved her and trusted her. She was with him everywhere. On his arm as a jewel when out for pleasure and at business conferences as an extra set of eyes and ears.

As he faced the last big spin of the wheel, Crosby made Marianne "the primary beneficiary of his estate and key figure in the struggle over the future of his company."

When time came for the fateful operation, the entire family gathered at the hospital: Suzanne, Bill, Henry, Thomas, sister Elaine as Crosby gambled with the worst odds he had ever known—50-50. The surgeon was going to go in and clean out Crosby's lungs which were closing up from emphysema because they had to make room for air. Marianne was totally against the operation. She didn't like the odds. As it turned out the outcome was classic: Jim's operation lasted five hours and was a success except the patient died immediately afterward from a massive heart attack at age 58.

The funeral of this secretive visionary who loved to dream up big promotions, big deals, and big plans was appropriately big with 20 limos and a litany of attendees that ranged from the powerful to the disreputable and from the luminescent to the shady. They buried Jim at Spring Lake at the Jersey shore where his 90-year-old mother still lived.

Crosby had been a man of enthusiasm and energy who loved to wake up colleagues in the middle of the night with grandiose ideas. His friends included Bebe Rebozo and Richard Nixon to whom he was devoted to the end.

He loved reading nonfiction and knew a lot about volcanos, architecture, and aeronautics and reveled in the glamour of his life. A barrel-chested man with thick black hair and proud of his virility, Jim liked attentive, feminine women and was notorious for his string of girlfriends, but he didn't have the time or temperament for children.

Still, he liked family and would bring his girlfriends to holiday gatherings at his sister Elaine's house until Jim got too depressed by all the good family feelings that were there and that he didn't have in his regular life. He tried to capture those feelings once when he got engaged, but his girlfriend crushed his feelings when she broke it off because of his obsession with business.

Crosby bought Paradise Island in the Bahamas in the mid-1960s, which was when Rebozo introduced him to Nixon and Jim started a gaming operation there. The island had originally been used secretly as a World War II base for submarines and was called Hog Island. It was rechristened and reinvented as a gambler's utopia. The U.S. Senate would, years later, investigate the charge that money was skimmed from Paradise Island gaming tables and laundered through Rebozo's bank to illegally finance Nixon's 1972 campaign. It was never proven, but widely suspected because of Crosby's great support for Nixon.

Crosby was always very closemouthed and frequently operated on the edge of legality or in the shadowy zone where one can't be sure of exactly where the line is. His close associates included Robert Peloquin, described by some as a "tough, charismatic Korean War veteran," who was hired to run Resorts's security operation. Peloquin was previously involved with Intertel, an international investigation firm, for whom he chased Clifford Irving around the world for client Howard Hughes; spirited Anastasio Somoza out of the U.S.; and slipped a fugitive Shah of Iran into hiding at Crosby's private Paradise Island villa. Peloquin was fourth in command at Resorts after Charles Murphy, I.G. "Jack" Davis, and Crosby himself.

The funeral brought all kinds of family including Crosby's older brother, Francis Peter Crosby, known as the family black sheep who spent a good part of his life as a combination playboy and securities swindler. Francis had done time, been on the lam and, at the time of Crosby's death was living in a low-cost New Jersey housing tract nurturing himself on dreams of a comeback. The two brothers had been estranged for a long time because Crosby didn't like how Peter conducted himself and said he could have been a great success if he had used his brains for something honest.

After the funeral and burial, the mourners gathered at P.J. Ruggles's restaurant in Spring Lake for late lunch and Charles Murphy went from table to table passing out copies of Crosby's will. Peter was stunned to learn he got 40,000 shares of Resorts stock.

Other happy inheritors included seven of Crosby's former girlfriends who each got a small number of shares: Virginia Coates, Marcia Dunn, Georgianna Farr, Hildegarde Flagg, Michelle Gerbino, Helga Weiss, and Becky Houchen. Of course, Marianne hit the jackpot because the girlfriend who wins is the one who gets the most when her sugar daddy dies.

She got all of Crosby's personal effects, $700,000 for a house, and 57 percent of the rest of his estate in trust, which included 190,000 shares of Class B Resorts International stock and 24 percent of the voting power.

The Murphys didn't like this bequest.

In the New York Minute it took for the word to get out about the bequests, the Wall Street raiders began circling almost immediately to seize control of Resorts International and they saw Marianne as the key player.

The day which ended with copies of Crosby's will being passed out was the point at which the people involved began their relentless pursuit of self-interest.

First, there was the very unhappy family, the Murphys. The Murphys and the Crosbys were inseparable for 40 years. They always summered together in Spring Lake, New Jersey every year. The men fought together in World War II. They married each other, had family reunions together, had family fights together, had family vacations together, but it looked as if they weren't going to inherit together.

The Crosbys had six kids: John, Jr., Peter, Billy, Elaine, Jim, and Suzanne raised in Washington, D.C. Jim went to Lawrenceville School in the early '40s and met Henry Murphy, the judge's nephew, heir to the funeral home in Trenton. They went to war together and came back and Henry married Jim's sister, Elaine in 1950. A few years later, Suzanne married Henry's cousin, Thomas. Charlie Murphy, Thomas's brother, became Jim's inseparable colleague for 25 years and his legal adviser.

Jim had been the smart one of the family. He was a graduate of Georgetown University with a degree in economics and began working for the stock firm of Harris Upham. Then he took over a small company, Unexcelled Chemical, in the mid-1950s, became a New York playboy, and in 1958 he became chairman of Mary Carter Paint, his father's company.

Jim loved the excitement and glamour of the casino-hotel business and was attracted to Paradise Island's casino-hotel complex in the Bahamas. In 1966 he paid Huntington Hartford $14 million for the 12-square-mile island off Nassau. It was a lovely place and appealed to Jim, but it also became a morass of suspicious money transactions, bribes, and influence peddling along with rumors of Mafia involvement. Jim didn't like this and thought it was bad for business, so he brought in Peloquin to check out employees and clean up the place.

In 1976 Jim shifted focus to Atlantic City. His friends in Las Vegas thought he was nuts to look at the rundown, has-been town, but Jim bought the old Haddon Hall Hotel and the Chalfonte next door for $5.5 million. In addition, he got an option on a nearby 56 acres for $5.7 million because Crosby was convinced Philadelphia people would flock to Atlantic City gambling casinos the way they once did to Atlantic City when it was a beach resort.

He spent $35 million renovating and converting Haddon into the posh modern hotel-casino that opened May 26, 1978 with Steve Lawrence and Eydie Gorme. The place was instantly jammed and began grossing $438,504 a day with a very happy effect on Resorts International stock. Resorts stock was at about 31 when he opened his Atlantic City complex. At the time, Wall Street analyst Andrew Racz estimated the stock would move to 50, but Jim said 150.

They were both wrong, it went to 208 and crazy Jim Crosby recouped his entire Atlantic City investment in four months.

In 1979 Crosby sold Chalfonte to Harrah's-Holiday Inn for $26 million and that year Resorts's revenues hit $407 million—they had been $61 million two years before.

Excited, Crosby kept getting new ideas for new projects. He leased ten of his 56 acres to the Showboat casino for $6.3 a year or more than he had paid for the entire 56 acres. He kept going and going and going, obsessed with the mental challenge of business and constantly hashing and rehashing his ideas with everybody.

But there was a time bomb ticking. He had been a heavy smoker for years and contracted lung disease first in his forties and it got so bad that they had to operate for the first time in 1978. They took out half of his lungs and left him tethered to a damn oxygen tank and unable to walk very far at any one time.

Then came some outside trouble in 1979. The

New Jersey Casino Control Commission raised the issue of his association with some questionable characters (Sy Alter and Cellixfni), which put his permanent gaming license in jeopardy.

Also, the U.S. authorities investigated him and a 1984 Bahamian royal commission discovered a trail of bribes from Resorts to Prime Minister Lynden O. Pindling.

The New Jersey Commission focused on two checks: l) $120,000 issued by Peloquin to Bahamian attorney Jack Duffus, February 1981, and 2) $700,000 to another Nassau lawyer, April 1980, as finder's fee for Crosby's $10 million sale of the Paradise Island bridge. Big parts of each check ended up with Everett Bannister, Nassau wheeler-dealer who was on the Resorts payroll as consultant for a decade and was said to have funneled over $420,000 into Pindling accounts.

In the end, New Jersey renewed Jim's license because it couldn't be proven that Crosby knew where the money was going, but it chastised him for consorting with Bannister. By the mid-1980s, his Atlantic City operation accounted for $248 million of Resorts total income of $468.

Unfortunately, the ordeal over the license renewal weakened him, but he kept plunging into deals. In 1985 he tried to help TWA executives fight off the takeover by Carl Icahn without success. Then he concentrated back on what he knew best — gaming. He plunged into a project to build the biggest hotel ever in Atlantic City, the 42-story Taj Mahal for $525 million.

During this period, something happened that would ease the tension in his life considerably. Crosby met the baroness at a Monte Carlo gala on July 6, 1981, hosted by Prince Ranier's uncle Prince Louis Polignac. They talked briefly during dinner but it was, as she said later, like a thunderclap. Ten days later they went for a cruise and ended at St. Tropez on Bastille Day where everything was jammed and he tipped the headwaiter heavily to get a table in a restaurant at the Byblos Hotel. That didn't pass unnoticed by the baroness and, during their talk, she asked him why he never married. He said he had been too busy with business. Pressing her opportunity, she asked if he had a girlfriend. "No," he answered and she said, "I am available."

Later, she visited him in the Bahamas, Miami, and then returned to her husband in Mexico and got a divorce. Crosby and Marianne began living together in Atlantic City, which she loved. They played backgammon until the wee hours, went to his New York City apartment in his private copter and visited the Bahamas, Côte d Azur, Italy, and Provence as part of their good life together.

She redecorated his East Side apartment stocking it with new tablecloths, furniture, Oriental carpets, and wall hangings and got him a new wardrobe. Friends admitted that she took very good care of him including planning wonderful family Christmas and New Year's holidays with the Crosbys and Murphys.

But that was then and this was now. Everybody carefully examined Jim's April 1986 will, which he had drawn to take care of Marianne and see that Resorts stayed in the two families.

At heart of the bequests was stock in Resorts International. There were 390,783 class B shares worth about $20 million at the time of Jim's death and 5.6 million shares of class A stock outstanding. But the trick was that the Class B stock had *100 times the voting power of class A stock* or 48 percent of the voting power in the company!

As they all discovered at the post-funeral lunch, Jim Crosby named Tom and Henry Murphy his executors and left 50,000 shares B stock to his brothers and sisters, Elaine, Suzanne, John, and Billy. The remaining 340,000-plus shares were split among former girlfriends and trusts for Peter Crosby and mostly for baroness Marianne Brandstetter with Charlie Murphy and Peloquin as trustees.

Wall Street speculators rushed to their calculators and figured out that, whether Jim Crosby had intended this or not, somebody could control Resorts with a relatively small number of Class B shares. Roughly, it figured out that spending a $100 million could get control of Resorts.

On August 4, 1985, *Wall Street Journal's* "Heard on the Street" column said, "Resorts International's Two-Family Control Could Be Broken, Some Say, If Price Is Right." The source was Andrew Racz who thought Marianne was key. Her 194,246 B shares in her trust gave her 24 percent voting control. If she is motivated by money, her trustees couldn't resist a serious cash offer, Racz said.

The B shares rose sharply on the market and Thomas and Henry faced a conflict. They wanted to keep Resorts in the family on the one hand but they had a responsibility to Crosby's beneficiaries on the other to maximize their profits and that might mean selling. Add to this a second conflict of interest in that, when Baroness Brandstetter died, all her shares reverted to the Crosby and Murphy families.

So, it was possible that a showdown could have loomed between Brandstetter and her trustees, Robert Peloquin and Charles Murphy, who wanted to resist a forced sale of Brandstetter's shares and yet, might be forced to in the best interest of Marianne.

The key man in this was Charlie Murphy, Crosby's right-hand man for a quarter of a century, who loved Resorts and wanted to keep it in the families. Henry Murphy, Charlie's cousin, was also torn. All of a sudden the Trenton undertaker was a big shot as chairman of the board [elected in May] of Resorts and no longer in the shadow of his brother, Tom, chairman of Cap Cities/ABC.

Tom, incidentally, was embarrassed over having shares in Resorts because it cast a shadow on his role as head of the ABC Television network and other Cap Cities properties. So, Tom turned control of his shares over to Henry.

Henry's motivation was simple. He wanted to keep his new celebrity status and that meant keeping Resorts in the family, but he really didn't quite know what to do, so, in spite of being chairman, he deferred to Charlie who knew how to run Resorts.

Enter at this point a Big Bucks Texan, Jack E. Pratt of Dallas, with hotels in Central America and the U.S., including the Sands in Las Vegas. He said he had $10 billion from backers and he wanted to buy Resorts. On August 22, 1986, he bid $85 a share for 585,000 Class B shares held by the estate and the families. The answer came back and Jack E. Pratt didn't like it. The estate and the family wanted at least twice that much. Pratt said he was shocked.

At that point, nobody on Wall Street could get a fix on Resorts per-share value because of the uncertain real estate values in Atlantic City. Merrill Lynch was rumored to have guestimated a price between $130 and $150 a share.

Pratt was still shocked, but also still determined and he came back in September with a jump to $135 a share. Plus Pratt had the extra advantage of already having a gaming license from the New Jersey Commission. If a deal was made, that would save the sellers 18 months in the settlement.

The baroness was, at the time, vacationing in Switzerland and didn't know about Pratt's latest offer. Charlie Murphy and the executors, Tom and Henry, didn't want to let Resorts go. But, as noted before, they also had fiduciary responsibility to Crosby's beneficiaries and could they ignore: 1) Pratt's $135 offer, and 2) the coming jump in capital gains taxes of 8 percent at the end of 1986?

Plus there lurked in the back of everyone's mind two things: a black pit and a giant albatross that was meant to be a beautiful swan. The black pit was the possibility that one of the beneficiaries of the trusts, particularly Marianne, could sue the trustees for failure to act in her best interests as legally required. The giant albatross was the dream unfulfilled by Jim Crosby when he died: the enormous, half-finished, way-behind-schedule-and-overcost $600 million Taj Mahal.

If the trustees were waffling, Brandstetter's lawyer wasn't. He contacted her in Switzerland and said that Pratt's offer was about three times what the stock was worth and, if the families didn't sell to Pratt, they were screwing Marianne, but not in the Biblical sense that Jim had been. He recommended she sue them to force a sale to Pratt.

At the same time, Pratt's people were singing the same song to Brandstetter to get her to pressure Charlie and the other Murphys to sell.

Marianne remained loyal to Charlie and the Murphys because she got along with them and she trusted them. Besides, whatever anybody thought, she had loved Jim and didn't want to do anything that would sully his dream.

However, the feelings were not mutual and it was here that the Murphys made a mistake. They clearly, if quietly, resented that Brandstetter got such a big chunk of the estate. And Charlie began doing things that robbed her of dignity and status, which Jim Crosby would have objected to had he been alive.

For example, Charlie Murphy told her to move out of the Atlantic City suite she and Jim shared for almost four years and he also wanted to sell the East Side coop because it was worth double the $700,000 Crosby had specified as the price of a home to buy for Marianne. So, you are dealing with an almost half-billion-dollar deal and you want to queer it just to save a couple hundred thousand? Petty minds make petty decisions and giant mistakes.

Meanwhile, Charlie, Tom, Henry, and Peloquin met regularly to consider the options they had.

Resorts was heavily leveraged to build Jim Crosby's last dream, the Taj Mahal, which now stood half built and that created additional pressure beyond the threat of some beneficiaries' greed that might force a sale that would rob the families of control.

They saw three possible options: 1) the family might buy up more Resorts stock; 2) they could organize an employee stock ownership plan (ESOP) to buy more stock; or 3) find a passive, white knight to buy in.

One thing they agreed on was that they didn't want to sell to Jack Pratt who they regarded as a loudmouth, low life who would chop up Resorts and sell it in pieces. As the Murphys fiddled and faddled around, two other offers came in, but fell apart before they could be acted upon.

Then the Feds jumped in. The Securities Exchange Commission looked into what was going on. Then a Philadelphia attorney named Greenfield filed a class-action suit on behalf of the stockholders claiming the executors and trustees were not acting in the best interests of the stockholders and were trying to buy Brandstetter's stock and that of other stockholders at well below market.

All this delay and fooling around unleashed a loose cannon in the form of Peter Crosby, the estranged brother whose life has been filled with troubles, swindles, indictments, jail time, and who had once been married to French actress Denise Darcel. He was married now, but he only spent weekends with his second wife, Suzanne, and their four children in Cary, Illinois, and lived the rest of the time in the New Jersey town of

West New York.

Peter sued Charlie, Tom, and Henry to force them to keep him informed of offers and other business details. The judge turned Peter down, but the suit unnerved the other three.

In the end, the blood-money war turned out to be too much for Jim Crosby's heirs and they finally sold out at the same price that Pratt had offered them, $135 a share but not to Pratt. Instead, they sold to loudmouth extraordinaire, Donald Trump, who did finish up the Taj Mahal.

Trump would get in a brouhaha with selling part of these holdings to Merv Griffin in 1988, he would be sued for fraud and settle for $16 million in 1991 and Griffin would take his part of what had been Resorts into bankruptcy.

So, even if the blood-money fighting has stopped among the Murphys, the Crosbys, and the baroness, it keeps going on with Jim Crosby's old Resorts International empire.

Twenty

Trumped

The Trump story is the story of a family that made good from immigrant beginnings, and one in which each of the five children was affected differently by the enormous wealth the Founding Father generated. Oh, yes, it was the Founding Father — not the insecure, egomaniac Donald created by the celebrity-struck media — who made it for the Trumps.

Frederick Charles Trump was sired by a hard-drinking Swedish-born father who ran a small restaurant in the Queens borough of New York City and who died when Fred was 11 leaving his wife, Elizabeth, to eke out a living as a seamstress for herself and little Fred.

However, that immigrant gene was strong and active in the Trump DNA and Fred began working hard at an early age to help his mother. He started as a "horse's helper" around construction sites. His tough and dangerous job was to help pull, push, and shove horses hauling building materials when it was icy cold and the horses couldn't get into the construction project alone.

In time, the boy became a journeyman carpenter and attended Pratt Institute in Brooklyn learning the building business so that by 1923, he started Elizabeth Trump and Son Company, a construction firm. He was legally too young to sign papers and his mother had to do it for him.

His first project as a new entrepreneur was to build a house in the Woodhaven section of Queens for about $5,000 and sell it for $7,500. He kept doing this over and over again for the next six years and, soon, young Fred was supporting their little family of two.

He was a conservative man because everything he had, he earned and he didn't want to chance losing it by rash deals. Except for a short time during the Depression when business wasn't good for selling new houses, Fred would be in the construction business for the rest of his life making lots of money following one simple maxim: give people a quality product for a fair price. Not too complicated, but often not understood by people in business.

This was the rule that Fred followed whether building low-cost apartment units or fancy, high-priced mini-estates in Jamaica Estates where he lived in a lovely home on Midway Parkway and raised a family with the former Mary Macleod. Married in 1936, the first patter of little feet came with Maryanne in 1936; followed by Fred, Jr. in 1938; and, Elizabeth in 1942.

Fred assumed that Fred, Jr. would become his clone and successor in both name and role in his increasingly successful business. Tragically, it wasn't going to work out that way.

Then in 1946, World War II ended and Donald John Trump followed two years later by youngest brother, Robert, in 1948, the year that Fred, Sr. launched his biggest apartment house project yet with the 1,400-unit Shore Haven Apartments.

Aside from learning about headers, foundations, studs, and siding, Fred, Sr. learned that one of the most important materials needed to make a real estate project a success is political influence. He discovered early that, if you give politicians money to get elected, they returned the support with tax-abatement deals, zoning changes, and housing subsidies. If it is done carefully, the politician gets elected and makes money while the real estate developer doesn't get elected and makes even more money.

Fred and Mary didn't want to spoil their kids, but the kids figured out pretty soon that they weren't poor because they lived in a big house, were chauffeured around, and went to a private school.

Each of them responded to their family wealth in different ways. The eldest, Maryanne, was kind of the surrogate mother and developed into a conservative lawyer who would later marry and become a judge in New Jersey.

Fred, Jr. was missing something in his makeup that made it impossible to become his father's hard-driving, hard-working clone. His main problem was the same as that of many sons of strong and successful fathers: he was afraid of his father. He was afraid he could not be as good as his father wanted him to be. His father wanted him to be a mirror image and Fred, Jr. desperately wanted to be his own person, but was conflicted because he also wanted to please his father.

That was not how Donald was structured. From the very beginning of his life, his focus was on pleasing himself and to hell with the rest of the world. Fred and Mary and the other kids agree that he was the most demanding brat of the bunch. He learned from the moment that he began suckling at Mary's breasts that screaming, demanding, bawling, confronting, and being imperious got him the most attention and the most of everything he wanted. Other people gave in to him either because they thought him cute and engaging or because they didn't want the hassle of dealing with the tantrums.

Half a century later, that's still true with Donald.

As a teenager, Donald went to the Kew Forest School as did most of his brothers and sisters, but the school wouldn't put up with his behavior and he was yanked out and sent to New York Military Academy up the Hudson River. There he did quite well in his grades and on the playing fields, but not so well on the dance floor and at the social gatherings. Girls from nearby private schools thought he lacked class and that he was too much of a brash, new-rich climber. Most of them refused to date him. It was a social rebuff from the old-money rich girls that the audacious Donald would never forget.

With the help of his politician connections, Fred, Sr. built a vast empire of low- to medium-cost apartment housing in the communities surrounding Manhattan. From his office at 600

Avenue Z in Queens, he reigned over a domain of thousands of rental units while ever building more homes, high-rise residential buildings, and specialized units for the elderly and other categories subsidized by the city, state, and federal government.

Donald was what his older brother, Fred, Jr., was not.

Donald was Fred, Sr. reborn. He inhaled the excitement of bulldozers on the move, the smell of fresh plaster and paint, the burr of whirling Skillsaws, and the pops of bolt guns all as part of the organized confusion that transforms a weed-covered plot into Bay Side Arms or Willowbrook Shores housing thousands of people.

Donald spent every weekend, every summer, and every vacation from school dogging his father's steps and learning, learning, learning about the real estate development business. Fred, Jr. tried, but he just couldn't cut it. His father had burdened him with too much and, indeed, Fred, Jr. had probably burdened himself with too much. Donald, on the other hand, listened and found out what his father did and continued to make noises and demand attention.

In Donald's own assessment of the difference between himself and his older brother, he said that he used to fight back with his father all the time. "My father respects me because I stood up to him." Fred, Jr. could not do that.

Knowing where he was going, Donald did his college work at the Wharton School of Business at the University of Pennsylvania. Much of the schooling was boring and he kept busy buying, rehabilitating, and selling property in Philadelphia when he wasn't home in Queens and Brooklyn treading in his father's shadow listening, gathering, and disputing.

His goal was to become a full partner in his father's business and move operations into the big time: Manhattan. The lucrative fields of New Jersey, Queens, and Brooklyn were solid and dependable for Fred, Sr., but they lacked glamour, they lacked panache, they lacked style and Donald wanted all those things. Most of all he wanted to be accepted by polite society. He hadn't forgotten the put-downs of those rich girls when he had been at the New York Military Academy.

Meanwhile, Maryanne had married a lawyer, John J. Barry, and was pursuing her successful legal career and raising a family in New Jersey; Elizabeth quietly went to work at the Chase Manhattan bank; Fred, Jr., called Freddie by most, found it increasingly painful to stay in the family maelstrom; and Robert, the youngest, hung around with Donald and was his best friend. Robert idolized Donald and was finishing college and looking forward to following around in the shadow of his brother as his brother had followed around in the shadow of their father.

Meanwhile, Donald finished at Wharton on May 23, 1968, and was so eager to get home and to the family office that he didn't wait around to have his picture taken with his class. He began working full-time with his father whose holdings now exceeded $200 million and annual gross rents $50 million. Donald did not have to start from scratch.

Donald plunged into becoming the Donald we

know today building on the Donald he had always been: brash, bawling, bratty. He got an apartment in Manhattan, began wearing burgundy suits with matching patent leather shoes and quickly established himself as a free-spending devotee of the "in" spots like El Morocco, Regine's, Doubles, and "21," entertaining an endless stream of beautiful, willing women who were trolling for a rich, young man just like Donald.

As Donald soared in his money-driven glory, his older brother, Freddie, plunged deeper into his own private world of depression over his failure to be what his father had wanted him to be. A critical Rubicon was crossed when his father announced that Donald was to become president of the Trump Organization. It was the official seal of disapproval burned upon Freddie's failure.

Freddie retreated, married Linda, a girl he had been dating, with whom he would later have a son and a daughter named after Freddie's father and mother. Freddie turned to getting high in two ways. He became a pilot for TWA, which would remove him from the day-to-day reality of his family and he began piloting assorted bottles of booze, which would remove him from the day-to-day reality of being Freddie Trump—Failed First Son.

The six-foot Donald, a nonsmoker and nondrinker, haunted the nightspots of Manhattan searching for new women and one night he saw three beauties waiting in line for a table at the East side'ss then-singles oasis, Maxwell's Plum, noted for Tiffany lamps and the launching of thousands of one-night stands.

He helped the girls get a table and immediately

sat down with them, which the three women anticipated and, indeed, expected. Ivana Zelnickova Winklmayr, a former Czech Olympic skier, was one of the three women on a vacation from Montreal where she lived with her boyfriend. Donald became entranced and began a whirlwind wooing campaign that would last for a time.

Three major business milestones marked Donald's life during this period of the late 1960s and early 1970s:

1) Convincing his father to leverage his properties and generate mountains of cash for an invasion of the Manhattan real estate market and then getting his dad to lend or give him — depending on which story you prefer — $50 million to get into Manhattan commercial real state. Donald's self-embroidered biography mysteriously seems to miss this boost from his father.

2) Alliance with Roy Cohn, the sleazy, well-connected legendary lawyer who first came to America's attention in the infamous Joseph McCarthy hearings. This was a connection made through his politically savvy father who had supported politicians such as Abe Beame and Hugh Carey over the years and understood the need for a strong fixer in one's corner. That's what Cohn was. Part of the right-wing, gay underground with tentacles throughout the New York political and legal power structure, Cohn was the Trumps' fixer. We saw him in the role in the chapter on the Goldman family-money feud.

3) The Penn Central deals, which allowed Donald to pick the bones of a fallen commercial giant with admittedly admirable audacity and contrarian vision.

This last deal made in 1974 established Donald as a key deal maker in Manhattan real estate and, in the process, startled the old real estate hands in town.

The Pennsylvania Central Railroad was broke, in a receivership presided over by the famous Victor Palmieri, and desperate for cash. It owned two gigantic waterfront parcels along the Hudson River running from 59th to 72nd streets and from 30th to 39th streets — a total of 21 blocks of waterfront property.

The City of New York was also on the ropes in 1974 and none of the real estate barons such as Zeckendorf, Helmsley, or Tishman were investing in Manhattan. Nobody wanted to put his money into the dilapidated railroad yards that would have to be rezoned for residential and commercial use if they were going to be put to any profitable use.

But 28-year-old Donald Trump ignored all of this and made the biggest Manhattan real estate coup of the decade. The total price was $62 million, which was a steal price by any standard, but the mind-boggling part is that he bought it with *nothing down*. The $62 million was to be paid out only as the property was developed and made enough money to pay itself off.

At this moment of Donald's triumph the rest of the Trump kids continued on their preordained paths: Maryanne moving upward as a judge and Elizabeth comfortable where she was as a secretary at Chase Manhattan. Robert, shadowed whatever Donald did as a vice-president in the Trump organization. And, far away in all senses of that phrase, Freddie continued his slide as his marriage disintegrated and he moved to Florida to work on charter boats.

The next great coup Donald built on top of his Penn Central deal was making another purchase from the bankrupt railroad colossus. This time it was the Commodore Hotel adjacent to Grand Central Station. The Commodore was decrepit and mismanaged, but in a fabulous midtown location.

Trump crafted the Commodore deal in this way: He got the Hyatt people to sign on as a partner and together they would pay $10 million to Penn Central with $6 million of that going for back taxes. Then they sold the property to New York's community development public corporation, the Urban Development Corporation (UDC), for one dollar and leased it back for 99 years. The rent would start at $250,000 a year and rise over the 99 years to $2,775,000.

By doing this, it made it possible to have the UDC use its power of eminent domain to force tenants out of the Commodore building who didn't want to leave. So, Trump was able to do whatever he wanted with the building.

Then Trump got the city to give him a 100 percent tax abatement for forty years. In other words, he and Hyatt would pay no real estate taxes on the property for 40 years. This, most experts agree, was like giving Donald a gift worth anywhere from $40 to $300 million.

Donald had made two gigantic deals with the help of the insolvent Penn Central that rocketed him to public attention as a major real estate player in Manhattan. He was 29.

Of course, he was in the public eye more and

more because of his flamboyant behavior, pronouncements, arrogance, and sheer gall. He was the Mike Todd of New York real estate and the crown prince of the media that drools over this kind of colorful character who speaks in sound bytes and makes a headline every time he opens his mouth. His burgundy suits and shoes, his lavish lifestyle, his boyish charm and appearance — it was made for television.

His father was quietly proud, if not a little bewildered, and his siblings were awed. By 1976, Donald was making all the major development decisions for his father's Trump organization. He was also in hot pursuit of the one thing missing from his castle — a princess.

He had been ardently wooing Ivana and trying to take her away from her live-in boyfriend in Montreal. In a way, the contest was like that between a cobra and a small domestic animal that becomes mesmerized by the weaving of the cobra until the cobra strikes. It was clear who was winning when Ivana began flying down from Montreal to spend each weekend with Donald. Friends and relatives knew Donald was smitten because he always met her at the airport. His arrogance wouldn't allow him to do that for most other people.

So, on April 9, 1977, the couple were quietly married in the Marble Collegiate Church on Fifth Avenue by the Rev. Dr. Norman Vincent Peale in a small family ceremony. Ivana would quickly turn out to be not only the glamorous model she had been, but a knowledgeable business associate working on Trump projects such as the conversion of the Commodore into the Hyatt Grand

Hotel (the only Trump project not bearing the Trump name) and the luxurious Trump Tower built on the Fifth Avenue site of Tiffany's. Along the way, she would also give birth to three children.

Life was not so wonderful for Freddie, the scion of the family, down in Florida. He thought working on charter boats would give him a new sense of purpose, but it didn't. His life continued to sour, his marriage collapsed and, in desperation, he returned home to live with his parents, which is where he faced the very feelings of inadequacy and failure that had propelled him on his downward slide in the first place. It was like putting a diabetic in a candy store.

Fred, Sr. worried about his eldest son and wanted to help him, but he didn't know how. Freddie couldn't communicate to his father what was wrong. It was as if they were two foreigners each speaking a language that was incomprehensible to the other and thinking that they had a hearing problem and not a communication problem.

Freddie's life would have been vastly different and so would have all the other Trump children's if they had been born in an ordinary middle-class family. They weren't. They were born into a family dominated by a father who believed that hard work and determination was all that was required to achieve financial success and that meant happiness. It was a blessing for Donald and a curse for Freddie. In many ways it didn't do much for Maryanne, Elizabeth, or Robert either.

For the two years that Freddie lived at home, Fred, Sr. brought him to the office every day and tried to get him involved in the business, but it didn't take. Freddie didn't understand it or like it. He went through the motions, but never caught the excitement and grasp that Fred, Sr. or Donald had.

The only thing with which Freddie found he could communicate successfully was his deep depression, which was temporarily eased by a bottle of booze. Doctors warned that Freddie's mental condition was getting worse and his physical condition going downhill with an enlarged heart.

The situation was one that upset Donald more than anything else he had experienced in his life. Regardless of his public persona, Donald cared about his brother and tried to reach out to comfort and encourage him. It was no use. On September 26, 1981, Freddie was admitted to Queens Hospital Center and died there that night. He had commited suicide in a socially acceptable way by drinking himself to death. He was 42.

Everybody had a theory about why it happened and what should have been done that wasn't, but it didn't matter, Freddie was dead. It would leave a mark on the family—particularly Donald and Fred, Sr.—that they would never forget.

Seven-and-a-half months later, Donald opened his triumphant landmark building of shops and condos on Fifth Avenue—Trump Tower. It was a lure to the rich and famous from around the world to buy one of the 263 condos in the building ranging in price from $800,000 to $10 million. He had gotten into a public brouhaha over destroying some of the classic statuary that adorned the previous building on the site, but Donald loved the controversy and the enormous press it generated for himself and his trademark building.

In the years to follow, Trump would continue as he always had in his flashy, ostentatious way as a symbol of the excesses of the 1980s along with Ronald Reagan, Ivan Boesky, and Michael Miliken. He reveled in the lavish media attention with his beautiful and competent trophy wife; the children in private schools; and the adoring attention of New York's beautiful people, rock stars, and celebrities.

His arrogance was underscored when the public objected to his plan, announced November 18, 1985, to build TV City, including the world's tallest building, in the old West Side Penn Central rail yards. Neighbors worried about the traffic and congestion the project would create and Donald's reaction to the people's concerns was, "What they think doesn't matter. They have no power." Marie Antoinette would have been proud.

Just like Marie, Donald was wrong. Those people did have power. They organized themselves into a community-action group called Westpride and descended on City Hall. They panicked the politicians and Donald's project was stymied and the land has lain dormant ever since.

He bought into the New Jersey Generals football team, the Eastern Shuttle, one of the world's biggest yachts, and the fabled estate of Mar-a-lago. If those rich girls from those upper state schools could only be with him now!

His biggest move was into the Atlantic City casino market in the farthermost cry possible from his staid, conservative father's approach to steady, solid apartment rentals.

Donald had written his self-promotional book, *The Art of the Deal,* which became a best seller. However, Donald was not the originator of the deal by himself. It was something that Fred had taught him every day over the last 25 years.

Witness the device Fred and Donald used to bail Donald out of his problem of meeting $3 million in bond interest on his Trump Castle casino in Atlantic City. The 85-year-old Fred had his lawyer walk into the Castle and stride up to the high-stakes blackjack table to buy $3 million in $5,000 chips. Then as the stunned spectators watched, he simply put them into his briefcase and strode out of the place without placing a single bet.

So, what happened? Well, the New Jersey law says that casino chips are always redeemable at full cash value. So, Fred gave his son's Trump Castle the $3 million it needed and got fully redeemable collateral. If, on the other hand, Dad had lent Donald the $3 million and the Trump Castle had to fall into a Chapter 11 bankruptcy, Fred would have had to stand in line with all the other creditors and probably settle for pennies on the dollar.

Yet, even with his dad's bailout, Donald was in financial trouble. The *Wall Street Journal* announced that Donald's financial empire was coming apart at the seams just as his marriage to Ivana had done.

With things crashing down around him, Donald gave an insight to his inner self when he was flogging his second book, *Trump: Surviving at the Top,* before thousands of booksellers at the annual American Booksellers Association convention in Las Vegas over Memorial Day weekend in 1990. His speech was an odd combination of lusting for success and anticipation of failure.

"My publisher knows how to turn me on, because I want to do that—keep going higher and higher—and then we die and nobody gives a damn. It is pretty futile when you get down to it."

One of Donald's close friends of which he has few, said this was vintage Donald: "There is in Donald a genuine need to self-destruct. In order to feel real, he has to exceed himself constantly. Underneath there's despair: Nothing I do is enough and it never will be."

A close personal friend of Trump's was quoted in *People* Magazine in 1990 when his marriage was on the rocks and his financial empire looked about to unravel. The friend said that Donald's main problem was that he suffered from the malady that afflicted many of the new-rich, the painful yearning for acceptance by the "in" crowd of the hereditary rich or the New York elite. It is symbolized by the origin of the famous "400" list of the socially acceptable established in New York decades ago. There were only 400 in Manhattan's elite in those days because that's all who could be accommodated in Mrs. Astor's private ballroom.

Donald wants to be part of that 400 and that's why he wanted to disassociate himself from the scruffy, blue-collar image of Queens and Brooklyn and establish a foothold in Manhattan. Even as a millionaire, he would sit by the phone waiting for the weekend party invitations to the toney

Hampton estates that never came.

He found to his sorrow something that today's hereditary rich found out generations before when they were the new-rich with names like Astor, Rockefeller, and Guggenheim. Namely, social acceptance can't be bought with money.

People commented that Donald says the old-line rich are frivolous and boring while the old-line rich say he is arrogant and coarse. They are both right, says, *People*.

The same thing happened to him when he bought Mar-a-Lago, the 58-bedroom estate of the late Marjorie Merriweather Post in Palm Beach with its three bomb shelters, movie theater, and antique furnishings. He actually bought it for $3,000 of his own cash plus an extraordinary *unrecorded* mortgage from the Chase Manhattan bank of $10 million. The banker who made this possible, Conrad Stephenson, was later able to buy an apartment in one of Donald's posh Manhattan buildings for a $50,000 discount.

While Donald and Ivana viewed buying Mar-a-Lago as instant access to the Palm Beach elite, it didn't work. The snobs of Palm Beach giggled and made fun of them. Trying hard for acceptance, Donald flew 40 members of the exclusive Palm Beach Bath & Tennis Club who were based in New York down to Mar-a-Lago for a fabulous time of dining, drinking, and dancing. They enjoyed themselves immensely and not a one of them reciprocated with the sought-after invitation to lunch at their club.

Even one of the maids at Mar-a-Lago, Reidun Torrie, quit because she couldn't stand working for the Trumps. "They have no class," she complained.

And everybody knows the Marla Maples story and very few are sympathetic with Donald about that. Most see Ivana as a loyal wife dumped for a shallow gold digger. What many didn't know is that Marla had been on the scene enjoying what she told the New York tabloids was the best sex she had ever had, for at least two years before the story broke as a result of a public confrontation between Marla and Ivana at Aspen where Donald had brought both along for his vacation.

The most bizarre twist of the Marla story came with the discovery that her publicist and adviser, Chuck Jones, had frequently invaded her 8th-floor apartment at the Trump Parc when she was gone and stolen shoes and lingerie along with some nude photos of Marla and Donald.

On July 15, 1992, Matt Calamari, Trump's head of security, confronted Chuck with a secret videotape of one of Chuck's tours of Marla's apartment. He held him hostage for eight hours questioning him about his sexual obsession and shoe fetish with Chuck protesting his innocence all the while until they went to Chuck's place and found the missing shoes and lingerie—but not the nude photos.

They turned Chuck over to the cops and he was arraigned while the tabloids in New York went ballistic at this new sexual twist. Adding additional spice was word that not only were nude photos of the golden couple missing, but so were Marla's diaries containing sizzling passages about her love affairs with Michael Bolton and an Arab prince in Aspen.

A few days later, Marla opened in *The Will*

Rogers Follies and did better than critics anticipated, but she and Donald continued to be worried about the missing photos. Jones threatened a
civil suit against them and Trump's security
people while rumors kept drifting in to Marla
and Donald that whoever had the nude photos
was trying to peddle them. It all seemed so con-
sistent with the soap opera life all the principals
were leading.

Meanwhile, Ivana dropped all her names and,
Cherlike, insists on being called simply, "Ivana."
Her novel, *For Love Alone*, hit the best-seller
list, she got a new boyfriend, she launched a skin
care and a jewelry line. She still overdressed and
was regarded with antipathy by the old-money
crowd.

Donald did well in the '80s because he was
buying into a rising market. As *New York Times*
architectural critic, Paul Goldberger, characterized it, Donald was doing it all mostly with
highly leveraged smoke and mirrors. The bill
came due in the '90s and Donald wasn't prepared
to handle it.

At this point in his baroque career, Donald has
lost his yacht, his plane, his airline, and half of
his largest Atlantic City casino. He is divorced
from Ivana, his mistress gave birth to a girl last
year named Tiffany, and most of his business
partners including the Hyatt chain are suing him.
Some bankers estimate his net worth as being a
negative $400 million and that most of his prop-
erties could be pulled out from under him in a
New York Minute.

The worse blow of all is that his father, now in
his late eighties, turned the management of his

affairs — valued at about $150 million — over to his youngest son, Robert. Robert used to worship Donald and worked for him for some years until he got disgusted and quit suddenly to go his own way. Now, he and Donald "don't see eye-to-eye anymore," as their father puts it.

In his book, *The Art of the Deal,* Donald says things that contradict the way he has lived. He set down such rules as plan for the worst; don't be too greedy; never pay too much; and, money is never much of a motivation.

Whatever is the motivation for Donald, it seems that being accepted as *somebody* is at the heart of much of what he does and has done.

Is that the echo from the rich girls of his youth? We'll see as a new chapter in the Trump Follies opened at the Plaza Hotel December 20, 1993 when the Donald finally married the Marla.

Twenty-one

Probate Potpourri

Under no circumstances do I want to ignore the following delicious tidbits about inheritances among the rich even if these morsels are not enough to justify an entire chapter by themselves.

For example, there is the mess that happens when people don't expect to die just when they did. That's what we started out with in this book when Howard Hughes died before he expected to and hadn't signed a solid will to direct the disposal of his estate. He had, you recall, drawn, redrawn, re-re-drawn will after will, but his secretary said he just never got around to signing any of them. Then boom. He was dead.

Joe Robbie in an example of dying too soon.

Blood-money feuds are not limited to arcane debates in hushed courtroom corridors and walnut-paneled law libraries. They are also out in the sunshine on the playing fields of America including the heirs of Joe Robbie battling over the Miami Dolphins and the heirs of Jean R. Yawkey scrapping over the fate of the Boston Red Sox.

Joe Robbie, a former governor of Nebraska who founded the Dolphins in 1966 along with actor/comedian Danny Thomas for $7.5 million, died in January of 1990, immediately igniting a blood-money feud among his widow and nine surviving children.

The estate was valued at $73 million and everybody was lined up to get his or her share including the IRS, which wanted $25 million because Joe didn't get around to structuring his holdings with the tax consequences in mind.

Elizabeth Robbie, the widow, wasn't happy the way three of her kids, Tim, Janet, and Dan — trustees of the estate — were running things and in March of 1991 demanded her 30 percent cut of the estate. In papers the three kids filed with Dade County Circuit Judge Edmund Newbold in September, the children said that she should be happy with the $300,000 a year she was getting under a "lifetime employment contract," or widow's trust, and if she were to get the total payout she demanded in March, taxes might wipe out the entire estate and Elizabeth would actually end up with nothing.

However, she was entitled to 30 percent of the estate under state law and, if she got that paid out to her, it would destroy the trust and she would have to pay most of what she got in federal taxes. At least that's what the trustees, Tim, Janet, and Dan, claim. Elizabeth's lawyer didn't agree.

Well, boys and girls, this sparked two other daughters into going public. Diane Feinholz and her sister Deborah Olson said they were, "horrified that they [Tim, Janet, and Dan] would suggest such a thing. She is their mother, after all."

Diane and Deborah then tipped the jar of beans and let the whole world and Canada know what started the family blood-money feud. It seems that the three trustees rushed to sell half interest in the Joe Robbie Stadium to the Blockbuster rental TV mogul, H. Wayne Huizenga, right after old Joe kicked his last point after touchdown.

This irritated Mom and the other kids—not because it appeared unseemly to transact business so quickly after Joe died, but because they didn't get enough money out of the deal. Huizenga only paid $5 million and assumed half the $90 million mortgage at a time when the family was running out of cash and needed dough pronto.

Besides, the family's remaining 50 percent ownership of the stadium isn't part of Joe Robbie's estate. It belonged to the Robbie family as a group. On top of that, Huizenga, who already owned 15 percent of the Dolphin football franchise, had an option to buy 10 percent more.

The IRS played a big role in this and part of the problem was figuring out the value of the Dolphin football franchise. The trustees said Joe's estate was worth $73 million of which $59.5 million was the value of Joe's share of the football franchise. However, tax experts said that the IRS can figure the value of the team anyway it likes without regard to what it sells for or what anybody else appraises the team's value. In the never-never land of the IRS, it can pull a figure out of thin air and require the Robbies to pay the tax on that. Of course, this can be appealed to the courts, which would tie things up for years and years and at the time when the Robbie kids were yapping for money like little kittens denied their mother's milk.

However, the Grim Reaper played a bigger role in the Robbie family feud than anybody when he stepped in and took Elizabeth Robbie a few months after he took her husband — much sooner than anybody would have believed she would have died. This meant that almost all of the estate was subject to a 50 percent federal estate tax because Joe Robbie failed to get an insurance policy to handle the tax problem or to create a tax sheltered arrangement as Nelson Poynter did with the *St. Petersburg Times* on the other side of Florida from Robbie's Miami. As one fan said, "If Joe had bought a life insurance policy instead of a running back a few years ago, his family wouldn't have this problem."

Now the whole picture changed, yet remained the same. Elizabeth's death changed the widow trust protection the Robbies had against estate taxes, but the hatred between the split groups of the children remained the same with the trustee group claiming the Dolphins were only worth $68 million and the opposing group of siblings claiming they were worth $88 million and that the trustees were cheating them. Of course, it ended up in Judge Newbold's court.

At one point in late July 1992, everybody thought they had come to a settlement.

In June of 1993, things got to the point that the trustees entered into a deal with Nelson Peltz and the DWG Corporation — parent company of Royal Crown Cola and Arby's — to sell the other

50 percent of the Joe Robbie Stadium and the remaining 65 percent interest in the team franchise. Originally, the deal included former Bears coach, Mike Ditka, but he was out of it at that point.

The short version is that the sale of the Miami Dolphins and Joe Robbie Stadium is being forced by a $47 million estate tax bill from the IRS and the exhausting family feud.

Wouldn't have happened if Joe hadn't died too soon.

Same thing, ironically, with Conway Twitty.

Country Singer Conway Twitty cashed in his chips unexpectedly on June 5, 1993, when he died following stomach surgery. He had endured stomach pains for three days and put off going to the doctor until, finally, the pain was too much and he went in. Then it was too late to save him, much as the surgeon tried.

His death was a terrible shock to Dee, his wife of six years, but was compounded when she found out she wasn't in the will!

The only legal, signed will in existence was one Conway executed in 1987 before Dee took him away from his second wife, Mickey, who had borne three of Conway's four children. That will left everything to Conway's children.

Dee had been Conway's secretary and she took him away from Mickey in a way that left Mickey and his kids very bitter. Twitty settled $10 million on Mickey when they divorced in 1985 after changing his will in 1984 cutting Mickey out entirely. But, as anybody who has been through that kind of situation knows, money is not the only issue or even the main issue in many divorces. In this case, it gave the players a chance to settle some scores.

Dee will get their house and cars and some other property the two owned jointly, but, at this point, not his $30 million estate in record royalties and his Twitty City entertainment complex.

Friends, including Hugh Carden, coexecutor of the will, say that Twitty had drawn a new will including Dee, but he just never got around to signing it. So, now the scene is set for a blood-money feud.

To get any of the $30 million, Dee will have to sue the estate and, if she wins, she might get a third under the Tennessee law doctrine called "elective share." At the time of Twitty's death, Dee was so torn up by Conway's death that she was suicidal, but in time that might change and she might see the value—$10 millions' worth of value—in suing. Mickey and the four kids, Joni, Kathy, Jimbo, and Michael, would probably resist.

Just in passing, Conway's first wife will get nothing and she now lives in a homeless shelter in Dallas, Texas.

It is a situation perfectly suited for a somebody-done-somebody-wrong country and western song.

WHETHER IT'S A CRIME OF PASSION
OR
A COLD-BLOODED MURDER—
PINNACLE'S GOT THE TRUE STORY!

CRUEL SACRIFICE (884, $4.99)
by Aphrodite Jones
This is a tragic tale of twisted love and insane jealousy, occultism and sadistic ritual killing in small-town America . . . and of the young innocent who paid the ultimate price. One freezing night five teenage girls crowded into a car. By the end of the night, only four of them were alive. One of the most savage crimes in the history of Indiana, the four accused murderers were all girls under the age of eighteen!

BLOOD MONEY (773, $4.99)
by Clifford L. Linedecker
One winter day in Trail Creek, Indiana, seventy-four-year-old Elaine Witte left a Christmas party—and was never heard from again. Local authorities became suspicious when her widowed daughter-in-law, Hilma, and Hilma's two sons gave conflicting stories about her disappearance . . . then fled town. Driven by her insane greed for Witte's social security checks, Hilma had convinced her teenage son to kill his own grandmother with a crossbow, and then he fed her body parts to their dogs!

CONTRACT KILLER (788, $4.99)
by William Hoffman and Lake Headley
He knows where Jimmy Hoffa is buried—and who killed him. He knows who pulled the trigger on Joey Gallo. And now, Donald "Tony the Greek" Frankos—pimp, heroin dealer, loan shark and hit man for the mob—breaks his thirty year oath of silence and tells all. His incredible story reads like a who's who of the Mafia in America. Frankos has killed dozens of people in cold blood for thousands of dollars!

X-RATED (780, $4.99)
by David McCumber
Brothers Jim and Artie Mitchell were the undisputed porn kings of America. Multi-millionaires after such mega-hit flicks as BEHIND THE GREEN DOOR, theirs was a blood bond that survived battles with the mob and the Meese Commission, bitter divorces, and mind-numbing addictions. But their world exploded in tragedy when seemingly mild-mannered Jim gunned down his younger brother in cold blood. This is a riveting tale of a modern day Cain and Abel!

Available wherever paperbacks are sold, or order direct from the Publisher. Send cover price plus 50¢ per copy for mailing and handling to Penguin USA, P.O. Box 999, c/o Dept. 17109, Bergenfield, NJ 07621. Residents of New York and Tennessee must include sales tax. DO NOT SEND CASH.